AF729994

Lowly Creatures

HarperVia
An Imprint of HarperCollinsPublishers

LOWLY CREATURES

A Novel

GASPARD KOENIG

Translated from the French by Stephanie Smee

Without limiting the exclusive rights of any author, contributor or the publisher of this publication, any unauthorized use of this publication to train generative artificial intelligence (AI) technologies is expressly prohibited. HarperCollins also exercise their rights under Article 4(3) of the Digital Single Market Directive 2019/790 and expressly reserve this publication from the text and data mining exception.

This is a work of fiction. Names, characters, places, and incidents are products of the author's imagination or are used fictitiously and are not to be construed as real. Any resemblance to actual events, locales, organizations, or persons, living or dead, is entirely coincidental.

LOWLY CREATURES. Copyright © 2023 by Editions de L'Observatoire / Humensis.
English Translation Copyright © 2026 by Stephanie Smee.
A Note from the Translator copyright © 2026 by Stephanie Smee.
All rights reserved. No part of this book may be used or reproduced in any manner whatsoever without written permission except in the case of brief quotations embodied in critical articles and reviews. For information, address HarperCollins Publishers, 195 Broadway, New York, NY 10007. In Europe, HarperCollins Publishers, Macken House, 39/40 Mayor Street Upper, Dublin 1, D01 C9W8, Ireland.

HarperCollins books may be purchased for educational, business, or sales promotional use. For information, please email the Special Markets Department at SPsales@harpercollins.com.

hc.com

Originally published as *Humus* in France in 2023
by Éditions de l'Observatoire/Humensis.

First HarperVia paperback edition published in 2026.

Designed by Yvonne Chan
Earthworm illustrations © akininam/stock.adobe.com
Emoji illustrations © Cali6ro/stock.adobe.com

Library of Congress Cataloging-in-Publication Data has been applied for.

ISBN 978-0-06-341682-6

Printed in the United States of America

26 27 28 29 30 LBC 5 4 3 2 1

It may be doubted if there are any other animals which have played such an important part in the history of the world as these lowly organized creatures.

—CHARLES DARWIN, *The Formation of Vegetable Mould through the Action of Worms* (1881)

1

"Earthworm. First of all, as far as names go, it's not a particularly kind one, more of an insult really. Better to call them 'lumbrics' and restore a little scientific dignity. Family: *Lumbricidae*. Species: *Lumbricus terrestris*. And these lumbrics represent the earth's most substantial animal biomass. In other words, if we put them all on a scale, they would far exceed the combined weight of *Homo sapiens* and every elephant and ant in the world. To give a rough estimate, there are between one and three tons of them in every hectare, assuming humans and their dirty paws haven't yet had a chance to interfere with the soil."

It was Professor Marcel Combe's short video doing the rounds on YouTube that had made Arthur keen to attend his lecture. But on entering the vast, almost empty, lecture hall and seeing a smattering of students in rows barely acknowledging each other, Arthur felt disheartened. The place still smelled new, with its plywood walls that were designed to add a touch of "nature" but only managed to draw attention to the steel and glass of the surrounding buildings. This was not how he had pictured his agronomy degree.

Arthur wondered what moment of madness had led to the AgroParisTech campus being relocated to the concrete desert that was the Saclay plateau. The previous year's cohort had still been able to spend their freshman year at the Château de Grignon, amid three hundred hectares of fields and forests. It was where generations of students had learned how to milk ewes and get laid in the underbrush. Instead, Arthur now had to swipe a card twenty times a day to get through security barriers and then find his bearings in a maze of indistinguishable corridors where the only things that differed were the numbers on the doors. He had never seen so little nature as in the six months he had been at college. The only chirping to be heard outside was the sound of bulldozers ripping up the earth. The students' dorms looked like the classrooms, which in turn looked like gym lockers. Sure, there were efficiencies to being on this campus where everything was at your fingertips, but efficiencies that allowed time to do what? Watch porn? Labor over perfecting chemical formulas? Who felt like going for a drink in a cafeteria that was cleaned twice a day, and who felt like being on display in their goldfish bowl of a student union room, located smack bang in the middle of the central thoroughfare?

Arthur had felt like he was in exile from day one. Previously one of the most fertile places in France, the Saclay plateau had been transformed into a functional desert, an interminable commercial precinct where instead of business logos there was branding for some of France's most prestigious colleges, the likes of Polytechnique, Mines-Télécom, or the École Normale Supérieure. It was supposedly a magnet for the best minds in France, students as well as researchers. But what happens to a mind confined by an unrelentingly geometric space, blinded by the neon pallor of the corridors, overshadowed by a forest of cranes? It turns into an atrophied supermachine, ready to reproduce with other supermachines in order to create a world of even more supermachines. Was this now the declared mission for future agricultural engineers from AgroParisTech? To learn the correct language descriptors relevant to regenerative agriculture, so they could feel better about transforming French farms into meat-processing plants covered in solar panels?

The most perverse thing about the layout of the place was the introduction of a few pastoral flourishes, as if by way of afterthought. After climbing an endless staircase from the train station of the RER B line, out-of-breath students would unexpectedly find themselves having to cross a little wooded area and then a field of reeds before reaching paved walkways and closely mowed lawns. On the campus itself, a carefully demarcated wetlands meadow preserved a few square meters of wilderness. Around the minuscule gravel beach, tufts of shaggy grasses had sought refuge alongside bulrushes sprouting clusters of tobacco-brown flowers and a few marsh marigolds floated on the water like giant daisies. A devil's pool for the Anthropocene visitor.

In any case, Arthur had sworn it would be a temporary exile. As soon as he had the degree society required of him, he would be out of there. Whenever people asked him which sector he was considering working in after college, he would say, "Working on my garden." It was vague but sincere.

Arthur was still standing at the door to the lecture hall, hesitant. He would probably have turned on his heel had he not noticed the boy with the well-groomed blond hair and pronounced cheekbones. Everything about him exuded good health and a calm state of mind, from the gray T-shirt that hinted at a lean, toned physique, to the laptop still closed on the desk in front of him, to the impassive expression on his face as he waited for things to start without shifting about in his seat or fiddling on his phone. There was something particular about him, Arthur thought, something quite different from the other students who were all fidgeting and distracted by one another. He headed over and unfolded the seat next to him. The blond boy moved his laptop to make room and readily held out his hand to Arthur, as if they had run into each other at a stand at some agricultural fair. Spontaneity of that sort was unusual, even among students. Especially among students.

"Hi. Kevin. No accent on the 'e.'"

Funny, thought Arthur. *He doesn't look like a Kevin, much less a Kevin with no accent on the "e."* He quickly chastised himself for the ridiculous thought before also introducing himself. Kevin smiled at him and said nothing. They both opened their laptops. The lecture was about to start. Its title: "Advances and Challenges in Geodrilology." Geodrilology, the science of earthworms. Suffice to say that for a talk not featured in any part of the mandatory curriculum, there was not much of a crowd.

"Maybe I shouldn't have come," muttered Arthur, feeling some last-minute regret. "I've got a seminar paper due tomorrow."

"Don't say that," came Kevin's reply. "Earthworms are really cool."

"Why? Because you can cut them up into little pieces?"

"No. You kill them if you do dumbass stuff like that."

"What's cool about them, then?"

"For starters, they're hermaphrodites. Which is not that common in the animal world. That's what fascinated me when I was a kid. They're male and female at the same time."

"If we're going there, let's not forget snails, too . . ." said Arthur, getting to his feet.

Too late. Marcel Combe, "world-renowned expert" according to the poster advertising the lecture, had just made his appearance. Arthur sat back down. After all, why not? He was already intrigued by the speaker. He'd probably been expecting some lab assistant type with a waxy complexion. But here was an old lion, eighty at least, with a curly mane of hair, blue eyes, a boxer's jaw, broad shoulders. He was well-dressed. His dark suit gave him an air of importance. His polka-dot tie was fixed by a silver tie pin. He was the Jean Gabin of earthworms.

Professor Combe relished the impact he made. He took in the scattered audience with an indifferent gaze and then eyed the state-of-the-art electronic system mounted into the stage's solid wooden lectern.

"Good heavens, aren't you kids spoiled?" he commented in a rasping voice.

Murmurs from around the lecture hall. Students at the selective *grandes écoles* secretly adored having their privilege called out.

"They must have killed some earthworms to build this campus!"

Silence. Arthur thought back to the scene from *Seven Years in Tibet* in which Buddhist monks from Lhasa save earthworms with their bare hands before pouring the foundations of a building. Western architects took no such precautions. Arthur watched for Kevin's reaction; his neighbor was upright in his seat, fingers ready to tap out the first morsel of noteworthy information.

"Let me introduce myself. We don't need to linger on my qualifications: I never received anything beyond my elementary school diploma. I started off as a gardener. Learned on the job. And then I became Research Director at INRA, which, if I'm not mistaken, is about to move out here, and take up position right next door to you people. They'll have some very fancy labs and be able to spend even less time on the land, in the fields. That way they'll come up with even more ridiculous things to say."

Stifled snort. INRA, the National Institute for Agronomic Research, was not, however, to be sneezed at. Arthur wondered if they were in the presence of a scientific genius or some conspiracy nut. Kevin was still at the ready, cursor flashing on the blank screen in front of him.

"Lumbrics, you realize, are responsible for ensuring the fundamental well-being of the soil. As a result of their continuous digestion, they ingest the equivalent of their own weight every day, breaking down organic matter into biogenic elements, which then go to feed plants. It is estimated that lumbrics swallow and excrete three hundred tons per hectare every year. Yes, you heard correctly, three hundred tons! Indeed, the earth on which you walk, the earth which provides us with food to eat, is, in large part, 'lombrimix'—also known as earthworm poo. Which is why the great Charles Darwin considered our lumbrics to be the most significant animals in the natural evolutionary process. Without them, everything collapses."

"Ah yes, Darwin," murmured Arthur.

Distant memories surfaced from a biography of Darwin.

"That's in his last book," he explained with some authority to his neighbor. "He spent years studying the earthworms in his garden."

Kevin nodded.

". . . two hundred and seventy tons per hectare per year!" exclaimed the professor.

Arthur had lost track of what was being said. He noted down the figure automatically.

"Darwin was happy just to calculate the weight of fecal deposits on the surface. I'm the only person to have calculated the total weight of lombrimix or fecal castings, which includes that found beneath the surface. The only person since Darwin!"

Arthur and Kevin exchanged an amused glance.

". . . so I hope that from now on you'll be more polite around lumbrics."

Marcel Combe had set the stage with figures, references, and formulas he had belted out a thousand times before, and which were probably sufficient to render dumbstruck a lecture hall filled with the uninitiated. But this audience remained skeptical. Agronomy degrees consist in no small part of having to listen to specialists explain the vital significance of their particular field and the injustices facing it, before they make a case for a funding hike. But then Marcel Combe played his trump card: the earthworm's reproductive system.

"The habits of the lumbric are utterly fascinating. Unlike their marine forebears, terrestrial lumbricids are hermaphrodites. Each individual is endowed with a male reproductive organ, sometimes in the form of a tiny penis, and a female reproductive organ."

Kevin gave a smile intended to catch Arthur's attention.

"Copulation takes place top to tail. It can last for up to several hours, which puts our own performance on that front as humans in perspective!"

Barely two or three stifled snickers. The students of AgroParis-Tech were clearly not the target demo for Marcel Combe's comedy. Arthur had only one, deeply held wish: that he not end up like *that*. A crusty old lewd scientist.

"The two partners exchange sperm without mixing them up. Then, on the female side of things, each one produces ova that are then entirely encased in a cocoon, which will be deposited on the ground. Fertilization is then left to progress, you might say, entirely on its own. In any case, it all happens outside the parental body. The embryo then turns into larva and, like billions and billions of others over the last two hundred million years, the hatchling worm will emerge from its cocoon to carry out its mission of looking after our soil, a mission for which we show so little gratitude."

The story's conclusion was neat enough. But then Marcel Combe had to go and spoil everything.

"Basically, the earthworm's reproductive cycle is like gay sex followed by an assisted reproductive procedure between girls."

Now the lecture hall was awake. "Is this old man an asshole or what?" exclaimed Arthur to his neighbor who was laughing out loud. Several students stood up, outraged. They were making it clear in no uncertain terms to Marcel Combe that when it came to jokes, especially jokes of that nature, topics like that were off limits.

"But there's no judgment on my part . . ." he defended himself awkwardly. He was more used to an audience of older farmers who reveled in his "politically incorrect" remarks, as he proudly described them.

Nobody would have imagined that a lecture on earthworms could provoke such a tumultuous response. AgroParisTech students being generally well brought up, most contented themselves with posting furious tweets hashtagged #lumbrifacist. Some left the lecture room threatening Marcel Combe with worse reprisals. Arthur considered following them. But a glance at his neighbor who was calmly waiting for the next installment, looking delighted, dissuaded him.

"Aren't you shocked?" he asked Kevin, nonetheless.

"Nah, I think it's pretty funny."

The professor ran a hesitant hand through his white mane. With their spots and lines, hands betray those who don't look their age. They wear the wrinkles that might elsewhere be spared. The spectacle of Jean Gabin, defeated and out of character, was no victory for anyone.

Marcel Combe sighed. "I will now share with you the results of fifty years of research . . ." he resumed, clinging, in a world he no longer understood, to that by which he could still justify his place in it. Fifty years in fields and laboratories, fiddling with, observing, measuring, dissecting earthworms. Fifty years publishing research read by a handful of obscure geodrilologists. Fifty years of enduring jeers or embarrassed looks every time he was asked what he did for a living.

His lecture, presented with a solemn rigor, supported by figures and graphs, left Arthur entranced. An entire subterranean universe opened up to him. The infinite spaces that captivate philosophers are to be found not over our heads but beneath our feet. Earthworms transform soil into a labyrinth of pathways, junctions, shafts, and hidden chambers. Every square meter of earth conceals five meters of tunnels, a network even more concentrated than that of the pyramids. It is these tunnels that allow the nutrient-rich elements necessary for life to surface from the bowels of the Earth and, inversely, that allow rainwater to drain and be stored in reserve. Absent this complex architecture, soil subsides, water runs off the surface, and plants starve.

Earthworms are blind pharaohs. They take the time to enjoy life, sovereign rulers over themselves and their domain, masters of their biological clock. Fleeing the light, they slowly traverse their kingdom, retracting and expanding like accordions. They're at no risk of suffocation: they breathe through their skin. Wanting for nothing, they store their own excrement and reingest it after it has fermented. In winter, they hibernate, rolled into a ball in a deep lethargy. In summer, they flee the heat and gather in the cool of their chambers, descending deeper as the soil's temperature increases. They chew the fat, waiting for the dry period to pass. When they die, two or three years later, and are summoned before Osiris, weigher of hearts, they emerge victorious; they have five of them.

Of course, there are earthworms and earthworms. Over five thousand species have been identified, across every continent. Professor Combe had studied them in detail. He had meticulously reconstituted their biopaleogeographic path according to plate tectonics. He had traveled to the far reaches of the earth to touch them. He had devised innumerable experiments. Kevin did not stop tapping his keyboard. It was the scientific humility shining through the orator's boastful front that Arthur found most appealing. Marcel Combe was constantly harking back to the fact that geodrilology, and soil studies more generally, were in their nascent stages. Clearly an intense focus on geodrilology, a field about which the greater public remained ignorant and one scorned by other researchers, lent itself to modesty.

"At this point in time, there is nobody who is able to describe the workings of a clod of earth," the professor explained. "A microscope reveals an unlikely diversity. No single thousandth of a millimeter resembles another. You'll find bacteria, yeasts, dead organic molecules, mineral particles, in short, millions of disparate elements, most of which we still know nothing at all about. And yet, this clump of earth functions! It breathes in oxygen and releases carbon dioxide. How? By what biophysicochemical miracle? Nobody can say."

In an era where every other geek claimed to be reinventing the world, Arthur found it comforting to discover in Marcel Combe a true scholar, an inquiring mind that knows what it doesn't know.

After a presentation of fairly technical information lasting more than an hour and a half, the incident had been forgotten, but the AgroParisTech students' interest had noticeably waned. Casting a glance around, Arthur noted that most laptops had a Facebook or Insta page open. He himself had started looking at emails.

The lecture hall came back to life during Marcel Combe's long summarizing, when he described with the dramatic emphasis of an aging actor the unfolding ecological disaster. Deep tillage and widespread use of pesticides have decimated the lumbricid earthworm population in most crops, reducing it to some dozen kilos per hectare. The ground then becomes soil-less, a compacted, devitalized substance, a giant shelf onto which fertilizers are poured in order to create commercial products in the guise of tasteless plants. Which in turn leads to landslides, the draining of water tables, and of course, the impoverishment of ecosystems at a dizzying rate. "Techno-science," as described by Marcel Combe, had turned its back on science; agroindustrial productivism had ruined natural fertility; and humanity had, in a matter of a few decades, managed to destroy the subtle equilibrium that was the product of millions of years of biological evolution. "No earthworms," resumed Marcel Combe, "means no more earth. It is no coincidence that astrophysicist Hubert Reeves describes the disappearance of earthworms as disturbing as the melting of the glaciers." Arthur felt overwhelmed. This was not about to help his eco-anxiety.

Yet, if one were to believe Marcel Combe, who was not fond of leaving his audience in a state of despair, the earthworm could become humanity's best ally. First off, earthworms are able to be reintroduced into soil using an inoculation method, a process discovered a century ago by a certain Mr. Ashmore, a New Zealand farmer. Better yet, they can be put to work processing humanity's waste. Professor Combe proceeded to sing the praises of vermicomposting, which involves feeding a colony of lumbrics organic waste, anything from cardboard to potato peelings; a few months later and it will have been transformed into a fine, odorless vermicompost, a black powder ready to be used as fertilizer for anything from houseplants to crops.

"These days there are some very elegant little setups for individual use that can be kept in the kitchen," explained Marcel Combe. "You stack up drawers, one on top of another, place waste in the top drawer, and extract compost from the bottom one, in both solid and liquid form."

"Imagine that thing in our dorms," murmured Arthur.

"You can bet some idiot would end up kicking a ball into it," continued Kevin. "Go explain that to management. Thousands of little pink worms squirming all over the place."

Arthur gave a forced laugh, attracting a disapproving frown from Marcel Combe.

"You won't be laughing so hard once you hear about the potential of vermicomposting on an industrial scale," the professor continued. "I'm calling it a *lumbri-polytechnic*."

It was the stuff of dreams. His dreams. Marcel Combe and his lumbrics saving humanity from its sins.

"You could build veritable factories where billions of worms would be busy in giant trays working for our common good. Lumbri-composting, lumbri-filtration, lumbri-recycling: with these creatures, anything's possible. I've done the studies. The results are conclusive. All you would need to do is invest one thousandth—no, one millionth—of the amounts spent on creating digital idiocies in order to fertilize the soil, recycle a town's waste, purify waste water, treat farming effluent, and eliminate liquid manure. In short, to solve the fundamental problems we're facing. There's only one thing that upsets me: I'm not going to witness it in my lifetime. I'll be feeding the worms before they feed you."

Arthur heard a few snickers. Marcel Combe had straightened up and was looking off into the distance, over the heads of the students busy scratching their noses or liking a post. He was alone at his dais. He knew nobody believed him. It was too simple to be true.

"What are humans?" exclaimed Marcel Combe, whom nothing now could stop. "Etymologically, nothing more than humus. Which is why humus will be the thing to save humanity."

This last statement was met with a round of desultory applause. Arthur clapped his hands enthusiastically. Kevin, too. Their well-meaning noise offered some small consolation perhaps to the patriarch of earthworms.

"I don't take questions," said Marcel Combe, haughtily, gathering up his papers.

* * *

The two boys hung back, chatting at the door of the lecture hall. The enthusiasm of one reinforced that of the other. Had they not met, that lecture would probably have been subsumed into the daily flood of material they were receiving. But it had given them the perfect pretext to become friends.

The long Saclay evenings were thus spent deepening their knowledge of lumbrics. They subscribed to some of the few specialized blogs and read the bible published by Marcel Combe. They rummaged through expert publications and shared their limited findings. Arthur expanded his research into the fields of history and literature, long his favored subject areas. He emerged empty-handed. After Cleopatra who, aware of the earthworm's role in fertilizing the Nile valley, accorded the creature semidivine status, the world's royalty came instead to prefer the eagle, the lion, the bee, or the salamander. As for writers more generally, they hardly seemed to show any more interest. Even the alexandrine written by Victor Hugo on the subject, giving literary life to an "earthworm in love with a star," was scarcely flattering. The earthworm referred to the lowly manservant, Ruy Blas, while the star, of course, represented the Queen of Spain. Only a romantic author could prefer a dead star to the source of all life.

Arthur and Kevin had the rare feeling of discovering an almost brand-new field of research. As a result, they quickly forged the complicity of explorers. They made a solemn promise to each other never to abandon their earthworms. To devote their careers, their lives to them, one way or another.

The two boys fell into the habit of fleeing their dismal dorms in the agricultural engineers' residential wing to have a beer in the evenings on the top floor terrace of the college's main building. They would make their way through the spaces dedicated to scraggly urban vegetable patches and lean on the terrace railing. From up there, they could just make out the woods adjacent to an old Benedictine abbey that had miraculously survived the suburbanization of the Essonne. In front of them, the dark mass of the forest was crisscrossed by the elevated tracks of the future Grand Paris Express transit line, and illuminated from afar by the glowing halo of the city. The natural world was on borrowed time, and it compelled them to philosophize. Unlike previous generations, they were not there to rebuild the world. They were watching it fall apart and trying to find a role for themselves in the pending collapse.

Arthur, then, wrote a thesis on the scourge of abundance with the faux despair of someone in their early twenties, that age when you can amuse yourself by believing in nothing because you still believe in yourself. An only child long accustomed to solitary monologues, he had at last found an audience. At night, on his feet, his face illuminated from below by uplights set into the terrace, he laid into productivism, condemned the endless multiplication of human needs, and extolled the virtues of general frugality in all aspects of life. In order to describe the current state of the world, Arthur recited the figures of Jean-Marc Jancovici, otherwise known as "Janco," the engineer idolized by an entire generation of conscientious youth seeking to understand the scale of the disaster bequeathed to them by their parents. In imagining tomorrow's world, he invoked Epictetus, Rousseau, Élisée Reclus. He was in no way conceited. Writers from the canon simply formed part of the pond in which he swam; he quoted them much as he would relay the drunken musings of a mate, without really knowing whether to take them seriously.

Arthur had a soft spot for Henry David Thoreau, who had gone off to live as a semihermit for several years on the shores of Walden Pond, in the heart of Massachusetts. Here was someone who had taken austerity to its ultimate consequences. He spent his time eliminating rather than accumulating, living in a single room with three chairs ("one for solitude, two for friendship, three for society"), giving up all stimulants (including coffee, which dashed a morning's hopes), refusing even the offer of a doormat (what use would it be? The ground is not dirty). Working on his little vegetable patch, he even unwittingly developed the technique of direct sowing without plowing. Was Thoreau a libertarian or an anarchist? A poet or philosopher? Arthur couldn't care less really. In his mind, he represented the ideal of a free man.

From his lawyer father, Arthur had inherited a facility for rhetoric, a taste for questions ending with an ellipsis, and a certain cynicism when it came to politics, which made him run a mile from any sort of activism. After graduating from the respected Henri-IV high school, he had taken preparatory classes for an agronomy degree, almost as if to make a point, cultivating an image that, intellectually, he was his own man. Everybody had told him: take the humanities prep classes and get into Normale Sup, the prestigious École Normale Supérieure, which would have been a natural fit for his distinct predilection for writers who'd been dead more than a century, whose egos were no longer anybody's concern, and whose opinions were thus able to flourish all the more freely. But Arthur was not fond of well-trodden paths. He held his future peers—apprentice philosophers ranting about degrowth yet all the while incapable of planting so much as a leek—in pretty poor esteem. He dreaded the thought of his private convictions being sullied by the herd mentality of champagne rebels. But more than anything, he couldn't see himself making a living in the sphere of critical thinking. He had no wish to become a professional in the field of exegesis, nor somebody fixated on injunctions. If the point of philosophy had long been to make sense of the world, its purpose now was to transform it, and it was time to roll up his sleeves.

So, Arthur had diverted to the STEM stream to study biology and earth sciences and, without too much difficulty, was accepted into AgroParisTech. At least there he was master of his own ideas, without having to transform them into some sort of crusade or career plan. Like Thales, proud of the yield of his olive trees, or Montaigne of the splendid alignment of his melons, he wanted to finish his days with dirt under his nails. Even if he was convinced that his efforts would ultimately be in vain and that a good number of species would disappear in the sixth mass extinction, he would do his part, heading up the front line, and not stash himself away among books and conferences.

Kevin, as taciturn as Arthur was voluble, would listen to his friend holding forth with the curiosity of a child watching a fly crash into a window. Kevin admired Arthur's erudition without really understanding his motivation. He always wanted to agree without ever feeling like exploring the opposite side of the argument. He wondered how exhausting it must be, this constant state of indignation, and offered his friend the most precious thing he possessed: a solid, loyal, reassuring presence. He absorbed Arthur's words the way good soil soaks up water.

There was nothing predetermined either about Kevin becoming an agricultural engineer. But for different reasons. His parents were simple farm laborers, his mother employed on a fixed-term contract at a cheese manufacturer where she spent every day packaging fermented sheep's milk, his father driving tractors for a cooperative for which he was paid according to the seasons and to demand. They rented a nondescript cinder-block house in a nondescript small town in the Limousin, a region where notwithstanding the many intervening years, they still felt like they were just passing through, much like they would always feel as if they were passing through life. They were the product of generations of pieceworkers and vagrants, shunted around according to the shifting winds of the economy, always ready to plug the holes in society. They remembered what it was like to own a bindle and knew they could always pack their own again should the work ever dry up. And so, they harbored no anxiety. They were a couple with no history, no attachments, no ambition, no resentment. Nothing noteworthy ever happened to them, which itself was never a source of complaint. Rather, it was as if fate had concentrated every share of their good fortune in this placid, unassuming child of theirs, with his Grecian beauty. They had overseen his education from a distance, refraining from undue interference for fear of unintentionally spoiling this unusual sapling that demanded only to be left alone to grow in peace and quiet.

Kevin managed to succeed at everything he encountered, without ever really trying. After middle school, he went to an agricultural high school, following the path taken by most young people in the area. When he did well, he was sent off to the STEM stream to study life sciences. When he did well at that, he took the preparatory classes for a technology degree in Limoges rather than the more traditional advanced technician's certificate. And when he did well at that, one of his professors registered him for the highly competitive entrance exam for AgroParisTech; only fifteen spots a year offered for the "pro" pathway. Because he did well at that, he was admitted. And so, against all expectations, there he was, mixing with the country's future elite. He didn't make a big deal of it but graciously made the most of his new surroundings. Not unlike his parents, Kevin tended to meander, but in a way that passed for ambition in the eyes of others.

His only disappointment was not to be living in Paris; he couldn't wait to get to know the city better. He almost didn't accept his offer when he realized the college was moving from its Rue Claude-Bernard location out to the Saclay plateau. But enrollment was already underway and everybody was offering their congratulations, so he didn't dare let them down. In any case, a decent half of the course was in the field, on site at businesses, in labs, or on farms. And he was not about to decline the funding he'd been offered, in his eyes a fortune.

Kevin was economical, unintentionally so. Whereas Arthur

preached sobriety in his fluoro Camper shoes and tortured himself in his attempts to define acceptable compromises, Kevin had no specific needs. A couple pairs of jeans, his laptop, the student refectory; he wanted for nothing. The rest of his funds went toward evening beers. For some, it was the definition of student insecurity. For him, it was the beautiful life.

To Arthur, Kevin was a sage who, without recourse to books or even thoughtfulness, instinctively followed the rules of virtue. He admired him for it, and was also somewhat resentful. What was the point of all this self-interrogation, punctuated by anxiety and epiphanies, if you could reach the same result just as easily, without any apparent effort?

When their discussions carried on into the night on the terrace, Kevin and Arthur often found themselves caught out by the 11 p.m. curfew. The security guards would be carrying out a quick round to check that the college was clear before locking the gates. The first few times, the two friends complied. Then they grew bolder and, concealed in some recess, allowed themselves to be locked in. The night was clear and warm. They still had a six-pack of beers and a thousand topics to discuss. They took turns pissing over the railing. At around one in the morning, they tried to make their way back through the deserted corridors. They amused themselves by prowling through seminar rooms where test tubes were stewing away and leaped over deactivated barriers like subway fare evaders. They gave themselves a scare trying to exit through the locked glass doors before finding one that opened from the inside.

Once out, they just had to get through the external gates to the campus. They wandered right through the freshly planted shrubs and found themselves at the wetland meadow. It was now or never. The moment had come to do what every student dreamed of doing on those days that were already insanely hot. They sat down on the little beach, removed their shoes, and plunged in their feet. Arthur mumbled some nonsense about Bachelard and the poetics of water while Kevin half dozed off. The cool of the water gently sobered them up. Overhead, a few stars could be seen in a sky still relatively free of light pollution. There was even the hooting of an owl from over near the future Électricité de France lab, which was still under construction. Wriggling his toes, Arthur generated a meditative lapping of the water.

"Come on, let's do it," said Kevin suddenly, emerging from his drowsiness. He took off his T-shirt, and then stripped right down with a lack of prudishness typical of the locker room. Arthur averted his eyes, a little embarrassed, but followed suit all the same. The pond was just wide enough for them both to splash around.

"It's the best part of this whole school," said Arthur.

Their legs sank halfway up their calves into the sludge. It was a curious sensation, being pulled down to a depthless bottom, spongy and organic, a living layer of earth that might suck them up and digest them in an instant. The edge of the pond gave off an acrid stench, like sweating vegetable matter. Dragonflies skimmed the water, oblivious to the pond's new occupants. Duckweed ran through Arthur's fingers, flashes of green gold. Even after being shunted into such a confined space, nature had reasserted its freedom.

Suddenly Kevin pointed to the intermittent beam of a flashlight. The two boys fled from the water stifling their laughter, pulled on their clothes while still dripping wet, and lay down on the pebbles. They heard steps approaching.

"It's the dude from security," whispered Kevin.

"I feel like we're in *The Great Escape*."

"We've gotta get out of here!"

Kevin made a move for the student union. Arthur followed. They managed to hide behind the wall just when the light would have caught them. They waited for the guard to head off toward D block and then raced over to the garden gates, which were a good six feet or so high.

"I'll give you a leg up," said Kevin, offering the palms of his hands as a step.

"What about you?"

"We'll see."

Arthur awkwardly hoisted himself up, grabbing on to the bars. As he tried to pull himself up, leaning onto his arms, his damp fingers slipped. He lost his grip and fell backward with a loud yelp. Kevin managed to grab him by the waist to break his fall, and they found themselves tangled up on the ground.

"You okay?" asked Kevin, getting up.

He reached out a hand to Arthur to help him to his feet.

"Yeah, but we're toast."

The guard had turned his torch onto them. In the crude light, Kevin looked like a water nymph with his pale, gleaming skin. The guard rushed toward them, shouting. After a lengthy discussion, Kevin and Arthur succeeded in opening the main gate, solemnly swearing never to do such a thing again, a promise that of course they wasted no time in breaking. Their nocturnal jaunts multiplied. They planted cannabis cuttings in the middle of the college flower beds. They also made it as far as Paris to puncture SUV tires, a high-profile activity prompting healthy competition among their peers. Little by little, Kevin and Arthur became inseparable. Everybody at the college associated one with the other. From parties to exams, they turned up everywhere together.

Orbiting around the duo were the feminine figures invariably attracted to Kevin. While Arthur, a poor errant male from Generation Z, ashamed of his desires, would deploy various byzantine seduction strategies without much success, flirting without annoying, urging without harassing, caressing without rushing, climaxing without dominating, all Kevin had to do was take a seat in the cafeteria in order to find himself surrounded by a veritable assembly of female students. His amiable indolence, accentuated by an incurable lack of imagination, lent him an air of refinement. In his company, women seemed suddenly to forget all the rigid strictures of #MeToo and reverted insouciantly to being lighthearted, chirping girls. Back in Limoges, Kevin's friends were often being paired off—some of them were even parents already—but here, nobody had any reason to fear the future, and youth was lived more overtly. All Kevin had to do was choose; an outdated privilege he exercised with a certain sensitivity, but which deprived Arthur of his evenings of fun and games and conversation. Arthur felt slightly jealous, without knowing exactly of whom. Of Kevin and his easy love interests, or of the girls his friend preferred to him?

* * *

Arthur soon had the opportunity to see Kevin at work. Both had received through friends of friends one of those open invitations to a gathering where the fortunate select of Parisian colleges converge courtesy of one plus one after another. No Facebook posts or Telegram chats. Evolution has proven that word of mouth is still the best way of ensuring the endogamy of the elite.

"Anne's place, Rue Gay-Lussac." Arthur knew how it would play out. Some parents' apartment temporarily transformed into a hippie camping ground, random playlists but nothing too loud for the neighbors, joints doing the rounds but please, use the ashtrays. Arthur was dragging his feet at the prospect of undertaking the long and unreliable crossing of the Essonne courtesy of a combination of night buses and the RER express train. Kevin, on the other hand, was keen. Especially after having seen on Google Maps that Rue Gay-Lussac was next door to the former site of AgroParisTech. He wanted his share of the renowned and mythical Montagne Sainte-Geneviève, home to the Pantheon in the fifth arrondissement. This was his long-awaited chance. Arthur would serve as guide.

It was Anne who opened the door, a brunette with a fulsome figure, and a pretty, round face that she was doing her inept best to desecrate. She had punctuated it with as many piercings as she could manage, and in the Andalusian curls of her hair she wore a bandanna sporting the anarchist "A." She welcomed them with a jaded smile. It took three sentences for Arthur to know exactly who he was dealing with. A nice second-year from Sciences Po who was ready to get down and dirty and whose anticapitalist sentiment was proportionate to the height of her ceilings. "Here's one for Kevin," he said to himself.

They drank, pretended to dance, and collapsed into a gigantic velvet sofa that was perfectly designed for pointless conversations. In this student environment that was anything but indifferent, where people were already keeping an eye on the anticipated trajectory of everybody else's career path, the Agro kids occupied a particular position. They had gone through the same ruthless selection process as all their fellow students at the party, and nobody was disputing their intellectual chops. But it seemed they were destined to deal with powdered baby formula or corn yields. Whereas the others were acquiring a form of generalized incompetence that would then allow them to occupy any position with the requisite confidence, the agronomists already had their hands in the dirt. They were the peasants of the engineering world, the commoners of National Administration School grads. All of which lent them a somewhat ambiguous aura.

Anne came and sat between the two boys.

"So, what is it exactly you do in agro?" she asked Kevin, resting a hand on his thigh. "Are you the guys who're going to save the planet?"

"Basically, we study earthworms," replied Arthur, who was determined to use any possible means to sabotage his friend's easy and inevitable success.

"You're joking, right?" She laughed, without taking her eyes off Kevin, as if she were speaking to a ventriloquist.

"Earthworms are humanity's future," continued Arthur. "And then there's the fact they're just adorable, sensual little creatures. They'd be right at home in this apartment. Good temperature, ideal humidity levels . . ."

This time, Anne had no choice but to turn to Arthur. He continued in his mocking tone, which, to his great surprise, didn't seem to irritate his target, who was always happy to be castigated for her way of life. She was only seeking to atone for her Parisian childhood, her weekends in Italy, and her studies paid for by the Bank of Mom and Pop.

"Agribusiness has destroyed the poor earthworms," asserted Arthur.

"True!" exclaimed Anne, who knew not a thing about it but could only imagine that agribusiness was pure evil. "Agribusiness and neoliberalism," she clarified. She wasn't at Sciences Po for nothing.

In the meantime, Kevin had picked up a conversation with his neighbor on the sofa, a pretty boy straight out of business school, hair gleaming with product. Arthur didn't have a second to lose.

"My mission," he confided in Anne, in all seriousness, "is to reintroduce earthworms into soil that has been stripped of its goodness. Using inoculation," he added, thinking back to Marcel Combe's remarks.

"Rad!" She nodded in agreement. "I'm all for it, reneger . . . gerena . . ."

"Regenerative farming."

"Yeah! Sorry, I'm a little buzzed," she lied. "You know you'll be up for a fight with the pigs from the farmers' unions."

"Well, yeah." Now it was his turn to lie. He knew perfectly well that the farmers' unions couldn't care less about some soft daydreamer wanting to try out alternative methods.

"So how do you do it?"

"How do you do what?"

"I mean, how do you reintroduce earthworms?"

Arthur was caught off guard. He mumbled some explanation randomly punctuated with scientific terminology. As he spoke, he looked at her lip piercing, a shaft of metal passing from one side of her bottom lip to the other with a gleaming ball at either end, and wondered what it must feel like. Then suddenly he interrupted himself. Anne followed his gaze. Next to them, Kevin was making out with the pretty boy.

Anne withdrew her hand, which, until then, she had distractedly allowed to remain on Kevin's thigh, and turned, resolutely, back to Arthur. And so their story began.

Half an hour later, Arthur and Kevin ran into each other in the kitchen amid a whole lot of wasted École Polytechnique kids who were busy spreading bread with tarama.

"Maybe we should get out of here soon," suggested Kevin, natural as anything.

Arthur didn't know what to say. A thousand questions were running through his head. Kevin seemed as relaxed and wholesome as ever.

Leaving the party, the two boys walked past the former, feebly lit, AgroParisTech buildings. The words "INSTITUT NATIONAL AGRONOMIQUE" could still be made out in handsome capitals on the facade. The building, which only a few months earlier had stood as a proud rallying point, now had the air of a historic monument. Scaffolding had been erected on the Rue de l'Arbalète facade. The new occupants, a private vocational college, were undertaking a complete renovation at significant cost. It was death in a display case.

"It's like a château," Kevin marveled. "In the very heart of Paris."

It was true: the monumental portal, the combination of dressed stone and gingerbread-colored brick, and even the onion-domed section of roof all lent the former premises the air of a seventeenth-century hunting lodge.

"Don't get too carried away." Arthur's response was more

tempered. "It dates from the late nineteenth century, when the Institute took over from the Faculty of Pharmacy. And before that there was the Apothecaries' Garden. It was full of bizarre plants . . ."

"You really do know everything, don't you," said Kevin, rubbing his shoulder.

Arthur tensed.

"Listen, I have to ask you something," he started off. "I'm sorry if . . ."

He was interrupted by a police car screaming up Rue Claude-Bernard. Once it had disappeared, the city felt suddenly silent.

"Are you gay?"

"No! Why do you ask?" answered Kevin smiling.

Arthur felt like he was being tortured. Ahead of them, a traffic light changed color, restoring some semblance of normality to the unsettled evening.

"Back there, on the sofa . . ."

"Oh yeah, every now and again I change it up. Otherwise things get a bit tedious, all that pussy."

"And you . . ."

There were things that Arthur didn't want to imagine.

"All bodies are made for pleasure," concluded Kevin. "You have to make the most of it, don't you think?"

"So, you're bi?"

"I dunno, I'd have to do some more homework. Didn't think I'd be painted into such a tedious corner in Paris."

Arthur was quiet, abashed. They set off again in silence toward the Port-Royal to take the night bus service. Kevin took his time, loitering. Arthur was laconically offering commentary on various landmarks as he chewed things over. He regretted his inappropriate questions, he whose upbringing had been steeped in a culture of battles against discrimination, thanks to the court cases in which his lawyer father would appear.

"And here we have the Garden of the Great Explorers. An extension of the Luxembourg. You can see the Senate, right at the end there. I like this view. It's calming."

Arthur felt uncool. It wasn't even about fighting discrimination. Kevin didn't belong to any group and was not claiming any particular rights. He was just happy being himself, "the universal man" as he had once read in Machiavelli's letters. So Kevin acquired a superior status; in Arthur's eyes he was beyond classification, beyond taboos and prohibitions. He ranked above common humanity by virtue of his very simplicity, his openness to being in the present moment, his complete acceptance of the desires coursing through his body.

Universal man, calmly sitting in the bus shelter on Boulevard de Port-Royal.

II

Kevin had found a seat at the back of the hall, next to the aisle. He was reserving the seat next to him for Arthur, just in case. He was not particularly interested in being at this evening commencement ceremony, but at least it was being held in the Grands Boulevards district in the center of Paris, which he hadn't had as much opportunity to discover as he might have hoped during these last three years of study, between courses at Saclay and fieldwork placements. The gilded scrollwork of the Italianate theater delighted him. He felt as if he were in a cocoon, cradled in the repeating folds of balconies and false ceilings. He would finally emerge as an adult, a fully qualified agricultural engineer. He was impatient not to have to justify himself anymore.

As was the case each year, or almost every year, a group of "career divergers" would take advantage of the occasion to denounce agribusiness and present their alternative plans to work on self-managed farms or for the Confédération Paysanne agricultural union. They'd be met with the applause of their peers who, for their part, would already have entered into agreements with Danone. It had become a tradition since the stunt pulled in 2022, when eight students had derailed the ceremony to expose the hypocrisy of an education, which, in their words, encouraged them to be participants in the "unfolding social and ecological devastation." With their long hair, and wearing open sandals, flowery T-shirts, or striped maxi-dresses, they had attacked the social conscience of businesses, government inaction, and society's inertia, inciting their peers each to look for their own way of diverging from the accepted path. By way of professional plans, they had declared their commitment to various protest movements, their occupation of future development zones, or their participation in farming collectives. Their calls for defection, springing straight from the heart of the system, initiated by the very people from whom answers were expected to be forthcoming, had generated considerable emotion in the court of public opinion. They had not attached themselves to the gates of the theater, they hadn't yelled vulgar slogans, they hadn't bared their breasts. They had calmly taken the microphone and, for seven long minutes, had listed off their precise and rational arguments. It was like watching some group project's bashful presentation. And that was what had made it so powerful. If good students were turning their backs on their studies, if the engineers were renouncing all efforts to find any solutions, if the agronomists no longer believed in agriculture, wasn't this truly the end of the road?

Of course, the end always takes a while coming. Once the YouTube video had duly made the rounds, everybody got on with their lives. Since then, this appeal for defection had become institutionalized. College leadership devoted fifteen minutes to "alternative futures." A dozen students called for the overthrow of capitalism, the journalists present took down the best punchlines, and then the ceremony continued peacefully on its merry way, with one presentation after another on sustainable development and testimonies from alumni having launched successful start-ups in the green tech space. An admirable way for the system to absorb its own internal challenges.

Kevin saw numerous parents around him, solemn and dressed in their Sunday best, for this ceremony marked the very official start of their own path to old age. He hadn't even considered inviting his own, who had just moved to the other side of the Limousin region where his father had been offered a position in a cooperative. His mother would once again pick up seasonal work, true to the precariousness that had always been her lot. They had settled in to a house that was as ugly as their last one and were planning to buy an RV so they could see out their days on the road. What would they have made of this Italianate theater? They were superbly disinterested in the career of their only son, "so long as he had food to eat and was not headed for prison," as his father had said once. It was their way of showing affection.

The head of the school appeared at the lectern in a suit but no tie, intending to convey a laid-back look but managing only to give off an unfortunate impression of incompleteness. The lights dimmed and the theater fell silent. Arthur still hadn't appeared. Kevin had hardly seen him during their third year. They had both selected "Biology and Biotechnologies relating to Health and Microbial or Plant-based Productions" as their majors, but were sent to different labs some distance apart. Kevin was continuing his easygoing existence, making himself readily available to anyone who was neither too ugly nor too stupid, male or female. From time to time he would be subjected to long weeks of abstinence, which didn't bother him in the slightest. However, for the first time, he had to admit he was missing something: Arthur, or more precisely, Arthur's voice that used to beguile him with ideas, and in the evenings would talk to him about Aristotle's definition of economics, of exchange and accumulation, of phronesis and mediety. It was better than Netflix.

Kevin dreaded seeing Arthur associate himself with the divergers. He was not keen on the idea of his friend demeaning himself in a discourse that would be less a discussion of Aristotle than of defection and struggle, slogans that Kevin considered beneath him. They had exchanged several WhatsApp messages on the topic.

They suggested I join them 🤣

Of course they did.
They ask everyone. 😠

They're right.

Yeah, and?
Why say it like that?
Why ruin the party? 🤔

Kevin was entirely on the same page as his peers when it came to concerns about global warming, loss of biodiversity, or declining ecosystems. He just didn't understand the point of the battle they claimed to be waging. Even if he had no other solution to offer, for the time being.

It's about raising consciousness.
And not supporting the
blahblahblah of corporate
social responsibility. 🤮
Social and environmental
responsibility is like sex:
The more you talk about it the
less you do. And vice versa.

Kevin took this last comment as a compliment. But still he had his doubts.

Isn't it a bit easy to say all
that when you're fresh
out of AgroParisTech?

Not at all. It's brave.
Nobody will ever want
to employ them.

I expect they all have the
means to support themselves
without working. I don't.

👍

Ever since finding himself moving in Parisian *grandes écoles* circles, Kevin had learned how, when necessary, to wield the social argument: a weapon of mass destruction that obliterated any conversation.

We need to talk earthworms.

I have a plan.

Me too! 😜

😍

Kevin sighed with relief when Arthur arrived and sat down next to him. So he wasn't going to take over the stage with the divergers after all.

"You were right," whispered Arthur, "they kinda act like spoiled brats."

On stage, the head of the school was addressing the new agri-engineers like they were "gifts to a sustainable planet."

"What does that even mean?" Arthur fulminated. "It's not the planet that is or isn't sustainable. The planet couldn't give a damn; it just exists, that's all."

"Chill . . ."

Kevin put a hand around his shoulder. Arthur relaxed and sank down into the seat. One agro student ten years their senior wearing jeans and a headset was now promoting his most recent product, a wireless soil analysis sampling probe. He was striding about, looking out into the hall like a person possessed, as he had probably been taught to do in his TED Talks training, presentations that were designed more to strike at the audience's emotions than to convince. "Soltech allows us to follow the evolution of soil properties in real time and provides recommendations based on progress of the crops. Volumetric moisture content, pH, amount of light, and even density . . . it's all processed." He ran through slides with the smiling faces of bearded cereal producers, looking just rustic enough to be authentic, but who were equipped with the latest MacBook Pro to track their crops from their living room. "The issue is not the number of fertilizers," he had the audacity to assert, "but the ability to administer the right dose at the right time." Graphs appeared on the screen, showing an increase in yield corresponding with a reduction in chemical inputs. "The day those curves intersect, we'll have done it!" Kevin heard Arthur snort. Personally, he thought the tech stuff was interesting but was careful not to show it.

"Our ambition," concluded their elder, "is to revolutionize farmers' quality of life. No need to travel kilometers across the fields every morning to handle a clod of earth. Soltech is more precise and more reliable than the human eye. Better knowledge of our environment for a more responsible treatment of our soil!"

"And nothing about earthworms, go figure," grumbled Arthur. "What's the point in knowing the pH if we don't know the number of lumbrics per square meter?"

Kevin acknowledged there were obvious limits to Soltech from a scientific point of view. Soil quality can't be summarized using a handful of parameters. It depends on thousands of factors, millions of microorganisms that are still, for the most part, beyond the grasp of humans. As Marcel Combe had repeatedly noted, nobody is currently able to carry out a complete biophysico-chemical analysis of a clump of earth. And it's in reference to this fundamental ignorance that human intuition, the product of a long evolution that largely exceeds what is known of consciousness, takes on more meaning.

"They should invent a worm radar," said Kevin, half joking.

"I'm sure any good earthworm would devour his probe."

Kevin was aware of Arthur's obsession and had followed its many manifestations. Ever since that evening in Rue Gay-Lussac, he had not deviated from his notion of lumbric inoculation. His relationship with Anne had ensnared him in the plan; as time passed, he had found himself playing along. What had started out as a vague attempt to flirt had turned into a vocation. He had rapidly carried out a survey of the few publications on the topic. They were able to be summed up in a bibliography only a few pages long. Everything remained to be discovered. Arthur had the impression, so rare in such a jaded era where every horizon seemed already to have been explored, that he was making inroads into a new continent where pioneers remained few and far between and everybody knew each other. Unlike the majority of his peers, who were joining communities of tens of thousands of researchers in order to scrounge for the crumbs of those still unresolved questions, he encountered no difficulties in accessing the best conferences that always featured the same dozen specialists, aware of their marginality but convinced they represented the avant-garde of scientific progress. Humanity had hurtled toward understanding the infinite expanse of the heavens but remained stammering before the infinite immediacy of the planet's soil.

According to Arthur, who never missed an opportunity to drown Kevin in cultural references, earthworms undermined La Bruyère's assertion that "we are thinking creatures and have been for more than seven thousand years. And we are too late; everything has already been said." Everything? No. Seven thousand years had proven insufficient to see what lay beneath their very feet.

Following his master's, during which he studied the degradation of organic matter, Arthur enrolled in a doctoral program at INRAE, the National Institute for Agronomic Research—recently rebranded to reflect the mood of the times and now known as the National Research Institute for Agriculture, Food, and the Environment—and was looking at three or four years of study and, in particular, carrying out experiments on the repopulation of earthworms. Anne was excited by his dissertation topic: "Agronomic solutions in the context of agroecological transition: Soil revitalization through lumbricid inoculation." And yet she was careful not to mention lumbrics in the ecofeminist groups she had joined at Sciences Po. There were battles to fight about the equal division of domestic labor and the deforestation of the Amazon. Earthworms could not be prioritized, even if they were hermaphrodites.

"I've found some land," declared Arthur, who seemed to be following Kevin's thoughts.

"Crappy land where you're going to be able to work your miracles?"

"Exactly. Turns out I didn't have to look that hard. I've told you about my grandparents before, haven't I?"

"I thought they were dead."

"Yes. But before they died, they used to own a farm in Lower Normandy."

"I didn't realize. You only told me you used to spend your holidays in the country."

Kevin felt almost disappointed. The land, livestock—that was *his* parents' world. A not entirely disagreeable world, but nor was there anything enviable about it, and he had imagined Arthur divinely protected from it.

"It's not something I'm particularly proud of," Arthur continued. "My grandfather practiced polyculture farming, like everyone else. Papi's method involved calculating the balance between the cost of inputs, Common Agricultural Policy subsidies, the interest rate on his borrowings, and grain prices on world markets. He managed to get by, more or less. But his land didn't survive."

"Did he find somebody to take it over?"

"No. My father left all that behind to study law in Paris and never had the slightest desire to get involved, either up close or from afar. The farmhand, who had started out as an apprentice and could have taken over the business with his eyes shut, ended up following a woman to Brittany. Papi finally put the farm on the market on some specialist websites. He had some interest, but it depressed him, these strangers who would ask questions about the water tightness of the animal stalls. So, he sold the bulk of the property to his idiot neighbor who keeps expanding. He's called Monsieur Jobard—I mean, can you believe he has such a ridiculous name? May as well have 'fool' for a middle name. Honestly you couldn't make it up. You know the first thing he did?"

"Pulled out the hedges to let a tractor through."

"Yeah. You get it! You'd think that sort of behavior was a thing of the past. Well, it's not."

"No kidding!" murmured Kevin.

As an adolescent, he had known a lot of guys who drove the farming equipment; they'd come back to his place to eat during their lunch break.

"Hedges can be annoying, though," he added.

"What?" asked Arthur, startled.

"Just joking."

"All Papi kept were the farm buildings and a few hectares with a bit of equipment, 'to keep his hand in,' as he used to say. He certainly did that. He kept pouring out pesticides until the day he died. Even though I must have explained it to him a thousand times. 'We're feeding the world' is what he used to say. Yeah right. All he was doing was killing the earth that was feeding the world. He was a kind man, though."

Kevin was quiet. Even if Arthur was unquestionably correct, he didn't like it when elders weren't given the respect they deserved. Especially those farmers who had been twenty years old in the 1970s and had changed their way of doing everything. They'd been sold progress and had bought it outright. It was the craziest gamble ever made by a generation. A gamble they lost, perhaps. But how could they be reproached for their audacity, their machines that looked like spaceships, their unquenchable thirst for knowledge, their wild hopes for a world without war or famine? Farmers had become mechanics, chemists, lawyers, financiers, and geo-politicians. Their failure was also the failure of humanism.

"My father is letting me have the property. It's not worth much," added Arthur quickly, trying to downplay his privilege, "but anyway."

"Not much, meaning?"

"I don't know. One hundred thousand, two at the very most."

Kevin smiled. His parents had probably never had ten thousand euros to their names. Becoming landowners was not in their realm of the possible. They were mere tumbleweeds, blown around at the whim of the wind. They left to others the task of putting roots down.

"We're moving there, Anne and I. As of this summer."

"Do you mean for vacation?"

"No, for life."

Kevin looked at him incredulously. He couldn't for one second imagine him fixing fences wearing overalls and rubber boots.

"I can live in the country, too, if I want," declared Arthur, dryly.

"And what are you going to do there?"

"We've discussed this a thousand times! Reintroduce earthworms."

Kevin knew all about Arthur's fantasies. He loved listening to them. But it had never crossed his mind that he would ever implement them. With his three-day beard, T-shirt sporting a cannabis leaf design, and corduroy jacket, Arthur looked anything but a farmer.

"That's not a profession."

"It's work. I'm going to do it using SGT."

"Using what?"

"Did you fail agroecology? Simplified Growing Technique."

"Oh yeah, that business involving no plowing . . ."

"Correct."

"Weeds, here we come!"

Arthur just raised his eyebrows. He rejected the notion that there were "bad" plants. He seemed sure of himself and his plans. Kevin knew that these days there were any number of techniques and combination crop farming methods that allowed a sort of natural equilibrium to establish itself between cereals and weeds. But why make life more difficult than it needed to be?

"So then, you're diverging."

"Sure. I'm diverging without actually spelling it out."

"I still don't see how you're going to earn a crust. With a few hectares and no plowing . . ."

"We'll be twenty-five next year."

"Yeah, so?"

"We can go on welfare."

"Something to aspire to."

"I'd rather be paid by society for doing something that will benefit the environment than be remunerated by some company to destroy it. And besides," Arthur added, as if to excuse himself, "I'll be doing my thesis."

"What about Anne?"

"She wants to write novels."

"What, all day long?"

"We're very much in love."

"You won't last six months."

Kevin immediately regretted his spitefulness. The whole situation was upsetting. He couldn't understand how Arthur could squander his best years with a single girl, a single body, a single possible future. In his view, heterosexual relationships like that were unbelievably tedious. Everything was a foregone conclusion: the desire, the coupledom, the children, the exhaustion, the boredom, followed by the only alternatives: divorce, or resignation—also known as "the love of my life."

"You could come with us," suggested Arthur timidly.

"And be the third wheel?"

Notwithstanding the high esteem in which he held their friendship, Kevin could not for a moment imagine living in Lower Normandy with two neo-rurals bewitched by butterflies.

"So what will you do?" asked Arthur. "You're not going to abandon me? You're still going to be thinking about our earthworms?"

Kevin was about to reply when he was saved by the divergers taking the stage. It was the moment the whole hall had been waiting for. Arthur was watching them intently, a little envious. They had improved since 2022. There were about twenty of them, holding hands. They were all wearing green T-shirts bearing the extinction logo, an hourglass in a circle. Equipped with clip-on mikes, they divided among themselves a text they had learned by heart, interspersed with English slogans chanted in unison: "Extinction rebellion!" or "One Planet!" Their discourse had become politicized. They wanted to make more of an impact than their overly timid predecessors. Saving the planet was no longer enough. Now capitalism had to be destroyed, to the great delight of their cohort. Banks, multinationals, Europe, governments, lobbyists, all of them were the enemy. Even the UN was complicit.

"They're going too far," said Arthur, as if to reassure himself. "I'd be happy just repairing the damage caused by my grandfather. The rest we can see about later."

"They're sort of cute. Like a happy band of orgy-goers."

"Minimal agriculture, minimal ethics," said Arthur, on a roll. "Tend your own garden first."

Kevin left his friend to his own thoughts. It was obviously not the time to be telling him about his own project. Kevin was planning to launch a little worm composting business. There were already some composting boxes on the market in which various sorts of waste could be broken down by worms, but nothing that was either practical or elegant. Kevin was convinced there was a better, low-cost solution. With his agricultural engineering training, he would create a simpler, more attractive product. The idea was that latte-drinking liberals with their smooth hands, worried about saving the earth but revulsed by the idea of digging their fingers into it, would never have to lift the lid on the squirming lumbrics. The slogan could have been: "Don't get dirty, get green."

Kevin had maintained sporadic contact with Marcel Combe after his lecture. He had asked him for advice in identifying the best species of lumbric. The old professor would have been dreaming of a young man taking on his plans for an industrial scale worm composter, but Kevin's ambitions remained more modestly commercial. Selling designer worm composters to city dwellers guilted by their mountains of daily waste would mean he could be independent, earn a living, and, most importantly, live in Paris, which, in his mind, remained a city of Babylonian nights and pleasures, crawling with insatiable reprobates. It would mean he could satisfy his principal requirement: to depend on nothing and nobody—neither man nor woman, professor nor boss, ideal nor doctrine.

The lights had come back on, and the audience was applauding the divergers with raised fists. Then the head of the school made his way onto the stage and resumed his speech. "Thank you to our young engineers for presenting us with this alternative vision . . ."

"Come on, let's get out of here." Arthur leaped out of his seat, insistent.

And the two boys made their way with a determined stride through the padded, double-winged doors that separated them from adult life.

Out on the boulevards, it was already dark. They bought a pack of beers at the first grocery store they came across and headed down to the Seine. Kevin was eyeing the café terraces he would soon be frequenting, while Arthur was bidding farewell to his city, head bowed. At the Pont Royal, they took the stairs leading down to the Quai des Tuileries. Only a few steps and they were in another world. The intermittent lampposts left puddles of deep shadow. The noise of Paris, suddenly muffled, gave way to snatches of conversation; laughter and insults ricocheted off the flagstones, dissipating at the water's edge. There were small groups of partygoers, solitary walkers, homeless people with their dogs. They had to be careful not to trip on empty bottles or stumble over a body splayed on the ground. Barely a stone's throw from the large department stores, the horizon obscured by the monumental facades of the Musée d'Orsay and the Assemblée Nationale, life continued away from the lights, away from any judgment. The slapping of the river interfered with an otherwise well-ordered universe. The modern city, illuminated and divided into sections, had somehow permitted the continued existence of this fantastical shadow zone, a place rendered all the more titillating by the sweet scent of marginality. Only occasionally would floodlights from barges catch these nocturnal strays unawares, fixing them like fugitives captured in the strafing beam of a watchtower.

The two friends sat on a stone bench. They hadn't thought to bring a bottle opener. Kevin grabbed the beers and, using the edge of the bench as a lever, removed the lids with a practiced gesture. They clinked their bottles, drinking to the future.

"Hey dudes. You gonna offer me a beer?"

A punk with pink tresses emerged from the darkness, a water nymph gifted from the river, punctured with piercings. Kevin felt Arthur tense, and sensed his discomfort.

"Take a seat," Kevin said to her, calmly.

The three of them shot the breeze. The punkette was clearly well on her way to getting wasted. She told rambling stories of railway stations, bungled deals, and, bizarrely, public law decisions, a subject she had studied for a couple of years, and about which she retained fond memories. Then Kevin took it on himself to explain his worm composting plans to her. She kept saying, "Yes, yes," despite not really understanding and, judging by her expression, was troubled by the idea that she had run into some dude even sketchier than she was. Worms in the living room, that was dodgy, no doubt about it. Having gotten her attention, Kevin plucked up the courage to outline his entire project. He didn't once look at his friend, who said not a word.

"All of Paris's waste," he concluded, embracing the city with a broad sweep of his arm, "everything that oozes out of this city's body, all its food, its fucks, every bit of it transformed into quality soil by millions and millions of earthworms! The city's excesses returned to nature . . ."

Kevin didn't recognize himself. He let himself be suffused by the atmosphere of the moment. He was convinced it would be easy. All he had to do was allow himself to be swept along, like the barges slipping under the arches of the river's bridges.

"Hark, I present you with Rastignac of the Seine!" Arthur spoke at last.

Kevin didn't know what to make of his friend's reference to Balzac's character from *The Human Comedy*.

"Sounds super, dude," added Arthur, with no hint of irony.

Relieved, finally, Kevin placed his hand on Arthur's. He felt the hairs on Arthur's bony fingers under his own palm.

"You guys are fucking weirdos," said the punk chick, as she picked her way, reeling, toward the Pont Royal.

III

Arthur and Anne had loaded into the trunk fifteen or so trash bags containing everything they thought they would need to set up a life. They had decided to devote the bulk of their year's carbon emissions to this long trip, knowing that once they were there, they would inevitably need a car. Arthur's father's old Volvo, with its low roof and rectangular lines, looked like it had come straight out of a Claude Sautet film. After turning off the A88 at Falaise, they switched off the GPS so they could "start to get to know the region," as Anne had said, as she disappeared behind the widespread map. She had circled their destination in red: Saint-Firmin-sur-Orne, where Papi's abandoned farm awaited them. They took their time losing their way on that warmish, end-of-spring day, meandering along smaller byroads that took them deeper and deeper into the countryside, like worms into their chambers. This was their neo-rural initiation rite, as they were drawn into the depths of the landscape in which they planned to introduce a bit of new life.

Through the Volvo's open window they discovered the real

Normandy, the Normandy with no name. Lying among the hedged farmland of Vire, the Caen Plain, Domfront and its surrounds, and the Falaise countryside, it was sometimes referred to as the "Switzerland of Normandy" due to its changing altitudes. Arthur was not fond of this expression, coined for tourism purposes. This made it no less true, however, that between Pont-d'Ouilly, Clécy, Athis-de-l'Orne, and Condé-sur-Noireau, where the Armorican Massif meets intermingled woodland and hedged pastures, the landscape hollows out, crumples and creases. Looming over clifftops and house facades alike, granite shatters the intoxicatingly peaceful Norman countryside. It sobers the spirit. The half-timbered houses in charming villages are replaced by dark stonework, heavy and menacing. The pleated rocks force rivers to divert, apple trees to form great knotted roots, cows to cling to sloping pastures, and villages to hunker snugly into the shadows. Every hollow conceals another, barely signaled by bell towers striking up to the sky like buoys in the sea, lest the scattered souls of their inhabitants be forgotten. And yet they are well adapted, these locals, to their environment. They have all that happiness requires. Every hamlet has its unrivaled view, its slice of the world, entitling every last villager to their noble ways.

At that time of the year, the countryside was all yellows and pinks. On the steepest slopes, expanses of wild broom were punctuated by eddies of loosestrife. Arthur took note of the uninterrupted hedges between fields and the dense foliage covering holloways that crisscrossed the road at regular intervals; so many veins still nourishing the earth. This precipitous country, largely given over to pasture, had seen less aggressive land consolidation than in other parts. Even though Arthur and Anne barely encountered another vehicle—or if they did, only vans pelting along at full tilt—everywhere they looked they saw a populated landscape, delicately strewn with stone houses, their granite lintels brightened by pink tones of schist. As if topographical chance had miraculously preserved the region from the lethal triumvirate of metropolis, housing estates, and dilapidated buildings.

Even though France was experiencing its umpteenth period of drought and the Loire was, in places, able to be crossed on foot, here streams spouted forth at every turn, fields remained regularly supplied by rains generated over the Atlantic. After a morning spent packing up their possessions followed by four hours on the road from Paris, Arthur and Anne couldn't resist the temptation of getting their feet wet. They pulled over onto the shoulder next to a stone bridge. A faded signpost noted the place as the Moulin de Taillebois. They headed briefly along a path of crushed stone before descending through a lush grassy jungle to the riverbank. There was no barbed-wire fence, no permanent picnic facilities, no hikers' waymarks; it was just open space. They knelt down and cautiously ran their hands through the water, like animals sniffing before drinking. Pompously claiming its title as a tributary of the Orne, here the Rouvre was content to be a clear, relatively shallow brook. Its bed was soft and silty, rays of sunshine danced strobe-like through beech tree leaves, and the current coursed across the pebbles. Arthur and Anne looked at each other, and, without a word needing to be said, undressed. They stretched out naked in the stream as if crawling between bedsheets, their backs supported by a mattress of sand. Tiny fish approached to tickle them. Every one of their senses was sated. Unusually, there was nothing, nothing at all to spoil things, no engine noise, no stale smell of muck-spreading, no concrete blocks in their field of vision, no unduly sharp pebble beneath their buttocks. Even insistent desire had been extinguished by the water's cool.

"This is paradise," said Arthur. "Everything humanity could need has been created . . ."

"Shut up," said Anne, as gently as possible.

They remained like that for several long minutes, without touching, lost in themselves, thoughts slowing, relishing the welcome offered to them by their new environment. The light's refraction rendered their bodies pale and misshapen. It was as if their heads were floating above the water, two masks adrift.

* * *

Arthur had been apprehensive about their arrival at Saint-Firmin. The farm, located a little outside the village, had been named "Farm in the Woods." Back then, one didn't concern oneself with finding sophisticated names for Airbnb tourists, such as "Key to Your Dreams" or "Hedgerow Heaven"; language naturally took the most efficient, the most direct, and, accordingly, the most authentically poetic path. It had been many years since there had been any woodland, but the Farm in the Woods remained isolated. Access was by way of a small road behind the church. A five-hundred-meter climb up a gentle slope was enough to dispel all trace of urbanization. The main farmstead with its slate roof retained a certain air of solidity, but the adjacent barns, which still housed farm equipment, like the old McCormick tractor with its dented wheel rims, were already significantly dilapidated. All around were fields as far as the eye could see, most of them now belonging to Monsieur Jobard.

Up on this high plateau, the wooded pastureland of hedgerows and copses had disappeared; wheat, barley, and oats in the blade stretched out in endless subtle shades of green. Arthur would have loved to have come across at least one venerable old oak, untouchable, saved by old-fashioned Norman beliefs.

But no. Amid a sea of showy, well-groomed cereals only two hectares of eyesore remained: the last plots his grandfather had held on to, on the verge of becoming a wilderness, already darkened by brambles, gorse, and ferns. They were adjacent to the farmhouse, the idea being that one could head directly from the kitchen into the fields. Except that now there was a barrier of thorny spikes in the way.

This was where Arthur wanted to create his Walden.

Arthur was struggling to imagine Anne in this environment. Their relationship was balancing on the tenuous thread of their ideals and there was every reason to wager it would quickly snap in the face of reality. Her enthusiasm at the prospect of being a future novelist borne of the land notwithstanding, Anne had grown up in the fifth arrondissement in the heart of Paris on the Montagne Sainte-Geneviève and considered the countryside as some sort of far-flung suburb populated by extreme right-wing voters and left to run wild. She was about to find herself in some fairly rundown building filled with Formica furniture from the sixties and impregnated with that inexplicable stench of fried onion so characteristic of every rural household, no matter how high-tech it might be. As for Arthur himself, he couldn't realistically conceive of how he was going to occupy his days. He had brought an entire library of the classics to ward off boredom. His thesis supervisor at INRAE had strongly advised him against "burying himself in that hole" and encouraged him to come into the lab at Saclay as often as possible to do his experiments. He had been told thousands of idealistic tales of his kind who foundered swiftly because of a failure to adapt, impatience, or hostility from the locals. Moreover, he had a degree in agronomy, rather than any technical agricultural qualifications, and he was dreading finding himself face to face with a plot of land, a real, tangible plot of land into which he would have to dig his hands, which he would have to inspect and care for every day, and which would require him to come up with solutions not found in any manual.

To his great surprise, the first weeks passed by in a sort of industrious harmony. Anne had taken to the job of refurbishment in earnest and with liberal recourse to YouTube tutorials threw herself into the tasks of rewiring, plastering, and plumbing, dressed without fail in denim overalls that gaped at her chest and showed off the curly tufts embellishing her underarms. She appeared astonishingly well suited to the work and was always wandering about with her tool kit, which she carried slung across her body in an old leather pouch. In this isolated house where nobody was able to hear her, she started cussing with evident delight. "It's breakin' my balls" featured prominently among her favorite expressions; she had been repressed for too long hanging out with her Sciences Po crowd. She would crack open a beer at day's end, slumping into the old Chesterfield sofa in the living room, and direct her man to the stovetop, a task he accepted with a certain pride, going so far as to demonstrate his enthusiasm by tying an apron around his waist.

Anne took visible pleasure in continuing the process of scarification on her body that had begun with piercings as she emerged from adolescence. Her hands were stained with primer, her arms marked by a thousand DIY gashes, her catlike features roughened by a mixture of sweat and dust. Arthur had never found her so attractive.

Once night fell, both of them would collapse onto a mattress placed directly on the floor. Anne would routinely put off any writing until the following day; she claimed that the hours spent with screwdriver and trowel were allowing her to continue her plot development.

The distribution of labor happened naturally enough without any discussion. While Anne put Papi's rusty drill to use, Arthur started clearing the area where he was planning on creating a rewilded meadow, the perfect biotope for his earthworms. He could already see himself with Anne in the coming spring, running through waist-high grasses. Hesitant about the idea of using a tractor and reckoning that he was, in any event, incapable of maneuvering it, he had decided to go about clearing the land using traditional methods. He had come across a basic scythe in the barn and had embraced the dandy spirit to the point of selecting an old checked shirt that would henceforth be his outfit of choice for work in the fields. Wasn't this in the order of things? Shouldn't land ravaged by mechanization be brought back to life by man's own handiwork? Arthur remembered a passage from *Anna Karenina* in which Levin, a wealthy, but idle, landowner spends an ecstatic day scything through the wheat and fraternizing with the peasants. Why couldn't he, too, experience the ataraxia of the scythe?

Initial efforts proved disappointing. Arthur approached the first brambles with determination, convinced he could demolish the enemy with a couple of well-aimed blows. He was stopped in his tracks by the resistance put up by this solid, tangled matter intent on proliferating and directing all of its prickles at the invader. Arthur was forced to go at it twenty odd times before managing to slice off the first armload of runners, attacking with an awkward motion that resembled more a thrashing than a calm swinging of the scythe. He finished off the messy murder with a pair of pruning shears before tossing the corpse of green matter to one side, a laughably small and misshapen pile. His hands were bleeding, having been lacerated by thorns. He stopped, out of breath, and raised his eyes to look over his plot of land, which suddenly seemed immense, a veritable fortified camp, the first barrier to which he had only just managed to breach. He chewed on a young, unripe blackberry, remembering it was supposed to have certain medicinal properties, even if he had forgotten what, precisely, they were. The taste was horribly sour. He spat it out, medicinal or not. The job ahead felt impossible, inhuman. The triumphant hammer blows sounding from the living room nonetheless commanded him to take heart. The scythe probably just needed sharpening, he told himself.

Arthur spent the following days hunting for a whetstone. He did not yet know anybody in the village and refused to make the slightest request for assistance from Monsieur Jobard, whom he regularly saw on his fluorescent blue tractor in the neighboring fields, but whom he had thus far refrained from greeting. Arthur discovered that the specialist stores were all several dozen miles away and all of them closed on the dot of noon. After several failed attempts in the gardening stores of Athis-de-l'Orne and Thury-Harcourt, he resolved, with death in his heart, to head to the DIY Cash store in the mall at Flers. He practically had to drive to Caen to lay his hands on what must have been the most basic piece of farming equipment for the last thousand years. Didn't anybody scythe their grass anymore?

Arthur felt a degree of vengeful satisfaction working the blade until it became sharp as a razor.

"Now that's a scythe," he declared triumphantly to Anne. "You could cut through granite with that."

"I think I've finished doing the bathroom," she answered, smiling, splattered with plaster from head to foot.

"Come on," said Arthur. "I'll show you."

They left the kitchen and headed toward the scrubby bushes.

"Watch this!"

Arthur gave a great circular sweep of his arm. Thorns flew off in front of him.

"That's how it's done! The old-fashioned way!"

He resumed his action, which ended in a cry of pain and with Anne running off to look for bandages.

The next day, Arthur, hobbling, succeeded in clearing a few square meters. He kept at it for close to eight hours straight, barely stopping for a bite to eat. It was backbreaking work beneath the summer solstice sun. There was nothing hypnotic or meditative about it.

"Tolstoy really was an ass," he mumbled, stretching out his muscles that were protesting at the sudden activity. He had the keen sense that the effort required was disproportionate to such a paltry result.

He set to studying his action. He found websites dedicated to the scythe and its reemergence.

Economical and pleasant to use, the scythe is an efficient, entirely ecological and environmentally friendly tool. This offered some comfort at least to Arthur and his endeavors.

The scythe must do the work, not you. He couldn't agree more.

With your scythe horizontal to the ground, place some sort of reference marker at point "A" at the edge of the blade. While keeping the tip of the handle against your boot, grip the middle handle and pivot the scythe around to the right, level with the ground, until point "p" reaches point "A."

If "p" ends up above "A," the angle is too open and must be reduced.

If "p" is at the same level as "A," the blade is considered to be in a circular setting. This setting is recommended for grass of thinner density, where "p" can be up to 3 centimeters beneath "A."

A setting where "p" ends up between 4 to 6 centimeters beneath "A" is required for thicker or tangled grass.

Why was it all so complicated? Did the peasants of the Middle Ages understand the relationship between "A" and "p"? Arthur was learning how to farm like an adult goes about learning a foreign language. He needed to study the vocabulary and understand the grammar. Nothing about it came naturally.

After making some adjustments and persevering, Arthur managed to clear a couple of hundred square meters of land in a month, the same time it took to grow the beginnings of a mustache. Every so often, he felt on the verge of that felicitous state where the body finds its equilibrium, where the blade seems to move of its own accord, where the mind retreats into a void. But very soon, some imperceptible incorrect motion would haul him back to his clumsy, hand-to-hand combat. Caught in the violence of the gesture, all he felt in those moments was a vague murderous pleasure as he methodically massacred hundreds of blackberry brambles.

Arthur also did his best to pull out the largest roots, the ones that would take several years to break down. Digging his spade into the earth always made him feel a degree of sadness; the clay-heavy, naturally fertile soil had been reduced to compact chunks giving off an unpleasant, acidic odor. The merest blow reduced it to dust, the slightest shower transformed it into a gigantic mud puddle, forcing Arthur to interrupt his work. The soil was a desert, stripped bare after forty years of pesticides, plowing, and fertilizer. Arthur knew Papi's recipe by heart: soil improvers in March, the NPK triumvirate of nitrogen, phosphorus, and potassium; then, when the plants were growing badly or too quickly, a good plant growth regulator in the springtime to stop them in their tracks. Papi was very proud of his dosages, which in fact called for considerable expertise and constant revision. His land had become nothing more than a receptacle for chemical products. When he held it in his hands, Arthur felt like he was in a laboratory. He had not yet spotted a single earthworm.

The bare plot of land was quite a repugnant sight. Very pale brown, it was more reminiscent of a clay tennis court than farmland. With a sparse scattering of debris and studded with twisted rootlets, it seemed even worse than wasteland. It was hard to imagine how this husk could ever take on new life.

To try to set his mind at ease, Arthur marked out a square meter of soil and sprinkled it with a mixture of mustard and water. Then he waited.

"Come on, little ones, come on!"

The minutes went by. Nothing appeared. The principle behind this well-known technique was that the nauseated lumbrics would come up for fresh air. Arthur had prepared several boxes to sort them by size and color so he could start to identify the species and subspecies on his land. He added a bit more liquid. The smell of the mustard tickled his nostrils.

"Are you sulking then?"

He called out to Anne, who was just back from sourcing new sanding disks in Athis. She set down her leather bag and came to kneel next to Arthur. They held each other like new parents leaning over a cradle.

"Come on, little ones, come on!"

Arthur launched into a long explanation to better prepare Anne for the spectacle that was brewing, taking his inspiration in large part from Combe's lecture. Lumbrics were divided into three main categories. Endogeics, quite pale, very shy, never emerge from the earth. It was a shame, though, given the good fortune of living on this planet, never to be curious enough to take a wander in the great outdoors. At the other end of the spectrum, the overexcited bright red epigeics leap right out of the soil, never happier than in a pile of manure. Their perpetual motion borders on vanity. However, the boss of all earthworms, *primus inter pares*, is, no contest, the anecic. Extending majestically to a length of several centimeters, its tail as spearhead, it comes and goes between the surface and its subterranean lair. It makes cautious sorties into the fresh air to consume some fresh produce, or conversely, to deposit its excrement in the form of castings several centimeters high, like sand pies. You even see them dragging leaves along with their mouths back into their tunnels. That's no easy feat; they have to roll up the leaf to slide it down into the earth where it will serve as food stores or strengthening material for their tunnels. As Darwin noted, the anecic is intelligent enough, when it encounters an obstacle, not to attempt the same maneuver again but to try different solutions. How many humans could you say that about?

"Then," Arthur continued, "you have to distinguish between geophages, rhizophages, or carnivores, then between the different subspecies, like *Ailoscolex lacteospumosus* or *Agastrodrilus monicae* . . ."

"Look," Anne interrupted him, "something's moving over there!"

They both leaned over. The earth was in fact moving in fits and starts. Something was pushing from underneath.

"There it is!"

The head was starting to emerge.

"An endogeic?" asked Anne, excitedly.

Arthur pulled a doubtful face.

"All I can say is it doesn't look well."

The worm took several long minutes to appear completely then lay lifeless on the surface, as if exhausted by the effort. It was about two to three centimeters long. Arthur picked it up with his fingers and examined it closely.

"Frankly, I've never seen one in this condition. As a general rule, they squirm about when you catch them."

The worm was almost inert. The clitellum—the bulge that appears on an earthworm during puberty—could hardly be made out on its grayish body. The worm appeared completely deflated.

"I can't even tell which end is which," Arthur said.

"That's its mouth, isn't it?"

"Or its anus. Not sure." Arthur mused aloud. "And yet it's not really time for estivation, even if it's starting to get properly warm."

For several days now, it had felt like summer had well and truly settled in. It was midmorning, and the sun was beating down right overhead.

"Time for what?" asked Anne.

"Estivation. It's a diapause: worms become lethargic. A sort of summer hibernation, really. But it's still early in the season. It's not normal."

A handful of other worms had appeared while they had been watching. They, too, were lying motionless on the stripped earth, done in, like streamers that had come down after a party. Arthur waited another ten minutes or so, long enough to allow three more of their peers to join them. He could make out none of the usual earthworm characteristics. There was no trying to identify an anecic or an endogeic from these exhausted wrecks.

"We've really pulled in the crowds here. It's ridiculous. Ten or so specimens from one square meter. That makes ten kilos per hectare. Which is to say, nothing."

"But isn't that good for you?" asked Anne.

"How's that?"

"For your experiments? You'll be able to start from a real blank slate. A completely dead area."

"Not completely dead," corrected Arthur, "let's say profoundly impoverished. But it's sad all the same."

He felt her pressing her mouth against his and slipped his hand behind the front panel of her overalls, directly onto her breast. She sighed and drew out her kiss. She started to unbutton Arthur's shirt while he hooked his lips to her piercing like a fish taking the bait.

"What if someone sees us . . ." he objected without conviction.

"There's never anybody around here. Just your earthworms."

"Which are blind."

She used her arms to push him onto his back. Arthur reacted just in time to shift to the side so as not to crush his poor lumbrics. As he pulled down his pants, she slipped off her overalls, then settled on top of him, legs straddled. She took the tool of her pleasure, rubbed it around the lips growing slick between her thighs, then slid it all the way inside her until against her buttocks she felt the two familiar little padded cushions, reminders of man's similarity to other creatures. In those moments, Arthur was fond of thinking he was nothing more than a simple mammal, no different from any other male of any other species. She straightened up, head raised skyward, hands behind her on her lover's legs. Her gaze was fixed on the distance, toward the granite cliffs, the dark ridges of which could just be made out. Her pelvis undulated smoothly, with a soothing regularity. Beneath her, Arthur enjoyed the deliciousness of being kneaded. The bramble branch tearing at the base of his spine only heightened his pleasure. Half dazzled by the sun, he saw Anne's breasts, taut and regal, amid a dancing constellation of yellow spots. They came quickly, as one, brightening the plateau with their moans.

IV

"But . . . won't it smell?"

"Absolutely not. That's a myth. Its cleanliness is what sets it apart from a classic composting unit."

"And yet I saw on some blog that lots of customers complain about that. Even if it is a myth, it becomes an issue for business, doesn't it, if it's such a widespread belief?"

"Well, obviously, if it's too hot for too long, that can happen. Ideally, room temperature should be between 15 and 25 degrees."

"So you have to have the air conditioner on all summer so these delicate little creatures stay comfortable?"

"No, it's not that regulated . . . everything is always a bit fluid when you're dealing with living things . . . you just have to keep an eye on it . . ."

"When you see what people do with their dogs during long vacations, I doubt they'll be paying much attention to their earthworms!"

Having suffered refusals from all the major banks, Kevin had waited four months to finally get this meeting with BPI, the public investment bank set up by the state to "service the future," if you believed its branding. He had been summoned to its head office on Boulevard Haussmann. After passing between two marble columns at the entrance, he had found himself in a monumental foyer with a green wall and sinusoidal sofas. A young woman who introduced herself as an "assistant" had then accompanied him through the labyrinthine corridors, swiping herself through each door.

Sitting opposite him now was a distinguished man in his fifties with unapologetically salt-and-pepper hair, sporting round, finely framed, silver glasses and a colorful pocket square in his tweed jacket. He had immediately clarified that he was a "business manager" and not a banker, that would probably be too vulgar. His sardonic smile never left his face and he took visible pleasure in tormenting the flailing young entrepreneurs who paraded through his office. Kevin had already learned how to recognize this particularly Parisian personality type: an executive with a linear career and an agile, but narrow, mind; one of capitalism's anonymous dogs' bodies, gathering up only crumbs, and compensating for the mediocrity of their career path by their conviction that they were at the forefront of social progress. They were five-thousand-euro-a-month revolutionaries—harbingers of disruption, oracles of corporate accountability, prophets of tomorrow's world, always ahead of any innovation. While the general public was still discovering artificial intelligence, they were already getting worked up about quantum computing. By dint of subscribing to newsletters and attending conferences, they ended up with a cross section of enough references and quotes to fuel a city dinner. The most determined among them had spent a few weeks disconnecting on retreat and elaborating their own theory of the universe, a hundred or so pages of material, alas, too innovative to interest any publisher, which would lead them to develop one ultimate virtue: modesty. Suffice it to say that all this unrecognized genius could not be wasted for too long discussing a loan of sixty thousand euros for worm composting.

"I just need financing for the design and production of the molds," Kevin tried to explain. "Then I'll be able to produce the boxes on demand."

"Boxes of what? Boxes of earthworms?"

Kevin realized that the round glasses had scarcely lingered on his file. Once again he attempted the perilous exercise of explaining his project, without letting his interlocutor realize that he had worked out the man hadn't understood a thing.

"That's a good question! In fact—and I apologize if I wasn't clear in my diagrams—the worm composter is made up of several boxes."

"Yes, I saw that."

"You put in an initial collecting tray with worms and biowaste. You close it back up, and you keep feeding it regularly. When the tray is full, you put a second tray on top, which has holes pierced in it to allow the worms to access it on their own. And so on. After several months, the first tray will be full of the best possible fertilizer, fine, black compost: you remove that tray, empty it, and then it's ready to be put back on top."

"But there'll be worms in the compost."

"No, they'll have gone."

"Gone where? They can't escape from the box, can they?"

"No, no, they'll have gone into the second tray."

"They can't get out? You're not going to have little worms squirming all over the living room carpet?"

"They'll be very happy staying in their boxes. They'd dry up and die in a handful of minutes on the outside."

"Good, I trust you. The main point is that the waste turns into compost, *am I right*?"

"I'm sorry?"

Kevin still hadn't grown used to the anglicisms that were bandied about the capital, understanding neither their meaning nor their point. The business manager looked apologetic but sympathetic.

"Compost and also worm tea," Kevin continued. "It's a very powerful fertilizer, you need to dilute it."

"*A cup of tea!*" the business manager said in English, and burst out laughing.

Kevin wasn't up to making repartee. This much he recognized, so he chose to remain silent, his face impassive, waiting for the other man to decide he was done with entertaining himself. The business manager gave up.

"And these worms, what do they look like?"

"First, they're not just any old worm. You need epigeics. More specifically, *Eisenia*. Same worms you use for fishing. They're a highly pigmented species, bright red. You can start with 250 grams worth."

"How many worms is that?"

"Between five hundred and a thousand. Then they get into a rhythm and autoregulate their population depending on their food. It takes ninety days for a worm to turn into an adult. Within six months, each of them could have a hundred or so offspring.

There can easily be three to four thousand worms in a fully operational worm composter."

"I'd rather not think about that. And who will supply the rootstock? The Adam and Eve of the worm composter?"

"I'm already in touch with partners involved in the vermiculture industry. They can deliver them through the mail. Twenty euros for two hundred and fifty grams. There are even companies who'll do it for free."

"Vermiculture! Even at my age, I'm still learning something new every day."

"Look, I brought you a packet . . ."

Kevin pulled a sealed plastic bag out of his rucksack and put it on the desk. The business manager pushed back his chair slightly. His verbosity suddenly vanished.

"Can I show you?"

"No, no need. Thank you, though."

"You'll see. They're adorable."

The business manager protested with alacrity, but Kevin had already zipped open the bag and plunged in his hand. He pulled out a handful of soil in which dozens of tiny snakelike creatures were all tangled up in a reddish, squirming ball. The manager let out a yelp of disgust.

"You can touch them, they won't do anything to you."

"No, no!"

"They don't bite, they don't sting, they won't dirty anything . . ."

"That's not the point."

The business manager nervously ran his hand through his hair, revealing a scalp that would soon be bald. What was the point then? Kevin was struggling to understand this phobia of perfectly inoffensive animals. Especially here, in this temple of economic rationality.

"There are three subspecies in this batch," Kevin continued, unperturbed, "*Eisenia foetida*, *Eisenia andrei*, and *Eisenia hortensis*. With a little bit of familiarity, you'll soon be able to distinguish between them. Can you make out the slight differences in their coloring?"

"Not really."

"Look, they're trying to get back into the bag. They're photosensitive. Poor little creatures."

"Yes, poor little creatures. Put them back, quickly."

Kevin allowed the torture to continue a few more seconds, just for the pleasure of seeing every trace of sarcasm disappear from the face of his interlocutor. He imagined, for a moment, how delightful it would feel if he were to toss the worms into the other man's face. His screams would be heard out in the street.

As soon as the little creatures were back in their bag, the manager let out a sigh of relief and remained silent. He was regaining his composure, hands clasped, mouth pursed. Kevin took the opportunity to glance about him. The wood paneling was buried under a jumbled collection of posters, prizes, and photos inscribed in bold type with the adjectives of the day: BPI's investments were sustainable, innovative, solid, responsible, committed, simple, benevolent, global, strategic, humane, and high-return. To read them, even the bosses appeared to be "activists." The room was bathed in the piss-yellow hue of BPI's corporate branding. *It's like rapeseed*, thought Kevin simply.

"Look, your thing is interesting," said the manager at last.

He was wondering if, finally, and despite Kevin's rough-around-the-edges appearance, there couldn't be some unexpected disruption here.

"And you can put all your waste into it?"

"Almost all."

"Which means?"

"You have to avoid dairy products, meat scraps, fatty products, citrus . . ."

"Are you serious?"

Realizing that yet again there would be no miracle, the business manager's expression changed.

"But that's far too complicated! Do you know how many people are able to recognize a piece of citrus these days?"

"They'll be given a notice with some diagrams. It's pretty easy to sort. You get used to it soon enough."

"So what can you put in there, apart from your stale bread?"

"Ah, you're better off not putting bread in."

"Listen, young man . . ."

"But coffee grounds, crushed eggshells, the . . ."

"They're really too picky, these earthworms of yours. I can't see who's going to enjoy crushing eggshells. Let's be realistic."

Let's be realistic. That was generally a bad sign. Nonetheless, Kevin made one last stand.

"Even if we don't get the whole world doing it, there is a young, urban population who wants nothing more than to get involved. There are already six thousand members in the 'Worm composters' Facebook group. I'd only need to sell two hundred boxes a year to break even."

The business manager looked distractedly at his telephone,

which was sitting on his desk in plain view. He didn't like modest projects. Kevin went all in.

"Look, isn't it at the heart of BPI's mission statement? Financing the transition toward . . ."

He was searching for the words. His eyes fell on a poster opposite, a cheat sheet for green values.

". . . toward a simpler, more sustainable, more engaged world?"

"You know," burst out the manager, cut to the quick, "there is nobody more conscious than I am of the environmental stakes. I was talking about it twenty years ago. The situation is serious. Very serious," he added, lowering his voice, his tone earnest.

Kevin nodded his head.

"Humanity must reinvent itself. Completely. It's a paradigm shift, in the Kuhnian sense. You know about Kuhn and his paradigms?"

"No . . ."

Kevin felt at a loss, his throat was dry. Arthur would have known what to say.

"It's very complex . . . It's not something I can explain in thirty seconds . . . Look, just quickly, it's a system of representations where everything refers to something else. Everything is then significant, see? So, there can't be any partial change. It's all or nothing. As our managing director said at our annual event, BIG, 'nothing will be like it was before, until the next metamorphosis.' Isn't that a cool way to frame it?"

Kevin mumbled. All he could think about was his loan. He knew it had just been refused but that good manners demanded that he not seek an explicit response. They are too polite, too kind, at BPI to announce bad news. Kevin would, however, have liked to say that in addition to crushed eggshells, you could also throw in other meal scraps, paper, vegetables, fruit . . . He didn't manage to get it out.

"You should go to BIG. A thousand participants, five hundred workshops! It would bring you up to speed. I can make sure you get invited, say next year?"

"I'd love that."

"Let's do that, then! Don't hesitate to contact me if I forget."

The business manager half stood up and held out his hand. Kevin thanked him, foolishly, and headed for the door. Before he left, he hesitated, then turned back one last time to the manager who was already busy responding to his many WhatsApp messages, a smile on his lips. Kevin took a deep breath to give himself courage.

"And the Innovation fund?"

"What?"

"I thought there were special subsidies . . ."

"My young friend, your project would need to be innovative! There's not even a hint of tech in your worm boxes. Next time, bring us a smart worm composter!"

* * *

Kevin decided to walk back to his place. He didn't see any need to hurry. To do what? After that last meeting, there were no more paths of inquiry to explore. He let himself be swallowed up by the crowds of the Grands Boulevards neighborhood, crossed the Place de la République where a dozen or so protestors were chanting incomprehensible slogans behind unrecognizable flags, then headed up the Canal Saint-Martin toward Buttes-Chaumont. He had taken a sublet in the upper nineteenth arrondissement, a windowless room in some miserable share house that suited him well enough. It provided him with the two things he considered essential: a bed and Wi-Fi.

Since he had moved into the neighborhood, Kevin had felt himself both drawn to and repelled by the canal. When he was studying in Limoges, he used to love going for walks along the banks of the Vienne. The old town dove directly into nature; the rushing river a constant promise of possible escape. Only a few minutes of being swept along by the current and one would end up in the fields. The canal did not serve the same purpose. Its water was stagnant, compressed between locks, merely a mirror to reflect the dressed stone buildings. The canal was not fleeing the city, it was trapping it. Moreover, local Parisians didn't walk along its banks; they clumped together there and idled, legs tossed over the wall, lost in interminable conversations. Anybody who fell into the water might well drown in it, but they would not be carried away.

Kevin sat down on the cold stone and looked at his reflection, still and serious, fractured by the crinkles of the canal like an ancient fresco. He felt no particular interest in himself. He made no attempt to look after his own appearance and left his straw-colored hair untended. He accepted compliments in the belief they were offered to everybody. Since moving to Paris, he had, almost unwittingly, been caught up once again in the merry-go-round of parties and clubs. He passed from one set of hands to another and rarely ended up spending the night alone. It felt like his body had, in a way, become public property, fingered, explored, handled by any number of different hands and mouths. As if his mind had dissociated and was looking down at these excesses of pleasure with a weightless voyeurism.

He shared his apartment with three other recent recruits to the workforce determined to continue their student way of life with all the benefits of a modest wage. Breakfast was often the occasion for introductions to passing guests as they emerged from one bedroom or another. Each of them ended up being able to identify their fellow tenants' tastes: bearded with tattoos, dreadlocked blend of races, or plumpish Asian women. Kevin had the distinct impression that he was the cause of some discomfort with his diverse tastes. In the easygoing atmosphere of Buttes-Chaumont, gays were perfectly accepted, understood, celebrated. Straight people, on the other hand, were pleasantly outdated relics. But those who thought it unnecessary to choose a camp were considered procrastinators at best, renegades at worst. Lending their allegiance to no single community, slipping beyond the boundaries decreed by social norms, including the most progressive, they forced people to confront their own lack of fulfillment. Nobody dared question them, but nobody knew either how to approach them. Their freedom was an unbearable and universal affront.

In Limoges, Kevin had remained as discreet as possible regarding the company he kept. Here, in Paris, he had believed himself free to display them straightforwardly enough, exhibiting neither pride nor shame. His companions' looks over breakfast led him to realize there was still a long road ahead. Sharing a croissant, one of his flat mates had earnestly asked him, with the best of intentions, if he went by "he" or "she." Kevin had replied with a shrug. He had never felt the slightest doubt about the matter and thought it strange to be suddenly required to explain himself.

The same awkwardness was evident with his partners. Straight people sleep with other straight people, gay people with other gays. They behave the same and are on the same wavelength. But those who are indifferent rarely sleep with others who feel similarly. They're constantly feeling like certain questions must be avoided, out of sensitivity, so as not to offend. They're living a lie of omission so weighty it prevents the forming of any real relationship.

Kevin saw himself often classified as "bisexual." He considered the word fairly ridiculous. He loved people's bodies, that was all there was to it, whatever organ was to be found between the thighs. He loved his fellow humans, regardless of their own idea of themselves. He didn't feel he changed, moving from boys to girls. He used the same gestures, the same caresses, the same tenderness, with some slight adaptations. Too much is made of the difference between the sexes; using the same materials, nature has simply varied the combinations. Kevin understood there was not the slightest difference between the swelling of a nipple or glans, not in shape, not in color. The same care had to be taken: make it quiver, create a feeling of impatient urgency, devour it, suddenly; then start over. Kevin understood that every fold, every opening in the body's flesh felt the same to the touch, burningly sensitive. Kevin understood that at the peak of desire, there is no longer any distinction between who penetrates and who is penetrated; like Plato's androgynous beings, unjustly cut in two by Zeus, people find their whole, without paying too much attention to the rivet that might bind one person to the other, or that might belong to either one. By what hypocrisy was it decided that lovers who are so wonderfully generous with themselves ought to be constrained to such a blunt duality, divided rather than united?

If he had to choose a category, Kevin's preference was "pan." Pansexual, somebody who loves without concern for gender. Pan, the god with the legs of a goat, protector of shepherds. Peter Pan, who refuses to grow up, who at the end of the story does not get married and does not have lots of children. Best of all, the advantage of being pan was that nobody acknowledged it. There was no P in LGBT, or even in the long version, LGBTQIA+. Kevin was neither lesbian, nor gay, nor bi, nor trans, nor queer, nor intersex, nor asexual. He slid into the +. It suited him, this discretion.

Kevin thought about all those worms crawling about in their little bag, who in that very moment, were languorously copulating, not fearful of anyone else's gaze. He had to set them free; they wouldn't survive more than a few days without a source of food. In any event, they were no longer of any use to him. His flat mates had been fairly firm in their refusal to set up the worm composter that Kevin was suggesting he construct out of some old plastic flower trays. Having initially demonstrated their enthusiasm for such an ecological process, they had then voiced the usual objection about smell, before also claiming a lack of space. Prejudices really did hide in plain sight.

He dragged himself up from the canal wall and set off walking again. He crossed one of the metal bridges so beloved by tourists then walked as far as the Buttes-Chaumont park. The sun was already setting on this warmish fall day, and the gates would soon be closing. It was that time of day when the English-speaking nannies of the neighborhood's chichi parents rushed into the park, using their strollers as battering rams to drive a wedge through the crowds. Kevin threaded his way through them against the flow, making his way briskly down the paths on the hunt for a home for his *Eisenia*. He headed over to a grove of trees and pulled out his little plastic bag. The suspicious looks of two joggers interrupted him in his task. He skirted the lake and noticed a pile of dead leaves in a dip of the path. It was the ideal spot.

"You are so going to love this," he murmured.

Then, for the benefit of the gardeners, he added: "You want compost, you'll get compost!"

He quickly tipped out his bag onto the leaves and watched the *Eisenia* squirm, panic-stricken, before finding their way to the banquet awaiting them. He windmilled his arms to ward off any opportunistic predatory birds and remained there long enough to see the last worm disappear, a dutiful shepherd boy watching over his creatures.

The security guards whistled to signify closing time. Kevin made an about-face and headed back around the lake at a more relaxed pace. The contours of the rocks gradually disappeared into the darkness, sketching haphazard shapes; farther up, lights were coming on in the windows of the fancy buildings that overlooked the park. It was as if, at that witching hour, the city was reasserting itself. It had played at this nature game all day. The show was now over.

Kevin was not prone to melancholy. Yet, that evening, he felt alone and at a loss. Into that pile of leaves he had also thrown away his first illusions. Despite his very economical lifestyle, his financial aid was running out and he would have to call it quits on this project that was going nowhere. Nobody was interested in his pleasant, humble worm composter, not bankers or their customers. After hearing so often that his worms stank, he was starting to feel that it was he who was on the nose. His failure on the entrepreneurial front was blurring in his mind with a vague sensation of not sticking to the rules, of not accomplishing what was expected of him. And yet all he was asking was to be able to live his life in peace. But because his ambitions were limited, they were doomed to fail. And having failed to conquer Paris, he would soon no longer have the means to live there.

V

"There'll be regrowth soon!" proclaimed Arthur, pushing open the door to La Lanterne.

A few regulars were drinking beers on the plank of wood that served as a counter. They raised their drinks to toast him.

"Bravo!"

"You ended up putting in some legumes then?"

"Clover," replied Arthur, proudly.

"Good for nitrogen, that is."

"If there are no earthworms pissing out any ammonium, you have to compensate!"

Arthur had spent the day sowing. He had finally resigned himself to putting the old McCormick 553 to use; it looked like a cartoon tractor with its tiny front wheels, its flat radiator, and its two widespread, owl-like headlights. The cab, open on all sides to the weather, was topped by a light piece of metal, the farmer's umbrella. Arthur had nicknamed his tractor Iron Man, in a nod to Jancovici, who liked to repeat, book after book, interview after interview, that gasoline had provided humanity with a superhero costume. A pensioned-off Iron Man 1.0, grumbling and doddery.

He had needed to find a slasher hailing from the same generation as the Iron Man. Hamstrung by pride, Arthur would never have asked anything of Jobard. Fortunately, he had gotten to know Louis, a farmer-baker of whom his grandfather, Papi, had always been wary. Louis lived in a long, single-story farmhouse outside the village, and for more than thirty years had been growing organic wheat and buckwheat from which he made his own bread, selling it from the farm door every Friday. Long considered a fringe-dweller, he had, reluctantly, become a forerunner. With his white beard, the thickset build of a man who works the land, and his incomprehensible tattoos, he regularly earned a feature in the local edition of the *Ouest-France* paper. Every Friday, Saint-Firmin would turn into a parking lot to welcome Louis's customers who would come from as far as twenty or thirty kilometers away and from all directions. This belated success had never led him to change his methods or alter his output. He stoutly refused to expand. When the bread in the shop had run out, it had run out. Try again next week.

Arthur had spoken to Louis about his plans when buying his whole-grain loaf, which he did his best to make last the week. Since then, Louis had been coming over to ferret about the farm and lend a hand, whether to help with plastering or to grease Iron Man's old bones. He asked for nothing in return, not even the pretense of affection. Helping out came as naturally to him as feeding the hens or trimming the hedges.

Louis, it turned out, had rustled up from one of his mates a slasher that was compatible with Arthur's model of McCormick, and even a disk seeder. Arthur would have preferred to do the sowing by hand, using that generous, life-spreading gesture, but he couldn't afford to be fussy. Louis helped Arthur hitch the slasher to the Iron Man's backside; it took a day, and then the two hectares had been cleared. Arthur contemplated the dry, bare, almost indecent earth surrounded by shimmering crops. His thesis supervisor had recommended dividing the land into four equal parts in order to carry out different experiments, keeping one control parcel fallow. He explained his difficulty to Louis, who couldn't see the point: natural pasture was obviously the best way of revitalizing the soil and attracting as many earthworms as possible. Why sacrifice half a hectare? Everybody knew what would happen if the land were left to grow wild. Arthur had nothing to say against this. He didn't pursue the matter and, carried away by the childish joy of driving a tractor, sowed his entire property with pasture grasses mixed with clover. In order to protect the worms, he refused to plow; in any case, direct sowing methods were coming back into fashion. The only land spared by Arthur was the strip of earth in front of the kitchen, which he had cleared with his own hands and where he planned to put in a vegetable patch. Iron Man faithfully carried out his mission, distributing fifty kilos of seeds across the whole surface. There was nothing more to do but wait.

Arthur and Anne had discovered an unexpected community at La Lanterne. Saint-Firmin's former bar-tabac had been closed since the period when Arthur would vacation with his Papi, but it had reopened the previous year in the form of an organic grocery store. Situated for more than twenty years on the village square opposite the church, the locals had found its boarded-up windows a depressing sight. Then one fine morning, a couple of thirty-somethings had turned up from Caen in a little van filled with boxes. They knew nobody in the area, had found the fixer-upper on the internet, and had launched themselves into it without any preparation. Laurent was a software developer and could continue his business remotely. Maria, a Romanian who had come to France to study, had meandered from postdoctoral contract to underpaid shiftwork after completing her sociology dissertation and wanted nothing more than a "real job," as she said. They had originally planned to set up the store as a cooperative, but initial discussions with the Saint-Firmin locals had rapidly dissuaded them of that notion. Between the laborers who had no time to get involved with the store, and the farmers who were not fond of the idea of a strictly equal distribution of shares, they had concluded that selling organic products in a village of five hundred inhabitants would constitute challenge enough. They had named their grocery after the old lantern of the dead, which, once upon a time, according to local legend, used to be affixed to the building. It meant the souls of Saint-Firmin's dead, passing through over the centuries when the square had been noisy with the shouts of children, the screeching of wheelbarrows, and the clanging of anvils, would be able to seek a little comfort in Maria's arms as she stood behind the cash register.

Timidly, customers had started to appear. They would come, as if to a performance, out of curiosity, giving the fresh cheeses and organic tomatoes one chance, and one only, before they returned to Leclerc, their usual supermarket. Maria recognized this and tasked herself with cajoling them with her rolling accent. She would sometimes put out a plate of *sarmales*, the stuffed vine leaf rolls she had learned how to prepare in large quantities in her childhood, and which the Normans were happy to taste, but not without some apprehension. She provided every possible service, setting crates aside for those who needed to store their apples, helping the elderly with their IT issues, and from time to time organizing ad hoc daycare for various children in the village. To begin with, people would ask about her charming, but clearly not-from-here, accent; little by little, the indisputable improvement she brought to the daily life of the Saint-Firmin locals triumphed over the most tenacious preconceptions. The cash register came to be hidden under a stack of flyers and the walls carpeted in notices announcing the various activities to be found in the area, hikes, concerts, canoe and kayak races, or maiden paraglider flights. It was the place people came to disseminate their news as well as to acquire it. Some people even made the trip from other villages in the area, intrigued to see this unlikely resurrection. They needed to see it to believe it.

Laurent and Maria had discovered that without a License IV—the administrative "open sesame" considered beyond reach of mere mortals—the grocery was not permitted to serve alcohol. But who could stop those customers who would take beers out of the fridge and consume them on the spot, in a nook where there just happened to be a few planks, some trestles, and some chairs? As luck would have it, there was a window looking out across the valley where you could contemplate the long bluish ribbon of the Orne River, and beyond that, the haphazard checkerboard of wooded pastures. The view lent itself to leisurely conversation, to monologues and syllogisms. And so it was that La Lanterne gradually reestablished its primary function of village café.

That evening, seated around the trestle tables were three regulars whom Arthur had already had a chance to get to know. First, there was Matthieu, a sheep farmer who used the ewes' milk to make his own cheese and who had a passion for carpentry. He valued his independence above all else, stubbornly declining any offer to join the dairy cooperative and refusing to sell his products in any supermarkets. When he wasn't in the sheep pen, he was scouring the area for raw lumber, which he would then keep in reserve. He would hunt down bargains in the sawmills or on internet marketplace sites and regularly made miraculous finds, oak boards longer than a man was tall, or square-meter cubes of elm being passed off by retiring cabinetmakers. Matthieu had taken five years to renovate a barn located not far from where his sheep were housed, making all the elements himself, from closets, to stairs, and even the external cladding. To amuse himself, he also made bowls and lamps using an old lathe. By working with different species of timber, he managed to create objects of contrasting shades that he would sometimes display for sale among his cheeses at the Flers market. Matthieu had the variable features of a forty-year-old: young man one day, cheeks still glowing vermilion red; hardy sheep farmer the next, face already furrowed by wrinkles. His wife, always on duty for the evening milking, was not often to be seen.

Next to Matthieu sat Salim, as voluble as the first was taciturn. He was the eternal seasonal worker, harvesting fruit in the fall, driving a semiofficial taxi in the winter, lending a hand on various building sites when the weather was fine. He always managed to land some welfare allocation to tide him over. He knew all the tricks: what day to gather potatoes in the fields, how to salvage refrigerators that had been dumped at the tip but were still working, where to source T-shirts and jeans for just a few euros that had fallen off the back of a truck. He still lived at home with his parents, Turkish immigrants who were shift workers at the nearby auto manufacturers. He didn't complain about it. He had a roof over his head, enough to eat, and ample time to binge-watch political talkfests and scroll through social media. Even if his Twitter account, @Enraged205, had only thirty or so followers, Salim would post dozens of times a day, taking issue with the slightest controversy and sharing 280-character anticapitalist theories. As a result of watching interminable interviews on Thinkerview, he had developed quite the expert vocabulary. He had an answer to every problem facing the world and knew that the cries he launched into the void that was the internet would, one day, be heard. His entire existence was geared toward generating likes, a clash, a storm that would prompt the masses, enlightened at long last, to revolt. Every evening he would fall asleep harboring this hope, his face illuminated by the pallid light of his cell phone.

Léa completed the gang. Having interrupted her medical studies, she had settled in the area ten or so years ago, working as a naturopath, and in time built up a sufficient clientele to support a comfortable life. She used local plants with magical names such as queen of the fields, hemp-agrimony, blue stonecrop, or navelwort to prepare all sorts of infusions. She rounded out her offerings with hypnotherapy sessions, auriculotherapy consultations, and Zen massages with incense and Tibetan music. Reconciled with their vital energy, those who felt healed convinced the skeptics to try it. In an area where doctors were scarce and the nearest hospitals an hour's drive away in Caen or Falaise, Léa's rooms, located in a dark, narrow alley a hundred meters from the church, offered a welcome space to be heard. People would go there with back pain and would end up recounting their life story. Léa allowed several hours between consultations, to recover her "mental space" as she used to say; it also allowed her to make time for those who wanted to unburden themselves. She had become a de facto confidante, confessor, and therapist. There were few Saint-Firmin locals who had not allowed her to fiddle with their ears or who had not participated in a gong bath. During the COVID pandemic, Léa had convinced a good half of them to refuse the vaccine on the basis that a well-balanced organism should generate its own antidotes. The prefecture had identified the village as a center of resistance and had dispatched a special mobile firefighter unit to carry out door knocking, a tactic that met with little success.

Léa was impressive. Pale and stick-thin, she had an ageless, two-dimensional face, like representations of the Virgin in Byzantine paintings. Her soft voice, an almost indiscernible murmur, called for silence. Her only adornment was a V-shaped tattoo at the base of her neck. Salim claimed it was a serpent's tongue, the creature's body unfurling between Léa's shoulder blades, its coils sliding down between her buttocks. The village was fairly divided about this hypothesis, about which everybody had their own firmly held, well-settled opinion.

Arthur did his best to fight his own skepticism. Everything in his academic and scientific training drove him to class naturopaths among the ranks of charlatans. But he reproached himself for his narrow-mindedness and forced himself to make way for doubt. He knew the extent to which Western agronomy had distanced itself from actual knowledge and could not exclude the possibility that this might also be the case when it came to medicine. After all, medications produced by pharmaceutical laboratories might be nothing more than poor fertilizer.

Arthur's triumphant arrival prompted Maria to pull some beers out of the fridge.

"This round's on me!" she announced cheerfully, setting them down on the timber bench.

Maria had paired with her jeans, as she often did, a brightly colored embroidered vest from her native Romania with a low-cut neckline. Her chest rippled with every step, a promise of consolation.

"Regrowth . . ." said Matthieu, pensively. "It's been a while since I've heard that word. The grass that grows back after the first scything."

"It's the energy returning," added Léa.

Arthur nodded his head vigorously. In those first months living in Saint-Firmin, he had felt as if he had been completely reborn. His lovemaking with Anne, until that point hesitant and guided by a certain mutual interest, had suddenly become a carnal, unbridled affair. Anne was insatiable in her demands of him; he accommodated her most unexpected desires, a sex toy in human form, discovering in this total submission a new source of pride, that of bringing somebody to orgasm. His daily existence came to be characterized by a certain placidness, brought on by his ever-replete, sometimes sore, body. He accepted difficulties, delays, and deprivations with equanimity. Paradoxically, at the very moment he was implementing his soil regeneration plans, he had never been so unconcerned about the fate of the planet. Seen from Saint-Firmin, it seemed less battered. In any case, not impossible to repair.

Despite their apprehensions, Arthur and Anne had made some genuine friends in the village, a meeting of equals, unfettered by the calculations necessitated by city life. Friendships based on mutual assistance, where each party offered what they could. Because they were constantly seeking advice and assistance, and especially from Louis and Matthieu, when selecting any material whatsoever, repairing any tool, preparing for any crop. Not once during their studies had they had to make such an intellectual effort, requiring them to call on every area of knowledge and adapt constantly to the needs of the job.

Arthur felt like he missed nothing and nobody. Even Kevin, who would update him at least once a week with the latest developments regarding his business model and loan applications, seemed a world away.

"In fact," said Salim, "they're a bit like us."

"Who are you talking about?" asked Arthur.

"Your earthworms, obviously. Aren't they the reason you're doing all this?"

"Yes, of course, but we hardly look like worms."

Maria burst out laughing. She had returned to the cash register to serve a customer but was still following the conversation.

"I'm serious," Selim insisted. "Who really does the work in this country?"

"Definitely not you!" laughed Matthieu.

"You kidding? I've been surviving on potatoes the whole month at Caligny!"

"One month of potatoes, two years of welfare . . ."

"That's not how it is. Anyway, aren't you getting benefits from the CAP?"

"It's hardly the same. If we were able to sell our products at the actual prices, we could get by without the CAP. It's a subsidy for the consumer, not the producer."

"You're just a right-wing idiot."

"And proud of it."

Matthieu had never made any secret of the fact that he alternated between voting for the right and extreme right parties. He just wanted to be allowed to sell his cheeses, for the government to stop using his taxes to subsidize deadbeats, and that he otherwise be left in peace. But instead, the powers that be continued to torment him. The Department of Competition, Consumer Affairs, and Fraud Prevention kept torturing him with labeling issues, the Departmental Directorate for Population Protection was asking him to fill out some nonsensical "declaration relating to the handling of foodstuffs," and inspectors appointed under the EU's Common Agricultural Policy kept poking their nose in when it came to counting his flock. The last time, they made a scene because one ewe born with stunted ears wasn't wearing the regulation identification tag.

"She's got no ears, so where do you want me to attach her tag?"

"It's mandatory."

Matthieu felt the persecution was pursuing him all the way into his own home. The Service for Inter-Commune Town Planning had refused to grant him a construction permit to create two windows in his barn loft. "In that case," he had calmly explained to the woman from Town Planning services, who was also one of his customers, "tell your bosses to go screw themselves." Matthieu had built the frames for his windows himself with leftover Oregon pine, a naturally rot-resistant material; he had picked up some brand-new double-glazed windows from a big construction site in Caen where the guys were flogging unused materials off the back of a truck, and he had installed it all over a few days when the weather had been fine. The woman from planning kept coming to buy her cheese from the farm gate as if nothing had happened, without ever so much as lifting her gaze to his windows. Matthieu had drawn his own immutable political conclusions from it all. He had never read a single leaflet from the far-right Rassemblement national party, couldn't give a damn about immigration, but unhesitatingly granted his vote to the people who, in his opinion, would "really create proper havoc." His hatred of the administration, its decrees, its interference, and its cowardice, trumped all other considerations. Anybody who profited from any of that was classified as a collaborator without further trial.

"Enough already!" Maria interrupted them. She had no desire to listen to the same argument yet again.

"All I'm saying," continued Salim, "is that we live underground, too. We get by doing this and that, we take a few steps forward and then we retreat into our little tunnels, not disturbing anybody, not drawing attention to ourselves. We scrabble together the scraps that get dropped. Everybody else walks over us without even noticing. We don't even resent them for it."

"Who's that then, who's 'everybody else'?" asked Léa.

"I dunno, everybody who has a permanent job and who goes to the supermarket on the weekend. People who live in the city and who work in glass office buildings. And everybody who then goes on TV and tries to tell us what we should be thinking. Everybody who wanders about in the fresh air pontificating to the rest of us. They think the world would stop turning without them. But the fact is, without us, they'd have nothing left to eat."

Arthur was listening in silence. He didn't trust himself, didn't trust his own propensity to pontificate. He was afraid of coming off as an impostor. Nothing made him prouder than feeling he had been adopted, that nobody had ever asked him about his background or where or what he had studied. He had moved to Saint-Firmin for good, he was renovating an old farm, he had a slightly bizarre plan; nobody was interested in asking anything else.

"It's true what you say," answered Léa, thoughtfully. "I heal them, Matthieu feeds them, Maria solves their little problems, you lend them a hand. Perhaps they just look down on us. Doesn't matter that we're the ones making their environment more habitable."

"We're earthworms!" proclaimed Salim.

"Sure, good enough for me," said Matthieu.

And they clinked their beers.

"Me too!" said Maria, coming back over to them.

"One day," said Salim, "we'll all come out at the same time, we'll guzzle our way through their tidy little gardens, we'll clean out their cupboards, we'll crawl our way into their bedrooms. What are we afraid of? We outnumber them, we're heavier, we're stronger. Just imagine the disgusted look on their faces. 'Ah, so there was something under there?' Well yeah, there was! That was us! Take a good look at us! After all those centuries of unacknowledged labor, we're coming to take our due."

Salim had turned to look out the window. In the distance, the setting sun lit up the cliffs.

"Here we go, he's off again . . ." sighed Matthieu. "I wouldn't mind being an earthworm, just so long as nobody makes me come to the surface. Leave me alone in my own shit."

VI

He had sworn never to set foot there again. And yet here he was, back on the leeward side of the Saclay plateau, barely a few kilometers from AgroParisTech. Through the windows of the bus, off in the distance, he could see gigantic harrows plowing the stubble back into the fields after harvest. A derisory attempt to reinject some organic matter into soil long since stripped bare that was, in any case, destined for more concrete. It was like performing mouth-to-mouth on a corpse. Then Kevin noticed a smattering of rectangular buildings, about as welcoming as warehouses in an industrial zone. Blue flags snapped against the sky, high above his new home: the École des hautes études commerciales, one of Paris's most prestigious business schools.

Kevin had gone back for a year. Unable to flog his worm composters, he had concluded he needed to acquire an attitude, a vocabulary, a network, without which he would never be able to build a business of any description. So he had applied for a Master of Science X-HEC Entrepreneurs where young graduates from the best families learn how to play shop while intoning key words of global-speak. During his admission interview, Kevin had managed to explain, without laughing, that lumbrics could change the world. He had then managed to secure a scholarship thanks to his magical "Level 7 Regional Student Assistance" status. With enrollment fees exempted, and on-campus accommodation included, he would need only a modest standard personal loan to finance his remaining expenses.

"The actual sciences are really not gonna like the sound of a *Master of Science*," Arthur had joked on the phone.

"I know. But what else am I supposed to do? I'm stuck. Nobody gives a shit about my *Eisenias*. I can't even afford the rent in my share house anymore."

"Using the HEC for emergency accommodation is pretty original."

Kevin felt wounded. As if he wasn't allowed to be left alone to cobble together his little business. As if he were being forced to be ambitious.

"You think I enjoy having to hang out with those kids? The Bank of Mom and Pop has shelled out a cool thirty thousand and they think they're hot shit. Half the guys are in suits, the chicks are in heels like it's 1980. They're all so buttoned up. And when they do go out and relax, they puke all over the place."

"You should just come to Saint-Firmin. We welcome every type of worm here with open arms."

"We've had this conversation a hundred times already."

"We've had the conversation, but I've never understood."

"It's just not my thing, that's all."

The fact was, Kevin was upset to see his friend waste his intelligence on two hectares that would never offer a return. He remained convinced Arthur's project would finish of its own accord and that Arthur would return to Paris. In the meantime, he had better things to do than count earthworms. What exactly that was, he couldn't have said. Something. Nothing specific. Kevin wasn't looking for fame, and certainly not fortune. But he had this thing in his head, this vague idea of a life less common. Too bad if, in order to work out what that looked like, he had to do a Master of Science X-HEC Entrepreneurs.

* * *

So, with little enthusiasm, Kevin got stuck into the accounting, retail, negotiation, and data management courses. Every day, generously remunerated external speakers came to announce some new revolution involving chatbots, horizontally integrated businesses, a participatory society. No innovative concept, no notion of progress escaped the redemptive power of business. According to them, the HEC was the breeding ground of saints ready to do anything to help their neighbor and save the planet.

The year was divided into four phases, each of which seemed as fanciful to Kevin as the next. The Learning Phase: start-up mission. The Testing Phase: project development. The Fastening Phase: soft skills. The Launch Phase: growth. His peers took it all very seriously, although he couldn't decide whether they were just pretending to believe in it all or if, when they went to bed at night, they really were wondering about their soft skills. And as for the dean of the master's program, with her impeccable blowout, did she truly think, as she had proclaimed to them on their first day, that this fresh year of study was "aimed at personal transformation through action learning based on a methodological approach" when the entire program was so deliberately designed with a single objective in mind: money would continue to circulate among the same hands? Novices must've asked themselves similar questions when entering religious orders to escape famine: Does brother Gauvain, praying here next to me, really believe? Does he really imagine, deep down, that there is a single God divided into three distinct entities, the Father, the Son, and the Holy Spirit? With the passage of time, and everybody continuing to copy one another, these questions dissipated of their own accord. What started out as harmless collective hypocrisy ended up becoming the substratum of personal beliefs.

Kevin now spent his evenings alone. As if his power of attraction, which had always come to him so naturally, had suddenly dissipated. His placid beauty was no longer sufficient. Couples formed along strategic lines that were probably unconscious but nonetheless efficient, according to each person's projects and core interests. In this partnership now known as love, Kevin had nothing to offer. His sudden abstinence did not make him unhappy but rendered his evenings on the plateau long and monotonous.

Despite all the prejudices Arthur had planted in his head, every now and again Kevin was surprised to find himself interested in his courses. As capitalism took on a human face, namely, that of the alumni parading before them, he found it less intimidating. As he grew to understand its mechanics, he also found it less questionable. As his macroeconomics prof—the only professor he truly respected—had explained, "the principle of capital is to set the world in motion, allowing new ideas to find old money." Kevin could not see any basis on which to reproach this definition. Seen through this prism, the notion of "sustainable development" so disparaged by his peers at AgroParisTech no longer seemed ridiculous. If it was so expensive to undo the mistakes humanity had made, why not go looking for funds from those initially responsible?

Kevin had unfortunately been allocated a less inspiring tutor. Mr. Vlaminck, a jumpy, overweight man in his sixties, introduced himself as an "expert in strategy and change management." His job involved convincing business leaders of their own obsolescence and of delivering them entirely new processes. He was a compulsive watcher of American TED Talks, eager not to miss the germ of any concept. After economic disruption had come the age of technological singularity, then ecological collapse. He modified his slides according to his findings, enthusiastic one year about progress in deep learning, depressed the following year when faced with the decrease in biodiversity. Like any other necromancer, he had to show himself to be as assertive and unequivocal as possible. Even the slightest doubt, the slightest nuance would have placed him immediately at a disadvantage.

Suffice it to say that Kevin's project did nothing to inspire him. The idea of a collapse was already starting to run its course, and composting had had its moment in the sun in the aughts. Most of all, Kevin could not manage to see a bigger picture. He continued to be hung up on his pathetic worm composter and to retreat behind his bank loan issues. His only plan for Launch Phase was to make a prototype.

"Well, it's obviously not Google," snickered Vlaminck. "But we'll probably be able to turn it into something slicker."

Vlaminck then got it into his head to have Kevin work on an online worm composter, a *smart worm* as he suggested calling it. All that was needed was an app to provide real-time information regarding changes in temperature, how full the trays were, the number of worms, the level of decomposition, etc. No longer any need to lift up the lid to admire progress: you'd receive an instant notification on your cell phone with specific instructions. No longer any need to see those disgusting worms, still less to touch them: everything would be controlled from a nice, clean screen. It would be more engaging for the customer, who would be able to share their experience in real time with the vermicomposting community; more profitable for the business, which would be able to sell the data collected to research bodies; and more attractive for investors, with whom a conversation could finally be had about big data and agritech. In terms of his master's, Kevin's project would fall into the "high touch" category, even if it didn't qualify for the Holy Grail of "deep tech." It was even possible to conceive of users receiving nutritional recommendations based on the quality of their compost!

"I can just see the App Store logo!" Vlaminck was dreaming aloud, aroused by his visionary concept.

Kevin was struggling to understand why anybody would be interested in the *smart worm*. Nothing could be more simple than to glance into the compost from time to time; it only needed a few weeks of hands-on experience to gain all the necessary expertise. That said, Kevin remembered the BPI business manager's emphasis on innovation and agreed to work on a prototype. He set to work designing a smart worm composter in the HEC fab lab. It rapidly became apparent that the sensors were only able to provide a very approximate measure of decomposition, inferred from the weight of each tray as well as humidity levels, and the whole apparatus relied on a fairly powerful battery that would need regular recharging. The *smart worm* would turn into a cumbersome and costly object, a far cry from its initial promise. As for nutritional recommendations, it would be unable to respond to any criteria that were even remotely scientific.

Vlaminck brushed these objections aside. A decent AI program, trained on lab data in the first instance, then data resulting directly from commercialization of the product, would allow progressive improvement in the precision of its measurements. All things considered, it could even be an additional argument in support of the project: "at the intersection of deep learning and regenerative agriculture." As for its price, it could never be too high. The *smart worm* had to feel like a luxury product of impeccable design, something one would be proud to display in one's living room.

"The *smart worm* will be for waste what Phantom speakers are for music," gushed Vlaminck, enthusiastically. "A sign of good taste, a status symbol. There's a market for that: it's niche, but lucrative. The wealthy no longer know what to do with their money. You have to position yourself—you have to go in hard, and fast!"

The prospect of a lucrative market left Kevin stone cold, and he met the suggestions with a polite, yet obstinate refusal. He was well aware that the *smart worm* made no sense from an agronomic point of view and that any recycling benefits would be largely outweighed by its energy consumption. Vlaminck chastised him for his arrogance. Who did he think he was, taking the moral high ground? But Kevin was not staking any particular moral claims. He just couldn't commit to a project he wasn't interested in, that was all. He apologized to his tutor for his lack of commercial nous. "I'm a lecturer in strategy and change management. You embody neither one nor the other," concluded Vlaminck in their final exchange of emails.

Kevin wondered about the meaning of that last sentence. He paid close attention to his peers who supposedly possessed both traits, a capacity for strategy and change, and who were prepared to invest all their youthful energy into responsible finance or the automation of human resource procedures. Try as he might to convince himself of capitalism's virtues, nothing about any of it caused him to dream. He would receive his master's like the rest of them but feared finding himself back at square one.

It was during the winter term, when most of his cohort were doing internships in Hong Kong or San Francisco, that Kevin met Philippine. He had noticed her immediately, a redhead with green eyes, slender and highly strung, pretty without being beautiful, always dressed in black and her only makeup a line of kohl on her upper lid. She walked the corridors at a brisk pace, as if getting from a business law lecture to a group discussion on engagement were a matter of urgency. She seemed determined, but to do what? The way she rolled her eyes, tapped her leg impatiently, doodled geometric shapes on the sheet of paper in front of her betrayed a healthy indifference to what she was being taught. On a number of occasions, she permitted herself to make cynical remarks in class about the dumbing down of consumers or the hypocrisy of corporate social responsibility. Kevin found it entertaining to listen to her loud, husky, almost masculine voice, which had come to disturb the muted peace of the global economy's future rulers. He noticed that Philippine frequently enlisted one or another fellow classmate in her confabulations, so they might serve as an accomplice. They would then form a loud, but temporary duo. Philippine regularly changed up her partners in mockery.

Lacking any other options, perhaps, it seemed this role fell to Kevin in that miserable January week. For a few days she didn't leave him alone. Kevin allowed himself good humoredly to be carried along, without really knowing what she saw in him, he who so often felt so drab. Knowing she would tire of him quickly, he made the most of her tumbleweed company, treating it as a welcome distraction. One day, as they were leaving a lecture on social capitalism in which she had doubled down on her mocking efforts, she suggested a game of foosball.

Heavy, cumbersome, expensive, and persistently resistant to digitalization, foosball, bizarrely, had taken over co-working spaces and the offices of Silicon Valley like a Nemesis from the ancient world. HEC found itself thus obliged to enliven its buildings with some tables.

They stood, facing off in reverential silence, ready to unleash. Kevin took a ball from the cache and eyeballed his opponent. Philippine stared at him through the arrow-slit of her kohl. She didn't blink. Her soul was nowhere to be seen.

Kevin tossed the ball into the center, ensuring it fell into Philippine's half. Foosball remained a significant initiation rite in the bistros of Limoges, and he had picked up some solid technique. He understood the tactical nuances of tackling, taking a fall, or bawling out. He certainly wasn't going to roll them out for this uneventful match that he planned on conceding to his opponent. But once the ball had dropped, Philippine went for it. She gave her midfielder a ferocious spin and scored cleanly, letting out a victorious whoop. Kevin looked on, speechless.

"Demi! You scored with your midfielder," he clarified.

He moved two counters along the scoring rods on either side of the table. The next goal would be worth two points in accordance with convention.

"No way, a goal's a goal!"

Having none of it, Philippine gave herself the point, sliding a red marker along and bringing Kevin's back to zero. Before he could protest, she had already dropped the ball back into play. Her furious tactics were disorganized but hard to contain. She leaped from one end of the table to the other, spinning the bars frenetically, shaking her fists and shrieking as soon as the ball breached her line of defenders.

"Pissettes don't count," smiled Kevin, after Philippine scored a goal with the wing forward closest to her hand. The play was against the rules.

"Don't fuck with me!" she answered without an ounce of irony.

Philippine was focused entirely on the game, exuberant at every point she scored, furious when she didn't. She addressed her metal players like a coach from the sidelines, cussing them out when they missed their passes or encouraging them just as Kevin was getting ready to shoot. When the ball was dead, lying out of reach between two players, she would blow on it shamelessly to claim it. Droplets of sweat appeared on her forehead, and red spots colored her cheeks. Kevin thought it was cute. He defended his goals as best he could but held back his attacks. Philippine was ahead in the score.

"Yes, yes, yes!" she exclaimed, taking her sixth point. "Admit it! I'm destroying you!"

Despite his every effort to play it cool, Kevin was starting to feel stung. He decided to take action. Now he started passing the ball to his forwards, controlled it, stopped it rebounding off the edge of the pitch, and amused himself by tapping it rhythmically before shooting. His flick of the wrist was crisp and targeted. He scored almost every time, effortlessly spotting the gaps in Philippine's feverish defense. The ball hit the back of the box with a distinct, heavy thud. Kevin was quickly leveling the score while Philippine, believing victory within her grasp, struggled furiously with her spinnies and unlawful midfielder plays. He let in another goal inadvertently, which he followed with the rapid scoring of more points.

"Match point," he declared.

"You'll never score."

Kevin again took control of the ball at his strikers' feet, dragging things out cruelly as he tapped it to and fro. Hunched over her handles, Philippine started to lose it.

"Come on, shoot, goddamn it!"

He shot. Thud.

"One more," she demanded, jaw clenched.

They changed ends without a word. Kevin had never seen her so serious. A little irritated by the drama of it all, he resolved to make it quick this time. Even when she lifted the table to make the ball roll in the right direction, even when she crushed Kevin's fingers when he dropped the ball back into play, she didn't score a single goal.

"Next round's on you!"

"I wasn't in form . . ." she grumbled.

Kevin slung a friendly arm around her shoulders.

"We can have a rematch . . ."

"No. No way."

"But it's just a game!"

"Yeah, and?" Her retort was swift. "Life's a game, too. That's no reason."

Kevin withdrew. She appeared to be serious.

"Sure, drinks on me," she said, suddenly recovering her casual vibe.

They walked in silence to the cafeteria where only three Chinese students were still hanging around, absorbed in some animated discussion that had them all laughing. They each helped themselves to a smoothie and headed for the register. Kevin took out his student card to pay for his.

"No, no, no!" Philippine interrupted. "Loser pays the round."

"I was joking . . ."

"Out of the question."

She elbowed him out of the way and swiped her own card. Kevin clocked her photo; she was wearing a deeply empathetic smile, the sort used on LinkedIn, and not one he had ever seen her use. They sat down at a table not far from the Chinese girls whose chatter was brightening the dreary atmosphere of the cafeteria. Philippine brought out a packet of chocolate-covered coffee beans. Kevin had already noticed this habit during class. She snacked on them constantly all day long.

"I'm Philippine."

"I know!"

"Wait, that's not all: Philippine with two p's. You mustn't ever forget the two p's."

"I'm Kevin. With a K. But I think everybody knows that."

"We've got weird names, you and I. We're not flying under the radar."

"What do you mean by that?"

She sighed without replying. He knew what she meant.

"Philippine" was a coat of arms. It was obvious, it represented the Haussmann apartment in the western arrondissements of Paris, the country house in Normandy, and winter vacations in Courchevel.

"So," she continued, "what's your project for Launch Phase?"

Kevin found the question abrupt, but he answered without batting an eye. He told her about the vermicomposting. The mold that would cost a good 60. (Kevin had well and truly worked out that in HEC metrics, the decimal point was assumed to have shifted three places.) The "market potential," to use the micro-economics prof's terminology. To his great surprise, Philippine seemed fascinated. She kept asking questions, going into the smallest details, never taking her eyes off his. Kevin was struggling to get used to those unblinking eyes, the perfectly still, green irises that carried him away to some cold, distant world. Sure, the loser might pay, but this round was taking on a curious feel, halfway between a hypnosis session and an admissions interview.

Philippine wanted to know everything about lumbrics. Their ingestion rate, their reproductive speed, their resistance to temperature variation. Kevin was of course using scientific vocabulary, which seemed to reassure her. Philippine then tackled the question of waste: what sort, how much? After all the enthusiasm for methanizers, which turned out to be not very profitable and of dubious ecological benefit, she thought it implausible that nobody had come up with the idea of earthworms. It was a simple, powerful idea, the stuff of entrepreneurs' dreams.

"Sounds sick," she concluded, hunting around for the very last coffee bean at the bottom of the packet.

"What?"

"Sick. Sensational. Man, where have you been, dude?"

"Nobody says that anymore."

"Well, I do. *Sssssick, sssssick, sssssick*! Can't you hear the snakes hissing? Doesn't it remind you of earthworms?"

Philippine whistled between her teeth, stood up, and took off like a shot, without even saying goodbye. He remained sitting for a moment, a little stunned. Sick?

Philippine disappeared for a few days. She wasn't the most committed master's student, but nobody seemed to mind. Kevin returned to his customary solitude. He heard talk of parties to which he wasn't invited, WhatsApp groups that nobody had thought to include him in, rumors about people whose names he didn't even recognize. Nobody showed him the slightest animosity. They were happy to just politely ignore him. In the great game of who-was-going-to-become-the-first-millionaire, he hadn't even made it to the starting line. When somebody really needed to refer to him, they called him "the agri-dude" or "the scholarship kid." He didn't take offense. He had no interest in becoming a millionaire. But he was starting to feel as if time were moving slowly.

A week later, in the middle of a lecture on how to read a balance sheet, Philippine came and sat down next to Kevin as if it were the most natural thing in the world. He could tell from her rapid breathing that she was about to bubble over.

"We have to talk," she murmured.

In the break, she grabbed him by the arm and dragged him into the cafeteria, as she had done previously. She opened a packet of coffee beans and started talking purposefully.

"I've read Marcel Combe's book, the one you told me about,"

she said. "It's sick, his whole thing. The lumbri-polytechnic. They digest pretty much everything!"

"Waste-water sludge, household waste, refuse from commercial zones, liquid manure from farms . . ." Kevin reeled it off mechanically. "That leaves only nonorganic matter to be recycled."

"Apparently Combe built a prototype to treat urban waste."

"Yes, apparently so. He shows a few photos in his presentations. He says he had to stop due to lack of financing."

"And nobody has tried again since?"

"As I've ascertained, lumbrics aren't very fashionable . . ."

Philippine took a deep breath.

"You realize that in two years' time, there will be laws making it compulsory to sort your organic waste?"

"No, I didn't know that. That's good. It'll encourage households to buy my worm composters . . ."

"Not just households. Everybody. Local authorities, industry. It's a huge market."

"That's another thing. My worm composters are made for individuals."

"Forget your plastic two buck worm thingamajigs!"

Her voice rang out through the cafeteria. A group of students at the next table turned around. They were keen for some domestic scene.

"We need to start thinking on an industrial scale," she resumed, her tone more confidential. "Build a factory. Factories, throughout the country. One day perhaps, throughout the world. Put billions and billions of earthworms in them. Digesting trash day and night. Producing thousands of tons of compost. Saving humanity from its waste. Saving the world from humanity. Say goodbye to dumps, say goodbye to incineration, say goodbye to methanation!"

Kevin burst out laughing. He couldn't even lay his hands on sixty thousand euros.

"That's the revolution, right there. Not these idiots' silicone gadgets," she said, pointing to the next table.

She wasn't wrong on that count, Kevin was happy to admit.

"It's feasible, isn't it?"

She looked at him with such intensity that he turned away. Maybe there was a reason for the fact that nobody had set up the lumbri-polytechnic outlined by Marcel Combe. Or maybe there wasn't.

"You'd have to first—"

"What I'm suggesting," she interrupted him, "is that we build this thing together. Both of us."

"I . . ."

She took Kevin's hands in hers.

"We're gonna change the world, dude."

VII

Not long after sowing the meadow, Arthur had a deeply unpleasant conversation with his dissertation supervisor. He had reached Arthur on his cell phone while Arthur had been driving the Volvo along a narrow local road that flanked the Orne. Arthur pulled over and got out of the car. The river at that point was hidden behind a curtain of fall-colored trees. Pushing through the lower branches, one was suddenly on the riverbank. A few lazy eddies had formed on the water's surface, spraying light. Clouds of midges streaked the air. The riverbed, pebbly and shallow, was visible to the naked eye. Impossible to drown there. Pasture sloped up gently from the far bank. A herd of Norman cows grazed nonchalantly. Their irregular red markings each sketched a map of a unique world. Some continued to graze, others remained lying on the ground, making the most of the last rays of seasonal sun. It all formed a tableau that lent itself to significant decisions.

Arthur had to confess to his supervisor that he had not varied the experimental protocol on different plots, nor had he retained a control area. He tried to explain to him the reasons put forward by Louis, which seemed to him to be perfectly valid: Why exhaust the soil using techniques you know are doomed to fail? He then was forced to listen to a long sermon about scientific rigor. Arthur was bold enough to reply that so-called scientific rigor was still doing nothing about the fact that even in this day and age, pesticide approval criteria still did not take into account the earthworms living in the relevant soil. Had they not earned the right to a little consideration by now? Didn't the common sense of farmers, acquired after a multitude of experiments carried out over entire generations, possess an intrinsic scientific value?

"You're heading for trouble, Arthur," scolded his supervisor.

"No, sir, I promise you I'm not. I'm feeling really good about it."

Arthur noticed a few dragonflies braving the cool air, performing aerobatics on the water's surface.

"It's impossible for you to carry out your work in these conditions. Even if you manage to rebuild the earthworm population across your two hectares, you'll have proven nothing at all."

"But I still would have succeeded."

"Succeeded in doing what?"

The herd of cows languidly approached the bank, probably attracted by Arthur's voice. Arthur explained that in any event, it wasn't possible for him to change the course of nature. The seeds were sown, and he would have to wait at least another year to change his crops. His supervisor reluctantly acknowledged his point and then insisted that Arthur get himself back to the main campus of INRAE on the double to discuss next steps with his protocols, and that in the meantime he pick up his lab work. He succeeded in extracting only a vague promise from his doctoral student.

After hanging up, Arthur filled his lungs with a deep breath, sat down on a stump at the river's edge, removed his shoes, and dipped his feet into the water. He amused himself curling and uncurling his toes, as he let himself be massaged by the current. The prospect of returning to the Saclay plateau, even if only for a few weeks, felt unbearable. All the more so as Louis had just given him some young chickens he had to look after, and Matthieu and Salim were supposed to help him build a basic hen house out of some old planks of pine he had found in his grandfather's barn. Arthur couldn't betray this burgeoning trust and just disappear off to the capital. He wasn't even curious to see Kevin again in his new business-school attire. He was too scared he wouldn't recognize him.

That evening, Arthur wrote a very formal email to his supervisor, taking care to copy in all the team members. Displaying an academic deference that revealed a slightly juvenile tone, he explained that he would be pausing his dissertation project to concentrate on soil regeneration. To concentrate "authentically" he added, after further reflection. In the future, he wrote, by way of postscript, people would be able to follow his work on a blog he had just created: *Even a Worm Turns*. He reread it back to Anne.

"Should I send it?"

"Yes," she said, giving him a kiss on the neck. "I'm so proud of you."

"Good, I'm sending it then," he repeated, stomach clenched, privately hoping to be persuaded otherwise.

"Send it," she whispered, nibbling at his earlobe and sliding her fingers over his chest. "You're looking really ripped, you know," she added.

Cocooned in the languid heat of desire, he used his thumb to press the key that signaled an end to his university career.

* * *

In the following days, Arthur checked his inbox only sparingly and with some apprehension, before realizing, half-irritated, half-relieved, that he would never receive a response. While he was at it, he published his first blog post, a long piece about his earthworm regeneration project that still bore the stamp of the entire agronomical lexicon. He shared the link on Facebook, conscious of the importance of this inaugural act that was going to spark the great soil revolution. He received six likes and three comments: one from his cousin who was wondering if he would be able to let her have the ceramic vase that used to sit on the mantelpiece over the living room's fireplace at the Saint-Firmin farm where, as she reminded him insistently, they had spent numerous vacations together; the second from one of his former future colleagues at INRAE who was taking issue with his graph charting the reproductive rhythm of lumbrics; and one last one from a complete stranger explaining that the disappearance of earthworms was part of a strategy to destroy the planet implemented by pharmaceutical laboratories and overseen by Klaus Schwab after Davos. *The revolution is going to take some time*, thought Arthur.

At La Lanterne, the little band of earthworms, as they were now calling themselves, celebrated the news with a round of beers. Relieved of the last link binding him to the elite, Arthur finally felt capable of completing his integration into Saint-Firmin, an exercise more delicate and arduous than any competitive state-run exams. He relinquished his infiltrator-observer status to become truly one of them. Only Maria, who, as it turned out, had defended her doctoral thesis at the Sorbonne, seemed to regret the speed of Arthur's decision. But having herself abandoned a university career to become a grocer and, moreover, the manager of a semi-unlawful café, she was not about to start preaching to him.

The primary job for this first winter was to plant a hedge around the land. As far as Arthur was concerned, that was a no-brainer. The ripping out of hedges during the land consolidation process of the 1960s to allow tractors easy access to the larger farms was these days unanimously considered a significant error leading to flooding and landslides. Even the most production-driven lecturers at AgroParisTech acknowledged the major role hedges played in safeguarding biodiversity. Up here on the plateau, it was his grandfather, Papi, himself who had gone ahead with this destructive practice; here and there you would trip over stumps that marked the former boundaries of the plots of land. In a cardboard box from the attic, Arthur had found black-and-white photos of the farm dating from the postwar period that showed a much more intimate and varied bocage landscape than the current monochrome palette of the grain grower. This was what he was keen to reinstate.

Arthur pictured his Papi at the steering wheel of the tractor, perhaps the same McCormick he was driving today, a tractor turned death machine, hurtling at full speed into the thick shrubs that still persisted after the lopping of the trees with the chainsaw. He imagined the panic, the massacre, and the exodus of the fauna that lived there. The shrews, voles, and toads were probably the first to be wiped out. The blindworms and weasels, finding themselves suddenly under attack, would have dived into their subterranean lairs to find some brief respite. The warblers, thrushes, blackbirds, and shrikes, abandoning their nests and fledglings, would have fled in a dreadful, disorderly flurry of wings. The adorable buntings with their yellow chicks' heads would not have survived their flight into the forest. As for the hedgehogs, they would have huddled up until nightfall, before proceeding step by step through the corpses, into the sudden silence of the ruins. And if the earthworms, those underground vultures, had hurried greedily toward all of this decomposing organic matter, their feasting would not have lasted long. A few years after it had all been ripped out, slowly, slowly, they would have been reduced to famine and eradicated from this portion of the earth's crust.

Arthur had thus resolved to make amends for the faults of his family. Thanks to some contacts of Louis, he came across a company backed by big business that financed such projects; all he was required to do was to send regular photos of the hedge—preferably featuring him posing in front of it with a blissful smile on his face—to illustrate the company's CSR reports. Equipped with his agronomic subject matter expertise, Arthur had no difficulty choosing a variety of plant species that would, over time, create a harmonious blend. Birch, hornbeam, oak, and walnut: canopy trees that, in a couple of decades, would form the vaults of this pastoral cathedral. Alders, beech, pussy willow: clumps of very fast-growing trees pollarded at the base and planted as outposts to protect from water and wind that would offer shelter to the first occupants.

And lastly, holly, medlar, elder, bushy shrubs to give volume to this otherwise rigid line, to create refuges where gnawing creatures could hide themselves away. Arthur knew that some of his seedlings would not take in that soil and would wither and die. But others, less choosy, would spread their branches as if after a long sleep and send out shoots. They would probably be joined by new arrivals, interlopers conveyed on the whim of the breeze, which would know how to make themselves at home, taking care not to create too much shade for the original inhabitants. When he imagined his hedgerow in the prime of its life, Arthur heard more sound and fewer images. The wind unsettling leaves, birds twittering from one branch to another, the rustling sound of life in the undergrowth. Arthur couldn't wait to turn forty. All he wanted to do was stretch out on the ground and listen to the concert.

In the meantime, he had to dig hundreds of holes, armed with only a simple shovel. He had drawn up a plan and was leaving nothing to chance. He carefully calculated the intervals: six meters apart for the taller trees, one and a half for the shrubs. He spent whole days out there, finding in the repetition of his gestures the satisfaction he had never managed to reach with the scythe. His sweat intermingled with the almost incessant drizzle; he had the impression of melting into the soft, damp, gray scenery. He was unsurprised to note how pale and brittle the soil was under the layer of mud. Each blow of the shovel was accompanied by an explosion of dust. And not a worm to be seen.

From time to time, Anne would come help him, digging silently at his side. She, too, was very attached to the hedgerow, but for different reasons. Indeed, she was nurturing a hope that their property—their "life cell" as she sometimes would call it to downplay any landlord-ish overtones—would one day be self-sustaining. She wanted to be self-sufficient. She was hugely persuaded by the very romantic notion of the Great Collapse, which numerous podcasts had convinced her was rapidly approaching. She had already installed rainwater tanks and, after endless DIY attempts, had managed to connect a miniature windmill to the living room lights, the random functioning of which she considered profoundly poetic. She intended to sink a well and had made contact with a water diviner on Facebook. According to her grand plans, the hedgerow could one day supply enough wood chips for heating once it was big enough; that way their life cell would only be generating the carbon it would previously have captured. Encouraged by her internet research, Anne was determined to transform their old oil-burning boiler into a wood-burning one. Arthur thought she was being overly ambitious but was not in a hurry to disabuse her of the notion.

Every now and again, the furtive figure of Monsieur Jobard could be made out in the distance through the gray gloom. Arthur thought nothing of it. He had not said a word to his neighbor since his arrival six months earlier. He would never forgive him for having bought Papi's land at such a low price. Arthur contemplated his handiwork, which was advancing every day like Macbeth's forest marching toward the enemy, woody stalks still fragile but already offering protection, living bulwarks against the poisons being poured into the adjacent field.

The very evening after the last tree had been planted, Arthur and Anne received a visit from Monsieur Jobard. After knocking summarily on the door, and without so much as waiting for an invitation, he came into the living room, which was only dimly lit by the open fire after the wind had dropped the previous evening. In this orange-hued half-light, his silhouette had lost its contours, a cylinder mounted atop rubber boots. The years spent on his tractor listening to Radio RMC had given him the physique of a Weeble toy, a soft stoutness that required him to swing himself along rather than walk, rocking from side to side.

"Ah, young people!" he said, eyeing the mess in the room, and not even bothering to offer a greeting.

He swayed on the spot. His flute-like voice was disagreeable and unsettling. The couple met his gaze without saying a word. He stared at Anne with a weighted insistence. Then he turned to Arthur, as if he had decided to address him alone.

"Haven't you grown up? I knew you as the baby of the family."

The last time Arthur had crossed paths with Jobard, during the last vacation he had spent at the farm, he must have been fourteen years old with his nose always in a book. Papi and his neighbor would regularly enjoy alluding to the most dreadful stories over an aperitif of Calvados and apple juice. Arthur would never have imagined that now, ten years later, he would be the one standing taciturn before Jobard.

"So, you've taken over the farm, then. What's left of it, at least. I've been wondering what you're up to over here, fiddle faddling around the place all day long."

"We're trying to repair the damage it has suffered," said Arthur, calmly.

"What are you prattling on about?"

"My grandfather destroyed the soil. As have you, by the way."

Jobard sighed scornfully.

"You're not about to tell me how to do my own job, are you."

"I know what I can see."

"Anyways, you're not about to fix anything with timothy grass," sneered Jobard. "You'd have been better off putting in rye grass. Timothy and clover, they'll never work. Foregone conclusion."

Arthur was taken aback. He had followed the recommendations from his agroecology course to the letter when he had chosen his grasses.

"Louis puts timothy in his pastures . . ."

"It's wetter down where he is. We're up on the plateau here. I bet he's the one who gave you the seeds."

"What of it?"

"Go take a look at his wheat. You tell me then if he isn't giving it a dose of glypho every now and again. That'll give his bread a bit of taste! You greenies, you're all the same."

Arthur felt unnerved. More than anything, he was keen not to come off looking like an amateur. While he was considering a more obliging response, Anne interrupted.

"So you came here just to piss us off, did you?"

"I came about the hedgerow," said Jobard, without so much as looking at her.

"It had to be done," Arthur reacted immediately. "It's perfectly suited to the biotope. In order for the soils to be able to regenerate—"

"It's your place," Jobard cut in. "You can grow stinging nettles if that's what tickles your fancy. You're just going to have to replant it all a little bit further back."

Arthur smiled, guessing at some sort of joke he wasn't getting.

"Thanks for stopping by, Monsieur Jobard . . ."

"I'm telling you, you're going to have to replant it all a bit further back," he repeated in a determined tone. "It's too close to my fields. It's going to get in my way. I'll lose at least a meter of crop. Across half a kilometer of hedge, let's say, that makes between five hundred to a thousand square meters. Almost 100 kilos of wheat."

"Peanuts, then," murmured Anne.

"I'm sorry," said Arthur, "but that hedge is here to stay for the foreseeable future."

Arthur tried to steer their visitor toward the door, but Jobard remained standing there with his arms crossed, still swaying from one leg to another.

"You've got your degree," he continued. "They must teach you the law in those fancy schools, don't they? So, the law says you have to plant it all a bit further back. And the law's the law."

"What law?" asked Arthur, getting irritated. "It's our property. It's all that's left of it, but it's ours."

"Sure, but you're still going to have to plant it all a bit further back."

The same refrain in the same irritating voice. Arthur lost his temper.

"That hedgerow is on our property, okay? Right on the boundary. I made sure I checked the land register."

"Well, that's the problem. I thought you'd be up to speed, though. I mean, what do they actually teach you at those bigshot colleges?"

"We learn about soil structure!"

"What they should've taught you is that a hedge like that, with tall canopy trees, should be planted two meters back from the property boundary."

"Whatever."

"It's in the Rural Code."

"I don't believe you!" shouted Anne. "What an asshole!"

Jobard froze for a moment, absorbing the shock.

"Now, now! No need for panic," he went on, without taking his eyes off Arthur. "You'll just have to replant . . ."

"Totally out of the question. I can't . . ."

Arthur's voice broke. He no longer knew if he was angry with Jobard for systematically pursuing his persecution of Arthur's family, with himself for failing even to think about checking something so basic, or with Anne, who was not helping matters.

"Law's the law," repeated Jobard. "No doubt about it. Still, we're not going to trouble a judge for something so simple, are we?"

"So why didn't you come speak to us sooner?" asked Anne.

"Didn't have time."

He really didn't give a damn about them.

"I'm sure we can find a solution," said Arthur, trying to control himself.

"Of course. I've nothing against hedges. They take up land, but that's your problem. I can help you move it with my transplanter."

Out of the corner of his eye he could see Anne shaking her head violently. Her piercings glittered in the firelight.

"A transplanter?" asked Arthur.

"I mount shovels onto the back of the tractor. Three blades at twenty-five degrees, like big soup spoons. I adjust them around the tree, the hydraulic arms push them in without any effort, it takes only a few seconds and then I'm able to pull out the root ball and put it back into the ground two meters back. It's neat, won't break a branch. It'll be done in a day."

Arthur hesitated. It felt like his hedge was being stolen, the hedge he had planted with sweat on his brow over weeks and weeks, the hedge whose roots were already tentatively exploring their new habitat. It wasn't just some prefab that could be shifted at will.

"I'll pay for the gas," noted Jobard, swaying faster now.

Was he going to have to thank him, too? Arthur hesitated, the sound of the fire crackling behind him. His pride dictated that he refuse, the same pride that had forced his Papi to hunt desperately for another buyer, resisting Jobard's offer until the last moment. However, caution was telling him to avoid a dispute that would be exhausting and about which there was no doubting he was in the wrong. Either way it would be a lousy day.

It's Antigone's dilemma, thought Arthur.

It was Anne who decided the matter.

"We planted that hedge right where it's supposed to be," she said, coldly. "We are not going to further violate that earth, which has already suffered enough. That hedge is a gift to nature."

Now Jobard turned to face Anne, peering through squinted eyes.

"And what do you know about nature?"

Then he approached Arthur. A sudden burst of flame illuminated his fleshy face. There was something constricted about him, like an animal raised on a battery farm.

"Does she wear the pants around here?"

Arthur had no choice. A single conciliatory word, and Anne would be lost to him.

"We speak as one," he said, regretfully.

"Why do you want to play when you know you can't win?"

"Now you can just get the hell out of here!" Anne sprang at him.

"Young people! Well, see you soon. In court!" Jobard threw back at them, retreating with heavy footsteps toward the door.

He shot a final look at Anne and muttered, "We put nose rings in our heifers around here."

"Did he just call me deaf?" demanded Anne in disgust as the door slammed. "Why deaf?"

"He said heifer," corrected Arthur. "Probably not a word you've heard very often."

Anne would never forgive him if he allowed such an insult to remain unanswered. Arthur raced out of the house, shouting: "Jobard, you asshole!"

The night was dark with bad weather and Arthur couldn't make out a single shape. All he could hear was the sound of steps growing fainter down the path. He shouted again, this time with all his might.

"Jobard, you asshole!"

His only response, the hoot of an owl. Arthur stood still for a moment. He had gone out without a coat and his limbs were trembling. And yet, he felt relieved, reassured. He had just done what his Papi had probably always dreamed of doing. He had drawn a line in the sand, without worrying about what was coming at him down the tracks. From now on he would fully embrace this existence of his, a life lived outside, whipped by the winds. It was as if, courtesy of Jobard, he had just broken off with every other asshole in the world. Not just the assholes of Paris, the asshole professors, the asshole engineers, but the asshole neighbors, farmers, asshole judges, the assholes who trampled all over a life that was so pure and so simple, a life that was open to them, just like it was to every other human. He felt utterly stripped of ambition, incapable of any resentment. After so much angst, he now felt certain of his choices.

Arthur closed his eyes in order to better feel the cold infiltrating his flesh. He inhaled deeply. Little by little, he managed to bring his shivering under control. He let his mind drift this way and that. His body felt at once curiously numb and dreadfully heavy. It felt as though he were sinking into the very soil of the plateau. The darkness around him, was that the sky or could it already be the earth?

When he went back inside, Anne had completely undressed. She was draped languidly on the Chesterfield in front of the fireplace, half turned on her side. Her breasts hung heavily like overripe fruit. Arthur contemplated her, moved by so much beauty, prickling with pins and needles as his blood resumed circulation through his veins. At last, reality felt worthy of those lines from Baudelaire he held so dear and that he now recited under his breath:

"As the hearth alone illuminated the room,
Every time it emitted a fiery sigh,
It flooded that amber skin with its bloodied plume!"

VIII

In less than a year, the two young partners made more headway than they could ever have imagined. In record time Philippine had laid the necessary groundwork to launch their project. She christened their business Posthumus, because "our worms promise life after death." She secured an initial million euros from her parents and family friends, which paid a wage to Kevin as Director, Technical Solutions, and allowed them to lease property where they could build their prototypes. She found an old factory that had fallen into disuse along the banks of the Seine, not far from Mantes-la-Jolie. Kevin spent his days there while she worked from home, a vast apartment in Paris's seventh arrondissement, dealing with all the legal and commercial issues.

Factory life suited Kevin perfectly. He enjoyed grappling with technical issues, finding the solutions to which felt like a constant game. No obstacle was great enough to deter him; he fell back in love with everything DIY, ordering secondhand machines that he would reconfigure with a soldering iron. He loved the solitude beneath those vaulted, echoing concrete ceilings. Whenever he needed a break, he'd sit down on a disused pontoon raised two meters above the river and watch the barges go by. They were hauling the raw materials the economy craved from Le Havre and would head back laden with goods intended for worldwide distribution. Their tranquil rhythm was the metronome of global commerce. Unlike the miserable monotony of cars, they each had their own personality, revealed in their lively colors and irregular shapes. Studying the bridge, Kevin would try to guess at the nature of the captain's life from the washing line, the potted plants, or the dog's kennel. Sometimes his feet would be splashed when the river's wash slapped against the banks. Returning to work he would feel reinvigorated.

His daily migration between Mantes and Buttes-Chaumont where he had returned to his previous share accommodation saw Kevin encounter the modern working class crammed into overloaded and unreliable suburban trains: secretaries, domestic staff, receptionists, cops, and construction workers, the damned of the megalopolis, compelled to work there and unable to live there, up at dawn and returned home amid the crush of the Saint-Lazare railway station. An awkward calm reigned in the dirty, overly bright carriages, as if everyone were ashamed to be conveying on their person a little of the world's ugliness. After a few weeks, Kevin decided it was preferable to move into a studio in the center of Mantes, above a kebab shop where he ate most of his meals. In any case, he was too absorbed in his work to resume his night life and had instead retained the monastic habits of his six-month master's at the HEC.

By dint of trial and error, Kevin had succeeded in developing a process he considered viable and able to be reproduced at scale. The raw manure from organic waste was first tipped with a little water into a mixer where an endless screw would transform it into a sort of viscous paste. A hopper moving along two rails would then distribute that paste along the entire length of the "Line," as Kevin had named the long rectangular tray where the vermicomposting took place. Why "Line"? Kevin couldn't have said. Horizon line, line of coke, lifeline: the worm composter was all of that, all at once. The Line was twenty or so meters long and weighed almost a hundred tons. Several million worms were discreetly working away inside. Once the hopper had passed through, Kevin would cover the Line with a tarp to protect the worms from the cold and light, pulling a curtain over the intimacy of their voracious private lives.

Kevin had sourced his first batch of epigeics from a supplier in Spain, explaining to the customs officials that he needed them for fishing; the number of worms had then decreased over the next few months. In order to harvest the fruit of their labor, he only had to run a blade along the bottom of the Line, as if cutting up a cake. The compost would drop onto a conveyor belt and, once dry, would be taken away for refining. Clusters that were still too hard to the touch had to be broken up. Then the conveyer belt headed off to a vibrating sieve salvaged from a coal plant that eliminated any scraps, pebbles, and residue. Only the best quality material passed through the metallic holes. All that was left to do was to bag it up and use it for compost.

The genius of the system lay in its extreme simplicity. Hardly any labor was required, and the Line could be infinitely extended and replicated. Kevin contemplated his homespun construction with a Promethean satisfaction, a small speck of a man in this cathedral of concrete and steel, alone amid tagged walls and broken windowpanes. The worms' digestion made a discreet and constant sound as the circulation of air bubbles accelerated, a sound not unlike the sparkling of champagne. There in the dilapidated vestiges of an industrial civilization that had ceased to exist, the Line was a living engine, producing energy on demand.

At the same time, Kevin was working to improve the liquid worm tea produced by the composting process in order to transform it into a good quality biostimulant ready for direct application in agricultural spreader piping. But this final step involved more complex chemical processes requiring other carefully selected, measured inputs. And so a mini-laboratory was born behind the Line with vats, drums, filters, and centrifuges, all linked by a labyrinth of steel tubes and, here and there, simple recycled guttering off-cuts. Kevin had not yet hit on an entirely satisfactory formula; there were always some remaining particles that were too compact, and that would risk blocking the pipes. Conscious of the vast market potential, Philippine was encouraging him to speed up research. She had already reserved the domain name: Posthumus Wormentino, with the biostimulant "worm wine" in mind.

Kevin had made certain to keep Marcel Combe duly informed of progress, and from time to time he would drop by. His expertise was no longer of any real use to Kevin, who these days was dealing more with engineering issues than agronomy. But he was fond of these moments of almost fatherly complicity. The Jean Gabin of earthworms would wend his way through the factory, a look of delight on his face. He would seize the worms to inspect their color, give the compost a good sniff, tap the hopper as if trying to make it belch. He would recount his memories of growing things, decades of digging holes and plunging his hands in to rummage through the soil. A life in the trenches.

Marcel Combe seemed overjoyed finally to have found a successor who was pursuing his own life's work and who, most importantly, was putting it into practice. He had been shunned by the academic world, as if he could not be forgiven for having started out as a gardener. In Kevin, he had found a co-conspirator.

Philippine, for her part, only rarely stopped by the factory. She worried about catching the train to Mantes "with all that lowlife riffraff," despite Kevin's protestations. She found the buildings themselves dirty and the temperature glacial; she only ever appeared sporting a thermos and a black puffer jacket. Most of all, she detested being around the worms. Only reluctantly would she approach the Line. When Kevin lifted the tarp to reveal a blackish, soupy mud, lumpy and glistening, along with dozens of reddish grubs panic-stricken in the sudden glare, Philippine would freeze, feeling nauseous.

Kevin loved to toy with his partner's delicacy. It was one of the rare occasions when he could take the upper hand. During one of Philippine's visits, he held out a fistful of earth; instinctively, she pulled away. Then he pulled out a worm with his fingers.

"Look how cute it is," he said to her.

"Put it back!"

"You're making it sad . . ." he pleaded, holding the worm up to her face.

"Stop it!" she shouted.

Her face had turned livid, her freckles lit up like paper lanterns. Kevin realized she wasn't joking. In fact, Philippine never joked. He didn't persist.

"Don't ever do that again," she ordered him in a trembling voice. "I'm . . ."

A total pain in the ass? he thought.

". . . I suffer from ophiophobia."

"What?"

"I have a fear of snakes, worms, anything that gleams and slides. It's called ophiophobia."

"You just have to get used to it. See, if you approach it slowly . . ."

"No, no! It doesn't help. It's genetic. A hangover from having been hunter-gatherers. I read it on the internet."

Kevin remained skeptical. As they walked slowly away from the Line, she recovered her composure.

"A third of all people are ophiophobic. That's why," she continued in a determined tone, "domestic worm composters will never take off. Even for businesses. We'd never be able to sell our lines."

"That would be the simplest option, though . . . Manufacture the lines and install them directly at the clients' business."

"People don't want to see them, don't want to know. All the studies I've conducted confirm it. We're going to have to treat the waste ourselves."

Kevin could sense the discussion heading in a new direction. Philippine wasn't just making a random assertion. He made a rapid mental calculation. France produced twenty million tons of biowaste every year, seven million of which were already treated by traditional composting methods, and another few million by biomethanation. A twenty-meter-long line would be able to treat approximately a hundred tons a year, assuming vermicomposting managed to take about half of the remaining market, that would mean . . .

"Five million divided by one hundred . . ." murmured Kevin.

"I've already done the sums," said Philippine. "We'd have to have fifty thousand lines."

"That's ridiculous."

"We'd just have to stack them up in piles of five."

"Madness!"

They had left the factory as they talked and were heading down to the pontoon.

"Technically possible?"

"Maybe, but . . ."

"One line takes up one hundred square meters, and that's being generous. So, fifty thousand lines, that would need one hundred hectares. With the equivalent of a significant agricultural holding, you'd be recycling a quarter of the country's organic waste."

"Seems crazy to me."

"Why?"

"Just the logistics . . ."

"Details."

They stood next to the Seine, looking at each other, immobile. Judging by the sound of backwash against the banks, Kevin guessed that a barge had just gone past. Philippine fixed him with a stare and took his hands.

"Kevin, we can do this. We're going to do this. And once we've done it in France . . ."

He realized, now, what had been preoccupying Philippine recently. She wasn't content to manage the administrative side of things and develop a commercial strategy. She was readying herself to build an empire. The global empire of the earthworm.

"For somebody who's opiophobic . . ." He smiled.

"Ophiophobic," she corrected him, gravely.

He looked away and saw another barge heading their way, its prow black and yellow, its two anchors sharp canines. It sat high, its water line well above the water, an indication it was returning empty. Kevin reflected a moment as he watched it progress. The vermicomposting lines didn't generate any heat and operated self-sufficiently. From an engineering perspective, he had no basis on which to oppose their large-scale deployment. He was already picturing how the conveyor belt could snake its way between the lines, providing constant material for the treatment room. And yet he felt uncomfortable, trapped in somebody else's ambition that was not his own.

"Of course," Philippine added, holding his gaze once more, "we'd start off more modestly. And then we'll see!"

"Sure, we'll see . . ." he repeated, as if to reassure himself.

Deep down, Kevin knew that everything had been considered. Philippine must already have drawn up nicely formatted slides that positioned their start-up on exponential curves.

"We have to be able to tell a story. I'm going to test it out with a few potential investors. I'll leave you to all your experimenting with those hideous worms. Just trust me for the rest of it."

Kevin watched the wake carved out by the barge. As always, he was allowing himself to be carried along for the ride with a mixture of inertia and curiosity.

"OK."

* * *

Kevin had started chatting about his days with the kebab shop owner, a Moroccan known as the Barber for the way he would delicately carve his lamb, like a hairdresser doing a layered cut.

On his best days, he could sculpt the meat into fleeting relief motifs: a triangle, a motorbike, even a face. He had attempted a portrait of Kevin but had been forced to acknowledge that his bleeding, greasy outline did little justice to the regular, pleasing features of his customer. He called Kevin "boss," a modest way of expressing his affection for this young man who was so much calmer than the other locals.

The Barber had a nose for business. In his younger days, he had set up a workshop repairing motorbikes in Rabat, and had then used his savings to settle in France thanks to a family reunification policy. He had first bought a grocery store before concluding that any margin would be made transforming products into meals. Now he owned three kebab shops in Mantes where his reputation for quality and his service had gradually dethroned his numerous competitors. Twice a week, he was on the road at two o'clock in the morning to source meat in Rungis from his usual suppliers. He haggled mercilessly over the price, coming and going from one wholesaler to another through the forest of carcasses in the meat pavilion, on the lookout for any price variability and unsold stock, returning with last-minute deals as the sun dawned. Such were the rules of the game at Rungis, where to pay with no negotiation would have been considered amateurish, insulting even. The Barber never left without the certainty of having clinched a good deal, which he would generally celebrate with a breakfast of offal in one of the market brasseries.

The Barber had no difficulty transposing his market experience to macro-economic issues and played the share market with a certain degree of success. When there was no soccer scheduled, BFM Business would play on the kebab shop's TV.

So the Barber was following Kevin's business plans with a keen eye. Producing earthworms seemed no more foolish a notion than selling lamb. Conscious that there was no future in the consumption of meat, he was already serving Mantes's first vegetarian kebabs. He had promised Kevin countless times that the day he wanted to start raising capital for Posthumus, he would be one of the first to invest. Five thousand, even ten thousand euros! "Count me in, boss," he would say to him, over and over.

That evening, Kevin shared his concerns with the Barber. He no longer knew what to make of his business partner, who was busily concocting extravagant strategies from Paris, plans from which he was explicitly excluded.

"It's good to want to expand," said the Barber. "Look at me: one, two, three kebab shops, maybe five or six one day, maybe even as far away as Rouen! If you don't grow, you shrink, that's the size of it. Gone are the days where you could rest quietly on your laurels in your own neighborhood."

"Yeah, maybe. But we're not ready."

"In our business, there's no such thing as ready. You learn on the job. If your girlfriend weren't there, you'd still be selling your plastic tubs on the street."

"Or I would have gone to help out my friend on his farm."

"Sure you would!" said the Barber, ribbing him. "Just like the young fellows around here who spend their whole day dreaming about their village back home. And then when they go back, they last two days."

Arthur, however, had lasted almost a year.

If it comes to that, I can always join him. I'm free to go. He found the thought reassuring. As if the Posthumus project were a simple wager, a parenthesis he could close off at any moment.

"I'll take more fries," he concluded.

A few days later, Philippine called Kevin to warn him that a delegation from L'Oréal would be coming to visit the factory the next day. He was busy in the lab diluting a seaweed blend designed to improve the quality of the Posthumus Wormentino branded worm wine.

"Why L'Oréal?"

"L'Oréal, an average of fifteen grams of waste for each product it has on the market, an endless supply of organic materials, a hyperaggressive CSR policy. It's the ideal client."

"Its products must be chock-full of chemicals."

"Didn't you say your worms ate everything?"

"They'd really have to be hungry . . ."

"Do you think you can be serious just for a minute? It's our first contract."

"What contract? We only have a prototype . . ."

They had never so much as mentioned a contract in any of their daily discussions. Philippine was putting it to him like it was a fait accompli.

"So, first up, it's not a prototype, it's an MVP, a minimum viable product. You're going to have to talk the talk tomorrow."

"I trust you to do that. You're bilingual in bullshit."

"Secondly," continued Philippine, without batting an eye, "it's a POC agreement."

"POC?"

"Didn't you retain anything from our disruptive innovation course? POC, proof of concept."

"Ah yes, test contracts."

"Exactly. If we convince them tomorrow, they'll shoot us two hundred grand for a one-year trial."

"Two hundred thousand!"

"That's not a lot. Getting L'Oréal as a client in my slide pack would be the real gold mine. There'll be three of them tomorrow: the woman who's head of CSR, the chief innovation officer, and an engineer from R&D. Let me handle the first two and you can look after the engineer."

Kevin looked around at the bursting cardboard boxes, the half-full trash bags, and the leftover compost scattered on the floor that in places had turned into veritable sludge. He was going to have to spend the whole day cleaning up.

"And how did you come across these—"

"See you tomorrow. Three p.m.," she interrupted him before hanging up.

The visit took place without incident. Kevin had been careful the night before to cut off a slice of compost that had had time to dry out and that he then passed through the sieve. His demonstration was sufficient to convince the engineer, who, as he himself acknowledged, "specialized more in packaging" and who appeared to be intimidated by Madame CSR, who sat on the group's executive board. Philippine was radiant, much as Kevin remembered her from the early days of their acquaintance. In a voice that was more serious and forceful than ever, she had the concrete walls resonating with figures and projections about which Kevin knew nothing. She provided so many technical details about the Line she might as well have built it herself, one bolt after another. She also spoke about earthworms with a passion, an empathy even, which drew moving and indulgent smiles from Madame CSR. The chief innovation officer who, for his part, was in the process of being frozen out over the last several years after a seamless career in management at L'Oréal Europe, scratched his chin slowly before declaring, much to everyone's general satisfaction, the worm composter to be "pioneering."

No more than an hour later, as the group was preparing to leave, Madame CSR turned to Kevin.

"And what about you, then? What's your background, my dear Kevin?"

It seemed as though she were making an effort to enunciate his first name. Kevin caught Philippine's expression, which was suddenly in free fall.

"We met at the HEC," she hurriedly intervened.

For once Kevin decided not to let himself be pushed around. While it might be all right for her to appropriate his work, she would not steal his identity.

"I started out doing an undergraduate degree majoring in biology in Limoges," he said, simply.

"Oh, really?" exclaimed Madame CSR. "Why Limoges? Do they offer a special curriculum down there . . . ?"

"It was close to home."

Madame CSR looked at him in astonishment. If the notion that one might be born and raised in the Limousin was an indisputable theoretical possibility, she had never yet met somebody for whom it was a practical reality.

"I'm a country kid, you know. My dad drove farm machinery," Kevin continued, for the pleasure of irritating Philippine.

"And after your first degree . . ." inquired Madame CSR, who was flailing a little, absent any obvious point of reference.

Kevin recounted his background as a scholarship student at one institution after another.

"Well, that is absolutely *maaaarvellous*! So the social ladder still exists in this country," she noted for the benefit of the rest of the group.

They all dutifully acknowledged their superior. Kevin remained silent. He never understood this business about a social ladder that people would so often mention to him. His own impression was more of walking from one adventure to another, with no climbing or falling involved.

"Kevin doesn't like to brag about himself," said Philippine, taking him tenderly by the arm, "but he's a real genius."

The visit concluded on a touching lengthy silence. Philippine had just understood, and made good, the point at which she had erred in her analysis. In a couple sentences, Kevin had become Posthumus's most precious asset.

After accompanying the L'Oréal team to their car, Philippine joined Kevin back in the factory. He was already busy dealing with one of the old hoppers that had turned out to be too narrow for the Line, and which the hire company was due to come and remove in the afternoon.

"Yes!" she exclaimed, making a fist. "It's in the bag."

She couldn't hide her excitement. Kevin carried on with his task, wordlessly. She slid up alongside him, resting her elbows on the edge of the hopper.

"They want to do a year's trial, with five hundred tons of waste."

"We'd have to build new lines," he said.

Every muscle in his arms was tensed with effort. Their blond covering of hair shimmered under the neon lights in the warehouse.

"I know. I raised the price to six hundred thousand. It didn't seem to scare them off."

Kevin stopped to take a breath and consider the news. He took a few steps, glancing around him at the factory: there would be space enough. The materials would have to be ordered as quickly as possible. Possibly another five meters added on to every line. Design a single conveyor belt. Move the lab. Nothing impossible.

When he turned back to Philippine to share his thoughts, he found her naked from the waist down, underwear and pants around her ankles, still leaning against the hopper in the same position. He was dumbfounded. The shift in ambiance was a little brutal.

"What are you waiting for?" she asked, a hint of annoyance in her voice.

There was nothing the slightest bit erotic to Kevin about that pale motionless pair of buttocks amid the machinery. Philippine had not even taken off her puffer. It was a coldly anatomical spectacle.

"I don't have a condom . . ." he said, piteously.

"It's not like either of us fuck very often."

It was hardly a very valid argument, but Kevin didn't have the strength to object.

"Well, then?"

Kevin approached, out of politeness. After all, he had never been very fussy in his choice of partners. Philippine arched her back on hearing his steps. *A true redhead*, he thought. As he came closer, he reached between his legs, trying to get a reaction. A waste of time. Nonetheless, he undid his jeans and pressed his limp penis against Philippine's buttocks. She wasn't moving and had buried her head in her hands, as if to avoid any eye contact. He rubbed himself against her in vain. He tried to slip a hand under her puffer, looking for a path to her breasts, but she squirmed, indicating to him to stop.

"Come on!"

She was growing impatient. How could she offer herself up with no tenderness, how could she come with no caresses? He was rescued by anger. Finally he felt his penis rise, not to love, but to wound. He gripped it like a weapon and pushed it into Philippine's moist flesh, who let out a husky sigh. Rather than letting their pelvises undulate, he seized Philippine's buttocks, bringing them violently toward him, in and out.

"That's it, like that . . ." she muttered.

The motion required a sustained effort on Kevin's part. He looked directly ahead of him, focusing on the Line. In that long metal tray, so mechanical in appearance, the worms must have been engaging in similar activities. There was a certain sensuality in the thought that neither Philippine's nondescript body nor her immodest moans aroused in him.

At last he tensed in one final spasm, burying himself in her as deeply and for as long as possible. Philippine fell abruptly silent, still gripping the hopper. He withdrew quickly. Her buttocks bore traces of their combat. She remained inert for a moment, collecting herself, then pulled up her underwear without turning around.

"You OK?" he asked.

He refrained from adding, "Feeling better?" like a physical therapist inquiring after a session.

"Yeah, I'm OK," she said, with as much indifference as she could muster. "We'll do it again, yeah?"

It was not a question requiring any response. She headed briskly toward the door.

"I'll keep you in the loop about the L'Oréal deal."

The memory of the visit seemed to be coming back to her.

"Yes!" she murmured again, making a fist.

Kevin watched her disappear down the path to the pontoon, a flash of red scorching everything in her path.

IX

When spring arrived, Arthur was feeling ready. He had taken advantage of the last few weeks of freezing weather to create a kitchen garden of one hundred square meters and to build an adjoining greenhouse, supposedly adequate to feed two adults. He had already agreed with Maria that any surplus would be sold at La Lanterne. Almost five hundred subscribers were now following his blog, *Even a Worm Turns*, and were waiting impatiently to see his soil resurrected. Arthur had even scored an interview in the journal *Reporterre*, published under the heading, "When an agro-engineer reinvents . . . life!" Anne's own relentless activity was starting to bear fruit, transforming their makeshift domestic arrangements into the beginnings of a cozy home. She had recently undertaken the task of repainting the walls and was sullying her overalls with every shade of primer and acrylic. Each morning, Arthur would have his coffee looking out over his future pastures, watching for every new stalk of grass. The first shoots appeared on schedule, filling Arthur with a wave of paternalistic emotion.

As the weeks went by, it became clear the timothy grass was

struggling. The blades of grass were short and sparse. The clover still hadn't pushed through the surface, depriving the soil of necessary nitrogen. Arthur placed all his hopes in the plants with thicker leaves, like sorrel, which were starting to appear in some places. Alas, amid the tufts of green, he saw a tough stalk appear and start to branch out, wasting no time in producing small magenta-colored flowers. It was rumex, a very invasive self-propagating weed, the nightmare of any organic farmer. It was known in first-year courses at AgroParisTech as a "bioindicator," a sign of poorly oxygenated, compressed soil in poor microbial health. Despite Arthur's best efforts at pulling them out, one by one, the roots appeared already thick and were starting to form rhizomes. Instead of the tall covering of grasses he had dreamily envisaged, Arthur's land looked more like a balding skull, marked with ropey patches.

"Rotten luck," Louis had said, coming over to examine Arthur's progress. "It's re-seeding and growing back of its own accord, that *doche*." Arthur worked out that *doche* was the locals' name for rumex. *Doche*, *Boche* . . . there was nothing pleasant about the word; it did not auger well. Louis had brought with him a curious-looking implement from his workshop. It looked like an inverted crucifix, with two parallel steel teeth at its tip.

"It's a *doche*-extractor," he explained. You push it in, as deep and straight as you can, and then you bring up the clump and remove the root. But you have to be careful, if you sever it, if you leave even the slightest bit in the earth, it'll take off again. I'll show you."

Despite all his experience, though, Louis had to try several times to release the whole root. It was half an arm's length, dangling like a rotten carrot, thin and grayish.

"You'll be busy with that," said Louis, casting an eye over the property.

He handed him the *doche*-extractor and left. Arthur stood there, slack-limbed. First the battle with the brambles, then the planting of the hedge. Was he once again going to have to spend days, whole weeks, digging?

To clear his head, Arthur decided to count his earthworms once more, this time using his cell phone to try to film himself so he could post it to his blog.

"It's the moment we've been waiting for . . ." he said to camera with a forced smile.

He marked out a square meter, poured out his mixture of mustard and water, then waited, holding his phone a meter above the ground.

"The grasses have been a natural source of food for the worms and encouraged them to reproduce," he explained.

One by one, the worms emerged.

"Here they are, hurray!"

Ten minutes later, he counted nine. One less than the previous summer. Arthur stopped recording and sat down. Tears welled up in his eyes. He had failed. Everything he had sacrificed appeared, for the moment, to have been utterly in vain. He also feared his subscribers' taunts, which he had no difficulty anticipating. He was overcome by an abrupt sense of disgust for the nine limp worms languishing before him. He gathered them up in his palm and with a furious gesture hurled them as far as he could. It was the flight of their life. "What does an earthworm make of flying skyward?" wondered Arthur. "Does it at least feel some frisson of the unknown?"

Just then, a thin figure in a black tailored suit appeared on the road leading up to the farm. Such attire was decidedly out of the ordinary in Saint-Firmin. Arthur stood up, intrigued.

"Bonjour. My name is Maître Frédéric de Lansdale, process-server for the court. I parked back there, I trust that's no bother? The number of times I've been bogged when visiting farms like this . . ."

They've made it this far, these inbred end-of-the-liners? thought Arthur. Up close, Maître de Lansdale's suit was quite worn. His shirt collar floated adrift around his scrawny neck. Arthur found himself unable to tear his eyes from the colored fish adorning his tie.

"Bonjour, Maître," replied Arthur, promptly recovering his sense of civility. "How can I help you?"

At Maître de Lansdale's request, Arthur confirmed his identity.

"I'm fortunate to find you in person. It's not always so easy, you know. I have to serve you with this," said the process-server, rummaging among the bundles of paperwork overflowing from his leather briefcase.

Arthur took the sheet of paper being handed to him. It was a summons to appear in proceedings before the local court of Caen. The claimant: Monsieur Jobard. The claim: an order to move the hedge abutting the claimant's property and award damages in an amount of ten thousand euros. The statement of facts: unlawful plantation of a hedge exceeding two meters in height and located less than two meters from the neighboring property, contrary to Article 671 of the Civil Code. Accompanying it was a thick file containing plans of the relevant allotments and photographs of the hedge. Arthur turned to the last page. For these reasons, the claimant asks the court to make the necessary findings of fact, and further find in favor of the claimant, namely, that in accordance with those facts, the respondent is in breach of Article 671 and must be ordered to pay damages. Arthur was trembling with rage.

"It's lovely, your land here," said Maître de Lansdale, taking a look around. "But you should clear that field over there. *Doche* really is a complete pain."

"I'm being accused of having planted a hedge," Arthur exploded, "in this day and age?! He should have proceedings brought against *him* for soil contamination!"

Maître de Lansdale adopted an air of contrition. He was accustomed to people using him to let off steam and even considered that service the most noble characteristic of his profession. Wasn't providing people with a face to hate simply the last trace of humanity in a completely impersonal legal process?

"I advise you to find an attorney," he said, laconically.

"The law is in thrall to polluters. The state is destroying the very thing on which it is built. Our society is completely rotten! It has been constructed on the exploitation of both man and the environment and will either be overturned by man or annihilated by nature itself."

Arthur was arguing with himself, carrying on a desperate monologue, into which he was unwittingly slipping several of Salim's expressions. Brought up to respect the law, he was loath to admit he now found himself on the wrong side of the courtroom. Until this moment, he had thought his ecological rebellion was being tolerated, even discreetly encouraged, by those from his own social background. Take his father, for example, who regularly attacked the state in the administrative courts and then posed before the media or at dinners about town as an intrepid defender of people's rights. Had Arthur chosen to go down the path of activism, had he become involved with the scientists of the Extinction Rebellion or the career divergers in his university cohort, he, too, could probably have claimed similar credit. But today, his unforgivable act was having joined the other side: the little people, the conspiracy theorists, the citizens who voted badly, the earthworms. He was a traitor.

"Anyone who is part of this system is a collaborator," Arthur concluded, staring at the man.

Maître de Lansdale savored the attack and smoothed his tie, making the numerous little fish quiver. He pulled a sheet from his briefcase labeled "Confirmation of service," ticked the "Service on the respondent, in person" box, and in the formal sections, affixed a generous and elaborate signature, a vestige of his aristocratic lineage.

"I will now file the application with the court. You will then have two months in which to file a defense in preparation for the hearing. The matter will then follow the usual course."

"Are you a robot or a human being?" Arthur lost his temper.

Without really knowing why, Arthur took a few steps and grabbed the *doche*-extractor, which he had tossed to the ground after Louis's departure. Then he turned back to the process-server. He felt like a peasant bearing arms, ready to revolt. Maître de Lansdale retreated cautiously. His selflessness did not extend to the assumption of any risk. He had colleagues who had suffered nasty blows from a pitchfork.

"All I can say is that generally speaking, a dispute like yours usually ends up settling amicably. You should work to find a compromise with your neighbor . . ."

"Never! I'm in the right," asserted Arthur, the evidence notwithstanding.

"At your service," said Maître de Lansdale, moving off.

Arthur was left alone with his resentment. He couldn't look at Jobard's fields without feeling a wave of hatred. The landscape, so peaceful in the eyes of a passerby, was now stained with violence. In his rage, Arthur went to unearth a stalk of rumex but managed only to pull out a section of root. He threw down his tool. Through the framed farmhouse window, he saw Anne busy applying the second and final coat of paint. He feared her disappointment.

Arthur started walking toward the village without really knowing where his steps would lead him. He approached La Lanterne. Maria had left the cash register to do a jigsaw puzzle at the table with two children from the village. Arthur realized it must be a Wednesday. He had lost track of dates; buried from one dawn to the next in the continuous march of seasons, he was no longer aware of the monotonous succession of weeks and weekends. He hesitated, then turned on his heel. He could guess what Maria would say: *move the hedge, go back to your dissertation*. He didn't feel like listening to the voice of reason. He turned down the cobblestoned lane barely wide enough for cars that snaked down to the lower village. He noticed a low door wedged beneath a heavy granite lintel, like the entrance to a burrow. Screwed on the wall next to it was a plaque: "NATUROPATH." He had never ventured in to see Léa. He pressed the bell, and the door opened.

"It's you," she said, as if nothing were more normal. "Just so you know, I'm in full energy recharge mode. My last patient emptied me out."

He followed her down a long narrow corridor through to the incense-heavy room filled with trinkets where she received her clients. The original ceiling had been removed; all that remained were the cross beams, which lent the room a sense of space that was unusual in these parts. Woven wall hangings muffled any sounds, their bright colors dizzying. At some point on the way from the front door, the old village cottage had morphed into an ashram. Léa pointed him to a cushion at a low table. He sat down cross-legged.

"I'll make us an elderflower infusion. It will help flush out any toxins."

"But I'm perfectly fine!"

"You're anxious, Arthur," she said, setting the kettle to boil. "Stress generates toxins. Trust me."

She brought over two intricately decorated, steaming porcelain teacups. Arthur noted her long, fine fingers adorned with disproportionately heavy rings. Her gestures were precise and considered, as if there were a risk objects might break in her hands. He recounted the misadventures of his day, his doubts on the topic of earthworms, his hatred for Jobard and "the system." She sipped her infusion without so much as looking at him.

"You need a gong bath," she said after a silence.

"Does that involve music?"

"We call it a holistic cleanse. The vibrations align your chakras, purify your magnetic field, and reorganize the emotional flow. The method forms part of the kundalini yoga tradition, introduced into Europe over a century ago by Carl Jung."

Arthur controlled his inclination to respond sarcastically. She glanced at her watch.

"We've just enough time. Lie down on the mat."

Arthur did so, courteously.

"Surrender yourself to the vibrations. Your energy will flow freely through the sushumna channel. You can think about whatever you want to think about."

"I'd rather not think about anything . . ."

"Don't expect to reach full consciousness today," she said in an expert tone.

Arthur smiled. His engineering training prevented him from giving any credit to such talk. But in studying earthworms, the limits of modern science had been so firmly exposed in his mind that he was compelled to grant the benefit of the doubt to practices that had survived the test of time over thousands of years. Chakras or not, there had to be some utility to gongs given they had persisted for generations.

Léa turned to face the wall on which two golden saucers were suspended, each about one meter in diameter. He thought he could just make out a dark shape through her linen top: a tattoo of a snake? She seized the mallet and struck a solid blow to the middle of the gong. The power of the sound took Arthur's breath away. Instinctively, he closed his eyes, as if projected in on himself. He felt the vibrations penetrate his body, from head to toe, as if his organs were unfolding and refolding like an accordion. It was a novel sensation. It almost frightened him. He felt as if his whole self might shatter into pieces at any moment, dissolving into the sound.

Léa knew how to manage her impact. Like the decrescendo of a percussionist, she reduced the intensity of her blows. Then she placed a Tibetan bowl on one outstretched palm and made it ring by stroking it in a slow, circular movement with a wooden stick. Arthur felt himself grow calm. The sound, less intense, more familiar, seemed now to be moving around him, passing from one ear to another, as if trying to carry him into its orbit. Arthur let himself be taken. In only a few minutes, Léa had broken down his resistance.

For almost an hour, Arthur's body was traversed by the whole range of vibrations made by the gongs Léa manipulated with dexterity. He thought first about all his worries, financial, legal, agricultural. Then various surrounding landscapes unfolded before him, as he passed rapidly through pastures, leafy woods, and along riverbanks. When, at last, he drifted off into a half sleep, he envisioned a giant worm approaching Maître de Lansdale, wrapping itself around him like a snake. The process-server suffocated without a sound, a foolish smile brightening his gray face. Then an even more imposing shape appeared. The worm fled slithering away but was soon joined by dozens, thousands, of other seething, panic-stricken worms. They seemed to be in good health, keen to be alive, sliding around easily, one on top of another, a living, ocher-colored jumble. Those worms, tossed into the Saint-Firmin earth, would have worked miracles. The shape kept moving closer and the worms started frantically moving faster. A strong hand reached out to grab a handful and slowly, implacably, crushed them as it clenched tight. The worms squirmed in terror before turning into a viscous paste and being tipped into a sort of hellish cauldron. As if watching a cinematic tracking shot, Arthur saw a bare arm appear attached to the hand, then a shoulder, and finally a face with pronounced cheek bones. Kevin. His lips were moving but his words were inaudible given the noise of the gong. Arthur was desperate to hear what he was saying. He focused intently on his full lips, unable to make out a single word.

"Stop!" shouted Arthur.

Léa set down the mallet and put her hand on the gong to stifle any further sound. Arthur pulled himself up, looking stunned. Léa knelt down next to him and took his hand.

"That asshole, Kevin . . ."

"Who's that?" asked Léa.

"A friend," Arthur replied, evasively.

Arthur had never so clearly acknowledged the schism between himself and his friend. It was no longer a game.

"A guy from my agronomy course who sold out," Arthur continued, melancholic.

"Sold out to who?"

"To the system. He wants to make a buck with his worms."

Léa stood up to put away her instruments.

"You mustn't judge. Everybody has their own vision of the world," she said, closing the gilt box containing the mallets.

Her gentle tone surprised Arthur. He was not accustomed to such tolerance.

"Kevin's not a bad guy," he conceded.

With her hands clasped, Léa bowed before a small statue of Buddha perched on a salvaged tractor seat. She murmured some unintelligible but pleasantly rhythmic words. Then, with a motion of her head, invited Arthur to join in.

"You should give thanks, too."

"But how?"

"However you want. The main thing is to express your gratitude. For being alive, for being balanced."

Arthur mumbled a few words of his own without conviction.

"The important thing is to take responsibility for your choices," she said, seeing him back to the front door. "Whatever they might be."

Instead of going back up to the farm, Arthur continued along the lane until he reached the edge of the village. He skirted the cemetery and headed down an overgrown path leading to the cliffs that was part of the national hiking trail network, and was punctuated sporadically by faded waymarks. Carved out by generations of farmers, the holloway was hardly ever used by twenty-first-century walkers with their fluorescent backpacks. Over the centuries, the trees had naturally formed an almost sealed, vaulted ceiling, protecting the route and shielding it from the sun. Their often-exposed roots clung to the edge of the path and created an indestructible braid. Having not been pruned, several branches extended halfway up, as if testing the space like a blind person's cane. Arthur made no attempt to avoid them, allowing his face to be whipped by the young, tender green foliage still damp from the morning dew. He walked as one might swim, immersing himself in the elements, eyes half-closed. Sometimes he would stumble over rocks and plunge forward without slowing his pace, holding his breath as if free diving. The light filtering through the vaulted greenery colored the air off-white. Arthur let himself be sucked along, taking the winding turns of the path as if in a toboggan. Oaks, beeches, birches, all of them took turns to slap at him with the sound of paper crumpling. The pain was delicious. Face scratched, clothes soaked, Arthur felt intensely alive. It was as if he were taking part in some ancient conversation, not unlike the comforting hubbub with which one is enveloped on pushing open the door to a bar.

Louis maintained that the trees spoke to each other, all day long. Having read academic papers on the topic of vibrations in the plant kingdom emitted at frequencies inaudible to the human ear, Arthur had allowed himself to be convinced. He did not understand what the trees were telling him, but their tone seemed to be courteous and high-spirited. He was being welcomed, wholeheartedly. He couldn't ask for more.

Back at the farm, Arthur succeeded in tearing Anne away from her painting, but not without difficulty.

"I'm almost finished," she said, with unfeigned excitement.

"Good job. Listen, I've been thinking . . ."

Arthur was frank with her, laying out his difficulties as well as his desire to deal with them. The time for compromise was over. He was going to pull out the rumex plants, one by one, then proceed immediately to inoculating the soil with lumbrics. He would devote himself in earnest to the kitchen garden, which would allow them to be more or less self-sufficient. He would not give in to Jobard's pressure and would ensure that the law found against the man. He would force the system to accommodate him. Anne appeared disconcerted by this sudden determination. She was meant to be on vacation here, not engaged in warfare.

"And also," he concluded, unexpectedly, "we've both turned twenty-five. We need to go to the welfare office in Caen and apply for our benefits."

"Why? My father is still sending me a bit of money . . ."

"Precisely. We shouldn't be depending on that anymore. Society gives us this entitlement. Sure, it's a right to not much at all. The right not to die of hunger. But all the same, we should apply for it. It's a question of principle. That will give us a thousand euros a month between the two of us. Enough to get by."

"All the same, I mean, welfare . . ."

"It's what we planned to do, isn't it?"

"Yeah, I suppose."

"What's the problem then?"

Arthur knew well enough what was bothering her. While Anne was perfectly happy proclaiming her desire to live on the margins, she had no desire at all to be officially reduced to the ranks of the poor.

"Nothing, all good."

She picked up her roller again, looking glum, and attacked the final wall without another word.

X

Kevin did not dare admit to Philippine that he had never traveled by air. Even while he was at AgroParisTech, he had always done his internships somewhere in mainland France and in places easily accessible by train. The notion of being abroad was still a fairly abstract concept for Kevin, one to which he felt mildly indifferent. He would happily have gone overseas had there been good reason to do so. Without such a reason, he saw no interest in spending so much time, money, and energy moving from one side of the globe to another. For those with the patience to take a good look around, the exotic was everywhere to be found. The most insignificant watercourse could resemble the Iguazu Falls, a mere encounter could fill a novel: it was a question of scale.

During his vacations, Kevin would go hiking in his native Limousin, often alone, camping by the side of a road. For the cost of a snack, he would make his way through ever-changing landscapes, listening to the village gossips as he filled up his water bottle, studying the comings and goings of animals once night had fallen. Every valley was a different world. As Arthur used to say, quoting Leibniz (or another one of those philosophers), no two blades of grass are the same. Why would he go searching for different ones in Peru or Thailand? Looking over his National Institute of Geographic Information maps, Kevin had realized, not without some sadness, that a single life would not suffice to explore every path in the Limousin. France itself, with all of its nooks and crannies, felt infinite, out of reach. Foreign countries, then, could be left for another lifetime.

Kevin followed Philippine through the labyrinth of Charles de Gaulle Airport, scrupulously imitating her every gesture. He had, from time to time, waited to collect friends at the airport but had never made it past the gates where tickets were checked. He was surprised to discover, on the far side, not a flurry of harried travelers, but rather a crowd of idle consumers, wandering from one shop to the next like children at a fairground. The space was saturated with signs, boarding gates, advertising, directions, sales promotions, notice boards, arrows pointing in every direction. One need take only a step before being snatched up by a moving walkway, titillated by the sign on a store front, or threatened by some directive to go here or there. It was perpetual motion.

"You're looking a bit lost," Philippine mocked.

"Can you imagine being stuck in here forever? It's hell. A modern hell."

Philippine didn't reply but quickly found her way to the lounge. Her gold card entitled her to temporary refuge. After a brief verbal joust with the receptionists, she managed to get Kevin in.

Once they left the lounge and had taken their seat inside the A350, Kevin felt no apprehension whatsoever. Spending twelve hours in a forty-centimeter-wide seat seemed perfectly harmless. He had no need for distractions; he was happy just to sit and stare at the plane's flight path on the screen in front of him in that semimeditative state that Arthur had so envied when they had to take courses on the structure of foodstuffs. While Philippine trembled at the slightest turbulence and gorged on coffee beans to settle her anxiety, Kevin allowed himself to be rocked gently by the aircraft's dance over the Atlantic. His only irritation during the crossing was his neighbor's insistence that he go over his role, again and again.

"The most important thing is just to be natural, completely natural," she carried on, worried. "Just introduce yourself, keep it simple. Tell them about how you were brought up in the middle of nowhere, about your biology studies . . ."

"Agronomy."

". . . and your passion for earthworms. Like you did with the chick from L'Oréal. But don't waste time talking about how you started out with kitchen bench worm composters. It makes you sound less convincing."

Kevin submitted. He spoke in confident but mediocre English, with none of the ill-considered babbling of those who try to reproduce the nuances of their native tongue. He didn't even try to mimic an accent. He was happy to enunciate his syllables with schoolboy precision and efficiency.

"That's perfect. And over there," she added, as if to reassure herself, "your name will offer some local color."

Especially with no accent on the "e," thought Kevin, sarcastically.

Arriving at San Francisco International Airport, Philippine launched herself effusively into the arms of Zoe, a distant cousin who would be putting them up for a week at her home in Redwood City. Kevin waited a moment until the two of them had finished embracing each other to screams of "Oh my god!" Knowing Philippine, he suspected not a single ounce of sincerity. He noted with some relief that cousin Zoe, raised in the United States by two French parents, was happier speaking American English; what's more, he was going to have to say Zo-*iii* rather than the Zo-*ay* of the French spelling with an accent on the "e." Kevin considered it an excellent excuse to avoid any conversation.

Redwood City was situated on San Francisco Bay, right next to Palo Alto. Discovering it from the back seat of a Hummer EV, Kevin thought he may as well have been in suburban Limoges. The single-story houses were laid out in monotonous rectangles. Each of them had its own garage and little garden with a closely mown lawn brightened every so often by a hydrangea bush. *Can't be many worms in that soil*, he thought. There were no shops to interrupt the implacable geometry of the place; at most a few children's playgrounds, completely deserted. The suburbs were punctuated by artificial lakes that somehow failed to create the slightest impression of anything remotely natural: the banks were too smooth, too clean, too geometric. Numerous signs prohibited access to them: no swimming, no fishing, no ball games, no unattended children, and so on. The only evidence of any human presence was a few bored-looking Latinos, each with a half-dozen dogs at the end of a leash.

"Dog walkers," explained Zo-iii.

Philippine made an effort to explain this detail to Kevin, who was stunned. So you could pay human beings to walk animals. Unless the animals were walking them.

On reflection, there were two aspects that differed from Limoges. First, the colors, a hangover from the whims of the early settlers. The facades seemed to be in a ferocious competition of gaudy tones. "You painted your house sky blue? Fine, I'll paint mine pink!" Then there was the price. Zo-iii proudly explained to her cousin the difference in valuation from one block of houses to the next. Estimates hovered around two million dollars. This was where Silicon Valley's *Lumpenproletariat* lived, working relentlessly simply to maintain the right to live there: engineers, IT specialists, designers, various types of managers. Ten years older than Philippine, Zo-iii had worked at Google as a labor and employment attorney (in other words, an expert in express layoffs) before setting up a headhunting agency. So she spent her time at conferences and cocktail parties trying to work out who could poach whom. With an appealing if unremarkable physique, she was on the verge of becoming the valley's madam. Already divorced, she was not interested in talk of love and was considering engaging a surrogate mother in a few years' time in order to raise a child, or rather, to have it raised by Filipina nannies, the equivalent of Latino dog walkers for humans.

In return for the promise of shares in Posthumus, Zo-iii had organized a tour for Philippine of the most significant Californian investment funds. Kevin knew the drill now, having done it repeatedly in Paris over the last six months. And with real success, since they had already managed to raise several million euros, opening up 20 percent of Posthumus's capital. Kevin thought these numbers were outrageous and was keen to close this round of capital raising so he could resume his work at the factory in better conditions. He had ordered the materials to build new lines, but assembly was at a standstill after he had run out of time. As for Posthumus Wormentino, which, over time, was supposed to become the flagship product of their business, its formula still needed to be tested. On that front, Kevin had called Arthur to discuss matters, easily convincing him to use the seaweed blend to stimulate his pasture. When he returned from San Francisco, Kevin would drop by Saint-Firmin to deliver some canisters of the biostimulant worm wine. A good pretext to see each other again.

Even if Kevin considered the funds they had already raised sufficient enough to kick-start their company's growth, Philippine dreamed of finding an American "lead investor" who would give Posthumus an immediate international profile. She had worked tirelessly on her presentation in English, her "pitch," even using her HEC contacts to engage a coach. She had prepared several versions depending on the time she had been allocated and the attitude of her audience. She could present the Posthumus project in three minutes or fifteen, with or without jokes, using the vocabulary of an engineer or that of a poet. Nothing had been left to chance, not even her black turtleneck sweater, an awkward allusion to Steve Jobs.

Zo-iii had arranged a series of interviews for Kevin and Philippine at Menlo Park, which according to her was "the richest place on the planet." Their first meeting of the day was being held at the Rosewood Sand Hill hotel, in the middle of the Jasper Ridge Biological Preserve. This was not how Kevin had imagined the global epicenter of risk capital. Cypress trees could be seen from the terrace stretching down to the swimming pool, beyond which tufted forests of sequoias continued as far as the eye could see. There were no fifteen-story buildings, or suited bankers, or any screens displaying stock market trades. It felt more like a peaceful luxury retreat in a natural environment overlooked by humans. Some of the ancient sequoias with their reddish trunks must have been there since precolonization. As if, at the heart of the most rampant capitalism, there was a need for this unexpected calm. The eye of the cyclone, and not a breath of wind.

After sizing up the badly shaven thirty-something-year-old in his *Star Wars* T-shirt sitting opposite, Philippine selected the poetic version.

"Worms will save the world," she announced, without further ado.

The man listened to her distractedly as he sipped on his coconut water, eyes riveted to his smart watch thrumming constantly with messages. He asked not a single question, followed nothing up, did not so much as nod his head. Philippine's studied enthusiasm, so effective in seducing the French, was falling flat as a tack. She showed nothing of her disarray, tapered off with a few grandiose formulas, then quickly pivoted to the engineer's version.

"I can show you some images of our prototype . . ." she said, pulling out her tablet.

"No, this is bullshit."

It seemed he might just as well have said, "This is genius." It was a matter of luck and humor. He put two twenty-dollar bills on the table to cover the drinks, stood up, and left without further comment. Philippine remained frozen for a moment.

"Welcome to America," said Kevin, sarcastically, in English.

"At least you can say they're direct," she retorted, her spirit returning. "We have to take it a little more gently. It's a good lesson."

Philippine plunged straight back into her preparatory notes, using the Rosewood Sand Hill Hotel's pen to cover them with arrows and comments. In that moment, Kevin couldn't help but admire her.

They wandered down the paths flanking the hotel toward their next meeting. It was here, among the pines and olive trees, in single story bungalows with glass facades and gently sloping roofs, that the biggest funds on the planet were to be found squirreled away. Kevin saw their names inscribed on elegant wooden plaques: *Sequoia*, *Schlumberger*, *Makena Capital*, *Andreessen Horowitz*, *Silver Lake Partners*, *Kleiner Perkins* . . . Security was extremely discreet. It felt like anybody could just walk in and try their luck. Tens of billions of dollars were hidden away in that Five Trident Club Med setting, ready to be poured into the four corners of the planet, wherever humans were attempting to create something new, for better or for worse.

The investors who met with Kevin and Philippine reflected their environment: direct, relaxed, nonchalant almost. They came in every gender, every color, every style: young and old, tracksuited or suited up, geeks and surfers, with nothing to hint at their role or rank in the hierarchy. It was as if every code had been abolished, keeping those coming cap in hand in a state of constant uncertainty when fronting up to the guardians of the dollar.

They always kicked things off by raising with Philippine any mutual connections they might have, including Zo-iii, and sometimes others. It seemed as though these shared networks allowed them a degree of trust; at least the money would be circulating from one friend to another. After that, their questions remained fairly vague. Most of them were only just reading into the file. They seemed to take their time, launching into off-topic monologues about government impotence in dealing with climate change, or the disappearance of bees. Philippine would nod her head with conviction before finding the opportune moment to pick up the thread of her presentation once more. Every sentence completed was a victory.

Kevin was initially astounded by the whole beach bar vibe; it was the complete reverse of the pathological professionalism he had been taught by the petty lords ruling the fiefdom that was the HEC with their ever-so-scrupulous due diligence. Then he realized that the relaxed dudes of Rosewood Sand Hill had moved beyond that primitive stage of commercial strategy. They knew there was every chance their investments would fail. Why waste their time and energy then on any analysis? It was enough for them to bet on one seed in a hundred turning into a giant, thereby paying for the others, a little like an oak producing dozens, hundreds, thousands of acorns in the hope of securing one or two descendants. Everybody had in mind Sequoia Capital's investment in Facebook, which made them four hundred thousand times their initial stake. All Philippine and Kevin had to do was simply convince these guys that worm composting could make them a fortune. The fact that this was highly improbable was of little consequence so long as the dream remained possible. The main thing was to keep the faith.

Philippine had an answer for everything. Not innovative? "Nature has given us the best ever tried and tested technology." No customers? "You know L'Oréal, right?" No precedents? "Welcome to the future." Kevin, for his part, as the moral and scientific backbone of the operation, felt like the ball being tossed onto the roulette wheel. Everybody was watching him, hoping he would fall on the right number.

The dudes generally brought the meetings to an abrupt close. They would confirm their conclusions with an exchanged glance, and then formulate a clear and negative response, barely more friendly than the bearded guy in his *Star Wars* T-shirt. They would then send their guests on their way with the same smile with which they had been received. "See you soon!" they'd say, without really believing it. Kevin and Philippine hated the feeling of being rejected from this happy world of free-flowing money.

The last fund of the day was Sequoia Capital. Philippine had once again rewritten her presentation to highlight the patents their R&D team were working on.

"What patents?" Kevin asked her.

"The worm composter."

"Bits of metal welded together in a hurry . . ."

The contrast between the Mantes factory, on the one hand, hardly more than a step up from a scrap metal workshop and, on the other, the chrome-plated steel and solid oak meeting rooms of Rosewood Sand Hill, suddenly felt dizzyingly extreme.

"The biostimulant, then!" Philippine was growing annoyed.

"It's not ready."

"That's what I'm saying. That you're working on it."

Dusk was already falling, setting the surrounding forests

aflame. For a moment Kevin wondered if he had to go along with all this imprecision. But he could summon no desire to object. He continued to be a curious spectator of his own life and found Philippine's script marvelously entertaining.

The entrance to the Sequoia building, more monumental than the others, conjured thoughts of a Japanese pagoda. The stylized design of the sequoia leaf, its needles distributed from each side of a central vein, lent it a sort of ideogrammatic intrigue. Most teams had already gone for the day. Kevin and Philippine went up to a living room plunged into half darkness and with no artificial light, where a fleshy man of about sixty, wrapped in a bathrobe, was waiting for them. He was sitting on a sort of ottoman, his legs crossed beneath him. His head was completely clean-shaven. From the window, the last rays of the setting sun could be seen diffracting through the swaying sequoia tops. *And here we have Buddha*, thought Kevin.

"Apologies, I've just come from the gym."

He had a strong Teutonic accent; German or perhaps Swiss, thought Kevin. Without losing her composure, Philippine raced through her presentation. This time she was met only with a long, considered silence. The Buddha held her gaze and invited her to continue. She slowed her delivery, then handed things over to Kevin, in accordance with the script they had planned out but which they had not yet had an opportunity to implement. She started out on the last part of the presentation detailing international perspectives, casting a glance at her watch: fifteen minutes exactly.

"Canada, the Scandinavian countries, and China have been identified as priority markets. The Chinese government has taken a particularly voluntarist approach to management of its ever-increasing waste, less than half of which is currently recycled. Given that the earthworm is still used in Chinese medicine, there should be less cultural resistance."

Kevin could feel Philippine hesitate before concluding with her dramatic slogan: "Worms will save the world."

Buddha shrugged his shoulders.

"Is that it?"

"Yes," said Philippine, proudly, satisfied with the fact that no matter what happened, she had done her best.

"I love it!"

Philippine was speechless.

"I love it!" he repeated. "I'm so over all the tech bullshit. I spend my day listening to young kids from good families wanting to put sensors everywhere. I see connected pillows, smart sex toys, refrigerators that are also dieticians. The worst of it all is that it all works! People pay to be put in leg irons. So, what do I do? I provide the financing. We bankroll modern slavery."

"That's a bit much," Philippine protested, without much conviction.

"A bit much? Take a look."

He held out his cell phone.

"This is an app to predict the time of your death. It suggests storing your best memories in an eternal cloud. And you know what? It's a smash hit. Take me, for example," he continued, opening the app, "I'm going to die around 2039. And every day, when I get up, *ping*! A little notification counting down. We're no longer even allowed to believe we're immortal. Want to try?" he asked Kevin.

"No thanks. I prefer not knowing."

"That's the spirit. Take it from me, I've had enough. I'd like us to leave people alone. Let them live and die without being constantly surveilled, measured, advised, guided, governed. Don't you agree?"

"Yes, for sure!" Philippine was getting impatient.

"And here you come with your ridiculous earthworms that are doing this genius work. This is the future."

"Worm composting is the future?" asked Philippine, incredulous.

"The earth. These worms produce earth, don't they? Good earth that runs through your fingers?"

"Particles so fine you could put them in an egg-timer."

The Buddha made as if to pick up some earth between his fingers and held his palms up over his head, pretending to cover himself in it from head to toe.

"Good earth that nourishes?"

"It's like compost in its purest form, ultrarich in nutrients," explained Kevin. "Chock-full of nitrogen, phosphorus, potassium, and even nitrate. And that's not even counting all the microorganisms."

The Buddha sighed with contentment.

"That soil, my friends, is gold. I'm convinced that soil is once again going to find itself at the center of our economy. Not tomorrow, but in five years, maybe ten. Regardless, thanks to all the cretins playing around with data who are bringing in millions, we're able to invest for the long haul. The eighteenth-century French physiocrats were right: all wealth ultimately stems from agriculture. When there's no more energy, when the supply chains are broken and telecommunication networks cut, when there's no more gas and no more batteries for our cars, what will people turn to? Will they be posting some outraged comments on their blank screens? No. They'll be thinking about surviving, the common lot of humanity prior to the Industrial Revolution. They'll be fleeing the cities like rats. They'll want some earth. Earth to live on and earth to feed them."

The Buddha unfolded his legs and stood up. He was round and imposing. Only his naked ankles, against which fluttered the belt of his robe, gave an impression of fragility, as if they were too fine to bear all that weight. Suddenly he raised his voice.

"So then, I'll buy in! I'll buy the fields, the forests, the uncultivated land, the abandoned houses, I'll buy it all! And you, too!" he thundered, pointing a finger at Philippine and Kevin, sitting shocked in their seats. "I'm buying you, too! I'm buying your gold!"

Night had fallen now. Their faces could hardly be made out. Through the window lay the dark mass of the forest and then, in the distance, the halo of light emitted by San Francisco.

"Great," said Philippine after a silence. "So, I'll send you a draft term sheet this evening, with our estimated valuation and governance clauses. We can discuss it at your convenience, but I should tell you that we're here in the Valley for two days only. We have to return to our provisional European headquarters to oversee production. I won't hide the fact that several of your colleagues have already expressed interest."

Kevin looked at her in horror. Why the bluff? And what headquarters? He'd never heard anything about them. Was Philippine referring to her bedroom in her seventh arrondissement apartment? The Buddha turned on the lights. The show was over and the actors' masks could fall away.

"Come on, I like you guys," he said, smiling, "but don't push it. I know they're too stupid."

Kevin noticed the patches of red on Philippine's face; she was blushing.

"It was lovely to meet you," she said, holding out her hand. "I'll send you the term sheet as quickly as possible."

As he accompanied them to the living room door, the Buddha took Kevin by the shoulder.

"She'll go far, that girlfriend of yours," he whispered. "Don't let her go!"

The following days were spent negotiating provisions in the term sheet. The Buddha had delegated the task, a job he personally loathed, to his juniors who considered the agreement a whim of their capricious boss and treated it in an appropriately off-handed way. Philippine took advantage of the situation to introduce all sorts of advantageous conditions that the juniors were quick to concede. However, in the claustrophobic atmosphere of Redwood City, relations between the two cousins were strained. Zo-iii, surprised by the rapid turn of events, was insisting on formalizing her commission on Sequoia's potential acquisition of a stake. Philippine was engaging in endless delay tactics. She had not the slightest intention of keeping her word nor of shelling out so much as a cent for "three little phone calls" as she said to Kevin, who took the liberty of objecting on moral grounds. Zo-iii tried every strategy, from intimidation to flattery, failing to appreciate the iron will she was up against.

Every evening, after enduring her cousin's recriminations over two steaming cups of organic lemon verbena tea, Philippine would go through to Kevin's room. She would enter without knocking, turn to face the chest of drawers, drop her silk pajama pants, and spread her legs. Kevin would press himself inside her, and they would draw mutual pleasure from this habit they had fallen into. She had never so much as looked at him, neither before nor after. She had led him to understand that her ophiophobia extended to the male genitals and that she would prefer not to look directly at that long twisting snake that gradually unfurled.

Over time, Kevin discovered numerous virtues in this brutish form of lovemaking. He reveled in being reduced to a simple object of pleasure, one man among so many others, reduced to the biological essence of his masculinity. And, provided they fell within Philippine's strict boundaries, he considered himself authorized to engage in every possible indelicacy. He manipulated the ass presented to him according to the numerous variations he had encountered in his ecumenical experiences. Philippine appeared to appreciate this inventive dexterity. In any event, she didn't object and moaned unrestrainedly, eyes closed, face generally buried in the hollow of her elbow. Her sighs were like her voice, deep and husky. The sounds of a seal. Kevin felt as if he were making love with neither girl nor boy, but with a disembodied pair of buttocks that might have belonged to anybody. This lack of differentiation suited him perfectly. Particularly as Philippine expected neither promises, nor fidelity, nor explanations of any sort.

Their brief and noisy capers served only to increase Zo-iii's discomfort, abandoned to finish her lemon verbena in the living room. Kevin genuinely considered inviting her in but as far as Philippine was concerned, a share in such pleasures presupposed a share in the capital. He had been chosen as a partner in both business and sex. Zo-iii would be neither one nor the other. As the days went by, her resentment grew increasingly palpable, to the point of writing to Sequoia in an attempt to stall negotiations and inject herself into the contract. Philippine was alerted by the Buddha, who forwarded the email exchange. Far from being outraged, she was instantly delighted with the perfect pretext to cry treason. Zo-iii had been the first to reveal herself, leaving a clumsy and indisputable trail in writing. Philippine could now strip her of her commission in all good conscience.

"To think I had drawn up your agreement," said Philippine to her cousin, in an excess of cruelty. "How could you stab me in the back like that?"

On the morning of their departure, Kevin went out for a walk, heading for what he thought would be the shores of the bay. At the end of the property, he came across a housing development. Limoges as far as the eye could see. Having reached the last street circling Redwood Shores, he still had to cross a wooden bridge in order to access the first sea wall. He walked up to the embankment. From up there he could finally make out the bay. But the view was still blocked by an artificial island, inaccessible by foot. Kevin could easily make out the whitecaps on the water a couple hundred meters away, but it was too far for him to feel the sea spray. It was as if, by colonizing what had for thousands of years been marshland and swamps, developers in the sixties had wanted to put as much distance as possible between themselves and that which remained wild and untamable.

Nonetheless, Kevin was able to walk along the embankment in what was a semblance of nature. He needed some clarity around the disordered emotions assailing him after the days of meetings at Rosewood Sand Hill with Philippine, who was more intense and nervier than ever. From what he had been able to make out on the final term sheet, the Buddha had put ten million on the table in exchange for a 20 percent stake, meaning Posthumus was now valued at fifty million. Kevin's first thought was for the Barber of Mantes, who for five, ten, or even fifteen thousand euros would never be able to invest. He had mentioned his promise to Philippine, who had just shrugged her shoulders. The kebab vendors of Mantes did not form part of her business model. This first betrayal bothered Kevin, modest though it was.

His second thought was for himself. With the shares he owned, he would become a multimillionaire from one day to the next. A virtual multimillionaire, since he would have to wait several years before being able to access his entitlements, when Posthumus was either sold or listed on the stock market. Nonetheless, a multimillionaire. The previous months spent working on the worm composter seemed to bear no relation whatsoever to the sums of money involved. Kevin had never dreamed of becoming wealthy and would in fact have been incapable of spending a fraction of that fortune. And yet, these extravagant figures were starting to dominate his thoughts. He had the nagging impression of having stolen something from somebody without having done so directly, the result of a misunderstanding perhaps. But from whom? From whom had he stolen? Nobody. That was the most curious thing: a victimless crime, exploitation without the exploited.

Philippine did not share his scruples. Once she had overcome her initial surprise, she had quickly gathered her wits. She was already onto the next thing. Kevin had come across her searching the internet between meetings for office space for Posthumus in central Paris. On their final evening in the Valley,

Philippine had fired a parting shot at Zo-iii, asserting that Sequoia's investment was, after all, entirely normal for underwriting a promising start-up. She was hopeful these first millions would increase ten or hundredfold. They should reach at least a billion and become a unicorn.

Kevin pulled out his cell phone and scrolled through the few names in his contacts. He was unable to share his turmoil with his partner, who would not have understood, nor with his parents, who would not have believed him, nor with Arthur, who would never have forgiven him. All he wanted to do was stare at the horizon. But he was deprived even of this meager consolation. The San Mateo Bridge was pitilessly blocking it from view.

XI

"This is Kevin," said Arthur, awkwardly. "He's brought me some liquid biostimulant made from worm compost. I'm going to use it for my oversowing. The grasses should like it. And the timing couldn't have been better. Kevin has arrived on the day of our hunt. He's going to give us a hand."

"Welcome!"

The whole crew from La Lanterne had gathered in Arthur's flayed field, Matthieu, Maria, Salim, and Léa, everyone but Laurent, who had taken his wife's spot behind the cash register, and Louis, who was busy with the first haymaking of the season. Anne had joined them, too; she was at loose ends after finishing her painting. Everyone was eyeing Kevin, who was looking more sculptural than ever in the dusty late-afternoon light.

The two friends' reunion, earlier in the day, had been hesitant. Arthur pretended his experiments were perfectly on track, while Kevin remained evasive on the topic of Posthumus and its activities. After a tour of Saint-Firmin, they had been reduced to fairly technical discussions about the composition of the biostimulant and the best method of spreading it. The presence of

Anne, who could not take her eyes off Kevin, was not helping to lighten the atmosphere. Arthur found his former classmate evasive. It was as if he had lost the sweet-natured insouciance that had made him so charming. The days of dreaming about their future on the terrace at AgroParisTech were well and truly over.

Arthur handed around the equipment for their hunt. Everybody had a headlamp, a pitchfork, and a bucket filled with soil and dead leaves.

"Let me just go over the goal," explained Arthur. "As you can all see, this soil is facing an uphill battle in its efforts to be regenerated."

"Only to be expected after what your grandfather did to it!"

"So I've decided to go ahead and inoculate it directly with earthworms. If we then oversow it, they should have enough to eat."

"I hope you'll be planting ryegrass this time."

Arthur was expecting to be constantly interrupted. He listened to each of them without showing any sign of irritation. He needed them.

"Yes, that's the plan. So, to start things off, we're going to look for worms already in the vicinity. Native species that should be well adapted to this environment."

"Are there different species of worms?"

"More than five thousand. I suggest you go into the woods," said Arthur, pointing to the trees a good kilometer away. "We'll have our best chance of finding some there."

"Beyond old man Jobard's field? He's going to be pissed."

"It's a communal wood, he hasn't got a leg to stand on. Once we get there, we'll be able to spread out, no point staying grouped together. We'll be trying to spot worm castings, clumps of earth no bigger than your thumb, pure worm waste . . ."

"Right. It's greasy, like mud. Sticks to your fingers."

"Then how do we get the worms out . . ."

"Simple. You use detergent."

"To make it easy, I suggest you use the vibration method. You get your pitchfork . . ."

"Detergent will work best."

"True, but it takes longer, and who's going to lug around the tubs of soapy water? We'll use a fork, you dig it in and swing the handle about from side to side to send waves through the ground. Worms hate that. They'll rush to the surface."

"Funny. Like apple trees in the fall. You shake them and wait for the apples to drop. Except that here, they're falling up."

"If you say so. Then you're going to catch them delicately between two fingers, preferably at the lighter end."

"So, by their ass?"

"You got it. Earthworms often retreat backward into the soil. But watch out, when you pick them up, you have to be careful not to break them in two."

"I thought worms grow back."

"Not easily. Then, you put them into the bucket where you can leave them to their own devices. If everybody can bring back between two to three hundred, that would be ideal."

"That'll take all night!"

"Precisely. In about an hour or so, you're going to have to turn on your headlamps. I've put in weak bulbs so as not to frighten away our little friends."

"Couldn't we be doing this tomorrow, during daylight?"

"Worms prefer to emerge at dusk and once night has fallen."

"This is going to cost you the worms' weight in beer, Arthur!"

They burst out laughing and set off, forks on their shoulders. The mood was lighthearted. Everybody was feeling enthusiastic about a shared adventure that was something out of the ordinary. Arthur positioned himself between Kevin and Anne.

"I came up with the idea when I was thinking about Mr. Ashmore."

"Who's that?" asked Kevin.

"Don't you remember? From Combe's lecture?"

"Maybe, yeah. The Australian farmer?"

"He was from New Zealand."

Mr. Ashmore, brilliant and underrated trailblazer in the field of earthworm inoculation. Combe had been particularly eloquent on the subject.

"Who's Combe?" asked Anne.

"I'll let you in on our big secret."

Arthur launched into an imitation of Combe, playing the raconteur: "In the heart of Maori land, amid volcanoes and meandering rivers, picture Mr. Ashmore traversing his parched fields, desiccated by southern hemisphere heatwaves, a perplexed look on his face. He's anxious about his livestock that are losing weight. This Eden, with its large numbers of wallabies and stoats, much vaunted in Europe for its perennial lushness, is not, he says to himself, living up to its promise. He has sacrificed too much to consider abandoning it; and yet, his prospects are hardly more enviable than those of a farmer from Kent. And it is then, through his dark thoughts, that he notices patches of moist, green grass on a section of land close to the forest. He goes over to them, kneels down and scratches at the soil, less out of curiosity than tenderness, seeking a little comfort from this rich, loose earth. Then he feels a living, viscous material beneath his fingers. He scratches around some more and takes a great fistful of earth. What does he find? A dozen or so distraught little grubs, squirming about. Why did Mr. Ashmore think more about it, instead of just releasing his clump of soil and putting his cows out to pasture? Why him, among the thousands, the millions of farmers who had also made similar observations, why did he decide not to let it rest there? We'll never know what went through Ashmore's head. We only know that he reintroduced earthworms, by hand, into his land, that his grass never again turned yellow, that the local authorities took an interest in his trials after the war, and that New Zealand developed a unique expertise in the use of earthworm inoculation for the purposes of soil regeneration."

Marcel Combe had recognized much of himself in Ashmore, a fellow autodidact, and must have nurtured the hope that one day posterity would accord them due recognition as trailblazers in the field of soil science. In the meantime, Arthur had made further inquiries with his former colleagues at INRAE, who had assured him that inoculation had been successfully trialed in vineyards of southern France that had been scorched by insecticides.

"You'll be the Mr. Ashmore of Normandy," commented Kevin.

"And Mrs. Ashmore?" asked Anne, coldly. "Does she ever get a mention?"

"No," admitted Arthur. "She doesn't feature."

After a short, embarrassed silence, Arthur tried to restart the conversation.

"Thoreau used to say that gathering earthworms was as entertaining a sport as fishing. We'll soon see."

"You and your Thoreau!" laughed Kevin. "I've missed him."

Arthur took Anne by the hand. She pulled away and he didn't insist. In jest, he took Kevin's instead, who let him do so entirely naturally. They walked along like two schoolboys, in gay abandon, among the green stalks of cereals doped up on fertilizer.

The woods covered no more than five hectares, the only paths those of animals passing through. The group dispersed upon entering. One could hear the sound of pitchforks being plunged into the earth, followed by a few exclamations.

"I've got one!" exclaimed Maria, laughing. "It's funny," she said, stroking her prey with her fingertip. "It's smooth in one direction but rough in the other."

"Those are its bristles," said Arthur. "Little hairs that allow it to attach to things on one side and to slip along the other. The way seal skins on skis work."

At the start of the hunt, Arthur made an effort to go from one person to the next to make sure everything was proceeding well and to encourage his troops. He noticed that each person had their own method. Léa had put on plastic gloves and was fighting her instinctive disgust as she picked up the worms. Salim, who was used to urban foraging, started by rummaging around under stones and leaves. Matthieu gave several violent thrusts of the pitchfork, and then struggled to catch all the worms emerging at the same time. Maria took her time, inspecting each worm closely. As for Kevin and Anne, who had set off as a couple, they were having fun waggling the shaft of the pitchfork around like the tiller of a sailing boat.

Arthur set to the task himself. The vibration method was effective in making the worms come out. Gathering them up whole, however, required a certain delicate touch. The worms were cautious, leaving the tip of their tail planted in the soil like a well-stowed anchor. As soon as they felt Arthur's fingers, they would scroll themselves back into their tunnels as quickly as possible. One either had to catch them by surprise or pull them out of the soil taking care not to break them. In this hand-to-hand combat, Arthur could feel all the strength of their muscles tensed against the predator, be it owl, woodcock, badger, or *Homo sapiens*. Sometimes, the mucus-covered worm would slip from his fingers, victorious. When Arthur finally managed to pick it up, it would squirm in the air, terrified at suddenly finding itself out of its natural habitat, furling and unfurling its coils like an accordion, trying to find something solid, anything in which it might continue its eternal labors.

Despite all the years he had devoted to earthworms, Arthur had never seen, or touched, so many. No two were alike. In what other species did one find specimens in which the size varied by a factor of five, from wormling to snake? There were slim ones, fat ones, lethargic and cantankerous ones. Their skin could vary across a broad range of colors, from caramel to fuchsia. Each one had its own iridescence, giving off its earthy shades from head to tail. In the face of adversity, some scampered off at a surprising pace, while some would play dead. For the first time, Arthur considered every worm as an individual, with its own history, its own survival strategy, its own subterranean hiding places.

Observing them up close, Arthur could make out their mouth. It had neither tongue nor teeth. It was a simple ringed void, like the hole shaped through the center of a ball of string. And onto this void was mounted a great set of shovel-like chops that would fill it, indiscriminately, with whatever it encountered, leaves, grass, rotting matter, residue of various kinds. The worm swallowed everything without chewing, and would then leave its gut to grind through the organic elements with the help of any little pebbles that came mixed in with it. It was a moving membrane, ingesting and excreting. Worms were the intestines of the earth.

What does an earthworm think about? wondered Arthur, tossing his squirming loot into the bucket. It finds itself in a blind, odorless, shapeless, tasteless, noiseless world. The only sense it possesses, that of touch, must be particularly highly developed. Ring by ring, worms can feel the slightest change in temperature or humidity. Always pushing, butting up against concretions in the soil, it marks out its territory according to zones that are more or less compact, more or less crumbly. One square meter of earth represents a universe, every nook and cranny of which it recognizes. It knows where it can squeeze its way through, and when it must beat a retreat. It even rediscovers little chambers it has created, where it chews through its own excrement like cheese, and where from time to time it gathers with certain chosen friends, skin to skin, seeing out the more inclement seasons. Much like great spaces with their fixed geometries have taught humans to reason causally, worms think in categories of mass and resistance.

How could human beings, with their infinitely more effective brains than the meager cerebroid ganglions of lumbrics, have been stupid enough to destroy billions and billions of earthworms over the course of recent decades by crushing them and starving them? In what mute, wounded, and bloodless suffering had they died? Whether useful or not to humans and their crops, were they not entitled to a simple right to live? Where Arthur was used to denouncing the scandal of the soil's impoverishment, now he was growing aware of a crime, the extent of which made him giddy, and the impunity of which appalled him. Beneath the neat rows of Jobard's blond ears of wheat, all he could see now was a gigantic common grave.

So Arthur put a word to his emotions. It was genocide. Or rather, since the law now recognized this offense, an ecocide: the irreparable destruction by humans of an ecosystem.

It came to him then, with a sort of moral clarity, the solution to the dispute with his neighbor. His father had started drafting the submissions for his defense ahead of the hearing. He was arguing that there were no grounds on which to bring the complaint as the hedge had not yet reached a height of two meters, and the Civil Code must be understood as applying to actual height rather than the hedge's potential height. Furthermore, there was no evidence the hedge would in fact grow. Given the law's disdain for the natural order, this was the logical conclusion to the argument. The lawyer was proud of his strategy and confident of its legal basis. Arthur had thanked his father unenthusiastically. He remained bitter about a prospective victory based on a legal loophole, as pedantic an argument as Jobard's own claim, and one that would bring credit to neither party.

He had come up with a much better argument on this current hunting expedition. Jobard was guilty of ecocide and Arthur had done no more than take preventive measures to minimize the harm. If need be, Arthur would bring his own cross-claim. Were he successful, the fate of all earthworms would be transformed. They would become a protected species, unable to be killed, much like the wolf or wood grouse. Killing just one, even just a little one, a completely gray one, would trigger criminal proceedings. Not a single farmer would be able to grow crops using conventional practices without being brought before the courts. It would no longer be an environmental issue but rather a legal question. Arthur would become a hero.

Night was falling, darkened by the clouds. Arthur switched on his headlamp and set off to join his companions, his bucket already full. They'd be somewhere in the five hectares of woodland. He walked in a straight line, unconcerned about the thorns catching at his clothes. He inhaled deeply, filling himself with the phytoncides emitted by the trees, the beneficial molecules he had learned about in his microbiology courses. The forest was coming alive with nocturnal creatures. Barn owls hooted as they took flight, and rodents scampered into the thickets. Arthur was at peace.

He felt like he was in a scene from a book. A wolf hunt, in winter, somewhere in an isolated village high in the Alps. Hundreds of armed villagers advancing through the snow, shaking their rattles. The hunt progressing, slowly, inexorably. The lighthearted camaraderie. The creature revealing itself by its absence, expressing itself by its silence, asserting itself by its cunning. The surging fear, absurd and tyrannical. The flaming torches brought at nightfall. The discouragement taking hold. More tracks appearing. The circle of men closing in along the wall. The creature cornered, calm, awaiting its fate. The sudden peace. The Grand Wolf-Catcher approaching and, at the same time, firing two shots. Blood on the snow. Death. And the ghastly feeling that the primary purpose of that whole spectacle was to be entertained.

This whole evening, with the earthworms, it's the same thing, thought Arthur, and yet it was quite the reverse. It was not about death, but about life. This obsession with murder, this aesthetic of oblivion—it was a luxury afforded by times of peace. Now, though, oblivion was knocking on the door, the oblivion of a sterile, dried-up, flattened world. There was no time left, no right to feel bored. The issue was not to be entertained, but to act. It was necessary to live: to live and bring to life.

Arthur spotted a glow in the distance. As he approached, he was surprised that it remained still. He didn't want to call out for fear of disturbing the voracious nocturnal hunt going on all around him. His eyes had grown accustomed to the darkness, and he wended his way comfortably through a thousand different shades of gloom. Skirting around a stand of birches, their tall silhouettes pale amid the darker beeches, he came across Salim sitting on the ground, his face glued to his phone.

"Anything interesting?" asked Arthur, hiding his irritation.

"Wait, wait," Salim answered, without looking up. "I'm replying to this asshole who's saying there's an increased security threat. It's unbelievable, the bad faith, these populist lies. You just need to look at the police figures! I'm going to post the link."

"Is it really that urgent?"

"If you don't address it, you know how the argument will go. Who's responsible for the security threats? Immigrants. It's always on us."

Arthur nodded without conviction. A year ago, he would happily have shared Salim's indignation. But now, people's struggles among themselves seemed of little significance.

"Asshole!" exclaimed Salim, tapping away.

"And who is this asshole?" asked Arthur, feigning interest.

"The Minister for the Interior. I'll give him a dose of his own figures. Ha. He's fucked!"

Arthur felt a form of disgust as he looked at Salim. The weak against the powerful, all well and good. But the weakest of weak, lost in the Normandy night with his thirty-five followers, against the most powerful of all, France's top cop? Where is the courage of someone with nothing to lose? The only person Salim was hurting was himself, an earthworm holding itself up in the middle of a field in an attempt to stop the plow. Not only was it a pointless, damaging waste of energy in Arthur's view, but it also suffered from moral laziness. Wasn't the best policy, at this point in time, in this forest, simply to contemplate the birch trees?

Democracy grants to its opponents the most deceitful privilege of all, thought Arthur, *the illusion of revolt*. A revolt that is tolerated, comfortable, and thus benign. At least in Russia or China you risk your freedom on a tweet. Here, you're content just to exhaust it.

"You know I'm an activist, don't you," said Salim, as if reading Arthur's thoughts. "I'm in charge of the cell here in Saint-Firmin."

What cell, of what minuscule group, doomed to what inevitable failure? Arthur moved off without seeking further clarification. Salim represented everything he didn't want to become. Arthur restored his spirits listening to the leaves rustle underfoot. He heard just one final echo from the pathetically imbalanced duel playing out beyond the birch trees. "And boom! My fortieth follower!"

Arthur walked on for another good ten minutes or so without

finding anybody. He was not afraid of the darkness. The medieval era of wolves and ogres had passed, replaced by an even more ancient consciousness of finding a safe haven from predators in this overgrown place. Brought together by the night, the trees coalesced into a compact mass, creating a latticework of branches, a complex architecture that transformed the forest into a Far Eastern palace. Arthur felt protected.

Hot on the heels of the peace he felt on his solitary meandering came the concern that his companions had deserted their posts. Arthur's fears were compounded when he came upon Léa, looking sheepish as she handed him her bucket. She had had enough. The place was overrun with bad vibrations according to her. She sensed something prowling around her, man, beast, or spirit, it hardly mattered, she felt threatened and was going back to her ashram. With her usual kindness, she thanked Arthur for the experience. He made no attempt to dissuade her.

A dozen or so meters farther on, Arthur saw a light swinging along in time with somebody's steps. It was Matthieu.

"I've finished," he trumpeted, and also brandished his bucket at Arthur. "I've collected a good two hundred."

If he were telling the truth, Arthur was completely delighted. He thanked him and Matthieu strode off in the same direction as Léa. The only ones left in the forest were Kevin and Anne, not counting the frenetic tweeter.

Arthur couldn't help but think back to the circumstances of his first encounter with Anne. He was very conscious that at the time he had been a second choice. An image of Kevin and Anne at the start of their hunt, their hands touching on the shaft of the pitchfork, flashed through his mind. He chased it away, shaking his head. He ran his hand over the bark of the first tree he came to. Plunged in darkness, Arthur discovered the full richness of his sense of touch. He felt the marked protrusions. He leaned into his strokes; the ridges intersected to form lozenge shapes, a persistent and regular tapestry motif. *Rhytidome with longitudinal crevasses*, he thought, automatically recalling his coursework. No question, it was an ash. Its wrinkles revealed that it was no longer in the prime of youth, but its trunk was still narrow, such that a man could almost have wrapped his arms around it. It must have been half a century old. In other words, emerging from adolescence, puny still, ready to take on another one or two hundred years of adult life, supposing that no cross carelessly drawn with the dash of a paintbrush came to signal a decree for its premature death.

Arthur continued to run his fingertips delicately over the bark, skin against skin. He reproached himself for his vulgar suspicions, the jealousy that had undermined his parents' relationship, this lamentably human desire for possession. He went back to his collecting. The fallen leaves at the foot of the ash offered up a stash of anecics. There was no need even to dig in the fork; there were plentiful numbers of worms, indulging insouciantly in their nocturnal feasting. They paid barely any attention to the commotion Arthur was causing. They must have felt protected from birdlife by the night's darkness and were happily indulging themselves aboveground, taking not even the basic precaution of carrying the leaves back to their underground galleries. Even the best biologically programmed animals have their moments of laziness. Some of them were making out, gluing themselves viscously to each other, with sometimes a third hopping in who had been greedily on its way to a particularly appetizing leaf. Others remained immobile, as if asleep mid-digestion. Sex and feasting. It was an orgy where the only thing that mattered was immediate gratification. Nature liberating itself from the most basic laws of survival. Arthur only had to help himself. The worms barely moved between his fingers, replete and indifferent to their fate.

As he was throwing the last worms into his bucket, Arthur suddenly stopped, mid-action, and stood upright. His ears, accustomed to the murmur of the forest, had picked up an unusual sound. It was like a hiccup, noticeably different from the nocturnal birdsong. Perhaps it was the grunting of a wild boar, a deer barking? No. The noise was too regular, every four or five seconds. There was an anxious edge to its husky rasp. What creature, what ghostly apparition could be moaning in the woods of Saint-Firmin? A dryad condemned to wander forever in search of virgin forest? One of Jobard's forebears despairing at his progeny? A village witch casting spells nobody believed in anymore?

Arthur was getting closer to the source of the noise. He had to stop frequently in order to listen. The sound played tricks on him as it bounced off the tree branches. Several times he set off in the wrong direction. It was past midnight when he started to tire; it was no longer fun beating a path through the brambles. He stumbled frequently and almost fell to the ground. Nonetheless, he persisted, intrigued. Finally he sensed that he was approaching the source.

It was Anne, seated on a fallen log and sobbing, her dark hair hanging over her face like a hood. Arthur felt both reassured and disappointed. He had feared a dryad and would now be faced only with a domestic squabble.

"Isn't Kevin with you?"

"Your Kevin! Is that all you have to say?"

My Kevin? wondered Arthur. He thought the possessive pronoun was quite flattering.

"What's the matter? Are you lost? Cold? Didn't you find any worms?"

"You're such a dick," said Anne, her voice suddenly more composed, as if he no longer even deserved her tears. "You don't get it."

"Get what?"

"See, that's just what I mean."

Arthur sat down next to her and tried to hug her. She drew away. He sighed. He hated these sorts of affect-laden conversations that, until now, Anne had spared him.

"Can't you see I'm a failure? A total failure."

"What are you talking about? The work you've done on the farmhouse is unbelievable. Nobody could have learned as quickly as you have how to . . . Of course, there are still the finishing touches, and the issue with the boiler, but . . ."

"The boiler!" She sneered. "Well, your hedge is going to take five years to grow."

"If you're referring to the earthworms," said Arthur gravely, "I think I'm on the right track this time."

"Are you kidding?"

"It's taking longer than expected, I admit. But we're getting there."

"You must be joking! I couldn't give a fuck about your dumbass earthworms! I can't believe I'm here, at the age of twenty-five, in the middle of fucking nowhere in Normandy, collecting earthworms for some loser on welfare!"

She gave the bucket a kick. Arthur turned on his headlamp and rushed to gather up the squirming soil.

"Were there many?" he asked anxiously.

"I don't have a clue, why don't you ask your Kevin."

Arthur didn't get angry; he was too focused on his task. He picked up the worms by the fistful, set his buckets down where they were safe, then switched off his lamp and returned to sit on the log.

"But we both had this dream."

A dream hatched on the run, to seduce her, Anne the activist. But she never needed to know that.

"You wanted to create a life cell . . ." Arthur insisted.

"Well, it's done. Now what?"

"Now nothing. We live in the life cell."

"Can I remind you the main reason I came here was so I could write?"

"You told me you were making progress on your plot."

Had Arthur ever believed in Anne's literary vocation? He had been very careful not to ask the question. His sensitivity had, inevitably, turned into indifference.

"I say that, yes. For months I've been telling myself that. The fact is I haven't written a line. Between fixing things up around the house, doing the shopping, the vegetable garden, the days go by. I don't know where they go, but they go. I'm going to be buried alive while I prep the walls with primer."

Arthur didn't understand. The fixing up, the shopping, the vegetable garden, didn't that represent life in all its strength and simplicity? A life that Anne, until now, had seemed to embrace with keen delight? Did it take only one moment of abstraction, a night in the forest, for her to abandon her convictions like this?

"But we have a beautiful life here," he protested. "A simple, healthy life. We love each other. I'm sure you can find three hours a day to . . ."

"And what do you suppose I should write about? Something about the colorways offered by the local hardware store?"

With his fingers, Arthur felt the water-logged moss that had taken over the log. It was like a ready-made pillow for the night. He knew it was pointless to keep talking. But he couldn't help but carry on.

"Everything around us is an inspiration. Look at the trees, learn how to feel them, how to smell them. There's enough here to fill a hundred books! Or," he added, trying to defuse the tension, "you could always write about earthworms . . ."

"You're not funny. Look at Kevin. He's getting ahead. His thing's working out."

And there it was, instead of the timid dryad with oak leaves for hair and fingers as long as branches, that worst of all monsters, vanquished by Arthur in a single email to his dissertation supervisor: ambition.

"Kevin is in business," said Arthur, scornfully, as if reminding Anne of his own principles.

"Maybe, but it's working out."

Suddenly the moon appeared between the clouds, illuminating Anne's face. Her eyes were red, her face sour. For the first time, he found her ugly.

XII

"Relax. Do something more personal. Rest your finger on your nose, maybe. Lift your elbow a little. There you go, that's better, darling—fab, fab, fab!"

For an hour now, Kevin had been playing nicely, posing in a studio in the Marais, dressed as always in his gray T-shirt. Mathilde, whom Philippine had engaged for her ballsiness to run communications at Posthumus, had landed the profile on the back page of *Libération*. In addition to the interview, the journalist had organized a session with, to borrow his words, a "renowned photographer." "You ab-so-lute-ly *must* do it, he's the bomb," Mathilde had insisted when Kevin was objecting to spending yet another day away from the factory.

With his greased hair, luxuriant beard, flannel shirt, and battered Dr. Martens, the renowned photographer was masking his fifty years with his hipster look, circling constantly behind his camera. He was flanked by a young, timidly beautiful, Indian assistant whom he addressed in English and who silently managed the lights and reflective panels, along with two other friends—or were they colleagues?—whose role escaped Kevin and who just stood there, as if watching a performance, offering commentary from time to time. Mathilde, keen to avoid any "dirty tricks," which only she could foresee, had also invited herself to the shoot and regularly came around to inspect the images on the camera screen.

It was not how Kevin had envisioned a photo shoot. Whenever he had needed to have his portrait taken, either for school or sports clubs at the start of the year, it had been over and done with astonishingly quickly. Sit down, smile, click, thank you. His beauty made the whole process easier for all concerned. Now, however, it was unsettling, forcing the renowned photographer to adopt all sorts of strategies to make this young entrepreneur who was all the rage look "less smooth." He assailed Kevin with an uninterrupted litany of contradictory injunctions: don't think about anything, imagine something positive, smile, don't show your teeth, look over to the corner but don't move your head, lean on the stool but stay upright, and most of all, *most* of all, look natural—perfect advice in circumstances where every other variable made that utterly impossible.

As usual, Kevin suffered in silence. He felt his lips tremble from the effort of pretending to smile. He could sense the renowned photographer growing irritated with his lack of cooperation. "It's cold, too cold," he fulminated. Kevin concentrated for the first ten minutes, doing his best to comply with instructions, after which he gave up, happy just to go through the motions. The renowned photographer recognized Kevin's reaction immediately and started manipulating him like a puppet, positioning an arm or shifting his chin. He sighed ambiguously; was it a sigh of fatigue, irritation, repressed desire? "Go easy," pleaded Mathilde, as if there was a risk of damage to her client and mascot. Kevin just let it happen, fully inhabiting his role as pure object, a role he did not detest.

Between flashes, he took stock of these last months. Their capital-raising success, and in particular, Sequoia Capital's investment, had surprised those in business circles and aroused the media's curiosity. Philippine had, in record time, taken a sublease on premises in the eighth arrondissement and employed thirty or so staff at their headquarters, while Kevin was constructing new vermicomposting lines at a rate of knots and had filed applications for approval of the biostimulants. There was now a small, permanent team on site at Mantes composed of two engineers and three technicians. Kevin continued to oversee activities at the factory, but his constant presence was soon no longer required. Philippine, on the other hand, was constantly at him to come into the city to represent Posthumus at dinners or press conferences. She was fully cognizant of the significant role Kevin's story played in a society that aspired to being a meritocracy. He was the kid from Limoges whom the great and the good of Parisian society wanted to fete at their dinners to prove that at long last, there was justice in this world, and they no longer had anything to reproach themselves for.

Once again Philippine suggested Kevin move. He didn't need to be begged. He still had unfinished business with Paris. He bid his brief farewells to the Barber, who was, as expected, offended.

"Pride comes before a fall!" He tossed the comment at his young customer while carving his lamb.

Kevin changed neighborhoods and, with it, perspective. He rented a three-room apartment in a Haussmann building next to the Parc Monceau, a fifteen-minute walk from the Posthumus offices. His sudden wealth, strange and largely still virtual, at least allowed him to breakfast alone. The seventy square meters were otherwise well and truly too vast for somebody whose possessions still fitted into a single large suitcase; he left one room entirely empty and camped in another, his old sleeping bag spread out on a bare mattress and an upside-down box as a bedside table. The ceiling moldings, which he would stare at lengthily before falling asleep, left him baffled. The estate agent had played up their "historical" character. At first Kevin tried to decipher any coherent shapes before concluding they were no different from the shapes tipped out of buckets at the beach, they were simply plaster instead of sand. There was nothing historical about it that he could see, except for human gullibility.

Kevin could not really have said how he was spending his days. He went from one meeting to another with a busy nonchalance. He met with researchers to improve his Wormentino worm wine, while waiting for results from Arthur's experiments using the biostimulant according to the dose Kevin had worked out in the lab. He lunched with investors, bankers, and wealth managers who all considered Kevin to represent a still very uncertain promise of profit, and who bombarded him with lengthy tirades on the topic of interest rates. He met with environmental defender groups who suspected him of serving the greenwashing interests of industrialists and interrogated him on the subject of the lumbrics' well-being. He saw to the induction training of a gaggle of communications people, policy officers, marketing specialists, PR managers, including the chief operating officer and other hangers-on who had joined Posthumus and had never seen an earthworm in their lives. He went to breakfast meetings in five-star hotels with writers of economic op-eds struggling for inspiration who asked for his thoughts on globalization. He accompanied Philippine to the offices of potential clients, especially the managers of local government authorities' administrative services terrified about the incoming law making the recycling of organic waste mandatory. He reassured the increasingly impatient "innovation" teams at L'Oréal via videoconference. Kevin felt like he was constantly having the same conversation, on the same topic, with the same forced enthusiasm.

"We're going to give something a try," exclaimed the renowned photographer, suddenly claiming all Kevin's attention. "Place your chin on the back of your hand. Like Rodin's *Thinker*, if you see what I mean."

Kevin didn't see at all. He dropped his chin against his hand.

The photographer sighed. "Ok, leave it."

Lifting his head again, Kevin caught the assistant's amused look. He smiled at her.

"That's it! That's the smile we want, hold it right there, hold it!"

She had the green eyes of Rajasthan, so pale in the middle of that smoldering face they seemed almost blind. Kevin scowled, eliciting a sigh of disapproval from the renowned photographer. He felt incapable of feeling any attraction even to that woman. During his first weeks of Parisian life, he had resumed some of his former habits in the Marais clubs where all he had to do was turn up and he would have his choice of candidates. He had quickly realized that even without flatmates to reflect back a distorted image of himself, he could not escape a particular image that in no way sat easily with him. He shared neither the etiquette, nor the struggles, nor the tastes of his bedroom companions. So he made do with a few girls but was unable to settle into any form of relationship. The most basic acts of tenderness, like holding a hand while walking down the street, felt like a painful charade. From dating apps to awkward dinners, any attempt to get together with somebody exhausted him. He concluded, with a certain relief, that much like earthworms, he was destined to be single.

From time to time, Philippine would come over in the evening to get her fix of sex, without ever staying the night. She had softened around the edges as a result of her predilection for bingeing on chocolate-coated coffee beans. Kevin found her less attractive but more comfortable. Ultimately, he considered their arrangement very convenient and resolved to be satisfied with it. Philippine, for her part, had no time to waste on romance; she would discuss Posthumus's affairs as she removed her underwear and then again as she put her clothes back on, barely interrupting herself to climax. Kevin would not have been surprised if, while flat on her stomach on the living room table, she was still thinking about the company's turnover. Their actions were orderly, refined even. Not a caress that wasn't strictly necessary.

Back in the office, the division of labor adopted at their first encounter continued to prevail. Philippine was responsible for strategy, and Kevin handled operations. Their discussions consisted essentially of keeping each other informed of their respective progress. They exchanged information and bodily fluids with the same mutual satisfaction, without feeling any need to get to know each other any better.

There was one thing that did bother Kevin. Philippine had promised L'Oréal they would process five hundred tons during the first year. For the time being, however, the factory had only been capable of receiving forty tons, divided between the two new vermicomposting lines. Kevin planned to commission another two lines that would be almost twice as big and equipped with moisture and density sensors, which would automatically trigger the cutting of compost that had reached maturity. He had even entered into a partnership with Soltech, the start-up that had featured at their graduation, and that had attracted both his own and Arthur's derision. Their product was perhaps not designed for complex soil, but it was largely adequate for compost.

Alas, construction was running behind. Having ordered the rails in a rush, Kevin was finding it difficult to locate hoppers of adequate dimensions; Sofia, the engineer responsible for site operations, had resigned herself to ordering ordinary models and patching things together with some complicated soldering. What's more, the sensors still needed some fine-tuning; the first tests had produced compost that still contained a number of worms, which required adding an interminable stage of manual sorting. In an effort to meet the deadline, Kevin had joined the team, spending two days removing worms from the compost, one by one. It was a peaceful enough task, almost meditative, far from the hustle and bustle of Paris, and it reminded him of weekends when, as a kid, he had picked out the rotten potatoes from the harvest. As far as the team was concerned, this fishing for worms was worth every induction seminar. But at this rate, L'Oréal would still be waiting in ten years' time. And Kevin was seriously starting to worry that Posthumus would not be able to honor its contracts, even as Philippine was accumulating commitments from businesses and local agencies keen to find a more economical alternative to methanation.

"All right then, darling, I won't make you suffer any longer. You're cute enough as it is anyway, don't worry."

The renowned photographer lowered his camera and scrolled through a few of the hundreds of photos he had taken. Leaning over his shoulder, Mathilde was vocal in expressing her preferences, which, as a point of honor, he ignored.

"You can pack up," he added carelessly to his assistant, without so much as a glance in her direction.

Kevin emerged from his torpor. He wanted to catch the blind gaze of the Indian woman once more, but she had her back turned to him now, busy packing up cameras into their cases.

"Thanks very much," he said awkwardly, as one would after a haircut.

He heard a muffled snicker from the two onlookers.

* * *

The profile in *Libération* represented a turning point for Kevin and for Posthumus. Titled "The Early Bird Catches the Worm," it dealt rapidly with the manufacturing aspects of vermicomposting, at a cost of some seriously exaggerated claims, like the assertion that earthworms could "devour *all* waste," or even patent untruths, such as the journalist claiming Posthumus had secured "millions of dollars from an American bank." Mathilde assured Kevin, who was stunned by such casualness, that the details were of absolutely no consequence, and he had no right to complain, given what counted for normal media coverage. The main thing was that the article emphasized the ecological attributes of the business ("a solution for the planet," proclaimed the subheading) along with the unusual characteristics of its cofounder, who miraculously escaped the anticapitalist jibes one might've expected of that paper. At the time, Extinction Rebellion activists were becoming ubiquitous; not a day went by without an attention-seeking sit-in or people supergluing their hands to the road to protest climate inaction. Nobody could guess where it was all going to end. Even at *Libération*, columnists writing opinion pieces had started to have a gutful. So profiles such as Kevin's, with their catalog of tedious but concrete solutions, were suddenly back in favor.

"Half ephebe, half boy from the country," the journalist concluded, "both brilliant and taciturn, Kevin is living proof that the glass ceiling so often encountered at the top of the social ladder can sometimes be smashed. Some end up having to pay for their name. Kevin, though, has avenged his own and all who share it. Here, at last, is an entrepreneur who does not consider himself humanity's savior . . . but who may be just that!" *Here we go again with the social mobility!* thought Kevin. He was more interested in the photo. It looked like he was scratching his nose while gazing at the ceiling. At least the renowned photographer had lived up to his promise of making him look unattractive.

Kevin felt curiously embarrassed when he bought a copy of *Libé* at the newspaper stand on the day the profile came out. It was a first; he rarely read the papers and never in hard copy. There was no doubt the person described on the last page resembled him. Uncannily so. But it suggested a coherence Kevin had never felt, having always allowed himself to be caught up in the events of the moment. It was as if his destiny were suddenly confined to this paper prison. And how unseemly to be distributed to households throughout the country! He imagined his mug beneath potato peelings or being devoured by flames in a fireplace. He would have liked to put a comic strip speech bubble over his photo: "Sorry, I'm just passing through, tomorrow I'm outta here."

In contrast, there was peak excitement in the open plan offices of Posthumus. Kevin expressed his astonishment to Mathilde.

"Are there really so many people who read this paper?"

Mathilde just looked at him, dumbfounded. He seemed to be serious.

"Well, no, nobody reads *Libé* anymore."

"So . . ."

"Nobody except other journos. They'll be hurling themselves at you. An entrepreneur who has received the endorsement of the guardians of the libertarian temple, it's gold. I've already had two messages, from BFM TV and from Europe 1's morning show. You're going to be a star."

Mathilde grabbed her cell phone, which wouldn't stop vibrating.

"That said," she continued, "I'm going to put the RTL morning show on standby. Just in case we end up on Inter. You okay with that?"

Out of habit, Kevin wanted to answer yes, yes. For once he refrained.

"I'm not sure if now is the right moment, but just in relation to our treatment capabilities . . ."

Just then, Philippine burst out of her glass-walled office and abruptly interrupted the conversation.

"Inter? That's great! And is it going off on the socials?"

"It's going crazy. The social media manager has done a great job. We've already got two thousand views on Insta and five thousand on LinkedIn. Given our positioning, the differential is nothing to worry about. There are some people making off-base comments about the circular economy, but all good, as long as it's positive . . . Others are posting photos of earthworms and poking fun. That still gets reach."

Mathilde showed Philippine a meme with Kevin's head on top of an earthworm's body, with the line: *You want to move up the social ladder, you have to dig deep. @Libe @Kevin #earthworm.*

"People are so predictable . . ." winced Philippine. "You're nice enough to provide them with something they can shit on, and they jump to it. Come on guys, go your hardest. The more they take us for fools, the more we'll treat them like fools."

"That's the nature of the beast, yeah," said Mathilde, to keep her boss happy.

Kevin had an old Facebook account followed by his parents and a handful of friends, an Instagram account from his time at AgroParisTech, and a Twitter account that he just used passively. The only influencers he followed were geodrilologists. Mathilde had let him keep Facebook "for personal stuff" and had taken over the others. "From now on," she warned him, "we'll be keeping a handle on what you say and how you say it." Kevin, who had never been overly fond of talking, had no problem with others doing it in his place.

Mathilde had not exaggerated. From one day to the next, Kevin became the latest green flavor-of-the-month entrepreneur. Everybody wanted him on their show or at their table. He very quickly grew familiar with the city's backstage corridors: the makeup rooms at television studios where he would be powdered up like a courtesan before going on set, bedrooms that served as changing rooms in overly narrow apartments, museums that had been emptied out for this or that gala, vertical gardens tucked away behind the double doorway of a building's unmarked porte cochere, the private mansions of ministerial offices where he was invited to brainstorm plans to transform the French economy into fifteen sectors, the terraces of company headquarters where it was good form to admire the view before talking business, the private clubs where Legion of Honor awards ceremonies took place. Kevin felt like a tourist on a VIP tour.

Philippine behaved as if she were his mother, or rather, his chaperone. She gave him his first and last tie. Sure, being young and owning a start-up came with the exorbitant privilege of holding on to your jeans and T-shirt, but there were some very particular circumstances, a round table meeting at the Automobile Club, say, when cool became careless.

"It really doesn't suit you at all," she said, deadly serious, as she looked at her dolled-up handiwork.

Philippine guided him, from time to time she would accompany him, but all the while she would remain as unobtrusive as possible, her discretion bordering on anonymity. Some people were surprised to learn that the famous Kevin had not scaled his mountain of earthworms entirely alone and that his cofounder was none other than the cousin of what's his name, the daughter of neighbors from the Île de Ré, the former classmate of so-and-so from the École Alsacienne. They would appear a little disappointed, as if the story they had been sold was too good to be true and, sure enough, there was a catch.

Like it or not, Kevin was adding contacts to his cell phone every day and, on Mathilde's advice, automatically accepting hundreds of LinkedIn requests. His repartee remained limited, but his sunny confidence was sufficient to endear him to people.

He found himself included in all sorts of networks that meant his evenings were filled with lectures and discussions and cocktails and canapés from which he would always take his leave with the same taste of warm champagne and gelatinous petits fours in his mouth. He who had never cultivated firm friendships, with the exception of Arthur, suddenly found himself in numerous Telegram chats and drowning in envious smiley emojis no sooner was his name mentioned in the press. People with the slimmest of connections would send him outrageously familiar messages, like they had known each other forever. All he had to do was open the correct door one day and SURPRISE! Everybody was a buddy, everybody was greeting him familiarly, giving him a kiss on each cheek, cozying up to him. Far from the affected universe he had imagined, Kevin discovered a form of camaraderie among the Parisian elite that had long since vanished from the rural regions of his upbringing, a mutual assistance that was all the warmer for the fact that deep down, none of them needed anything from anyone.

This tribe had its rituals. First you had to specify which clan you represented. After several minutes of conversation, you would inevitably be asked, directly or in a more roundabout fashion, about your tertiary qualifications.

"Agro."

"Is that a *grande école?*"

Yes, he had learned to reply, it's a *grande école*. Not as *grande* as Centrale, Normale, Polytechnique, the ENA, the HEC, or the Holy Grail, the double-feathered headdress: X-Mines. But, a *grande école* nonetheless, with an address out at the Saclay plateau and an increasingly desirable name. It was the clan from the distant forest, with the enviable fresh blood and rustic mores, even if it had not yet been completely accepted as one of the ruling families.

Next question: "It's not that place with the divergers?"

That part felt a bit much. The environment? Sure, all very well. Lefties? No thanks. "That's not how things get done." Kevin would nod in agreement. Fundamentally, he was on the same page, and he was not about to make excuses if his opinions happened to coincide with his own interests.

Kevin also had to get used to the codes governing the tribe, fairly simple but not always obvious. Proclaiming the death of the patriarchy but nonetheless waiting for the mistress of the house to pick up her fork before making a start on your own plate. Using English words with an air of regret, as if you had no choice in the matter. Affecting a blasé disdain for politicians while noting their every minor misstep. Proudly claiming your provincial roots, Limoges in Kevin's case, which would have given his parents, who came from nowhere and were proud of it, a good laugh. Always introducing yourself by your first name, a sign of modesty among people who are well known, or at least think they are. Quoting radical authors provided they're dead and thus inoffensive. Never wearing a black belt with lighter-colored shoes, despite the most disheveled outfits being permitted, even encouraged. Mocking pretentious restaurants where the menus say: "Titillate Your Tastebuds" instead of "Appetizer" and "Gourmet Delights" for "Entrée." More generally speaking, criticizing every attribute of success down to the last detail, in order to demonstrate that you, too, possess those very features. Not speaking about money, including and especially the amount of any capital raised, in order to maintain the illusion that money follows a natural course, finding its way to everybody. Being indignant about inequalities with a fatalistic gloom. Laughing at the most banal crude jokes but fucking as little as possible. And most of all, *most* of all, rule number one: making out as if there are no rules, and that everybody just happens to know each other; they've fallen in with one another in the most perfectly spontaneous way.

Kevin slipped into this new mold without any difficulty, as he had always done in the various social circumstances in which he had found himself. He found this one no more ridiculous than any other. Just a little more perverse perhaps in its perpetual negation of its own existence.

Coming out of the Europe 1 breakfast show, Kevin had twenty odd messages pop up on his phone when he turned it back on. They pinged one after the other, like slot machines coming up with three bananas in a row. His spot on the show, to which Mathilde had finally agreed, had been endlessly pushed back due to war breaking out, some famous actor dying, or a government announcement about retirement plans, current events that in Mathilde's opinion were unforgivable given the resulting delay to their own revelations around worm composting. Kevin felt comfortable for the seven-minute-long interview itself, but not before and not afterward. Hardly had he settled into his chair, microphone adjusted at mouth level by a pair of tattooed arms, when the presenter took advantage of an ad break to coldly go over her questions as well as the answers she was expecting. Then, after a very soft interview, she resumed her delivery of the news without giving him another glance when he left the studio. It was like the mics needed to be on for her to be friendly.

Among the messages of congratulations Kevin was still naive enough to consider sincere, and to which he nonchalantly replied from the taxi ordered by the studio, was a more laconic text from Sofia: "Come into the factory when you can." He called her immediately. "We'll talk when you get here" was her only response to his requests for more information. Sofia was not one to panic. Ten years older than her boss, she had pursued the same course of study before taking various management jobs in the agri-industrial space. She was a no-nonsense professional who, far from being seduced by Kevin, seemed to treat him like a kid who'd gotten lucky. Whenever he met with her, he always doubled his efforts to be serious and tried not to get bogged down in technical terms.

Kevin redirected his taxi toward the Gare Saint-Lazare and took the first suburban train to Mantes, an all-stops, which almost killed him. He tried in vain to imagine what might have gone wrong. Lumbrics don't get sick, they reproduce easily enough, and are happy to stay in their corner of soil with no need to roam in search of fresh air. In short, they do very well left to their own devices. It was this economy of means that constituted the beauty of vermicomposting, as Kevin had asserted repeatedly on the airwaves.

Sofia was waiting for him on the jetty. She led him inside without even a greeting. The third line appeared to be ready. Still empty, its monumental metallic form stretched all the way to the back of the warehouse. The hopper was in place, well fitted, with no obvious sign of soldering work. The recent coat of green paint evidenced an eye for the aesthetic that was entirely pointless and all the more appreciated for it.

"Nice work," commented Kevin in passing.

Sofia didn't react.

"For the last few weeks we've noticed a continual drop in production. There's nothing coming out of the lines anymore. We're feeding them as much as we can, but it's like the worms are on strike."

"Is there an issue with the L'Oréal waste?"

"That's what I initially thought, but I've tested it on some minicomposters and that all worked well."

"And the temperature—?"

"It's at twenty degrees," she interrupted him, irritated. "This morning I put on the suit and moved everything around. I found lots of tunnels."

"That's weird. Epigeics don't normally dig."

"Precisely. So I started poking through it with a pitchfork. And one of them came out."

"A worm?"

"A rat. We managed to catch it."

With the tip of her shoe, she flicked over the corpse that had been stabbed through its abdomen. Its tail, at least as long again as its body, sketched a question mark. Its digits, pink and wrinkled, looked like those of an infant. *Ninety-nine percent of genes in common*, thought Kevin in disgust.

"There are scores of them, possibly hundreds," continued Sofia. "All the lines are infested."

Kevin couldn't bear the sight of the white, round belly, stuffed with worms, his worms. He gave the corpse a hate-filled kick. He would have liked to destroy the rats, the way bulls and pigs used to be hanged for killing children in the old days. He felt guilty and powerless. The slaughter was continuing in silence right in front of him. How many worms were perishing in the jaws of these rodents at that very moment? He pictured them, alerted by the movement of the earth around them, frantically trying to escape further into the soil they had thought was infinite. But there was no way out, and there they were trapped, caught, ripped apart, bitten through, devoured, digested.

"We can't catch the rats one by one, nor, obviously enough, can we lay poison through the compost. The only solution is to empty everything out and buy new stocks of worms."

"That's one hell of a job! There are a hundred or so tons in there."

"And then install antirodent mesh."

"I should have thought of it before," muttered Kevin, somberly.

"We talked about it when I first got here, but the two of you were in such a hurry."

Sofia could have spared him the reproaches mid-crisis. But they were no less valid. She had wanted to secure the lines, and Philippine had been against it, railing against unnecessary precautions.

"It will take weeks before we can rebuild the colony," noted Sofia.

The rest of the team had gathered in a circle around them, heads bowed. Kevin realized then what it signified. It was not just a loss, it was a bereavement. The lines, once teeming with life, had been transformed into coffins. Over time, the worms, which one could neither see nor hear nor smell, had become companions. They filled the factory with a particular silence, like a crowd praying. With no conflict or drama, that silence had become an absence. Kevin saw that his troops were looking to him as one might to the relatives of a deceased, hoping for the first smile.

He granted them one with his instinctive grace and found a few simple phrases, which were enough to prompt them back into action. Then he picked up a shovel and started the thankless task of undertaker emptying out the lines.

XIII

At the start of that fall, morale in the Saint-Firmin farmhouse was growing weaker with the daylight. Arthur's father had refused to take on the ecocide claim formulated by his son against Jobard. He had no desire to compromise his professional reputation as a lawyer by bringing a case that might be politically astute but legally unsustainable. "Law is not theater" had been the bold reply from a man who had built a career around staging his pleadings.

"So, the undocumented immigrants, the sex workers, the Salafists, you're happy to defend them, but not earthworms?"

"Earthworms, as such, do not have legal standing. To the best of my knowledge, they have never brought proceedings. That might be a source of regret, but that's how it is."

"And nor will they get any television coverage, will they?"

Relations between father and son, which had not been particularly warm since the death of Arthur's mother, had then broken off. Arthur had decided to draft a counterclaim himself, the legal term for a counterattack where the defendant becomes the claimant, and doubts are raised about the original applicant.

Arthur painted himself as the victim of a criminal act: he would never have had to plant that hedge if Monsieur Jobard had not pulled out his own and polluted the surrounding soil. In addition, Arthur drafted a letter to the public prosecutor denouncing his neighbor's ecocide. He would thus launch a three-pronged attack: civil claim, criminal proceedings, and media campaign.

Arthur spent entire evenings with his head buried in legal textbooks trying to frame his anger in words that society and its judges would be able to understand. In the room next door, Anne was working on her novel, refusing to reveal so much as its subject. From what Arthur was able to make out, she was sighing a lot and typing very little. When they both found themselves back in bed, he full of bitterness, she of frustration, their bodies, sensibly packaged up in pajamas, drifted away from each other in a single movement.

The earthworms, for their part, were still sulking. Every week Arthur would conduct an accurate inventory deploying the most rigorous of methods: digging up a cubic meter of earth and counting. No pitchforks, no mustard; he wanted precise results, down to the last unit, even if it took a good day's work, sitting cross-legged, fingers in the soil. His blog was now being followed by half a dozen INRAE researchers, and he had his heart set on commanding their respect. Alas, it was evident his soil revitalization project was still not progressing. The number of worms remained desperately static. From time to time, Arthur found a dozen or so more. Hope would carry him into the following week, but the trend would never be consolidated. Neither Kevin's biostimulant nor his springtime reinoculation attempts had borne fruit. Arthur felt at the end of his tether. The rumex was returning, ever more abundant and invasive, signaling his failure for all to see. It was as if this earth was lost for good. As if, defying the laws of biology, life refused to return.

Léa, who regularly stopped by the farm despite Anne's visible hostility, explained Arthur's difficulties on the grounds of "too narrow an intentionality."

"You're trying too hard to force things. The day you stop wanting them, they'll appear on their own."

The comments of his former future colleagues at INRAE were less metaphysical but just as ineffectual.

The summer has been so dry it must have killed them off.

Oversowing doesn't work without a bit of plowing.

You should see if there's a history of Agrostis stolonifera in that field. It kills all the other grasses.

If the earth is too compact, externally introduced lumbrics won't have been able to burrow through it. They'll have died by suffocation.

You've introduced only a few hundred of them. It's far too few. You should try with several thousand.

It takes longer, of course, with clay-based soil.

Why not try ramial chipped wood? Works a treat. Makes mushrooms come back immediately.

Lumbrics that are native to wooded areas aren't necessarily adapted to fields. We don't know enough about subspecies' characteristics.

With no control plot, you can't do any serious analysis.

It could be the clover. I think I'd have used legumes.

There's probably remnant pesticide. Meaning no mycorrhizal fungi, or not enough. With no mushrooms to finish off the job of decomposition, I can't see what the worms are supposed to do all on their own. Personally, I'd be letting the soil recover for another four or five years.

The only definite conclusion was that the worms gathered during their search, far from reproducing in their new territory, had either fled or perished. Of hunger, heat, loneliness, or crushed? Who could say? By depositing them in holes he had dug, Arthur had buried them alive, condemned them to death. He who had aspired to being the earthworms' hero had become their executioner.

The only bright spot on the horizon was the kitchen garden. By applying in scholarly fashion now well-established permaculture techniques, Arthur had managed to produce a significant crop. Over the summer, Arthur and Anne had come close to self-sufficiency. Eggs from the henhouse provided them with the necessary animal protein. They sold their excess to La Lanterne and thereby pulled in the equivalent of a third welfare allowance, which Arthur stashed away for the winter months. Inspired by Thoreau, who itemized the cost of everything, Arthur kept very precise records of the hours he worked, his expenses, and his income. He wanted to demonstrate that it was fairly easy to achieve a subsistence lifestyle by reducing your needs to the basics and trading with one's close neighbors at least in a very rudimentary form of a division of labor. "With one hundred square meters of land, and two hours' work a day," he concluded, "everybody can feed themselves. The rest is just a bonus. We have to reconsider the physiocrats, those Age of Enlightenment economists who believed the earth was the source of all wealth." These blog posts, supplemented by practical advice on the selection of salad seeds or natural ways to eliminate slugs, had significantly more success than the traffic responding to his earthworm posts, which were both more technical and less encouraging. Arthur felt a little ashamed of them. The material he was writing about the vegetable patch was in no way innovative, it was perhaps even the antithesis of innovation, a display of knowledge accreted by humans over thousands of years. But in an era where memories were so short, where anything organic was still considered to be some extraordinary novelty, Arthur was forging his own small community.

A subsistence living? Yes, Arthur was probably managing that. But living contentedly? That was still work in progress. The day he could look out from the kitchen with his morning coffee to a lush meadow where earthworms were having the time of their lives would be the day he felt perfectly at peace. It was Anne who was balking, finding deficiencies.

* * *

One day, late in the afternoon, somebody knocked at the door. Anne went to open it, only too happy to be distracted from her vain search for inspiration. From the sound of her voice, Arthur could tell it was no courtesy call. He, too, stopped what he was doing and found a small, short-haired lady dressed in a myriad of colors, manifesting by her outfit a rainbow-like cheerfulness entirely belied by her words. She didn't come across as very old, but her wrinkles were already deep, as if life had taken a head start. He thought at first it might be Madame Jobard, whom he had only ever seen at a distance.

"I'm certified by the court," she explained to Anne, holding a plastic-coated card under her nose.

"A bailiff?" wondered Arthur. It was unlikely. Proceedings were following the usual course, with the first hearing set for the start of the following year.

"Madame is an inspector, apparently," whispered Anne, turning to Arthur. "I don't understand why anybody would be inspecting me."

Arthur was well familiar with this tone, which he found infuriating. Faced with any obstacle, Anne immediately resorted to the arrogance of her education. By way of counterreaction, he himself felt a degree of sympathy for the inspector. She looked like Nathalie Arthaud, representative of the political party Lutte Ouvrière, who in turn looked like her predecessor, Arlette Laguiller. There had to be some Trotskyist gene to which Arthur was sensitive.

"Of course, you're entitled to refuse access for the inspection," said Arlette, "but you would risk losing your welfare payments, as well as being found liable for wrongful payment and fraud."

It was thus with greater deference that Arthur gestured her to come in. She had been sent by the CAF, the office responsible for their welfare payments. She had sent them a letter a fortnight ago warning them she would be coming, but, as Arthur explained to her, nobody ever went to empty the letterbox, which was located at the end of the road, which was usually stuffed with nothing but advertising and other circulars. Regardless, Arthur remained calm. He and Anne were perfectly entitled to receive the amounts the people's representatives had decided should be paid to those who, by choice or misadventure, were not receiving any income. It was their right. He was neither ashamed nor proud of the fact. He often thought that if people knew how to value the cost of regenerating a piece of land, society would be in *his* debt.

"You've got a good setup here," said Arlette, looking around.

"We've spent a year doing the renovations ourselves."

"Both of you?"

"Yes, we're a modern couple."

"I know the type."

"And what type is that?" Anne was unable to contain the aggression in her voice.

She was still wearing overalls, but they were clean now, and today she had put on a plain turtleneck sweater.

"The bougie-in-the-country type," Arlette replied, unceremoniously.

"We don't look poor enough for you, is that it? You're being paid by the taxpayer to insult us?"

Arthur tried to calm things down. To be fair, Arlette was not helping matters. She refused to sit down and had adopted the disembodied tone of an answering machine to deliver her monologue.

"First of all, I am required to inform you of your rights. The right to have somebody present at the interview if you do not speak sufficient French . . ."

"We'll manage."

"Not everybody is so lucky. The right to bring along any necessary notes, observations or requests for modifications . . ."

"Still fine," said Anne. "We have the right to speak."

"The right to obtain a copy of the investigation report on written request to the director of the Caisse d'allocations familiales."

Without drawing breath, she listed the supporting documents

she would need to inspect: identification, family record book, tenancy agreement or lease, proof of residential homeowners' insurance, water, electricity, gas, landline and cell phone bills, most recent pay slips and employment contracts, social security cards, bank statements, tax assessment, land tax notification.

"That's for starters," she specified.

"We've just finished our studies. We've had internship contracts, but not employment agreements."

"I'd like to see them. And your degrees, too. With the date on which they were conferred."

Anne remained standing with arms crossed conspicuously to demonstrate that none of this had anything to do with her. Arthur went into the next room, which served as their office, and tried to gather together all the documents he could find. The silence between the two women in the living room was palpable, interrupted only by the sound of the printer spewing out paperwork.

Arlette scanned the documents bearing the header RÉPUBLIQUE FRANÇAISE, which were still warm, taking notes in a random fashion. Arthur got the impression she was pretending. She was looking for something else.

"What are your current professional circumstances?"

"None. That is exactly why we . . ."

"Novelist!" declared Anne, gazing off into the distance.

"Please be so good as to provide me with your publishing agreements. Are you registered as an artist or author with the Organization for the Collection of Social Security and Family Benefit Contributions? Have you received a contributions payment schedule? Are you registered for automatic deductions from your rights entitlements?"

"No . . ."

"You're not registered for automatic deductions?"

"I know nothing about it! I couldn't give a damn! I'm a novelist! Like Yourcenar, like de Beauvoir, like Sagan! Were they registered for automatic deductions?"

"I can't say. I'm not responsible for their files."

Anne snorted in an explosion of disdain.

"Do you receive artist-author welfare payments?" Arlette insisted.

"Anne is not yet really . . ." Arthur tried to explain.

"Really what?" Anne burst out, turning on Arthur. "I'm not really a novelist, is that it? That's what you think, then. What you've always thought."

Her voice broke and she collapsed into the Chesterfield opposite the fireplace, burying her face in her hands.

"If you'd prefer," said Arlette, "we can limit ourselves to purely administrative matters."

Arthur was really starting to appreciate Arlette.

"So, you haven't yet signed a publishing contract?"

Anne remained mute. The only thing visible was her curly hair tumbling over the back of the sofa.

"Yes, that's right," Arthur replied. "Anne is a novelist in the making."

He heard a sigh of rage from the sofa but decided to finish up with the inspection, which seemed to him to be coming along nicely.

"Right, then," said Arlette, in an encouraging tone, automatically shuffling the pile of papers into some sort of order. "Still, we'll have to regularize your living arrangements. If I understand things correctly, the dwelling belongs to your father."

"Yes, but he has agreed . . ."

"Precisely. You will have to sign a commodate."

"A what?"

"A loan for use agreement documenting your rent of the property free of charge."

"OK." Arthur smiled.

Keen to be done, he adopted the approach of being entertained by all these classifications conceived by the bureaucracy to contain, control, and regularize life. *When it comes down to it*, he thought, indulgently, *all these people are afraid*. Afraid of what is being said, of what might spill out, of how things are. They're like farmers with their pesticides: they want to work on a surface that's all smooth and neat; deal only with matters they understand and can control, following foolproof protocols; and then watch as perfectly aligned citizens sprout in front of them, like ears of wheat.

"One last thing . . ."

Arlette suddenly lit up, her eyes glittering.

"What is the nature of your relationship?"

Arthur looked perplexed. It was a valid question after all. But he was certainly not about to undergo couples therapy with Arlette.

"As you know," she continued, "welfare payments vary according to household circumstances. You're currently receiving two full entitlements, in accordance with your respective declarations. Now, if it is determined that you constitute a household for social security purposes, the amount will have to be recalculated on that basis."

"I'm not sure I'm following. We're not married and nor have we entered into a formal civil partnership."

"I know and I'm not suggesting otherwise."

"Thank you for that," said Arthur, sardonically.

"Nonetheless, there is evidence of cohabitation. If that's the case, you'll be subject to an adjustment in the order of several thousand euros."

Any semblance of goodwill Arthur may have felt toward Arlette dissipated. It was the moment she had been saving up. Fake bourgeoise empathy? Not on your life.

"What exactly do you mean by 'evidence of cohabitation'?" demanded Arthur, keeping his cool.

"It's very simple. Fortunately, the law is very clear on this point. First of all, you're living under the same roof."

"Like many people, friends, flatmates . . ."

"In addition, Mademoiselle here has indicated that you have both been renovating this house. Can you confirm that?"

"Yes, so?"

"So, you're sharing household costs. Further evidence."

"You're not serious . . ."

Arthur was still entertaining the illusion that there was a human being somewhere inside the inspector. Yet that which rendered her human, fully human, was precisely the delight she was taking in exercising her administrative power.

"So then, I'm going to have to ask you a rather delicate question. Do you share the same bed?"

"That's enough!" screamed Anne, standing up abruptly. "Get out!"

Anne grabbed the poker from the hearth and with thrusting, hate-filled chest, advanced determinedly on Arlette who, for her part, remained impassive. Arthur intervened.

"I'll take that as a yes," concluded Arlette. "Thank you very much. I have everything I need. Good evening to you both."

The rainbow dissipated in an instant. Anne stood facing Arthur, poker in hand. She was staring at him with the same fury. He approached slowly, hands half-raised, adopting the natural gestures of somebody seeking to disarm a lunatic.

"Anne, it's me, everything's all right, she's gone."

She stepped back abruptly and raised the poker. He stopped short.

"Everything is not all right, not all right at all."

Her voice had dropped. She was speaking calmly now in a voice that was even more terrifying.

"I have never been so humiliated."

"You mustn't take it like that. That's what they want. Don't give them that victory."

"You've turned me into a beggar."

"What are you talking about? We have rights, as citizens, and . . ."

"A beggar and a maidservant."

"You don't mean that."

He felt embarrassed for her. He was certainly not about to launch into the all-too-familiar litany of who does what.

"The beginning has been harder than expected . . ."

"The beginning? It has been two years. My friends from Sciences Po are parliamentary aides. And what am I . . . ?"

"You're accomplishing your own dream. Our dream. It won't be long before we have our own Walden."

"And what exactly will we do in our Walden? Will we just sit by the fire and stare at each other?"

"Precisely."

Arthur didn't believe it himself anymore. These days he could hardly look Anne in the eye. As for the next fifty years . . .

"You're truly a loser."

"You've already said that. You're wrong. You're only a loser if you accept society's criteria."

"You haven't even managed to do what we came here to do. Even the earthworms are refusing to comply."

"Maybe Léa is right. I'm trying too hard. I don't have enough of the loser spirit in me . . ."

Anne shook her head, sighing. Arthur knew then that they were done. Where there is hatred, there is still room for love. But when hatred turns to pity, there is no room for anything anymore. With an anxious pang he felt that old enemy, loneliness, start to surface.

"I am not some loser," murmured Anne as much to herself. "I'm a novelist."

"The jury's still out on that, really."

With nothing left to lose, he was exercising his ultimate privilege, honesty. Anne appeared stunned, frozen in her belligerent stance, clutching her risible poker.

"You've been no more successful writing than I've been reviving the earthworms. We're even. And it would appear," he added, spitefully, "that words do no better in soil that is too hard."

Anne stood speechless for another few moments, then, gathering all her strength, struck him with an abrupt and violent blow to the chest. He had neither the time, nor perhaps the will, to protect himself. The poker hit him cleanly on the ribs. He collapsed in pain, without a sound, winded, his last image being Anne's look of murderous rage.

* * *

When Arthur came to, he saw Matthieu. He had made a fire and was on his feet, glass in hand. Arthur felt a cushion under his head and a blanket covering him. His shirt was torn down one side. He wanted to shift himself to get up but could only groan in pain.

"Don't move," said Matthieu, coming over.

He brought the glass to Arthur's lips, supporting his head. Arthur recognized the powerful whiff of Calvados.

"Can't hurt."

"A doctor . . ." Arthur begged.

"No! You're crazy! You'll spend all night in the ER at Caen on a stretcher."

"I'm going to be paralyzed."

"Ha ha! Some joke! You've got one or two broken ribs at worst. You'll hurt for the next four or five weeks, but they'll heal on their own. We're not calling a doctor for that. My old man did five ribs falling off a scooter. Didn't stop him from doing the milking, morning and night."

Arthur felt his spirits slowly lifting. He had never heard Matthieu talk so much.

"Anne?"

"I drove her to the station. She told me you absolutely had it coming. I'm not judging."

Arthur started sobbing. He felt abandoned, broken, incapable of continuing his life here. He was not far off agreeing with

Anne. A loser. The easiest thing, the most natural, would be to return to the fold. For him to take the train back to Paris, too. To return to INRAE, tail between his legs.

Each sob wrenched his insides, as if somebody were burying a knife in him. He quickly dried his tears.

"Have another mouthful," said Matthieu.

Taking regular little sips, Arthur emptied a good quarter of the bottle, listening to the crackle of the fire. Matthieu watched him, saying nothing, poking the coals from time to time. Night had already fallen. The first frost would soon arrive.

Arthur let himself be numbed by the warmth of the alcohol. He was getting to grips with his emotions. This rupture had brought with it a certain clarity. He was no longer on extended vacation in the country with his girlfriend. He was going to have to take his mission seriously or leave.

Settled deep in his armchair, Matthieu had fallen back into his usual torpor. Calm, heavy, immutable. And with that innate ability to think about nothing that would take Arthur and his peers several years of meditation courses to achieve. Arthur pictured the Saclay plateau for a moment, the RER train, the labs, the canteen lunches with his colleagues. It felt inconceivable now. What had started as a postadolescent wager had turned into his life's purpose. He was gripped by a certain excitement at the idea of the challenge ahead. Finally, he was going to have to pit himself against himself.

"They're right," he said at last. "I'm going to have to inoculate the soil with more worms. Maybe buy more stock. And combine rye grass with beans."

Matthieu groaned.

"No?"

He groaned again. That was a no.

"Just let it be, leave the land alone."

"But nothing will happen!"

"Precisely, nothing at all."

Arthur hauled himself upright with difficulty. He looked through the hole Matthieu had cut into his shirt. His skin looked like a galaxy seen through a telescope: purple at the center, where Anne had struck him, then concentric circles of color radiating outward.

"Next week I'm going to bring you some manure. With all the sheep's litter, I have so much of the stuff I don't know what to do with it. We'll spread a good layer over your two hectares. Like cream on a cake."

"Good idea, yeah. Organic matter."

"Worms are no different from anyone else. They'll turn up for a feed."

XIV

"We're not going to let our weekend be ruined by a strike," declared Philippine, adopting a belligerent tone.

Their train to Verneuil-sur-Avre had been canceled so Philippine was now deploying her customary ingenuity to track down a luxury car service that was prepared to defy the gas shortages.

"We'll charge it to the company account. In any case, given the guest list, it could be seen as a work trip."

They settled into a fully charged Tesla and left for Perche on Saturday morning, having been invited to spend the night there by Madame CSR, their most significant supporter at L'Oréal. Their driver, Yacine, was dressed in an impeccable suit and demonstrated an appropriate degree of deference, ready to feign complicity when his client was in a chatty mood but also to adopt the role of mute and obsequious servant when necessary. Personally, he didn't really give a damn, provided he received a five-star rating. He quickly sized up who he was dealing with and selected a playlist of Mozart's sonatas as background music.

"I'll go via Concorde to avoid the demonstrations," he explained, heading off any debate. "The General Workers' union will be leaving Villiers and heading up to Clichy. We'll lose twenty minutes but there's no chance of getting jammed."

"It's crazy messing people around like this," complained Philippine. "You're all right, you've got an EV, but your colleagues, they can't work anymore!"

Yacine nodded his head vigorously. He had learned to agree with his clients' opinions. That way, he gave them the comforting feeling, for free, of finding themselves on the right side of things, of communing with the immigrant working class. On one occasion, he had driven a radio announcer who, half an hour later, when he was back on air, had quoted him in order to back up his own arguments. Yacine had had a good laugh. He thought it strange the way the wealthy were always keen to invoke principles of fairness to make themselves feel better. They could content themselves with just defending their own interests and nobody would hold it against them.

"At least there's less traffic," Philippine continued, after a moment's reflection.

"Absolutely, the ride should be a smooth one."

The Tesla slipped noiselessly through a furious France. Beyond their tinted windows, Kevin and Philippine saw trash cans accumulating in the streets, riot police lined up in their vehicles awaiting confrontation, demonstrators in yellow vests occupying the toll booths, posters and banners draped over bridges and strung up at intersections. Even taking minor country roads they had to pass through a few good-natured roadblocks, getting away with a honk of the horn. Extinction Rebellion activists mixed with protesters, as they did now on every such occasion, viewing the general woes of the people through the filter of the environmental crisis. In village centers, failing bakeries bore witness to the ravages of inflation, their shop windows obscured by slashes of white paint.

"It's so miserable, a village with no croissants," commented Philippine. "I don't know how people live in such a place."

They passed through one last roadblock that was hardly intimidating, where two pensioners were shooting the breeze, thermos in hand, haplessly waving a placard making some statement about purchasing power, and finally arrived, fifty meters farther on, in front of a steel-reinforced wooden gate. Philippine said her hellos to the video surveillance camera, the gate's mechanism kicked into gear, and the Tesla's tires crunched over the gravel drive leading to the manor. Elegant, bucolic grounds unfolded on either side. There were donkeys grazing in meadows, orchards in blossom, streams straddled by stone bridges, carefully restored hay barns, and even an old ivy-covered bread oven. In the distance, the former feudal mound could just be made out, now covered in a forest of deciduous trees.

"It's just to the right," Philippine directed.

"Have you been here before?" asked Kevin, surprised.

"A couple times, yes," she replied, blushing lightly.

"But . . . did you already know . . ."

"She's a friend of my parents."

"I'm starting to understand."

"There's nothing to understand! We went through all the usual processes at L'Oréal. It's a small world, that's all."

They drove over ancient moats filled with brackish water and emerged into the courtyard. The facade, just a single story, was a substantial fortified structure. Its mullioned windows gave an impression of stately opulence, without the pretension of a château. An outer wall mounted with bartizans extended on either side, becoming living quarters that had probably been built at some later period. The slender roofline of a turret, like an inverted champagne flute, could be made out at the far end. Madame CSR, positioned on her front steps, came down the flight of stairs with the solemnity of a head of state welcoming her counterpart.

"Darling!" she exclaimed, on seeing Philippine, who launched herself from the vehicle.

Kevin thanked Yacine and confirmed their pickup time.

"What the hell sort of a pad is this," he said, his parting comment to the driver.

By expressing his astonishment with quite such candor, Kevin hoped to convince Yacine these were not his people, that he did not belong to this crazy world. Yacine's only response was an artificial smile. Too late. He already belonged.

"You didn't have too much trouble, with the strikes?" asked Madame CSR.

"A nightmare," replied Philippine.

"You'll see, it'll be worth the effort. Guess who I've invited!"

Philippine listened expectantly.

"Well, you know I sit on the board of the French-American Foundation?"

Philippine did not know, but was unsurprised. Madame CSR was involved with so many foundations and think tanks. The French-American Foundation was an influential organization that brought together the young French elite on the pretext of forging links with the United States. Every year, a dozen or so thirty-something-year-old "Young Leaders" were selected and promised, absent any mishaps, a pathway to senior appointments.

Previous members included a number of captains of industry, ministers, and even presidents.

"Well then," continued Madame CSR, clapping her hands, "I decided to invite the whole of this year's new cohort this evening! Only young people."

Philippine appeared just a tad disappointed. She would have preferred some older types who had already made it.

"My darling Kevin . . ." Madame CSR continued, taking him by the hand, "we can drop the formalities, can't we?"

As he was in the process of acquiescing, the handshake turned into a kiss on each cheek. Kevin felt enveloped by a heavy scent of vanilla.

Madame CSR accompanied them to their respective rooms. They made their way through a string of rooms furnished with a rustic elegance, well suited to the manor's agricultural past: wrought iron chandeliers, former presses converted into pedestal tables, bookshelves of solid oak, monumental Norman armoires, farmhouse tables with feet worn down by generations of diners, chairs reseated with straw at great expense . . .

"All upcycled!" commented their hostess. "Nothing but vintage finds. It's unbelievable. Nothing's worth anything anymore. Take this Henri II walnut dresser, coiled columns, layered molding, Acanthus foliage, bas-reliefs, carved medallions. Hundreds of hours of cabinetry work, extraordinary expertise, and most of the time it goes for half the price of a piece of melamine furniture from IKEA."

"People don't recognize the value of things anymore," Philippine expressed her regret without so much as a glance at it.

They went through to the rear courtyard where they got a

sense of the extent of the structure's semicircular layout. Madame CSR pointed out her recent renovation works and enjoyed the principal privilege of any host, namely, to bore one's guests to tears with plumbing stories.

"It cost me an arm and a leg, but it has all been redone to last, using environmentally sourced materials. It's now a surplus energy house, consuming less energy than it produces. All the windows are double-glazed. The toilets are plumbed to rainwater tanks, and the radiators run on a heat pump. There are solar panels on the other side of the roof producing ten kilowatts and also a windmill behind the turret that fortunately you can't see from here!"

"Yes, they're pretty ugly," Philippine went the extra mile.

"Same principles for the land, of course: zero pesticides, zero fertilizers. Only compost and desiccated donkey manure. You'll see the kitchen garden, it's largely sufficient to meet our needs here; any surplus is given to the local school cafeteria. It's all permaculture based, of course. You two will be very pleased, it must have tons of earthworms!"

"I'll go take a look," said Kevin, who was getting into the swing of these social events and their small talk. "I'll"—he switched quickly to the less formal form of address—"I'll bring you some back for predinner drinks. They're full of protein."

Madame CSR burst out laughing.

"They'll be perfect on some little crackers! Of course," she resumed in a more serious tone, "the regenerative agriculture we're implementing here is more labor intensive. And given expenses, our maintenance costs run to a small fortune every month . . . But I wear it all! I won't have it said that I don't practice what I preach. This manor house is one hundred percent sustainable. When I think of the greenwashing allegations I have to put up with in the press . . ."

She sighed deeply, ensuring Kevin, Philippine, and the rest of the world were all witnesses to the extent of the sacrifices she was making and the injustices she had to suffer in return. Then she led them through to the south wing, dedicated to guests. She showed them to their rooms and announced in an authoritative tone: "Free time!" before turning on her heel.

Feeling a little grubby after the car trip and dreading the thought of Philippine bursting into his room, Kevin went out for a walk in the garden. He followed the banks of the main stream and found the orchard, a multicolored carpet underfoot. The spring blossoms were rushing to bloom before being cast into shadow by the fruit trees' foliage. Kevin reached the spot where the water was bubbling up from the ground, channeled through granite ponds and bamboo furrows. The considerable volume pointed to a healthy water table. Farther up, a large area, about half a hectare in size, had been given over to mound gardening, an old technique that had recently come back into fashion by proponents of no-till farming. Seeds were planted directly into pyramid-shaped banks created from piles of dead wood, bark, and manure extending for dozens of meters. It was a reverse field, where the furrows had been turned inside out like gloves and humans entered a Lilliputian world.

Kevin wended his way through the mounds, delineated by rounds of logs and aligned in a way that allowed for the occasional path through. He had never seen so many, and so well laid out. They had recently been covered in mulch, both to feed the soil with nitrogen and to limit the growth of weeds. A land of plenty for earthworms! Despite the weather, several shoots had already appeared through the soil. The nourishing heat generated by the mound was compensating for the weather. Kevin recognized peas, lettuces, even a few potato plants. Farther on, two gardening huts filled with tools were evidence of regular and meticulous upkeep. He nodded appreciatively. Evidence of fine handiwork.

Kevin could not resist the temptation to dig his hand into the black, moist earth. It went in with no resistance, all the way up to his wrist. He stayed like that for a moment, kneading the lumpy clods. It was warm, warmer still than the sun on his skin, as warm as a sauna, moist and stupefying. He allowed himself to be seduced by this original womb, with no wish to leave it. The sensation brought back memories of others he had experienced. Flesh softening within, dripping beneath his fingers, flesh that carried him away into its secretive folds. A stark contrast to his engagements with Philippine, always so dry, painful almost. Kevin sighed. He needed this tenderness. He glanced about to ensure he was alone and sank his entire forearm into the earth. He fingered it passionately, intoxicated by the imaginary pleasure he was giving it, his pelvis pressed into the mound.

Kevin felt a swarming sensation around his hand, then hesitant, viscose contact. He withdrew gently, breathing deeply, forcing himself to remain still so as not to frighten the worm climbing up his hand, probably attracted to the mineral salts exuded by human skin. For want of anything better, Kevin was making his own small contribution to the ecosystem. Word must have passed around in the tunnels that some rare and succulent juice was on offer. Kevin was quickly assailed by an entire colony of worms snaking their way voraciously across his palm. They sucked at his skin with their toothless mouths like so many miniature plungers. He let himself be massaged for a while, spreading his fingers to provide them with new pathways. When, finally, he withdrew his hand, it was gleaming with mucus.

Kevin headed back to the stream to gather himself. He sat down among the rushes growing along the bank and dipped his hand into the cold water, then dried it off against lush grassy tufts. His thoughts were cradled by the sound of the current. Everything here seemed so harmonious, prosperous, and virtuous. Notwithstanding Madame CSR's vanilla-scented perfume, and her endless clichés, she was correct in saying that she was turning her principles into action. In fact, Kevin reflected, she had succeeded in implementing Arthur's dreams.

All afternoon, he looked out from his bedroom window and watched the Young Leaders arriving. He was intimidated, a rare feeling for him. They were older than he was, but not so old that he could shelter behind the comfortable image of being only a young boy. They were all beaming, so confident, so alert with their cabin luggage bags festooned with the gold tags of airlines. Among them Kevin caught a glimpse of somebody who looked like Thomas Pesquet. "The astronaut?" he wondered to himself, in a low voice. "What the hell is he doing here?" He couldn't imagine that media celebrities might also have a real life, and had even greater difficulty imagining that he somehow might feature in it.

One couple had brought their young children and their Filipina nanny, who was obviously under instructions to speak English with them. Kevin watched them play in the rear courtyard. The nanny was keeping a distracted eye on them while watching a series on her cell phone. Bundled up in their Bonpoint outfits, corduroy pants and checked shirts, they were running around as all children do, quibbling as all children do, whining as all children do, but quickly recovering their good humor, as if already conscious of the fact that nothing could be that serious.

"Move on," said the sister, in English, to her brother, who was complaining about a deflated ball.

When it came time for dinner, Kevin took off his gray T-shirt and put on a collared shirt, his only collared shirt, which he had carefully folded to avoid creasing it. He realized that from now on, his beauty would no longer be adequate. Going through to the salon, which was already abuzz with the sound of the Young Leaders' conversation, he was offered a glass of champagne by Madame CSR, who delicately steered him to one side.

"My dear Kevin, I don't want to spoil the evening by talking work . . ."

Kevin tensed. He knew the schedule of waste treatment had slowed considerably after the episode with the rats. Just how delayed they were he could not have said. Philippine had taken on what she called accounts, which included, according to her, commercial matters. She was now directly responsible for the L'Oréal relationship and together with Sofia was coordinating the arrival of trucks to the factory. This meant Kevin was able to concentrate on assembling new lines, perfecting the Wormentino, and, of course, doing media.

"The problem has been resolved," he said hurriedly, "and we'll soon be launching . . ."

"What problem? I just want to tell you that our experience with Posthumus has been judged very conclusive," said Madame

CSR. "Proof of concept has been validated. We're ready to move on to the next stage."

Kevin was taken aback. Madame CSR raised her glass, holding his gaze.

"A true partnership! Three thousand tons of waste per year, from all our factories across Europe. I'm very pleased. It will serve as an industry-wide model."

They clinked their glasses in a toast to earthworms. Philippine joined them, all smiles. Kevin asked no further questions. He was ready to redouble his efforts.

They made their way over to the guests on the other side of the room. A dozen young people were slumped on low-slung sofas that looked like they would be difficult to extract oneself from. Opposite them, a log was slowly burning down in a granite hearth fitted with the latest model fireplace. Crossing the room, Kevin stopped to examine the oak bookshelves that covered the back wall. They were filled with books on art, illustrated coffee-table books, old vintage leather-bound books, gardening manuals, and a handful of contemporary works, prize-winning novels, and bestselling essays. Since meeting Arthur, Kevin was able to recognize the library of somebody who didn't read.

The Young Leaders already knew each other and were bantering away. They greeted Philippine and Kevin with easy cordiality. Of course, they were all over their spectacular capital-raising efforts. This initial success made them look quite normal in the eyes of people who were not. They deserved their place in the tribe.

The topic on everybody's lips was the strike. Everybody was talking about their various efforts to get through the roadblocks. Victor took the prize, having landed his helicopter in a field that Madame CSR had left for rewilding. Victor had set up a renewable energy investment fund and, having passed his pilot's license two years earlier, had bought his own chopper, "which wasn't that much more expensive than a Porsche Cayenne," he clarified, modestly. The rest of the group was teasing him about his carbon emissions. Half serious, half mocking, Victor maintained that a helicopter consumed less fuel than a car if you considered the route taken by each of them rather than the distance. Laughter all around.

"What sort of crap are you talking?"

"You're not being interrogated by some investigative journalist here, you can say it like it is."

"You could say the same, I suppose, for sexual harassment, you have to take into account the route of the hand to the ass, not the actual distance. That's well accepted."

"But I swear," said Victor, defensively, "you just have to compare consumption from any point A to point B. The chopper takes a straight line. So, even if it emits more CO_2 per kilometer, it still comes out on top."

"So you're financing choppers with your fund to save the planet?"

"Choppers for all! Great slogan."

"I hope you received your one hundred euro green energy allowance?"

"You guys are starting to piss me off," said Victor, burying himself in the cushions.

"Ah, that's more like it!"

"What do you say, Thomas? If we're talking about the route, a rocket is even more economical, right?"

"It appears that Hidalgo wants to bring in self-service electric rockets."

"That'd be like rocket-sharing."

It was indeed the astronaut, Thomas Pesquet. All of France was keen to know how he took a leak in space. He, too, was playing along, enjoying the banter.

"For the small minority who don't own a chopper, the strike really is a pain in the ass. And most of all, pointless. You know what some trade unionist on the BFM network told me?"

The conversation was now being monopolized by a certain Gaspard, an essayist who prided himself on being in with the media; Kevin had never heard of him. Gaspard was outraged about a televised debate that clearly had not gone according to plan and was now going on about some "paradigm shift," which reminded Kevin about the incomprehensible nature of his meeting with the manager from the public investment bank. But then the tone turned serious for a moment.

"Yet again other countries are going to think we're idiots."

"The French don't know how lucky they are."

"They've got it all and still they complain."

"They detest change."

"Every time somebody suggests an intelligent reform, they blockade the place."

Kevin had no real opinion about the strike. His parents had never been involved in any social movement. With no fixed employment, they were not the slightest bit concerned about wage increases or the legal age for retirement. They knew they were poor, and they were going to remain poor. To them, going on strike was a luxury that would always remain firmly out of reach, reserved for those who had a permanent employment contract, owned their own home, and holidayed in Spain in August.

What did astonish him about the whole discussion, though, was the way people were speaking about the French in the third person. His parents would never have done that.

"We're the ones building it, the wealth," said Philippine suddenly in her husky voice. "And they're the ones destroying it."

Madame CSR used the embarrassed silence that ensued to fill empty glasses. Philippine had just crossed a very fine, almost imperceptible line, one that distinguished meritocratic self-satisfaction from class-based disdain. A faux pas that could be put down to her youth. A few people looked to Kevin, who remained impassive, anxious not to break ranks openly with his cofounder.

Victor then took out a sort of snuffbox, prompting relieved exclamations. He opened it with great ceremony. In the grooves of the wooden tray were a dozen or so ready-rolled joints.

"You spoil us!"

"Are we worth it?"

"Now I understand why you go by helicopter. So you can avoid the dope tests!"

Victor turned to Madame CSR with an inquiring look. She pouted extravagantly, pursing her lips with mock severity and holding back a smile. The Young Leaders waited for her acquiescence like naughty schoolchildren in front of their teacher.

"I'll go look for some ashtrays," she finally said, after a drawn-out silence.

Everybody applauded. Victor circulated two joints to start with. The same etiquette applied here as in the stairwells of Seine-Saint-Denis. You had to pass it around. The conversation split into small groups. Kevin talked earthworms with the guy sitting next to him, a colorectal surgeon, who in return showed him photos from his surgeries.

"You and me? We're both in the gross business," he commented. "We shift the shit that nobody else wants to see. Among my patients, there are the sick people, sure, they're not there for the sake of it, the poor bastards. But they're not the only ones. A good portion of them are weirdos. You cannot imagine what people put up their ass. Just last week, I pulled out a fan. And it's all covered by social security, of course."

"The funding hole must take on quite a new meaning for you," Kevin chanced his luck.

The surgeon clapped him on the shoulder and rushed to appropriate the joke for himself, repeating it to the others. Kevin took the opportunity to listen in on other scraps of conversation. From what he could make out, in addition to the consultants and financiers who turned up everywhere you looked, the women in the group included a high-profile publisher, an Iranian architect, and a sports commentator who had just returned from the Soccer World Cup, and among the men were a chef who had just received a Michelin star, an officer in the Navy commando unit, and an opposition member of parliament . . . The youthfulness of their appearance—young enough in any event to still want to poke fun at their elders—belied the respectability of their positions. Some had come with partners but most had come alone, as if looking for the circle of buddies their careers had not allowed them the time to find. Kevin wondered whether he, too, could apply to join if Posthumus were to do as well as Philippine was hoping it would.

A clamor grew, gradually taken up by the whole group.

"Mélanie! Mélanie! Mélanie!"

A tall, blond girl with a sickly appearance stood up, looking punished.

"Sure, all right . . ." she said.

She went through to the entrance hall and returned with a violin. She had an awkward gait, as if trying to correct a limp.

"She's concertmaster at the Radio France Philharmonique," murmured the surgeon in Kevin's ear. "Just wait, she kicks ass."

Mélanie tossed her hair to the side, wedged the violin against her neck, and played a few strings to tune her instrument. Kevin realized what it was about her face that had intrigued him. Graceful though it was, her features were asymmetrical. Part of her mouth slid off to one side, an eyebrow to the other, as if reflected in a distorting mirror.

"Tell us it's a Strad, at least?" joked Gaspard.

"Yes," came her nonchalant reply. "Now, shut up all of you. I'll play something simple, otherwise it'll be wasted on you."

"Why don't you tell us we're all Philistines straight up."

"The *Chaconne* from Bach's Partita No. 2."

The Young Leaders nodded, delighted and knowing. Kevin felt caught off guard. He didn't know how to react. Music had no place in his life whatsoever. If he wanted an aural distraction, he just put on some background noise and let himself be lulled by the streamer's algorithms.

Kevin glanced across at Philippine and sat up straight, adopting an expression of concentration. The first notes seemed like questions marks. He didn't understand any of it. He found the tune muddled, arduous even, as if neither Bach nor Mélanie knew where they were going. He decided to grin and bear it, as he was so good at doing. He took a drag from the joint and passed it to Philippine.

Then suddenly, after a few minutes, the violin took off. Notes raced upward, fell back to earth, then started climbing again. Mélanie's expression was painful, even more tortured than it had been. Kevin had the embarrassing feeling that he was watching a pretty girl sitting constipated on a toilet. "We must be done now. Here we go!" he said to himself. But no. Everything stopped, and then came the question marks again. Kevin noticed Gaspard discreetly checking his phone for messages. At least he wasn't the only Philistine.

The second joint made it around to him. He took a few drags. His head was starting to spin gently. Just then the notes started climbing again, but this time they didn't come back down. Having arrived at the summit, they started repeating themselves. *Mezza voce* at first, then louder and louder. Mélanie was no longer grimacing, her fingers ran over the strings without any apparent effort, as if she were pretending to play and the sound had detached itself from any physical foundation. Arched slightly over her instrument, her face at last looked harmonious.

Kevin felt quivers running from his neck to his anus. He sank into the sofa, head tipped back, deliciously baked. The same theme repeated itself, climbing again up the octaves, accelerating. His mouth pasty, his body in a drug-induced languor, his mind adrift, Kevin felt as if he were seeing the sound, as if his senses were blending, one into another. It was neither an image nor a hallucination, but an incarnation as insistent as it was indescribable. Before his eyes he saw the broken cry of a madman wiser than the sages, of a sage madder than the lunatics, despairing of ever being understood. At times, Mélanie lingered on a deep note, a solemn, drawn-out deceleration, a return to reason, but the madman always broke free with a vengeance, galloping through the streets, singing at the top of his voice before the drawn shutters. The keeper of a message nobody wanted to hear, *vox clamans in deserto*. There was nothing for it, he had to die. Kevin was longing for this moment as much as he feared it, longing for the collapse, the execution, the final chord. But it never came. Instead, a second voice intervened, screaming the same story, then a third, maybe even a fourth, Kevin was lost. The message reverberated as an echo off deaf walls, a carousel of notes spinning furiously in a never-ending return to the point of departure. The madman was dancing above him. He didn't want to die. He had abandoned the notion of losing hope.

Kevin felt the heaviness of his limbs. Such delicious torture. He watched Mélanie. Her skin was pale, the color of moonstone. Her eyes were half-closed. She knew what she was doing. The Young Leaders all appeared paralyzed. Even Gaspard had put down his phone. A handful of latecomers took a seat at the back. Kevin could only make out their silhouettes, including the outline of a woman with dark curly hair who quickly concealed herself behind the others.

By now Kevin understood that any conclusion was impossible. There would be no collapse, no final chord. Slowly, slowly, the madman fell silent, exhausted. One by one the voices disappeared. All that remained was a pure and despairing lament, clinging unforgivably to life. Then it, too, dissipated in an interminable trill, the madman's death throes as he fell to the ground, an ellipsis prolonging an indecipherable message.

What followed was nothing more than a long and pointless

consolation. Again, Kevin recognized the question marks he had heard at the beginning, which Mélanie now seemed to pose with a certain weariness. They felt hypocritical. What point was there in asking questions if one were incapable of understanding the answers?

Everybody returned to their senses. There was whispering. Kevin turned to Philippine who was also buried deep in the sofa. He saw a tear on her cheek. A single tear, perfectly round, leaving a damp trail as it slowly fell. Kevin could not believe his eyes.

"You okay?" he asked her softly, resting a hand on her wrist.

She extricated herself swiftly and wiped her cheek.

"Yeah, I'm fine. Leave me alone."

Kevin repeated his gesture, this time more firmly. She didn't resist. She opened her eyes wide, clenched her teeth, trying to hold back her tears.

"Me too," he said, "that music . . ."

"It's got nothing to do with the music."

He stroked her bare forearm lightly.

"I'm just happy about the L'Oréal contract," she murmured.

He withdrew his hand, shocked.

"Maybe my father will realize I'm not so stupid after all," she continued, as if to herself.

Kevin, tactfully, didn't react. He didn't want her to feel he might take advantage of this confidence, which she probably already regretted. He let her believe he'd heard nothing, understood nothing, would remember nothing.

Mélanie dropped her bow to her side and acknowledged her audience with a hint of amusement, as if this standard conservatorium repertoire was undeserving of so much attention. Kevin felt briefly jealous. Not of the Radio France orchestra, but simply because she knew how to read music. He was growing increasingly aware of the many gaps in his knowledge.

"Bravo!"

"How are we meant to get up after that?"

"These fancy Roche Bobois sofas are the pits."

Mélanie slipped away to a corner, once again lopsided and awkward.

"Where's that joint?"

"Gaspard's fallen asleep on top of it."

"Must be looking for inspiration."

Madame CSR invited them to go through to the dining room. She had prepared a vegetarian meal comprising exclusively vegetables sourced from the garden. Everybody applauded her for the charming notion. The Young Leaders hauled themselves out of the sofas with difficulty and made their way in disorganized fashion toward the door, keeping up the relentless banter. Kevin exchanged a few words with the surgeon and turned around to find Mélanie. He would have liked to sit next to her at dinner. To ask her what she was thinking about when she played the *Chaconne*. About nothing? About God? About billings and company registration issues?

But instead of Mélanie, he saw Anne.

She was clearly trying to avoid him. Trapped in his gaze, she made her way slowly toward him.

"Anne!" Kevin had identified her instinctively without managing to quite recognize her face, like seeing a friend who had suddenly aged. She had removed her labret stud and all her other piercings and replaced them with a diamond pendant. She was no longer wearing overalls but instead a silk wraparound top that emphasized her chest in a flattering way. Her heels lent her a yuppie-like tilt.

They both blushed, like two friends running into each other in a soup kitchen queue after having once upon a time dined out in more upmarket establishments. Kevin knew she had returned to Paris but had not otherwise tried to catch up.

"What are you . . ."

Anne was there with her new boss, a Young Leader who had set up a crisis management communications consultancy. Kevin had hardly registered his presence. The others called him Lupus because of his sharp canines. Although he might well have denied it, he had a face to match the business.

"And the two of you are . . ."

No. She confirmed the situation firmly and with a look of outraged dignity in which Kevin recognized her militance. He didn't pursue the matter.

"The last time we saw each other . . ."

In a forest, yes. On all fours, gathering earthworms. They smiled. If they hadn't kissed that night, it was only because Kevin had left.

Madame CSR interrupted their reunion. She had taken up the rear and was encouraging her little flock to take their seats at the table. Curious, Philippine made the most of the general movement to insert herself. Kevin introduced the two women. They greeted each other coolly. Once in the dining room, which was housed in a vast country kitchen adorned with earthenware, Kevin tried to maneuver himself so he could sit next to Anne on his own. Philippine immediately worked out what was going on and changed direction without further ado. She simply whispered into her cofounder's ear: "I'll leave you to it. If you want to fuck her, go right ahead. One day we might need some help with crisis comms."

Surprised, Kevin thought he spotted a note of wistfulness in Philippine's expression.

During dinner, Kevin and Anne absent-mindedly caught snatches of various conversations about the latest gossip overheard at Davos, a new brand of Made in France organic cotton socks, the respective merits of Megève and Zermatt for winter vacations, the future of the metaverse and the protection of marine resources. All peppered with the most politically incorrect banter. In this select inner circle from which nothing would ever be leaked, people could unplug and give free rein to remarks that would no longer be acceptable in general society. Indeed, the opposition member called out to Gaspard mid-dinner.

"Promise you won't write a word about us all just having a bit of fun?"

Gaspard smiled but made no promises.

Between ass jokes, everybody was pitching ideas. The publisher suggested to the chef that he coauthor a book with the essayist; the essayist convinced the member of parliament to put forward an amendment to animal rights' legislation; the parliamentarian signed the navy officer up for the next hearings of the National Defense Commission; the officer suggested to the sports journalist that she cover a marines training exercise; the sports journalist invited one of the financiers to attend a conference she was chairing on the business of soccer; the financier insisted to Philippine that he get a chance to participate in Posthumus's next funding round; Philippine, always self-absorbed and the ultimate hypochondriac, asked the surgeon for a good referral to a doctor who could give her a base-line mammogram; the surgeon, keen for experiences beyond the reach of his public hospital salary, secured a spot in Victor's helicopter for the return journey; Victor sought advice from the architect about an investment he was hesitating to make in a construction company specializing in low carbon apartment blocks; the architect persuaded the violinist to play at the opening of his most recent building; the violinist secured an appearance by Thomas Pesquet at her next fundraising concert for Ukrainian children; Thomas Pesquet discussed his proposed autobiography with the publisher. Everybody seemed to be delighted and was posting smiling photos of themselves on the group's WhatsApp chat.

Kevin didn't ask Anne a single question about her change of heart. He now knew how the Sciences Po grad network operated. Anne would not have had to look very hard to find a well-paid job requiring no particular expertise. He understood her reasons well enough and was not out to judge. She was the one eager to justify herself as she munched away on her dandelion salad. She explained how her new job would allow her to carry on her fight for gender equality in the workplace, forcing businesses caught up in a media maelstrom to implement far-reaching change.

"Don't you believe me?"

"That's not the point. I think it's great *you* believe it."

Kevin was charmed. Anne's ingenuousness clearly knew no bounds. She was capable of applying herself just as effectively to her neo-rural attempts to settle in Saint-Firmin as to her communications consultancy job.

"Wait, you have a dandelion stalk on your cheek."

He delicately pulled it off, then brushed her lips with his finger. She half-opened her mouth. Kevin looked at her pensively while the Young Leaders all laughed at some scatological remark made by the surgeon. With Anne, he felt like he was with family, bound to Arthur. If one day he wanted to have children who said, "Move on," he was going to have to make a choice. In any case, did anybody still believe in love these days?

XV

Spring had returned and Arthur hadn't even noticed. His land still looked unappealing. Brambles had once again taken over. A scuff of the soil was enough to raise a cloud of dust. Arthur had done an estimated earthworm count for form's sake: numbers remained pitifully stable. He'd drafted some definitive lines for his blog.

"After two years, I can confirm the following: the soil is dead. It is not depleted, it has not deteriorated—it is dead as a doornail. Beyond resuscitation. And what of the much-vaunted clay-humic complex with which we were bored to death in our agronomy courses? It's a joke. There are no more fungi to decompose organic matter, no more roots to break up the rock, no more lumbrics to bring it all back tougher and elevate nutrient levels. Papi always used to talk about 'his earth.' But what earth was he talking about? It has morphed into mineral. How am I supposed to bring stones back to life? I'm not God. And even God created man from clay. Prometheus, Allah, Khnum, Parvati, Viracocha, for once all of them agree: to breathe life into something, to mold Golem, you need clay, mud, shit, something elastic and absorbent. There's nothing like that left on this plateau.

"Éluard has that ridiculous line: 'The Earth is blue like an orange.' This century of ours has ultimately proven him correct. We humans have peeled the Earth the way one would peel an orange. We've removed the zest. There's nothing left but a pebble with silver flecks.

"Of course, in order to cover up the great damage we have caused, we maintain the illusion by pouring on fertilizer every year and growing genetically modified corn. City dwellers driving past in their cars see fields undulating in the breeze and feel happy. Farmers feed everybody, and that makes them feel happy. Yields down a bit? Give everything a bit of a spray. And one day, in a few years' time, maybe a few decades, which is to say, in the blink of an eye on a geological scale, there'll no longer be enough oil for all their chemicals. And then we'll work out, just like I've worked out here at Saint-Firmin, that there's no more soil. And those yields, the beloved yields that are supposed to keep increasing, ad infinitum, aren't just going to drop: they're going to collapse. To nothing, zero pounds per hectare. The emperor is naked. Who are they going to feed with soil that is hard as concrete? Nobody.

"They'll say: What if we reintroduce some earthworms? Good luck with that, friends. See, lumbrics don't like being pushed and shoved around. In the time it would take to convince them, there'll be a famine. An alimentary apocalypse. Climate change, tsunamis, droughts, and floods, all of that is just a little appetizer. None of it goes to the essentials. It's not temperature that determines humanity's fate. It's the soil. Imagine a summer when cereals refuse to grow. When grains remain withered in the bunkers we still call fields. Just one summer. Cows, sheep, chickens, our entire established meat supply will be the first to go. The whole world will be forced to become vegetarian. Groans from the people. Silos will be emptied in order to make bread. When reserves run out, there'll be riots. There'll still be some greenhouse vegetables: people will be killing each other for a leek. Imagine the following winter, when phreatic zones stop filling up, as rainwater no longer flows through earth that has become mineral, barren. We'll turn on the tap: nothing. We'll go visit the neighbor: nothing there either, that's strange. We'll wait a day. Not two. Towns will be empty of people in only a few hours of indescribable chaos. There'll be nobody left to maintain the telephone, internet, and electricity networks. The planet will be plunged into darkness. The masters of the universe, those who have a vegetable garden and a well, will stave off the marauding hordes of executives, engineers, and blue-collar workers who've been forced to flee the cities.

"The Romans were alive to all this: *Homo* comes from humus. *Homo* lives on humus. Then *Homo* destroyed humus. And without humus, there's no *Homo*. Simple.

"So, then, you'll have worked out that, for my part, I'm throwing in the towel. I've seen my experiment through to the very end and I've ascertained that we were all doomed already. We're still enjoying, while blind drunk, the reprieve we've been given by the last few drops of oil. Organic matter that has taken three hundred million years to decompose in sedimentary basins and that has been guzzled down in just two centuries.

"As for me, I'm going to save my skin, for what it's worth,

tending my garden. And maybe I'll save yours, too, if you follow my advice in the vegetable patch."

Unsurprisingly, that post earned Arthur several thousand new followers and was even picked up on the *Reporterre* site. Not a single comment, however, from his former future INRAE colleagues. He had tumbled into another world.

Arthur wondered if Anne would read his piece. He couldn't help imagining her in front of her screen, impressed, and won over. He could not understand why she had fled.

His concluding remarks were anything but metaphorical. The kitchen garden and henhouse were now an essential means of subsistence and his only source of income, a few hundred euros a month. He had refused to accept any payments from his father after their falling out over the ecocide issue. He no longer wished to be dependent on that self-proclaimed hedonist whom he had always called by his first name, an antiracist profiteer, a rebel, perhaps, at twenty, but these days congealed in his image as a righter-of-wrongs, incapable of understanding the new battles ahead. At some deeper level, perhaps, Arthur was afraid of ending up like him, a fanatic for his cause to the point of cherishing the injustice that rendered the fight possible. His father needed racism in order to exist. Arthur, for his part, would never need pesticides. His desire for victory was sincere.

Furthermore, Arthur had received notification from the CAF that his welfare payments had been stopped, a penalty all the more inopportune now he was officially single and would have been entitled to the full rate. Arthur, however, had neither the inclination nor the courage to pursue the matter. He would rather plant potatoes than return cap in hand to Caen to beg from Arlette and her ilk. He wanted to disappear from the administration's sight. He no longer wanted to be registered anywhere, or owe anything to anyone. No longer did he wish to tap in his identification number or password. He wanted to live, or survive, entirely unobtrusively.

In his sudden solitude, Arthur could barely even rely any more on support from the gang at La Lanterne. Two young gendarmes, locals and fresh out of training, had come to carry out an inspection of the store, probably after somebody had made a complaint. They had noted the illegal service and sale of alcohol, a criminal offense subject to a penalty of imprisonment.

"But we're only having a beer among friends," Maria had pleaded.

"Beers bought and drunk on the premises? You need a License III for that."

"We're not doing it to make a profit. It just creates a bit of community in the village."

"You'll have to entertain your friends at home in future."

More sympathetic and embarrassed than anything else, the two gendarmes had agreed to turn a blind eye provided this serious violation of public law and order ceased. Maria had retained an acute fear of the police from her Romanian childhood. She saw no limit to the state's capacity for arbitrary regulation and assumed the worst was always a possibility. So she took these threats very seriously and put away the trestles once and for all. She did her best to organize a few drinks at home with the group, but without success. An invitation, a schedule, a gathering behind closed doors: nobody had anything to say in such a formal environment. Very quickly they stopped seeing one another. Salim doubled down on his tweets, claiming that the fascist state was responsible for breaking up spontaneous socializing.

The only breath of fresh air in the monotony of Arthur's daily life came when he regularly stopped by Matthieu's place for some afternoon carpentry lessons. Conversation was limited to their treatment of the sapwood or the handling of the jigsaw. Arthur especially appreciated the fact that in those moments he was able to focus on a single task. Faced with a plank of untreated oak, the scent of wood shavings in the air, his fingers covered in fresh sawdust, he would forget the world's tragedies. Being in contact with the wood gave him a feeling of equilibrium. To begin with, though, he felt uncomfortable about the idea of cutting up the dead corpse of a tree, whose rings represented the phenomenal life force it had once harbored. By sanding it, then varnishing it, he was preventing this corpse from returning to nourish the soil through its slow decomposition. He was mummifying it, interrupting nature's cycle.

Then, however, plane in hand, Arthur discovered a form of sublimation in this dialogue between life and death. If the tree drew its strength from photosynthesis, then a cabinetmaker was giving an almost eternal shape—be it a birdhouse or a chair—to light that was already several decades old. The only thing that truly pained him was the felling of trees destined for the indignity of cremation.

One morning, while he was pulling out radishes, Arthur was surprised to hear a distant ringing sound. "That'll be Jobard and his machinery," he said to himself, thinking no more of it. But when the noise didn't stop, he was keen to get to its source. Astonishingly, however, the volume remained constant. Having made it as far as the hedge, he turned away to take a leak. Then he realized the ringing had turned with him. He started to run, stopped: the ringing came with him, he couldn't leave it behind. Indeed, it was coming from within, from his left ear to be precise. It was as if his own body were slowly deflating, like a punctured balloon. After an initial moment of uncertainty, Arthur went back inside the farmhouse and put on some music at full volume. The algorithm of the music streaming service, Deezer, always fed off the hip-hop playlists Anne had created, and soon enough the words of Eminem were blasting through the countryside. Arthur spent a good half hour listening to them. They radiated a certain savage anarchy that corresponded neatly with his current state of mind:

> To all the friends I used to have, I miss my past
> But the rest of you assholes can kiss my ass.

Alas, as soon as Eminem fell silent, the ringing resumed. Neither more nor less intrusively. A sort of uninterrupted buzzing, a constant alarm. Dejected, Arthur barely had the strength to go upstairs to bed. He told himself he'd never manage to fall asleep. He buried his left ear in the pillow: pointless.

He fell asleep nonetheless. When he woke up the following day, the ringing woke up with him.

Arthur decided to see a doctor. The first available appointment with a GP on Doctissimo was an hour's drive away, in a village on the Caen plain. In order to save gas, Arthur took the regional bus that passed through Saint-Firmin twice a day. Time was really the only thing he had in abundance.

"Simple tinnitus. I could send you off to an ENT for further tests, but there wouldn't be much point."

The young doctor with his sporty physique who'd just set up shop after completing his residency looked disappointed. Yet another benign condition. People really did complain about anything and everything.

"Is there a treatment?"

"I could suggest a hearing aid, but they're very expensive and don't work very well. Other than that, there's medication. Worst case, I can prescribe you antidepressants."

"But it'll disappear after a while, won't it?"

"Generally speaking, no. You'll have to live with it."

"For the rest of my life?"

Arthur felt overwhelmed by a sudden anxiety. Had he been diagnosed with cancer, he would at least have had a chance of beating it. This thing he had was much more disheartening. It was both ridiculous and incurable.

"And what causes it?"

"A minor loss of hearing. The brain is trying to compensate for the sound it's no longer registering. Have you been exposed to high decibel noise? Nightclubs, for example?"

"Impossible."

Arthur was astounded that anybody could still imagine him frequenting a nightclub; he thought it was obvious to all that he was an antisocial small-time farmer.

"Well then, it's age-related."

"I'm not even thirty!"

"You're a little ahead of the game, that's true. Do you have your health insurance card for payment?"

In the bus on the way home, Arthur leaned his head against the window, feeling sorry for himself. His own flesh was manifesting his mortality, which until now had never been anything but a very theoretical topic for consideration. Of course, he was still young but he had already started down the path of a long, very long, deterioration. His body was starting to fail, little bit by little bit. He could no longer even savor his melancholy in peace and quiet. The ringing was a constant reminder of his unhappiness, like an evil spirit whispering a litany of reproaches. Was he really supposed to live with it? For days, months, decades?

Arthur recalled the definition of good health offered by René Leriche, a surgeon from the prewar years: "life lived in the silence of the organs." He must have read that quote in a book by Georges Canguilhem and it had stayed with him. So be it, then, he would never again know the silence of his organs. He had lost his health, that happy ignorance of present or future maladies. He looked around rather jealously at the other passengers on the bus. They could rest, daydream, mull things over. Forget, for a moment, their mortality.

What was there even to complain about? Arthur was disabled without a disability, ill without an illness.

He consulted various websites and Facebook pages that discussed tinnitus. He recognized the tedious banality of his condition, affecting as it did 10 to 15 percent of the population. Everybody described a ringing, a murmuring, a continuous low rumbling, a crackling or humming. Arthur found himself among a community of sixty-year-olds comparing hearing aids. He felt as though he was dealing with dozens of Doctor Knocks: Does it itch or does it tickle? Does it whistle or does it crackle? Notwithstanding a few tips of a prophylactic nature, listening to white noise or relaxing your jaw, Arthur quickly concluded that no treatment was going to work. Every renewed hope of those on the internet matched their despair. Tinnitus was a condition as common, ludicrous, and insoluble as the human condition itself.

So, Arthur abandoned the medical route and instead sought advice from his philosopher friends. After Anne left, he had taken the time to pull out some boxes of books and sort through the several hundred classics he had brought with him when they had moved. This collection of books endorsed by posterity was enough to sustain a life of reflection. Arthur now spent his evenings in their company. He imagined himself as Montaigne in his tower, opening one tome or another depending on what he fancied, and as Montaigne said, "taking from books, here and there, the phrases which please me." It might have seemed surprising, in the age of TikTok, to see this young man leafing through Malebranche in his Chesterfield. It was there, however, that Arthur felt the least miserable. Who knew, perhaps one day his own words would join their ranks. For the time being, he felt profoundly inadequate to that task and limited himself instead to blogging about his kitchen garden.

To tame his tinnitus, Arthur started with the Greeks. Pythagoras, in his theory of the music of the spheres, alleged that the cosmos emits a sound, including on Earth, a sound that is so homogeneous and continuous that it is impossible to hear it. Like a refrigerator humming, noticeable only when it stops, the sound of the world that lulls us from birth is so well assimilated by our body that our consciousness can no longer access it. An intriguing, cheering even, perspective linking us to the universe in a way that goes beyond our fumbling senses.

Pythagoras offered Arthur a perfectly simple solution: turn the tinnitus into music of the spheres and thus render it inaudible. He first tried ignoring it, a paradoxical, almost impossible task, much like trying to think of nothing. Arthur was counting on carpentry, an activity capable of utterly absorbing his mind; indeed, he sometimes spent several hours on it without feeling any discomfort, but he needed only to congratulate himself on the success of his strategy for the ringing to reappear at precisely the same levels. Pornography had a similar effect, but for a shorter period, and he couldn't jerk off all day long. Arthur wondered if in those moments when he wasn't paying it any attention, whether the ringing even *existed*. Could it be emitted by his brain then ignored by that same brain? Or was the simple fact of not listening to it enough to banish it?

The fact remained that as the weeks and months went by, Arthur debated with himself without making any real progress. He found respite only in sleep. Every evening, he would be less troubled by it. And every morning, upon waking, the ringing resumed. At least his dreams provided him with the illusion of a normal life. He started sleeping longer and more often. He took increasing numbers of naps, and would feel so numb that any notion of day or night grew blurred. Neither the lengthening days, nor the pollen turning the air outside into one gigantic orgy, nor the birds busying themselves with building their nests, none of summer's promise alleviated Arthur's suffering. On the contrary, the general good cheer only sharpened his frustration at finding himself isolated in a prison of sound.

Arthur also tried out the Stoics. Epictetus, Seneca, Marcus Aurelius. A slave, a politician, and an emperor. Doubtless humanity's three least enviable conditions: no power, insufficient power, too much power. And solitude, always. No surprise that they'd sought a solution to the question of suffering, physical as well as moral. Keep things at arm's length. Think of ourselves as another. Be mindful of the emotional states that affect us. And remember always that death may, at any moment, deliver you. "The key of life," as Montaigne wrote, suffering from his kidney stones.

Arthur found neither comfort nor consolation in the Stoics' writings, but instead a reason to resist, to toughen up. This approach, however, did have one considerable inconvenience: he could not stop thinking about death. He spent the whole day imagining his own demise. The idea of nothingness both terrified and attracted him. He took this vertiginous feeling for what it was: not a fear of falling, but a desire to jump.

Arthur pondered the most efficient means at his disposal. He had no wish to fail, like Seneca, who, after slitting his own veins, then suffered interminable death throes. Nor to carry on as Montaigne had done, too interested in the good life to think seriously of suicide, and incapable of putting an end to his days when he continued to suffer from ill health. In the countryside, hanging remained a popular method among farmers; everybody had a friend, or a friend of a friend, who had resorted to that solution. But Arthur felt he would be too clumsy. He just knew his knot would fail, and he would only succeed in falling flat on his face.

So Arthur turned to pills. He installed TOR on his computer, a browser enabling almost total anonymity, and proceeded to scour the dark web looking for lethal substances. It took two clicks for the laws in France to disappear, leaving him in a space of unbridled freedom where trafficking of any kind became possible.

Nembutal seemed to be very fashionable among the older population, but it took too long to work. Arthur was more tempted by cyanide, particularly as it reminded him of a family story. During the war, Papi's father had belonged to Hector, a Resistance network based in Calvados and associated with Free France. Arrested and tortured by the Gestapo in Caen, he bit on a cyanide capsule rather than denounce his comrades; local Saint-Firmin mythology had it that his heroic deed saved the landings. Cyanide, therefore, enjoyed an excellent reputation in those parts. Modernity having left its mark here, too, there were no more capsules to be found on the dark web, only ordinary little white tablets not dissimilar to aspirin.

A little irritated, all the same, at having to resort to chemistry, Arthur investigated ways of manufacturing cyanide from apricot kernels or even apple seeds. He found some convincing recipes, but the amygdalin thereby produced needed to be digested before metabolizing into poison. He gave up on the idea of an organic death, too much work, and ordered the little white tablets through the post. They were delivered two weeks later. When Arthur wanted to stop the ringing once and for all, he would know which drawer to open.

That left the issue of his body. In the mornings, Arthur would look at his naked self in the mirror, imagining what would become of this rather nondescript, pale and hairy flesh. He imagined himself desiccated, tough, green. The thought of a coffin bored him. Too claustrophobic. Cremation? Two hundred and fifty kilos of carbon released into the atmosphere. What was the point in leading an existence as abstemious as his, only to ruin it all at the last moment? So Arthur grew curious about a new method, humusation, originating in the United States and recently approved in France, which involved the transformation of the corpse into humus. Wrapped in a biodegradable shroud, the body is placed directly into the earth, then covered with a burial mound of carefully selected vegetable matter. Bacteria and fungus are left to run riot for several months, accelerating decomposition of the flesh. At around the halfway mark, a New Age undertaker comes to recover the bones and grind them up. A year later, all that remains is a small, dark, moist mound, the only remaining trace of a derisory existence. Heirs will receive a few square meters of excellent fertilizer, which they'll be able to spread about as they wish, much to the earthworms' great delight. And humans, rather than exhausting themselves in their vain efforts to get to heaven, can return peacefully to the earth, following in the footsteps of billions of creatures every day, and providing nature with a way of continuing its unlikely adventures in a corner of our galaxy.

It seemed an obvious solution to Arthur. He would gift his body to the plateau, a final attempt to regenerate the soil. For the avoidance of doubt, and to avoid any nasty surprises, he wrote down his last wishes in a password-protected PDF. Just as he was about to send it off to his father, he hesitated. His father was quite capable of sending him off, as a matter of pride, with a mass held at Saint-Germain-des-Prés, and then on to the cemetery. Arthur preferred to send the email to Kevin. In a lighthearted tone, he explained that he was taking an entirely hypothetical precaution, and noted that the password would be in a tea canister on top of the fireplace. With that, everything was settled. Arthur could now take his chances to continue to live a little longer, just to see, no obligation. "You could have put the will straight into the tea canister," replied Kevin pragmatically.

Having made these arrangements, Arthur once again found the necessary motivation to get up in the morning. Now he had the key of life in his hands, to quote Montaigne, every day became a bonus offered up by time itself. Nothing like preparing oneself for death to quell any further desire for it.

One afternoon, when delivering the season's first crate of new potatoes to La Lanterne, Arthur came across Léa, who had just been buying some ginger for her infusions. As there was no longer any chance of having a beer, Léa invited Arthur over to her place. He politely declined. These days he was happy with a silent dialogue with the dead friends from his bookshelves. She pressed him, insisting with the concerned tone of a therapist. He relented and followed her with heavy steps, determined not to confide in her about anything. He would down his elderflower infusion and leave.

Nothing had changed in the ashram. They sat down cross-legged on the cushions. He observed her impenetrable Madonna with Child face and said nothing. She let him look at her without batting an eyelid. She seemed accustomed to such silences. It was Arthur who cracked and started the conversation with the usual questions.

"Things are really going well," answered Léa. "My appointment book is full two weeks in advance."

"Just from Saint-Firmin?"

"No. Word of mouth is taking off. These days I might have patients coming from up to fifty kilometers away."

"What is it exactly you do for them?"

"They complain about a thousand minor aches and pains

when all their problems are in their head. I listen to them, calm them down, and rebalance their internal energy."

Arthur was struggling to imagine all those taciturn Normandy folk stretched out on the floor listening to the gongs. He couldn't help but pull a skeptical face.

"I know what you're thinking, Mister Rational. Perhaps you'll be surprised to hear I agree with you. The plants, the instruments, the aural massages, they're all a pretext. The fundamental element is time. I offer people time, which is theirs and theirs alone, as well as absolute discretion. With or without any words. In that time, they are able to regroup. There's nothing new in it. We've had priests, Communist Party section leaders, shrinks. They all represented the belief systems of their era: God, the People, the Self. Now, it's Nature's turn. So people like me have stepped in."

"I didn't realize you were so disillusioned."

She shook her head. "Quite the contrary. You could benefit from it, too, Arthur, but I can see you're in a state of extremely powerful resistance. I'm not even going to try. I can only feel sorry for you."

"I don't need your pity. Nor do I need your gongs."

Nowadays Arthur dreaded having to listen to sounds that would inevitably focus his attention on the ringing.

"Every now and again," she added, as though it were the most basic thing in the world, "I also practice orgasmic meditation."

Arthur's eyes widened. He had always imagined Léa was some sort of asexual creature, divinely spared any libido.

"Our society makes people sick with desire. It's the most deeply buried, the tightest, the most painful knot. They talk to me about one thing and another, they beat around the bush, when really, it's all they can think about, all day long. So, I take my sword of Damocles and cut to the point. Now I've worked that out, I've been able to take my art to the next level, to where it ought to be."

Just like the priests, the Party leaders, the shrinks, thought Arthur. He thought back to certain scenes in Saint-Firmin that now seemed to make much more sense.

"Do you sleep with them?"

"No! Not at all. There's no need."

"What do you do to them, then?"

"It's complicated. There are several possible paths. A bit like Tantrism."

"Matthieu?" he asked.

"That's different. I don't take him for sessions anymore. He wants something more, something I can't give him."

Arthur understood better why Léa was successful.

"I'm not a hooker, you know."

"That would never have even entered my head."

"That said, it wouldn't bother me. But there is a fundamental difference."

He looked at her with new respect.

"Prostitutes arouse the flame of desire, again and again. I, on the other hand, work on it, refining it to the point where ultimately it subsides. It's all in the technique. My patients are suspicious to begin with, then they come back wanting more. When they return to their own beds, with their girl, their guy, their vibrator, or their pillow, I hope there's something left. If only people knew how to make love properly in this country, there'd be far fewer problems."

Arthur remained speechless. It was a topic he had never considered and one his dead authors barely broached, or if they did, it was in awkward and convoluted formulations. Two thousand years of philosophy, spilling over with free will and moral precepts, and not a single word on humanity's principal preoccupation. What a waste! Sure, there had been Freud, but after him? Sex had been confined to psychoanalysis. Tidied away in a separate box.

"I'm not sure why I'm telling you all this. Perhaps I need a session, too . . ."

Arthur gently took her hand.

"Anyway," she joked, "I've got plenty of dough. I don't really know what to do with it now I've finished my renovations. I'm giving a bit away here, there, and everywhere, to whoever asks. If you're in trouble, you'll tell me, won't you?"

He shook his head. What sort of trouble? He still had a roof over his head and enough to eat, well, almost enough.

"There's really nothing to be done with you." She sighed. "You're about as uptight as they come."

Arthur thought it was a good thing to have put off hanging himself. He would never have gotten to know this splendid version of Léa.

"Well, then," she resumed talking, a little irritated, "the thing I really wanted to talk to you about was Jobard."

"There's nothing more to be said."

"I'm up to speed with all your dramas."

Arthur pictured the Weeble toy in this room, mid orgasmic meditation. He tried to stand up. Léa grabbed him by the shoulder and forced him to sit back down. He wondered how she had such a strong grip. She seemed so fragile.

"Listen! He's just as pissed off as you."

"Oh, poor him! Who was it who issued proceedings? Me or him?"

"If you hadn't given him the cold shoulder from the outset, you wouldn't be in this situation."

"What?"

"You arrive with your girlfriend from Paris who's never set foot on anything but asphalt . . ."

"Anne had a highly developed environmental awareness!" Arthur protested, unconvincingly.

"We saw her work . . . And so you settle in, you don't even say hello, you ostensibly turn your back on this fellow who is not only your nearest neighbor but also your grandfather's best friend."

"You've got to be kidding! Papi hated him. Jobard stole his land."

"The truth is that Jobard bought it from him when nobody else would, and at well above market price. In other words, he provided him with his pension. Everybody in Saint-Firmin knows it. Your grandfather was so ashamed that he cooked up this business about an argument."

Arthur remained silent. The fact was, he could remember evenings from his childhood when the whole family had been invited over to the Jobards, and then the invitation had been reciprocated. They would discuss crops, play dominos, and drink Calvados.

"Jobard never got on particularly well with your father, but he was always very fond of you and your mother," Léa continued. "He would walk you around the fields and point out various things in the natural world to you. From what he's told me, you'd all go fishing in the Orne, the three of you."

At the mention of his mother, taken too young by an invasive cancer, Arthur felt his eyes well up. He remembered the folding chairs, the hooks that used to frighten him, the earthworms they would collect by tapping their feet, and the warm, sweet sense of boredom sitting next to his mother, those moments of grace stolen from his father's temper. He wanted to reply but his voice caught in his throat.

"When he saw you come back with your mustache and your convictions, the know-it-all little agronomist, you can imagine how he felt."

"So he's the victim now! I don't believe it!"

But yes, he believed it. Arthur was intelligent and honest enough to recognize another perspective. Now all he had to do was reconcile it with his own. He stood up and Léa didn't try to stop him. He paced about the room. Picking up a random mallet, he approached the central gong and struck the copper disc with all his strength. The sound resonated in powerful waves. He staggered and turned back to his cushion where he curled up like a cat in its basket. Léa had blocked her ears with her fingers. They waited several minutes for the reverberations to subside.

"Sorry . . ."

"If it makes you feel better!"

It had. Even the ringing had stopped for a few seconds, beaten into submission by the gong. A few precious seconds of respite.

"So then, admit it. Whichever way you look at it, the guy is a polluter. The planet . . ."

"Enough already with your generalizations! Jobard belongs

to a lost generation, trapped by the banks and farmers' federations. But he's had the courage to ask the right questions. He's committed to transitioning to responsible farming."

"Bullshit! That's just a term invented by agribusiness to assuage its conscience."

"The fact remains he's reducing his inputs, year after year. He's plowing more shallow furrows, a centimeter at a time. He's spreading his land with green fertilizers in winter. Who knows? Maybe the earthworms will come back to his land first."

She was provoking him. Arthur's determination was faltering.

"He's a good guy. Go see him. Take a glass of something. Have a competition about enriching your soil. Make peace. He'll withdraw his claim on the spot. You have a thousand things to learn from each other."

Arthur wanted to mention the ecocide claim but didn't dare. His submissions in defense were ready, though, and his letter to the prosecutor, too. He felt foolish.

XVI

Kevin picked nervously at some peanuts as he watched the bubbles rise in his glass of San Pellegrino. He had asked his PA to find him a "little place" for his lunch with Arthur. Which had resulted in her making a booking at Le Petit Lutetia, a long-standing Left Bank brasserie that had become dull and pretentious thanks to the evil influence of the new owner, one of the two Costes brothers. This dynasty of restaurant owners had, over several decades, specialized in trashing the most mythical Parisian establishments, turning them into temples of fake luxury with pounding playlists, desserts drowning in Chantilly, and wannabe models for waitstaff. Its menu, featuring burrata from Puglia, spaghetti with lobster and miso salmon, now looked no different from that of any airport café. The calf liver had been retained for old time's sake, but made a loss. The new look Le Petit Lutetia had been an instant success with hip actors, gullible tourists looking for engineered authenticity, and bankers' wives who had spent the morning shopping at Bon Marché. Its decline was all the more flagrant given its unaltered decor of white linen, leather banquettes, and bucolic artwork, an insistent reminder that it could have been otherwise.

It could not have been a worse place to which to invite Arthur. Kevin, who was growing used to his role as boss, was sending appalled WhatsApps to his PA, accompanied by emojis in an attempt to soften his tone.

I said "a little place" 😠

It's listed as a traditional bistro 😜

Notwithstanding the fact that secretaries were now "personal assistants" and addressed their employers informally, they were still young, female, and useful for letting off steam. Some things had remained unchanged over the centuries.

Kevin, looking peeved, set his phone back on the table. Best he get comfortable with the situation. This new life of his was playing out in an endless stream of Costes establishments. He didn't know any little places, and he shouldn't have to be sheepish about his own success.

He considered his reflection in the mirror opposite. He now appreciated the value of the sharp slope of his cheekbones, of the lips made for pleasure. The wrinkles discreetly appearing on his forehead in no way interfered yet with his fine ephebic features. He needed to make the most of it all. This sort of beauty didn't last. When it deteriorated, his look would be more old dandy than old lion.

The restaurant door opened. Spying Arthur's flannel shirt, the maître d' rushed to intercept him. Arthur pointed over to Kevin.

"Nice place, this," he said, taking a seat.

"Wasn't me who chose it," Kevin defended himself.

Arthur immediately abandoned all his resolutions. His heart was beating fast.

"Just kidding. It looks like it'll be much better than my usual diet of potatoes, onions, tomatoes, and scrambled eggs. This season's fare. Plus bread from my neighbor, Louis."

"At least you're eating organic."

"As organic as it gets. But twice a day, seven days a week, it gets a bit old . . . It's been ages since I've been back to Paris. I have to say, it's not unpleasant. I could get used to it again very quickly."

Kevin felt relieved. What was it exactly that he'd been afraid of? They ordered a bottle of Brouilly and made a toast to earthworms, like old times on the terrace at AgroParisTech. Kevin grilled him about news from Saint-Firmin.

"A failure on all fronts," Arthur summarized in a lighthearted tone. "Romantically, financially, agriculturally."

Kevin pretended to look at the menu.

"Don't worry," Arthur continued, to set him at ease, "I'm happy there, with my chickens and my books."

"That's the main thing."

"So they say, yes. I've made my peace. With myself, and many other things."

"Could you leave?"

"Not sure. To go where?"

Kevin noted his answer. It augured well for what was to follow. Their waiter was about to take their order when suddenly he froze, pencil midair. An invisible tremor coursed through the room, progressing from one table to the next. A brief, almost indiscernible silence, then a murmuring as chairs squeaked. Thomas Pesquet had just come in.

"You know who that is, don't you—he's the astronaut!"

"Do you think that's him? He looks bigger in real life."

"France's favorite celebrity."

"Nah, that's Jean-Jacques Goldman."

Cell phones started to appear. Some people tried to sneak a selfie, deformed face in the foreground, a lock of Thomas Pesquet's hair barely visible in the corner. Some guy in his forties in a tailored suit with shadows under his eyes, looking like a coked-up corporate lawyer, stood and asked him for an autograph for his son who'd seen him on the cover of *Sciences & Vie Junior*. Thomas Pesquet played along before being escorted by the maître d' brandishing his white napkin as if chasing mosquitoes from his famous guest. Kevin recognized the publisher from the Young Leaders event accompanying him. He looked down, not daring to make himself known, fearing they would snub him. However, as he walked past Kevin's chair, Pesquet gripped him firmly by the shoulder.

"Kevin! How's it going? Recovered from that crazy weekend?"

Kevin muttered something.

"Catch you later!"

Pesquet disappeared into the back of the restaurant, leaving all eyes focused on Kevin, officially anointed.

"That's not the earthworm dude, is it?" asked somebody, hesitantly.

"Google him."

Kevin remained upright in his seat, looking straight ahead,

an impervious look on his face, a look he had mastered well for times of uncertainty. The restaurant's customary buzz picked back up, and the waiter, who had also now recovered from his own astonishment, took their order.

"You're a real star now!" Arthur exclaimed, kindly feigning having been impressed.

"It's just a coincidence . . ."

Kevin took a swallow of red, giving himself a moment to reflect.

"You know, I haven't turned into a dick."

"Even if you must spend a lot of time with dickheads."

"Yeah, even if I do."

Kevin was weighing each of his words. Arthur remained silent, tacitly encouraging him to continue. Kevin gave him a simple, factual rundown of Posthumus's progress, barely interrupted by the waiter who wished them *bonne dégustation* as if to emphasize they were in a Costes restaurant, and not some common brasserie where staff would permit themselves the familiarity of a *bon appétit*. In a society that believed it had conquered hunger, it was no longer a question of eating, but simply a matter of tasting.

Kevin told him everything: about the capital raising, the contracts, the clients, the goals. The factory at Mantes was no longer adequate to handle the growing number of orders. Kevin had located a site in the Limousin, fifty odd kilometers from his parents' village. About thirty hectares of pasture and uncultivated land sold by a farmer who was retiring, which Kevin was looking to convert into a giant worm composter. He had to do a presentation about the economics of the project to the local municipality authority and, most importantly, to the regional environmental regulator, the DREAL, about its environmental merits. After that, anything would be possible: hundreds of waste treatment lines, billions and billions of lumbrics constantly gorging themselves.

"Epigeics," Arthur specified.

"Yes, of course, less noble than your anecics . . ."

"That's not what I said!"

Arthur had polished off his steak tartare in record time and downed three-quarters of the bottle, like the periodic festival feasting of farmers before they returned to their frugal daily habits. All at once, he stretched back on the banquette, replete.

"So you've become a true capitalist. A captain of industry!"

"That's one way of looking at it. I could also tell you, as I say to journalists, that I'm in the process of saving the planet. The truth lies somewhere in between."

"Kevin, we're buddies. You can spare me the bullshit. I'm happy if you're making a few bucks."

Kevin gathered all his courage. He had always proceeded on the basis that Arthur was right, without ever putting up any real resistance to his arguments. Except for this time. He mustn't, he couldn't waiver.

"We're going to recycle tens of millions of tons a year. Without emitting an ounce of carbon. I don't know what more you want."

"Sure, let's agree on that. Let's not even think about the trucks' emissions, the construction of service roads, the land take. Let's not even try to flip the reasoning and ask if we couldn't instead reduce our waste. I'll grant you all that."

"So?"

"So, the planet. It's fucked anyhow. I've seen it with my own eyes. There's no more soil. What it needs is a prolonged fast from humanity. It's not even close to happening. Not before we all die of hunger, in any event. Then, we'd need several million years to reconstitute the fauna and flora. Like after an ice age. There'd be plenty of new species. It ought to be interesting, but there'll be nobody left to write the reports."

"We've never fed so many people on the planet . . ."

"But at what price? 75 percent of the earth's land surface is degraded. According to the IPBES it'll be 95 percent by 2050."

"According to who?"

"An international body on biodiversity. We heard about it in our agroecology course, don't you remember? Pollution, deforestation, intensive crop farming: the soil is toast. The less it produces, the more we try to boost it. It's a vicious circle. We're buying ourselves a bit of time so we can carry on with all this," he gestured to the neighboring tables, to the burrata from Puglia, the Patagonian prawns. "A few dozen years, maybe. *Bonne dégustation!*"

Kevin set down his fork. At a theoretical level, he was happy to admit the truth of all that, even the banality of it all, for an agronomy student, but he no longer had many opportunities to think about it. He poured himself some more San Pellegrino to give himself time to consider.

"So what should we do? Nothing?"

"I didn't say that. Papa Kant's Categorical Imperative remains valid. We need to do what we'd like others to do. It's the morality of the intention. Even if from a consequentialist point of view, it would be pointless."

"Arthur . . . I don't understand."

"How should I say it? I'm certain my actions are pointless, but I'm going to see them through nonetheless."

"Just in case?"

"No. In spite of everything."

"Like the hummingbird dropping a few drips of water on a forest going up in flames?"

"You're not going to wheel out Pierre Rhabi's crappy metaphors, are you? Generosity is truly a human perversion. There's nothing like it in nature. I prefer Thoreau's story of the squirrel. It hunts grubs and insects. It's not especially trying to do good in the forest. It's just doing its job as a squirrel. And along the way, it stores seeds with which it feeds itself. And it follows its little routine without worrying if the chestnuts will still be producing fruit the following year. What will be will be! I, too, am doing my job, my job of being a human on his plot of land, avoiding having to look too far ahead. Ever since realizing this, I feel lighter, sprightly, like a squirrel. I'm even ready to patch things up with my neighbor."

"That fat Jobard?"

"He's not as terrible as all that. He's just a bit of an idiot, like the rest of the world."

The waiter, extremely attentive to any friend of Thomas Pesquet, wasted no time clearing their plates.

"Dessert?"

"Pavlova," said Arthur.

"Make that two."

"If everything's fucked anyway, we may as well enjoy ourselves!"

Kevin focused his gaze on the table crumber whose hands

and arms were moving back and forth across the tablecloth. He wanted to be sure he had properly grasped Arthur's meandering musings in order to catch him in his own net.

"So, in the context of this behavior of yours, which is, let us say, both useless and necessary . . ."

"That's precisely what it is."

". . . in that context then, is effectiveness still a valid criterion?"

Arthur reflected. He had not asked himself that question.

"In other words," Arthur rephrased the comment, "am I trying to reduce in some marginal way the profound and irreversible pointlessness of my existence?"

"Exactly."

"I expect so. It's a bit the same as natural evolution. Life, in all its forms, is working phenomenally hard to adapt, to progress, even though in a few billion years it's going to disappear, broiled to death by a sun that will have transformed into a red monster. But it will progress nonetheless, because what else is there to do? The birds aren't sitting there saying to each other: we're all doomed, let's stop laying eggs."

Kevin gave a sigh of relief.

"So, what's the best way of trying to reduce this pointlessness in some minor way? Covering France in worm composters, or trying to put three earthworms back into a field?"

Arthur attacked his pavlova and didn't reply. He shoveled it in, leaving whipped cream all over his now very bushy, almost Nietzschean mustache. Kevin had never found him so touching.

"You don't want to hire me, though?" Arthur finally asked.

"In fact I do."

Kevin felt his stomach knot up. It was like a marriage proposal.

He hurriedly started talking again for fear of receiving too rapid and definitive a response.

"Let me explain. We need an R&D director to focus on developing the biostimulant."

"The Wormentino?"

"Yes. Trials haven't been very conclusive up to this point and approvals are lagging . . ."

"I can confirm that, it didn't alter anything on the plateau."

"Your environment was a little extreme. We got better results in less damaged soil. Nothing spectacular though. It's a question of dosage and refinement. It's not rocket science, but you have to put in the time and devote a considerable amount of gray matter. It's the key to the company's financial viability and its very success. Just imagine, with the thousands of hectoliters we could produce and sell every year . . ."

"Imagine the money?"

"Yeah, the money, sure, but also the soil, Arthur! What could be better for its regeneration than a biostimulant that's 100 percent organic? You just told me 75 percent of the earth's land surface is degraded. Let's say that's right. With Posthumus Wormentino, we could reduce that to 74 percent perhaps. Your existence would be marginally less pointless."

"Why me? I'm ensconced in the hole that is Saint-Firmin, checked out of the academic circuit. Nobody knows me. There must be a ton of brilliant agronomy dudes in Paris who would kill for that job."

Kevin knew that Arthur must not in any way suspect the slightest hint of indulgence. And yet, that's all this was. A gift for Arthur, for himself, for both of them.

"Back in your hole, to use your words, you've gained experience and a degree of legitimacy that nobody else has. I don't need yet another lab assistant. I need somebody who's knowledgeable enough to read a chemical formula and also knows how to get their hands dirty in the earth. They're not lining up for the job."

"It's true that the pseudo-science coming out of labs is largely responsible for the bullshit of the last fifty years. Soil is much too complex to be summed up by a few experiments carried out on a lab bench. We know hardly anything about the bacteria that make it up. You have to keep going back to the land, again and again."

"There you go. And then . . ."

"And then?"

Arthur had put down his spoon.

"And then, we could have a few beers after work."

He smiled.

"Two months ago, I would have said *no* right away. In fact, I wouldn't have said no, I would have spat in your face and left."

"I was fully prepared for that scenario, which in fact I thought was the most likely one."

"But now . . . I'm feeling calmer, more resigned. I'm telling myself none of it's that important. And I have to say, I have to say the evenings are sometimes long."

"You won't be missing out on anything. You've got your whole life to live like a hermit. Perhaps it's the best choice, I'm making no judgment. But you could still give yourself a few years to make sure."

Kevin could tell from the look on Arthur's face that he had gone too far. He changed tack immediately.

"My partner is on board, of course. Philippine would be delighted to have you on the team."

"About that, are you two . . ."

"Not really. Not anymore, anyway."

Kevin was lying in anticipation. Philippine still turned up to titillate him from time to time. He no longer took any pleasure in it but had not yet found the courage to resist. He felt a nagging stigma about it, a sense of shame almost. Arthur was the last person in the world with whom he would have shared any of this.

The waiter came over to offer them the inevitable selection of tiny desserts to accompany their coffee, the secret to any restaurant's profitability.

"To treat yourselves," he added, automatically.

They accepted one plate to share, like an old couple.

"I know this isn't the issue," added Kevin, awkwardly. "But I'll say it anyway: we can offer you shares in the company and a very comfortable salary."

"I'll think about it."

The deed was done. Kevin relaxed and let Arthur tell him all about his discovery of Spinoza. "*Deus sive natura.*" God or Nature, God and Nature, God is Nature. Power, necessity, immanence. Kevin nodded his head, not even trying to understand. He had never had such an exhausting conversation and was feeling done in. "Beatitude," explained Arthur. That was the word for it. Kevin was stricken by a sense of bliss. The thought of having Arthur around lit up his world with a joy he suddenly realized had been missing.

Kevin allowed himself to be lulled by Arthur's explanation of the three kinds of knowledge. He overheard Thomas Pesquet's laugh from the back of the room. The Young Leaders and the rest of that whole scene now felt like something relegated to the distant past. He had been caught up in their game for want of anything better when at heart, what he cherished most were moments like these, this friendship, a thing perpetually reborn. There were enough books on the history of philosophy for this monologue à deux to last a lifetime.

Kevin was doing his best to cut the mini chocolate éclair into halves when his telephone vibrated on the edge of the table. A name came up on the screen in large font: *Anne*.

Arthur stopped talking abruptly.

Rudely hauled out of his lethargy, Kevin hurriedly shoved his phone into his pocket.

"I'll answer later."

His cheeks, usually so pale, had blushed livid. There could have been no worse confession. Arthur was looking at him in horror.

"Are you sleeping with Anne?" Arthur asked in an emotionless voice.

"No!"

He was hardly lying. He felt no particular desire for Anne. But he was having to do a good job of pretending in order to live with her, as he had been endeavoring to do these last few weeks. In order to satisfy the ridiculous dream of having a bourgeois relationship with children who say, "Move on." But now Kevin had woken up, he was happily going to abandon all that madness. Never again! He would resume his aimless wandering this very minute.

"It's what was supposed to have happened that very first night," Arthur continued. "I'm such an idiot."

"No, no, that's not at all what was supposed to happen!"

Kevin couldn't carry through with the rest of his thought. And yet all he wanted was Arthur, his ideals, his doubts, his words. Arthur was still the person he was looking for, even through Anne.

"So this was the plan. Get me to be the third wheel. You must have both felt a bit bad abandoning me at Saint-Firmin. So you found a solution. A consolation prize. That way, we could all call it quits."

"That's not true!"

Anne was not feeling at all shitty about the situation. Quite the contrary, she was brimming with good humor, infinitely relieved at having left Bumblefucknowhere, as she called it. Every evening she was out with her girlfriends from Sciences Po or her work pals from her comms job. She never so much as mentioned Arthur.

"I hope you'll both be happy. Now that I think about it, you're made for each other. You're both ambitious and unscrupulous."

"Arthur, I beg you, listen to me . . ."

Happy? Not likely. Kevin was already bored to death. He went into the Posthumus office early in the morning to avoid having to eat breakfast together, or having to discuss the grocery shopping or plans for the weekend.

"I'm listening."

"I . . . I'm sad."

Sad about this huge mess when they were so close to beatitude, to endless beers on the terrace, watching the night sky, with no timetables or security guards. So sad. He didn't know what else to say.

"Is that it? I'm not. I'm not sad. I'm completely lucid. You're just an asshole, like every other asshole in this asshole of a town!" Arthur had raised his voice. Some other diners were casting him dark looks. Kevin was familiar with these outbursts and was expecting the worst.

"To think I might have been wavering . . . might have let myself be sucked in . . . thank you, Anne darling, for having called."

Arthur turned to the neighboring tables.

"What are you staring at, assholes? Get on with mopping up your plates, carry on with your sterile little discussions about finance and politics, make the most of it, down to the last drop! It'll be all over soon enough, all this bullshit from a bunch of assholes! You'll remember your meals at Costes when you're groveling along the roads. And I'll remember you when you come begging for bread and water."

After an initial moment of outraged astonishment, the other diners buried themselves back in their plates, as if they were in the Metro, eyes glued to their cell phones, waiting for the homeless person to finish their litany. The waiter rushed over to Arthur and took firm hold of him, friend or otherwise of Thomas Pesquet's friend.

"Monsieur, please. Let me see you out."

"Don't you worry, I'm out of here! You won't be seeing me again, not with the likes of you!"

Arthur was steered forcefully toward the exit. Kevin saw his flannel shirt disappear through the door, which the waiter closed firmly in his wake.

Kevin caught himself in the mirror, his face crumpled, eyes red, ugly. His cell phone started vibrating again in his pocket. Anne must have forgotten her keys.

A moment later, he felt a pressure on his shoulder. He jumped.

"See you soon, I hope!"

It was Pesquet, calmly taking his leave amid a sea of raised phones.

XVII

Arthur returned to Saint-Firmin, rage in his belly. The long journey from Montparnasse, on a slow train running on rapeseed oil (*Yet another rip-off*, thought Arthur), had allowed him to set his thoughts in order. It was no longer a question of patience or of reconciliation, Judeo-Christian notions that reeked of laziness and compromise. Arthur was reproaching himself bitterly for having let himself be softened up, by Léa as much as by Kevin. It was time to let rip. To punish the assholes from Le Petit Lutetia along with everybody else whose conceited indifference rendered them blameworthy, culpable, unforgivable. It was no longer the time for discussion, for persuasion, for begging. It was time to strike. That was how evolution in the natural world worked: resist the invasive species, eradicate the ones hindering life, destroy the destructive ones. If the system wasn't ever going to change, it would have to be broken. And if that could be done soon enough, there would still be a chance to save nature from humanity, and humanity from itself. In any event, it was the only possible route. There was no time for hesitation.

To start with, Arthur filed his counterclaim with the judge and sent a claim based on ecocide to the prosecutor. He posted the two documents, whose texts were not dissimilar, to his blog, accusing Monsieur Jobard of causing serious and irreversible damage to the plateau's ecosystem. The legal submissions overflowed with agronomic references and politico-philosophical arguments. Arthur was mindful that the legal system would likely dismiss the matter and made sure to notify local and international media outlets of his claims, both by letter and by email. All he could do was hope that one evening, in a news bulletin following the rest of the day's stories, a journalist less harried than his colleagues would take seriously this declaration of war by earthworms against farmers.

Arthur had not the slightest regret. Maybe Jobard was a good guy, as Léa had suggested. So what? How many good guys had swelled the ranks of idiots responsible for subjugating the peasantry with impunity, burning witches at the stake, enslaving the Blacks, exploiting the workers, exterminating the Jews, and driving out the indigenous? Good guys are just criminals who can't come to terms with the fact. Jobard felt some remorse, he had sensed the mood of the times, he was going through the motions to show willing, no longer using one or two pesticides. Truth be told, though, nothing was less rational than sustainable agriculture. It was the banner waved by those who knew what had to be done and were pretending to do it. Arthur would almost have been more sympathetic toward a good old grain producer from the plains who was genuinely convinced of the benefits of chemicals.

Jobard was not the only one. No question. But he would pay for the others. No quarter given.

In a hurry to share his rage and foment his revolutionary plans, Arthur had started hanging out with Salim. Although to begin with, admittedly, it was by default. He was staying away from Léa, who, in any event, was keeping her head down after the government's launch of a public campaign targeting naturopathy, which required digital platforms to block or to remove any reference to almost all practitioners. Maria was a changed person since the police had paid her a visit and was no longer interested in any talk about overturning anything or hearing about any alternatives to anything else. Matthieu had been reined in by his wife, who suspected something was up in the ashram and so kept him at home every evening where he consoled himself gaming. As for Louis, age was getting the better of him, as he himself said. The gang from La Lanterne had officially disbanded. The earthworms had been caught up in the great plow of the established order.

Only Salim had not changed his tune. He continued his tireless preaching for the abolition of capitalism and had, triumphantly, broken through the one hundred followers' barrier. It was apple season so he was busy in the orchards, but he would drop by the farm at sundown. Arthur would bring out the homemade cider brewed every year by Louis, who then distributed any surplus to a few acquaintances in the village ("provided you bring me back the bottles"). There was no danger of getting drunk. The cider lent itself perfectly to long conversations about politics, even if Salim, who was doing in his back lugging jute sacks around all day, was starting to feel a certain resentment toward both apples and their by-products.

Arthur was quickly forced to admit that he had totally underestimated Salim, which he put down to age-old prejudices relating to class, race, you name it. Somewhere between tweets, Salim had developed an encyclopedic knowledge in the narrow but inexhaustible field of revolutionary thought. More particularly, he had carved out his own path, shifting from one undercurrent to another with application and rigor. He had abandoned the Trotskyism of Pierre Lambert for the Critical Theory of the Frankfurt School, judging it to be better adapted to the world of modern labor in which the subject is responsible for his or her own alienation, moving on to his current favoring of Hartmut Rosa, whose calls for a "slow down" resonated with him. He had then discovered the political ecology of Ivan Illich and André Gorz, which enabled him to reframe the question of exploitation of the land in relation to the world more generally. Reification of the worker went hand in hand with exploitation of nature as an inert raw material. The fight against bureaucracy and the rehumanizing of intersubjective exchanges were becoming preconditions to the eradication of productivism and the emergence of a true ecology. "That's where my drift to libertarianism started," he confided in Arthur, deadly serious.

Salim's current spiritual father was Murray Bookchin. Arthur was ashamed to acknowledge he had never heard of him. He had spent too much time in the company of Montaigne and Marcus Aurelius. Salim lent him a few, already considerably dog-eared, books that he had picked up from the very sparse anarchist network in Normandy. He felt all the more aligned with Bookchin given that his ideas had largely informed the libertarian municipalism of the Kurdish separatist movement, the PKK, to the point of steering the organization of autonomous villages in Rojava. Even though he had never set foot in Turkey, and had inherited neither its language nor its nationality, Salim could only sympathize with the oppressed minority in his parents' country.

Salim spoke slowly, weighing each of his words and citing his sources. As is so often the case with autodidacts, he seemed anxious about mangling a name or misrepresenting a concept. He was as scrupulous in his expression as he was impulsive in his endless tweets. He was a rabid follower of political affairs, including knowing the details of parliamentary debates, and never missed an opportunity to express his disagreement. He had his own theory for it: "perpetual attack." Power would inevitably collapse of its own accord as a result of being constantly subjected to a barrage of rage from around the country.

In Bookchin, Arthur found the doctrinal structure he was lacking. The concept of social ecology brought together an absolute respect for nature and maximum decentralization of the decision-making process, with the municipality or city being the critical level of society. There would be no more nation-states, only self-managed assemblies operating in direct democracy. For all that, Bookchin didn't reject technology or advocate for a universal return to the land, nor was he suggesting that the entire human species should commit hara-kiri. He considered that humanity needed to organize itself according to its natural tendencies, namely, by association, consensus, and mutual assistance. In the same way that nature tended intrinsically toward freedom, individual emancipation could only result from a harmonious relationship with the environment. To be integrated with one's ecosystem was also to construct the optimal form of sociability. Far from stifling them, communities would thus foster the emergence of individual personalities. This anarcho-pastoralism was a good match with Arthur's life philosophy. He would have been perfectly able to apply it to Saint-Firmin, having first rid himself of the Jobards and any other parasites.

Running parallel with the development of his theoretical beliefs, Salim already had an entire background of activism to his credit. He had swiftly abandoned traditional unions, including the most hardline of which, under the pretext of changing the world, would fold at the first wage increase. He had attended the meetings of a few anticapitalist parties, enough to make him realize they wanted to assume power rather than abolish it. He would gladly have joined an organized group protesting development had there been one in the area. Alas, Norman pastures hardly lent themselves to revolution. He had also considered joining the black bloc protesters in Caen, but the thought of finding himself with an iron bar in his hands terrified him. So he had become involved with countless small eco-anarchist groups. Those he hadn't left of his own accord had dissolved themselves as a result of violent internal disputes. Salim had concluded that the propensity to break up was inversely proportional to any actual ability to influence. And so he found himself these days lacking any structure even remotely collective. He had given up haranguing the other seasonal laborers during their lunch break, as he had done initially. His convictions always earned him the most challenging picking conditions. He would be sent to those hillside orchards where the apples would roll all the way down the slope.

In Arthur, Salim had at long last found a temperamentally well-matched comrade in arms, peaceful and dependable. Not some adrenaline-seeking degenerate. "Two people is the start of something," he would repeat, mysteriously.

Arthur's agitation had exacerbated his tinnitus. But far from driving him to despair, the ringing now acted as a stimulant, urging him to action. For the time being, any such action was limited to writing his blog. He had turned it into an almost exclusively political platform. Advice on mulching now made only sporadic appearances among his anarchist-leaning diatribes. He would develop his arguments, systematically replying to his ever-increasing subscribers. He had certainly lost a few grandmas along the way who used to consult *Even a Worm Turns* as an alternative to the Rustica Project, but little by little, he was winning over a whole eco-libertarian community looking for a voice, and for whom his status as a defrocked agricultural engineer was worth any number of medals.

As for the farm, Arthur was concentrating his efforts on the kitchen garden. Little by little, he had transformed it into a true market garden that extended over a decent one hundred square meters or so, with a mix of greenhouse vegetables, mound gardening, and mulching techniques. He had carefully marked out rows using old tiles found in the barn, which gave a rather comforting sense of clarity to the chaos of his thoughts. With Louis's help, he had installed some rainwater tanks that worked by simple gravity and were sufficient to meet most of his irrigation requirements. He germinated his seeds in pots for the first few weeks before relinquishing them to the soil, thereby increasing their chance of survival. He went about methodically applying his AgroParisTech training, alternating crops according to the special features of each group of plants: leaves, seeds, or roots. He had not gone down the very fashionable agroforestry path, instead contenting himself with well-proven techniques. With La Lanterne no longer able to move all his produce, he now supplied the Caen Biocoop organic market with fresh products once a week. His reputation was growing in the area, to the point where strangers would sometimes stop by to purchase cabbages, potatoes, or carrots directly from the farm. With almost no costs and largely insignificant personal expenses, Arthur considered himself, if not rich, at least prosperous; in any event, able to meet his needs.

The Biocoop was encouraging him to register as a grower to allow them to regularize their contractual relationship; even Maria, who had become very legalistic, thought their little black market dealings were increasingly risky. But Arthur obstinately refused to regularize his situation. He had no need for contractual specifications to guarantee the quality of his products. And his experience with the welfare system had been enough for him. The state had ruined and humiliated him. He was not going to pay it another penny. Much like his hero, Henry David Thoreau, who refused to pay his taxes to a federal state that supported the slave trade, Arthur did not wish to contribute to the vast system of citizen surveillance and soil destruction. In his eyes, civil servants were in cahoots with agribusiness, and in league with the farmers' union. There was no way he was going to pay their wages.

Only Maria still tried to reason with Arthur. She defended social democracy. Complained about public services, solidarity, citizen participation, the whole classic conceptual soup of left-wing reformist graduates. Arthur could no longer bear such discussions. He recognized neither the Republic, a mere screen for ruling-class interests, nor the supposed public services, mere lures used to control the population. Little by little, Maria abandoned her efforts, upset by his radicalism. She asked him to come with his crates only very early in the morning in order to avoid attracting inquisitive looks.

Arthur gave up plans to grow any other crops aside from the

kitchen garden, which constituted the essential element of his autonomy. He no longer wished to interfere with the movement of life, even if it would support him. Humans were too fallible, the science was too new, their horizon was too limited for their actions to be relevant. So Arthur left his two hectares of field uncultivated. The forest would end up reclaiming it after several decades and the earthworms would return of their own accord. Given enough time, nature would address the problem that he had almost killed himself in vain trying to solve.

At the start of fall, however, Arthur couldn't help but notice the earthworms making increasingly audacious sorties from their tunnels, their turgescent clitella bright red, illuminated for love like a lantern at a brothel door. One evening, he pulled out his headlamp and crossed the kitchen garden just to be sure. He saw dozens of couples on the ground, so absorbed in their business that his presence went entirely unnoticed. Their tails were still buried in the earth, ready to recoil the rest of their bodies back into the depths at the first sign of danger. However, the interlaced worms no longer seemed particularly preoccupied by their survival. Neither the vibrations of Arthur's steps nor the glow of his lamp disturbed them. Arthur touched some of them with a finger, apologizing for the inappropriate gesture in a hushed voice: no reaction. Only one couple detached themselves with a sucking sound, like two ashamed lovers caught in the act. The others must have considered their desire to take priority over all other considerations. Arthur stretched out on his belly in the middle of a row of scallions, voyeur more than mere observer, curious to discover, in real life, the subtleties of lumbricid eroticism about which he had only a theoretical and rather vague knowledge.

What struck him initially was their immobility. Here were two fine anecics with a brown body, head to tail, attached to each other by their respective clitellum, which was secreting a slimy mucous. Their first fifteen segments were stuck together, with the exception of their heads, which were modestly turned away. These creatures that, ordinarily, were constantly crawling around on the hunt for food were suddenly immobilized. Unlike humans who writhe around in every direction, the worms' segments had stopped contracting and were quietly darkening with pleasure. No stroking, no thrusting. Arthur considered this way of doing things far more judicious. Why did love have to be such a breathless, contorted struggle? Would it not be better served by this placid, languorous union?

Marcel Combe had referred to the homosexual reproduction of lumbrics. Indeed, their male organs must release their sperm into their partner's spermateca, a sort of temporary storage space prior to fertilization. The worms ejaculate against each other, into each other, and preferably at the same moment. But what Marcel Combe had not understood and what Arthur now clearly observed, was the profound unity of the two lovers, forming a new body, over and above any sexual difference. Humans only climax in the back-and-forth movement, each individually. They draw closer only then to draw away. Worms, for their part, unite in a total embrace, with no space between them. Gradually they're covered in a frothy foam. They pull this whitish comforter over themselves to combine into a single organism, neither male nor female. The perfect androgyne, as conceived by Plato. Such an abundance of languor.

Arthur grew lost in contemplation. He had all the time in the world: lumbricid copulation could last several hours. He felt his sex harden beneath him but remained still, his pelvis riveted to the earth. He didn't want the moment to end.

He thought of Kevin. He had taken time to reflect on their abrupt separation at Le Petit Lutetia. Several conflicting emotions coursed through him. Jealousy, with its procession of crude images. Anger, the sort of anger that doesn't dissipate, nagging, impotent. And also, a vague sense of regret, at having left too quickly, of not having made space for the complexity of emotions.

Arthur laid his cheek against the soil. The onion stalks tickled his lips and gave off a gentle cooking odor that blended with the peppery scent of humus. He felt heavy, pulled to the surface like an astronaut returning to Earth. He wanted to be encased, interred, crushed into the organic matter.

He remembered his very first conversation with Kevin. He was looking at them now, right in front of him, these hermaphrodite creatures, choosing their partners from among all the possible worms, with no thought of gender. It was as if a sort of original lack of differentiation was surging forth from the depths of the Earth. "Was this not the meaning of Genesis?" wondered Arthur.

> "Then the Lord God formed man from the dust of
>   the ground
> and breathed into his nostrils the breath of life,
> and man became a living being."

What man was it talking about? A big-balled, single masturbator? Most definitely not: God would not have been so cruel. Especially as he left Adam alone for a good little while, taking his time to make a garden, trees, rivers, birds, and wild animals.

He even asked him to start working. A bit. To look after the garden. In other words, when Eve appeared, Adam was not yet a farmer, but he was already gardening, pruning, taking cuttings.

Arthur concluded that the man pulled by God from the humus was Man before the division of the sexes, Machiavelli's universal man, man with neither wants nor desires. And when Eve was finally created from one of Adam's ribs, God also carried out a little surgery on his protégé.

> "He took one of the man's ribs
> and then closed up the place with flesh."

In closing up Adam's flesh, God had to take the opportunity to fit him out with his genitals. He did it quickly: a pretty clumsy effort. It's hardly surprising if, on the day of sin, Adam and Eve blushed when they looked at each other.

> "And they realized they were naked;
> so they sewed fig leaves together
> and made coverings for themselves."

And then they were heteros. They were bound to have had a hard time of it.

> "Cursed is the ground because of you!
> Through painful toil you will eat food from it all the days of your life.
> It will produce thorns and thistles for you, and you will eat the plants
> of the field."

Which is exactly where Arthur found himself. On cursed soil. Surrounded by thorns and thistles. Everything was becoming clear.

Arthur plunged back into thought. A sort of creamy colored sleeve was now developing around the clitellum of each worm: the future cocoon. It was hardening imperceptibly, forming a protective wall amid the shapeless goop.

After an incalculable and delicious amount of time, Arthur saw the worms start moving gently, sliding up and down, one against the other. Regretfully they detached themselves, bit by bit. Arthur knew what this maneuver signified. The denouement was approaching. With a hasty gesture, Arthur pulled off his pants and buried his sex directly into the loose soil of the vegetable patch. He felt the damp earth against him. He no longer had any thoughts running through his head. He was in a state of complete chthonic ecstasy. He needed nobody else. He was making love with the universe. He came almost immediately, immobile, moaning in contentment.

The worms extracted themselves delicately from the cocoon they had made around their bodies. They proceeded cautiously so as not to damage it. In the same movement, they were going to deposit their own eggs by opening up their female pores and would release the sperm held in the spermateca. Once the worm had withdrawn completely, the cocoon would reseal. Baby lumbrics would start to form inside, in vitro, and with a bit of luck the offspring would emerge from it in a few weeks' time. In the meantime, each of the worms, endowed with its double parenthood, went on its way. They returned to their respective tunnels to recover from the wild night during which they had both ejaculated and released their eggs.

Arthur rolled over awkwardly, his balls facing up to the stars.

"Neither God nor master," he murmured, before dozing off.

XVIII

It was the big day. Posthumus had been selected as one of the "Next 40" start-ups, a ranking instituted by the Ministry of Economics to promote young businesses that would one day take over from the grandpas of the CAC 40 index. Posthumus had even received the environmental award, in large part due to the presence on the jury of Gaspard, who knew absolutely nothing about any of it but whom Philippine had bombarded with messages. The two award-winning cofounders of Posthumus had been invited to lunch at Bercy with the Minister of Economics. For Philippine, it provided the perfect opportunity to settle their administrative issues.

That morning, Kevin put on the made-to-measure suit he had ordered on Anne's advice. Ever since his very dramatic split with Arthur, his relationship with her had firmed up. He had accepted his fate as part of an established couple. Simply put, he no longer saw any alternative. Could he hope for anything better than this pretty, cheerful young woman who used her free time to agitate for a fairer world? He was well aware that Anne was doing her best to appease him. Whenever he felt the need to pack it all in, she would find the words and gestures to extinguish his vagabond flame, much as she had, for so long, consoled Arthur in the face of his failures. The only difference was that she had abandoned even the vaguest desire to do any DIY home improvements and, within the four walls of their apartment, had instead lapsed back into a deeply classical femininity, rather like secretly pulling on some old piece of clothing that was entirely unfashionable but so very comfortable.

Kevin had also grown used to their Parisian weekends: groceries, protests, drinks. He no longer had any objection to the fact it summed up his entire life.

Once at the office, Kevin was primarily concerned with the organization of the stacked vermicomposting lines that were supposed to be installed in the future Limousin factory. The engineer in charge of the project was going to be presenting him with his initial plans. It would be a crucial stage in the industrialization of the worm composting process, leading to a reduction in their reliance on space by a factor of three or four. The earthworms would be moving into a housing project, thereby joining the ranks of aquaponic fish in their urban farms or Chinese pigs in their concrete towers.

Kevin crossed the open space. He greeted, as he did every day, his thirty or so work colleagues, who had of their own accord assigned themselves fixed workstations, much to the great despair of Philippine, an advocate for hot desking. They ribbed him about the banker vibe of his outfit. Kevin was still looking for a comeback when he heard a commotion in his cofounder's office. He made his way over. Suddenly the door opened and Sofia exploded out of it, almost knocking him over.

"Good riddance!" shouted Philippine from her lair. "We don't need traitors here!"

Sofia grabbed her bag from one of the tables where she had left it and charged off to the lobby with not so much as a backward glance. Kevin wasted no time hurrying after her, much as he had always rushed after wounded animals. He didn't have to go very far. He found her hunched on a step in the stairwell, her eyes dry, trying to gather her breath. He sat down next to her.

"Well, I'll be able to switch my LinkedIn profile to green: *open to work*."

"Don't say that. Anybody can lose their temper. Especially Philippine. I'll sort it out . . ."

"No, I'll never set foot in this place again."

The stairwell of this residential building that had been taken over by legal offices and dentists felt like the backstage area of a theater. Red carpet, golden flame-shaped wall lights, the cast iron cage of the elevator, bad paintings of a bygone Paris. Sofia looked like Antigone stripped of her makeup.

"I told her I knew," she continued. "Of course I knew! To the extent it remained discreet, when it was just small quantities, I could understand and look the other way. I'm not a fool, I know how businesses work. But I can't anymore. Even the team suspects something's up."

"Knew what?"

Sofia looked at him, taken aback.

"Incredible!"

She burst out laughing.

"God, would you look at that face!"

Her laughter became hysterical. Her eyes filled with tears.

"I guess you've at least given me a laugh, the two of you. And as for you, you really are a sucker!"

Kevin held out a tissue without saying a word.

"My poor little heroic entrepreneur," she said, wiping the edge of her eyes. "So, you don't know where the trucks with the waste are going?"

"To the factory . . ." he mumbled without conviction.

"Yes, to the factory, for the photos. The rest are diverted to the incinerator at Thiverval. That's the closest now Guerville has shut down. A half hour tops by road. And once you're there, it's easy street: four furnaces each burning ten tons an hour."

Ten tons. Meaning the equivalent of a year's work for one vermicomposting line, in one day.

"It's a bit different from earthworms!" she continued. "And it costs nothing at all. France! Europe's leading incinerator!"

Kevin knew immediately that what she was saying was true. He felt overwhelmed, but also relieved. Now everything was becoming clear.

"How do you think we got through the test phase with L'Oréal? After that bullshit with the rats, we would have needed another six months, at the very least."

Kevin had never understood how the team had managed to meet the deadlines. He had put that achievement down to new, more voracious worms, and had suppressed his doubts.

"So Philippine, the super businesswoman, didn't hesitate. She went to see the boss of the haulage business. She offered him a sweet deal. It's entered under 'general expenses' on the balance sheet."

Kevin put his head in his hands. He knew the statistics around incineration: more than a ton of CO_2 emitted for every ton of burned waste.

"And since then, let's just say that habits are difficult to break. It's so easy! It means we can meet the needs of so many new clients! Why make it harder?"

Kevin undid his tie, which was strangling him. He felt like such an idiot in the suit, playing some role.

"L'Oréal was one thing; we didn't really get a chance. But now? The amounts going to Thiverval are indefensible."

"How much is it?" he managed to articulate.

"Two-thirds, easily. We've become a laundering business. Or rather, greenwashing."

Sofia gently put an arm around Kevin's shoulders, who was paralyzed. She gave him a jiggle, as you would a child.

"Hey, you're the one who's the millionaire! And I'm the one who's back on welfare. I'm not about to console you."

Kevin's first thought was neither for his investors nor for his clients nor for the journalists, all of whom had been misled. It was for Arthur. His friend would have killed him.

"The fact remains that I can't continue to cover up for you. First, it's repugnant. Second, it's becoming conspicuous. And most importantly, with all the seriously juicy contracts you've signed left, right, and center, I don't see how you're going to stop the machine. Fraud is now just part of the model."

She kissed him on the cheek and left.

"Fraud." Kevin took a moment to associate the word with his actions. It was a dirty word, pathetic, stinking of petty calculations and big lies. Kevin knew fraud was a crime. He wasn't afraid of the thought of losing everything. Rather, he was ashamed. He had betrayed his youth, his beauty, his insouciance.

He walked into Philippine's office without knocking. She was at her computer, exchanging emails with the minister's office.

"The guy with the flying taxis will be at the lunch, too. It's going to be fab!"

She changed her tone on seeing Kevin's scowl.

"Did you speak with that lunatic?"

Kevin put his clenched fists on the desk and leaned toward Philippine with a threatening air.

"Don't worry," she said quickly. "She signed a confidentiality clause. She won't say anything."

"I hope she does say something, and that you'll be hung out to dry!"

Philippine rolled her eyes, as if she were having to manage an annoying and pointless setback. She switched her computer to sleep mode and spun her chair around.

"I had no choice. I wanted to protect you."

"You absolutely did have a choice and the last thing you were trying to do was to protect me. You've been using me since the get-go. For the idea. For the media. For the fucks."

"As to your final point, I think we're even, you piece of shit."

The last time Philippine had offered herself up to him, it had been in that same office, one evening when they had stayed late to look over the monthly accounts. She had positioned herself, bare assed as usual, flat on her stomach on the conference table, tipping over one of her bags of coffee beans in her impatience. She had waited. Kevin had looked at her in disgust. Then he had left without a sound.

"Listen to me for once, for the first and last time," said Kevin, containing his fury. "I'm going to walk out of this office. I'm going to send an email to all our contacts, internal and external, no exceptions. I'm going to tell them everything."

For a moment Philippine looked scared. Then she regained her composure.

"With what proof?"

"Sofia . . ."

"That was burnout."

"The trucks . . ."

"If anybody's responsible for operations around here, that would be you. I think you're going to have some difficulty getting your version to go down. And frankly, who's going to be believed? The guy from the Limousin whose story was a bit too good to be true? Or the nice daddy's girl manipulated by the horde of dominant males around her?"

It took considerable effort on Kevin's part not to slap her. Her face contracted as if anticipating the blow. Eventually, he stepped away.

"That's right," she said. "It wouldn't help your case. You're the one who's going to listen to me now, Kevin. Sit down."

He let himself drop into the swivel chair.

"We're not about to start threatening each other, the two of us," she resumed, her tone sweeter now. "We're friends. It's true, I should have spoken to you about it. I'm sorry. Truly."

Kevin gave a vague snort. Philippine's eyes were alight again and she was staring at him, unblinking.

"Our system is working. Your system, the one you developed. We're now familiar with the timing involved in treatment and compost yield. When the Limousin factory opens, there'll be no more problems. But in the meantime, we have to make do. A few more months, a year at most. With our cash reserves, we'll be able to get production rolling very quickly once all the permits have been issued."

"I don't know what production you're talking about. We've lied. Everything has to stop."

"Hey partner, don't get into a huff! It's fair game. As they say in the Valley: *Fake it till you make it*. We haven't hurt anybody."

"Incineration, it's the worst of . . ."

"Sure! What does it represent in the end, what we've burned? A drop in the carbon ocean. Whereas our project is going to change the world for good."

Kevin curled his lip.

"The world of waste, in any case. That's precisely what Posthumus is going to do. Put an end to all these godawful repugnant furnaces. We can't commit hara-kiri with success just within reach! I'd even go so far as to say, we don't have the right to. Morally."

Kevin felt himself yielding. He would have liked to reflect on this notion. "Morally." At Le Petit Lutetia, Arthur had spoken to him about two types of morality: one of them intentional, the other consequential. But he couldn't really remember what he'd said. He changed tack.

"Why did you get us into this mess in the first place? Could you not just have told L'Oréal the truth?"

Philippine held back a smile. She had won. Too easy.

"If you hadn't screwed things up with the rats, we wouldn't be here."

She drove home her advantage. She was enjoying herself. Kevin stammered in astonishment.

"But you're the one who . . ."

"I wasn't the one who signed off the quotes. Failing to install antirodent mesh was negligent. I don't hold it against you, but you can't deny it. I was the one who was then left to sort it all out."

Kevin had no interest in being hauled back into that game. He chose to ignore her.

"So, L'Oréal, let's agree on that. And what about the other clients?"

"We couldn't have them hanging around on a wait list! In our game, if you don't jump, you're dead."

Kevin searched in vain for a response.

"Honestly," concluded Philippine, "I acted in the best interests of the business. And we both know what this business is worth. For us, and for the planet."

Kevin stood up and paced the room. He knew very well what the correct path was, but he couldn't pinpoint any of the right reasons for taking it.

"Kevin, you're so virtuous, it's why I adore you. Give me a hug!"

Philippine stood up and wrapped her arms about him. He remained paralyzed, arms outstretched, as incapable of returning her fake affection as he was of escaping her embrace.

* * *

In the taxi taking them to Bercy, Kevin repeated his course of action to himself. He was not going to allow himself to be intimidated. He was going to this lunch as a matter of courtesy, nothing more. His parents had always considered politicians with a disdain that was both discreet and enduring. They had never requested voter registration cards, or participated in public meetings, and they carefully avoided greeting the village mayor. What did they have to fear from power, seeing as they owned nothing and had little need for more?

Sitting next to Kevin, Philippine was going over her notes aloud. The minister's CV: parents both alumni of the ENA, the prestigious National School of Administration, an ENA alum himself, senior auditor acting as a judge of intermediate rank on the Court of Accounts, consultant at Boston Consulting Group ("my private sector experience" as he was fond of saying), economic adviser to the prime minister's office at Matignon, centrist representative in Orne's third constituency, respected in his local area for bailing out an auto parts manufacturer, had his moment of national glory tabling draft legislation (rejected) for female quotas in start-up investments, appointed minister in the most recent reshuffle, fierce advocate for CSR policies that were, in his words, aimed at revolutionizing capitalism.

"Classic tech, moderate progressive," commented Philippine.

She had trawled Google to dig up a few personal passions: windsurfing, running, chess. He had written a book, *At the Heart of Power*, which had sold three hundred copies, distributing another three thousand or so himself; every one of his visitors received a signed copy. Other than that, married, two children, a mistress, and hair implants.

"And these are our country's leaders," sighed Philippine.

Philippine had also had Mathilde prepare talking points. Posthumus's figures. The company's targets. Focus points (responsibility, sustainability, inclusivity). Specific sticking points that need tackling. And even a few entertaining anecdotes in the event conversation stalled. Why not mention the rats?

Pulling up in the forecourt of the Ministry, they looked up at the edifice, a sort of giant Lego construction set on pylons, one side burrowed deep into the twelfth arrondissement, the other moored in the Seine.

"I'm beginning to understand why it's called the 'lifeboat,'" said Philippine.

A lifeboat that's run aground, thought Kevin. A rust-colored skeleton. A bureaucratic tollbooth barring entry to Paris.

They went through the security check operated by uniformed officials, then continued down the central walkway through to the courtyard of the grand building that housed the ministers' offices. As they made their way down the gravel path, which was a good hundred meters long, they automatically lowered their voices. The suited male and female silhouettes moving from one building to another looked peculiarly as one might have imagined them to look, wan faces, clutching files, heads full of ingenious tax-related proposals with which to impress the chief of staff. It was like some futuristic city populated by people organizing other people's lives. Kevin felt his confidence ebbing. He had always slipped into any situation with a silent grace, but this felt as if he had reached his limit.

"I don't understand how those chicks manage heels on this gravel," said Philippine with what had to be acknowledged was a refreshing dose of cynicism.

"My dear Kevin!"

Kevin turned. One of the shadowy figures was approaching him, an unsettling smile on his lips.

"You don't remember me?"

Kevin recognized him by his tweed jacket. It was the manager from the BPI, the public investment bank who had refused him his loan way back when. Sixty thousand euros. An amount equivalent to Posthumus's daily expenses.

"I work here now. Helping the state define its investment strategy. We need to reimagine a France ten years from now. It's fascinating!"

Kevin nodded his head, waiting for the follow-up. Was he going to apologize? Express any remorse at all?

"In any case, I'm thrilled you followed my advice. Innovate, innovate, and keep innovating!"

As Kevin took his leave, he just happened to mention his meeting with the minister, which barely seemed to register with the former manager.

"Keep innovating!" came the echo behind him.

Kevin caught up. Together he and Philippine passed through the final security barrier and entered the courtyard. The sky opened over their heads, framed by an array of European and French flags. A meager stand of trees planted in the middle of the courtyard served only to emphasize the harsh stone surfaces of the rest of the place. Three black Citroën C6s waited patiently out front of the Ministry's tall glass facade, together with a handful of police on motorbikes. A gray-suited porter with a white goatee and the profile of a Roman emperor greeted them at the entrance and accompanied them to the elevators. Their steps rang out between the concrete pillars of the foyer. They passed through a vestibule where every past Economics Minister of the Republic peered down at them from behind a glass frame. On the sixth floor, another usher was waiting for them, this one decked out in a silver chain that harked back to the ancien régime. He led them through to a fairly shabby-looking waiting room with two imitation leather sofas and a few cheap prints on the wall designed to cheer things up. Government brochures dealing with public spending in the green energy sector lay scattered about on a scratched coffee table.

"Can you imagine working here?"

Kevin saw from the expression on Philippine's face that her ambition was not about to stop with Posthumus.

"It's a bit like a cross between the post office and an Ottoman palace."

"I'm not familiar with Ottoman palaces," replied Kevin.

They waited. Philippine leafed nervously through a brochure then closed her eyes and crossed her arms as she did the breathing exercises recommended by her yoga app. Not a sound escaped through the padded doors. The appointed time for their lunch came and went. Five, ten, twenty minutes. Nobody came to apologize or even to alert them to the delay. In this place, one bent to the state's time. There was no such thing as a diary appointment. One was simply available. Philippine's breathing grew increasingly noisy, with sudden eruptions of irritation. Even Kevin felt his hands grow moist and his pulse accelerate. He was forced to acknowledge an incomprehensible rising anxiety that had become apparent the moment they had crossed the Ministry's threshold. He was horribly annoyed with himself. He had nothing to fear and little to hope for. It was a courtesy visit between people among whom there was no governing hierarchical relationship, some of whom were in public affairs, others in general civil society. And yet, Kevin couldn't shake the feeling of having been summoned by his boss. It was as if the decor, the ushers, the waitstaff, all of it, had been conceived to force people irresistibly into the state of being required of them: allegiance.

The door opened abruptly. Philippine and Kevin leaped up in a single bound, like two soldiers called to attention. The minister walked quickly past, followed by a gaggle of advisers. He looked the same as he did in the photographs: ordinary. Indeterminate age, nondescript, no obvious flaws. So banal as to be indescribable.

"Bonjour Minister . . ." they both mumbled in unison.

"Come on then, what are you waiting for? We're eating upstairs!"

They followed him to the elevator at a trot. The minister was catching up on emails. He didn't seem to think much of the people communicating with him.

"That guy's such an idiot! And this one, who does he think he is?"

"Are there things you need to deal with . . . ?" Philippine started to say.

"Delphine," said the minister, turning to his chief of staff, "I'm going to need ten minutes on the phone with the PM this afternoon to deal with this ridiculous business about the planned layoffs."

"The PM's the prime minister," Philippine breathed to Kevin.

"Leave it with me," said Delphine.

"He has to understand that I'm not going to take the rap for it on my own. After all, it's his show, not mine."

They all piled out of the elevator, still trotting. Kevin might just as well have been invisible. "I don't give a shit about this guy," he repeated to himself. And yet, here he was, trotting along, too.

There was nothing about the dining room on the seventh floor designed to make anyone feel more comfortable. It was as if the furniture had been thrown together from a period film set, with a

Louis XV console table and a timepiece featuring a golden cherub. The walls were portable partitions, ready for a change of set. In the distance, through the bay window, the same barges Kevin had come to recognize from the factory pontoon in Mantes could be seen plying their way upstream.

They took a seat. The minister was still absorbed in his texting. Maxime, the entrepreneur who had started the flying taxi service between Roissy and the new vertiport at La Défense, appeared, completely out of breath. He and Philippine exchanged a few words in hushed voices, anxious not to disturb the great man in his textual letting-off-steam. A gloved waiter started serving immediately. Kevin looked out to the barges.

The minister put down his phone and sighed noisily.

"So, my young friends, how happy I am to meet you all! You're a nice change from all those fusty old bald guys . . . You represent the youth, energy and ambition this country needs! Now, you, my dear Nicolas . . ."

"Maxime," he corrected, awkwardly.

"Sorry, yes of course, Maxime!"

The minister patted him on the hand.

"You, Maxime, are going to send the nation up into the air! No more traffic jams! Speaking of which, I must ask you a favor. There's an old heliport on the roof here at Bercy. Yes, right over our heads. We've never managed to land a single thing on it. Wind issues, apparently. But with your megadrones, we ought to be able to make it work, shouldn't we? What do you think? It would send a great message about modernity: the minister in the flying taxi! What do you think? It's a good idea, isn't it? And it would be fantastic publicity for you."

"Yes, yes, we'll have to look into that, absolutely."

"Great, excellent, I'll let you sort out the details with Delphine." He took a great swig of white wine then turned to Philippine and Kevin.

"So—earthworms! Excellent! What a box office hit this is going to be! A recyclable box, of course!"

Philippine laughed noisily.

"And as I always say, there needs to be equality between the founders of any business. Isn't that right?"

Kevin had never envisioned his partnership with Philippine in this way.

"Often, men, and I don't say always, but I will say often, men are the ones driving the business. Women bring something else. A sort of honesty, I'd say. No bullshit. You're going to say I'm talking in stereotypes, that I'm just an old fool . . ."

"No, no . . ." Philippine and Kevin protested together.

". . . and yet, that's what I've observed! I'm still entitled to say what I see, aren't I? The left just doesn't understand that. They deny biological facts, it's a very serious thing, you know. Like Camus said . . . naming things correctly . . . uh . . . misfortune comes from . . ."

He turned to Delphine.

"Misnaming things . . ." she started off.

"Yes, that's it. Back to the earthworms . . ."

He stopped suddenly. He was clearly looking for inspiration on the topic. Philippine threw herself into the breach and with stupefying speed started setting out the advances made by Posthumus, allowing not a single pause between sentences in case somebody else stole her opportunity to speak. Kevin focused on his plate of smoked salmon, doing his best not to listen. He wondered if there was something more serious about lying to a minister. He decided there wasn't. Perhaps even the contrary was true: everything was fair game. He saw Delphine consult her cell phone and scribble a note, which she passed to the minister as unsubtly as possible.

"Oh, already!" he exclaimed, delightedly. "He must be in a mad rush. Young friends, I'm so sorry, I have to be on a call with the prime minister in ten minutes."

"Of course, of course," they all assented.

Philippine couldn't hide her disappointment. She had not yet made it to the heart of the matter. She should have cut down her introduction. Responsibility, sustainability, inclusivity: it sounded good but was too long.

"I'm going to have to eat my main course on a tray with my files. What a life! Still, I wanted to pass on an important message to you all. This government is a friend of all entrepreneurs. I'm relying on you to create jobs here, on French soil, and to help us promote the French brand. Of course, if you need anything at all, don't hesitate, get in touch. Delphine will give you her personal contact details. If there are any issues regarding tax audits, industrial relations issues, or whatever else it might be, please don't hesitate. We'll do whatever is necessary. Bureaucracy can be very hidebound in this country."

Philippine received this message loud and clear, her face lighting up at the prospect of speeding up the approvals process. The minister stood and acknowledged them in turn with a nod of his head, careful to say each of their names: Philippine, Kevin, Nicolas.

"Delphine," he added, "don't forget to give them a copy of *At the Heart of Power*."

"Thank you, thank you," they answered in unison.

The minister leaned in to Kevin as he left and in a serious, mysterious voice said, "I'd like a word with you in private . . ."

Kevin felt himself blush.

"Don't forget to talk to him about the DREAL," Philippine whispered to Kevin.

The minister took him over to a corner of the room.

"Look, this is a bit delicate, but I think you know Thomas Pesquet quite well. I'd love to organize a meeting here at the Ministry. Do you think you'd be able to arrange that?"

For a moment Kevin was taken aback. No, he didn't know Thomas Pesquet quite well. And no, he couldn't organize anything. Moreover, he couldn't imagine a minister having the slightest bit of difficulty tracking down somebody's phone number.

"Yes, of course," he heard himself answering.

"Excellent!"

"I also wanted to alert you to the fact that we're waiting on an authorization from the Regional Directorate for the Environment, Development, and Housing for our vermicomposting megafactory in the Limousin . . ."

It was Mathilde who had suggested using the term "megafactory." And using it exclusively when talking with politicians, local and national. For the press, it was better to say: "composting site."

"Ah, the DREAL! Nightmare! You're right to put me on notice. Send the details to Delphine and I'll speak to my colleague for the Environment. It's a promise!"

The minister escaped into the corridor as a waiter put a metal cloche over his steaming plate and placed all of it onto a tray. Before returning to his seat, Kevin walked over to the far end of the room and stuck his forehead to the bay window. He heard the conversation at the table sounding suddenly cheerful, less constrained. He spotted a barge on the Seine with a load of sand. He pictured the bargeman at the helm, well-accustomed to this orderly but no less impressive task of transporting his cargo beneath the bridges of Paris. Noiselessly moving through the heart of the capital. Aiming between the arches. Ignoring the tourists' ridiculous waves. Glancing up at the monuments from below. A time and a place where dreams could flourish and imaginations run wild.

And what about his own purpose in life now? Was this what it amounted to? Arranging a meeting between a time-poor government representative and a celebrity astronaut. Philippine would probably say the future of earthworms was at stake. He sighed and went back to his seat for the cheese course.

XIX

One morning, Arthur found out, via a text from Salim, that the *Ouest-France* newspaper had published extracts of his legal claim under the heading: "J'accuse! An Agro in agri-land!" The full version was available online. The newspaper was not taking sides but had presented Arthur's battle as a matter to be taken seriously. More than three months after sending his missives, Arthur had given up expecting anything to come of it. He had to concede that regional publications still had an ability to resist the neoliberal machine, to use Salim's words. The news circulated on social media throughout the morning. Arthur was swamped with messages of support sent by everybody in the area. He was under no illusions: Jobard must have received the same messages. Normans are a prudent people.

At noon, Agence France-Presse issued a dispatch: "First claim for ecocide filed against an individual." An hour later, most national newspapers had picked up the story on their websites, quoting AFP more or less directly. Salim hurried over to the farm.

"It's going off!" he shouted.

This was the moment he had been waiting for his whole life. He requisitioned the downstairs room to use as a crisis management HQ, fired up his old PC, which sounded like a washing machine, and declared hostilities open. He changed his social network profiles to describe himself as Arthur's spokesperson, tagged every journalist following the story and managed to be retweeted by some of them. He was smart enough to clear his own history.

"We don't want to detract from the story," he explained to Arthur. "When the time's right, we'll expand the discussion."

Arthur started to see the names of former friends from Paris and fellow agricultural engineers pop up on his cell phone. Their congratulations were better expressed but more sarcastic. Arthur was becoming the "Che of worms" or "the David of Normandy." It was as if he had suddenly reappeared on Earth's surface, having been washed clean of his stains by the grace of the media. Now it had been posted on *Le Monde*'s newsfeed, his radicalism was legitimized. Kevin was the only person not to have reached out. Without admitting as much, Arthur was hoping for some sort of sign, if only for the satisfaction of ignoring it. Nothing appeared. Arthur had been famous for a few hours but was still just as lonely.

In the late afternoon, Jobard started up his tractor and gave every appearance of getting on with his winter plowing, even though it was much too early in the season. He wanted to prove to Arthur, to the rest of the world, and probably also to himself that nothing had changed, nor would it ever change. Arthur took a few photos. The dust rising in thick clouds behind his machine was evidence of his crime. Healthy soil does not fly up in a thousand pieces at the first strike of the plowshare.

A journalist from *Le Point* magazine, smarter than the others, had worked out who Arthur's father was and had sought a comment from the great human rights defender. "It's a very noble cause," he had replied. "Alas, from a legal point of view, there's nothing in it." That quote, too, gained traction on the web, amid a thousand other harebrained theories. One of the most popular described Arthur as a left-wing radical academic, currently on sabbatical and seeking to discredit conventional agriculture with a view to nationalizing farmers' property.

In the days and weeks that followed, Arthur and Salim worked on building their community, which naturally came to be known as "the earthworms." Apple season had ended, so Salim had moved in, going back to his parents' place to sleep. He remained glued to his screen from morning to night, only getting up to stoke the fire in the hearth. He replied methodically to the thousands of messages received through the "contact" link on Arthur's blog and organized regional action teams. He identified the most motivated sympathizers and called them individually. The explosion in the number of political parties allowed him to recruit willing people from all sides. He was also in contact with a whole bevy of heads of nonprofits looking to get Arthur involved in their respective causes. Salim listened to them all but promised nothing to anyone.

For his part, Arthur fed his blog with very targeted posts and accepted requests for interviews on an almost daily basis. He always gave the same answer: ecocide, earthworms, justice. He followed Salim's advice to the letter. "Don't try to be clever. Stay focused on the message. Repeat, repeat, repeat."

Arthur even earned a portrait of himself on the back page of *Libération*, which of course appeared with the heading "Even a Worm Turns." The newspaper sent over a photographer, a "photographer of some renown" as specified by the email. Arthur and Salim set strict parameters. The photograph was to be taken outside and in front of the offending field. On a day when the weather was bad, if possible. And no smiling. They didn't want Arthur turned into some laughable, neo-rural romantic joker by the whole exercise. What was required was a tough, somber, controversial image.

Arriving at Saint-Firmin, the photographer looked well and truly sheepish. His Dr. Martens were not made for the winter sludge, nor was his canvas jacket with its white stripes made for the Norman drizzle. He started by complaining bitterly that his assistant hadn't been able to make the trip; the paper would only pay for one round-trip ticket, not two.

"It's the crisis facing the press," muttered the renowned photographer battling the wind as he tried to set up his reflectors.

Arthur and Salim watched him struggle, hostile, saying nothing.

"We don't have much time for this," ventured Salim.

Cursing, the renowned photographer abandoned his reflectors.

"Matter for you, I guess, if you're happy for me to shoot you with a filthy look on your face."

That was exactly their intention. To give the eco-bourgeois socialist *Libé* readers who'd never set foot in the country a look at their filthy dials. Force them to face up to their intolerable hypocrisy.

"Guys who get off on earthworms," continued the renowned photographer, "they're their own sort of special. I shot another dude like that a year or two ago."

Arthur stiffened.

"Yeah, good, a dark look, like that. May as well run with it as far as we can."

The renowned photographer didn't persist for long. The rain was carving channels in his greasy hair, and he was shivering with cold. He took a few more shots and then took off, taking great strides in a vain attempt to avoid the puddles. His steps made a spongy sound.

"He'll wear rubber boots next time," laughed Salim.

The rushed headshot, which would do the rounds largely due to a lack of any other photos of Arthur, would provide him with the image he was still missing: that of the furious farmer.

At Salim's encouragement, Arthur drafted a manifesto of about a dozen pages that skillfully combined the soil issue with the question of political oppression. After describing with a certain degree of agronomical precision the tragedy of the lumbrics' disappearance, and denouncing the administrative aggressions to which he had been subjected, he expanded his arguments to encompass a greater degree of generalization. Refusing to reduce the environmental movement to a calculation of carbon emissions, he deplored humanity's impact on intricately balanced ecosystems, which had the effect—and at an extraordinary rate—of undoing tens of millions of years of natural evolution, at least since the Cretaceous-Paleogene extinction, the most recent mass extinction event. He was equally critical of humans' influence over their fellow humans, steering clear, nonetheless, of neo-Marxist platitudes about exploitation. The fact was that everybody exploited everybody else, across race, gender, and class.

"Ecocide," he wrote in his first draft, "is not limited to animals. It's happening with the same violence to humans, culling any sort of originality, undermining spontaneous cooperation, stifling any joy. We're concreting over our hearts as well as our land. Society is planting human beings in nice straight rows that are kept weed-free by glyphosate. Legislation is our herbicide, the market our plow. We fell old trees much like we send our parents into nursing homes; we pull out weeds as we jail people living on the margins of society; we fence in land as we install barriers at railway stations and cameras in the streets; we stuff our fields full of fertilizer as we gorge ourselves on useless information; we cage our chickens as we make employees clock on and clock off; we attach stakes to our young seedlings as we discipline children in school. Single-crop farming extends across our landscape as much as in our own heads. Traceability and identification procedures are two sides of the same obsession with labeling. We want to control everything, nature and human beings, because we're no longer in control of ourselves." And so, it went on.

Arthur then proposed a new ethics, linking the eco-anarchism with which he was aligning himself to the traditional themes of Stoic philosophy. "The first moral act of a free woman or man is to distinguish, as Epictetus advocated, the essential from the nonessential. To define what is sufficient and to forgo the rest. The second moral act is to disobey the law, deliberately and over the long term. To break the bonds of allegiance that we cover up by calling them the social contract. The third moral act is to reeducate the senses in order to communicate with our surrounding natural world. Once these three foundational actions have been accomplished, the rest will follow of its own accord."

Arthur concluded by setting out the conditions of a collective transformation, formulating a vague call to action. "All together" and so forth. He was quite pleased with the result.

"It's not bad," said Salim, reading over the text, "but you'll need to remove the technical terms at the beginning, and also the names of those philosophers, you'll lose everybody. The most important thing is to give them something more solid at the end."

His authorial self-esteem mildly ruffled, Arthur defended the need for precision. The need for correct terminology and accurate references.

"You can't assume people are idiots. You can be revolutionary without having to compromise on rigor."

"Sure," agreed Salim, "but take another look over that last part, at least. *All together* we'll do what? Flatten all the GMO crops? We're way beyond that! We need to smash the system!"

Arthur conceded the point and added a final paragraph. "I call on all remaining earthworms, those left in this country of ours who still have a clear conscience and a valiant spirit, those who have no desire to renounce their own inherent humanity or the natural world around them, I call on them to join forces with us. Ignored, humiliated, and crushed today, tomorrow we will be hailed as the artisans of renewal. Wherever our land, we must emerge from our tunnels, our leaf mulch, our holes, and destroy the machine that is crushing us. We don't have much time. But we have the best of all allies and the most irrefutable of arguments: *life*."

"Better! I'd just get rid of the part about conscience and spirit. Sounds a bit Catholic. And then . . ."

Arthur rolled his eyes. He wasn't used to being lectured about his writing.

". . . you need to whip people up a bit at the end."

Irritated, Arthur bashed out: "Long live life and love, death to the living dead!"

"You happy with that now?"

"Perfect. Almost 1–2–2."

"What?"

"The perfect sequence of syllables for a slogan. Gives it rhythm. Half note, eighth note, eighth note, and back to the beginning. Long . . . live life . . . and love! Death . . . to the . . . living dead! Well, it's almost there."

"You try and do better!"

Salim and Arthur chanted together for a good minute. Two was already a small crowd. It gave them goosebumps.

* * *

Arthur's posting of the manifesto on his blog prompted only a few responses in the media, despite Salim's persistent retweeting. The text was both long and radical, two good reasons for journalists to ignore it. And soon the press had already moved on to the next big story: the Minister for the Environment's use of a private jet to go on vacation, allegedly justified on the grounds that it was the only way he "would be able to get back to Paris at the drop of a hat."

The manifesto was, however, gaining considerable traction, and quickly, on social media. Salim counted more than 500,000 views on the blog page in a single week. A few romantics took Arthur's injunction to join him at his word and fetched up at Saint-Firmin. First one, then two, and in the end a good dozen.

They included all sorts: retirees from the civil service who'd participated in the protests of '68 and who were now reliving their hippie years, outgoing executives craving purpose, students using their gap year to do some WWOOFing, moving from one farm to the next, welfare cases looking for a roof over their head. Arthur was initially reluctant to take them in but Salim reminded him that an anarchist worthy of the name couldn't shelter behind the bourgeois notion of private property. "All the same, it's my home," grumbled Arthur, who did manage to negotiate a strict separation between his living room and the barely heated outbuildings into which the self-proclaimed "earthworms" crammed themselves.

All of them wanted to help, but in midwinter all the vegetable patch needed was a chance to rest, while any internal work required skills that, as soon became apparent, the executives and WWOOFers were lacking. Some of them left, to be quickly replaced by new arrivals. After exhausting the possibilities for taking a walk and available topics for conversation, boredom quickly set in. They were reduced to playing cards as if they were in barracks and pooling a kitty for groceries, "each according to their means." Which was as much to say that the communal meals remained frugal. Everybody had counted on the generosity of the retirees from '68 who contributed, however, less than expected given their frequent absences for the purpose of secretly exploring the region's gastronomic restaurants.

The wanderings of these semivagrant earthworms in Saint-Firmin brought on the winds of panic. The "plateau's protesters" were the sole topic of conversation among locals bumping into each other at La Lanterne. Maria did all she could to fan her customers' malicious views. "I've always said it would turn ugly up there," she explained to anybody who cared to listen. Even Matthieu and Louis had distanced themselves. They felt they'd been duped by this Parisian who had pretended to be one of them and who had, in the end, done what they themselves would never do: attract attention.

One incident in particular turned the locals hostile once and for all. Jobard woke to discover the front wall of his farm slathered in childish slogans: "Old fart Jobard," "Farmers = polluters," "pesticide ecocide." Despite the sympathy some may have felt for Arthur's cause, this public attack brought the villagers out swinging in solidarity. Faced with an external threat, they were accustomed to putting their quarrels to one side and sticking together. Jobard refused to involve the police. This apparently magnanimous attitude only increased tensions. The lack of action on the part of the authorities meant taking justice into their own hands.

Anxious about all this negative energy, it was Léa who proposed a mediation to salvage the situation. She turned up at the farm. From the moment she saw Arthur buried in the Chesterfield, face drawn, beard bushy, she realized the situation had deteriorated considerably since their last conversation. She didn't try to reason with him, or convince him of anything in particular. She simply offered to help. She stopped by several times a day to this phalanstery that had come adrift. With the sweet-natured authority that came so naturally to her, she imposed a set of more reasonable visiting hours on Salim and managed the little group as best she could, creating some semblance of organization and division of labor. Back in the village, and in the company of her clients, she was reassuring; there was no need to get worked up about the band of idealists. They were mindful of the anger they had stirred up and wouldn't be starting up again.

Léa didn't believe a word of what she said. She had a real sense that Arthur had passed some invisible point of no return. He was now operating in a universe that was new to him, a somber, serious, uncompromising world from which there would be no turning back.

Salim was contacted through his networks by activists from Extinction Rebellion. They insisted on a meeting with Arthur, "face to face, with no telephones in the room." Salim was hesitant. Arthur was fearful after the business with the graffiti. He took the matter in hand and agreed the time and date himself.

Displaying a punctuality that was quite remarkable to these merry activists, two Bonnie-and-Clyde-like envoys appeared at the farm door, a young man and woman. They could barely have been twenty years old and were dressed very conservatively. His hair was nicely groomed, she wore a woolen beret. No tattoos, no piercings, no ponytails, not even a little goatee. Serious faces. Seeing them, Arthur realized he was their senior. No longer was he the new generation.

They politely satisfied themselves that Arthur's telephone had been put away and came straight to the point, without even taking the time to introduce themselves. They spoke with an outdated affectation, maintaining the formal use of address with Arthur that bothered him but that nonetheless he felt obliged to reciprocate.

"Are you familiar with Extinction Rebellion?" Clyde began.

"Of course."

"We've followed your cause with great interest. You're the face of a movement needing visible representation."

Arthur felt flattered. From Saint-Firmin, he was not in a position to assess the true extent of his influence. Had this not been his dream since the beginning: to become a guru?

"You've gathered a community ready to follow you. The difficult question you must now address is this: follow you to do what?"

It was hard for Arthur to dissimulate. He had absolutely no idea how to answer his band of squatters when they asked him the same question.

"Everyone must be autonomous in their search for finality," answered Arthur proudly.

Clyde did not rise. He was familiar with the theory.

"We'd like to propose a way we could work together."

Arthur was prepared for this offer. He fired off his response.

"Listen, my young friends, if you want to attach yourselves to the gates of the Ministry of the Environment, you're on your own. My aim is not to entertain the gallery with media stunts financed by billionaires in search of meaning."

Clyde smiled.

"We expected no less from you. And we completely agree. That sort of activism is just a screen to reassure the system. The intellectuals and the muckrakers adore us, we make them feel like they can engage at little cost to themselves. From mashed potatoes thrown at artworks to sit-ins on the freeways. Nothing too bad."

Arthur felt discombobulated.

"What I'm about to tell you must remain strictly confidential."

"Obviously."

"There's nothing obvious about it. I'm asking you not to speak to anybody, not even to your friend, Salim."

"I don't see why I would keep the slightest thing from Salim. He was my first fellow traveler . . ."

Clyde threw a querying look at Bonnie, who shook her head.

"Salim has a history," she now commented, coldly. "He has been involved in a half dozen organizations. There's been a cloud over his departure from every one of them, which has involved him venting all over social media and spreading ill-founded rumors."

"He had thirty followers at the time . . ."

"Doesn't matter. He's a security risk."

"You're wrong about his personality. These days, in any case, he has his house in order."

"Maybe, but there's no guarantee that's the case. We have extremely strict procedures."

Guarantees? Procedures? wondered Arthur. What was this new bureaucracy? He reflected for a moment, irritated by the turn the conversation had taken, yet at the same time, his curiosity was piqued.

"All right then," he said, rolling his eyes.

"You give your word?"

"Spare me the histrionics."

Bonnie appeared to hesitate then raised her chin approvingly in the direction of her sidekick.

"Extinction Rebellion," Clyde resumed, "is the Disneyland cover version of a much more serious organization: Extinction Revolution. Our objective is crystal clear: the destruction of means of production that are detrimental to living things. There is only one possible path to achieve this: seizure of political power."

"Are you going to run in the European elections?"

Bonnie sighed heavily.

"I told you he wasn't ready," she muttered to Clyde. "We don't believe representative democracy is capable of bringing about the necessary rupture. The electorate has been alienated by growth. The conscious expression of their will is thwarted by the constant titillation of their desires. Their political lion's skin, as Marx would say, is draped over their consumers' flesh. They say things must slow down but then go out and buy the latest cell phone. Gasoline is the opium of the people."

"So what are you proposing? Tyranny?"

"Our assessment is simple. First, without revolution, there's no transformation: all this talk of 'transition' is aimed solely at preserving the status quo."

"Agreed. On that point."

"Next, if we consider the last three hundred years, a revolution's success is determined by one necessary, if not always sufficient, factor: the number of fatalities. The French Revolution, the Bolshevik Revolution, both involved true carnage. But today's sweet little revolutions, your Arab springs, your colored revolutions across Asia, they're doomed to failure. Nobody gets taken seriously if no blood gets spilled."

"That's what Kojève said about May 1968: nobody died, so nothing happened. But that always felt a little radical to me."

"Humans have slain and continue to slay hundreds of millions of living beings. Is that not radical?"

"Of course it is! I'm the first to say so."

Arthur was irritated that his own arguments were being used against him.

"In order to redeem itself, humanity will have to consent to making some sacrifices."

"Sounds like Christian speak to me!"

"Let me reformulate it in the language of historical materialism: there can be no shift in consciousness without the sudden manifestation of tragedy."

"Sure. Agreed."

"When our revolution is over, Extinction Revolution—which will be renamed Extinction Now—will oversee the destruction of all energy sources: factories, power plants, even so-called renewable energy. See, we have come up with an entirely new revolutionary doctrine. Rather than pulling down the whole edifice, stone by stone, you just need to remove the keystone. Rather than furiously trying to remodel society, we need to create conditions for its reorganization. Bring about a brutal shock. Force humanity to wean itself off the drug that is eating away at it. The withdrawal will be quick. In a few weeks, we'll be able to bring the nuclear reactors to a complete halt, we'll be able to dynamite the dams, burst the gas pipelines, and bring down the wind farms. There is a threshold of irreversibility inherent in the collapse: the more that is demolished, the less one is able to repair. The main game is to preserve our ability to see through our plans to execute the dismantlement. That's what our engineers are working on. The last car must be used to switch off the last generator. One by one, the lights will be turned off, making it a physical impossibility for capitalism to survive. Once the servers supporting the internet are down, society itself will collapse. We'll prioritize disconnecting company headquarters, banks, and insurance companies. Insurance companies will be the first to go! No more insurance, no more risk; no more risk, no more capital; no more capital, no more production. There will, of course, be considerable human damage. Just think, Paris with no electricity . . ."

"At least it will be done," murmured Arthur, who was always imagining apocalyptic scenes brought about by the destruction of the soil.

"Precisely! We mustn't sanctify human life; it counts for as much and as little as an ant's life."

"And the day after? An enlightened dictator?"

"No. The day after, Extinction Revolution will enter its final phase: Extinction Extinct. The provisional government will abolish itself and leave humanity to work things out. It will be chaos, out of which will emerge the worst and the best. From the thousands of problems that will emerge, one hundred thousand solutions will burst forth. Political governance, the satisfaction of basic needs, means of communication, moral standards and beliefs: all of it will be reinvented. Humans will find their place in local ecosystems once more. Evolution, interrupted by the industrial age, will resume its natural course."

"I quite like the idea. A plan to end all plans."

Bonnie clapped in appreciation.

"Nonetheless," Arthur continued, "you haven't dealt with my objection to tyranny."

"We don't believe in notions of self-management. There must be leaders. We call them Predators. When we have brought about the revolution, they'll withdraw from their positions."

Once again Arthur recognized the gap that already separated

him from this generation that had grown up with Andreas Malm's manual for insurrection, *How to Blow Up a Pipeline*. In his era, nobody wanted a leader. People still dreamed of anarchy, and of consensus voting.

"It's a bit like what the Leninists wanted to do with the state. And what happened? They never relinquished their power."

"We've considered that. That's why the Predators will have to make a solemn undertaking to disappear."

"And what, return to their vegetable patch?"

"No. To pass to a state of unliving."

"Commit suicide?"

"That's a bit of an anthropocentric idea but yes, you could call it that."

"And if they back down, giving in to the perfectly normal desire to preserve their state of being?"

Clyde looked embarrassed. Once again, Bonnie took over.

"They'll be killed by their comrades," she explained. "Each Predator will be assigned ten Suppressors selected from the least charismatic members of the group. If the Predator is still alive one week after the launch of Extinction Extinct, the Suppressors will have orders to carry out the deed."

"And who selects these Suppressors?"

"The Predators themselves, each for another. If they don't want to be the only ones to die, it's in their interests to choose well."

Silence hung in the air, disturbed only by the familiar sound of the fireplace crackling. Arthur gave a faint smile. It all sounded like a schlocky science fiction plot. Bonnie and Clyde were standing still as stone. Just as Robespierre had succeeded Rousseau, Arthur realized that the generation of divergers who had proclaimed their ideals with greater or lesser degrees of conceit had been succeeded by this generation of terrorists.

"Extinction Revolution currently has around a thousand carefully and discreetly recruited members per country," Clyde continued, anticipating Arthur's objections. "Every member must be able to mobilize fifty or so sympathizers, aiming for infiltrators inside big corporations and the civil service. Fifty thousand well-armed humans, using surprise tactics, ready to kill and be killed, and able to seize the institutional controls of any European capital. Just look at the chaos caused by positioning fifty or so black blocs!"

"Sure, in any given country. But energy and communications infrastructures are interconnected."

"They are. That's the strength of the system but also its weakness. If a sufficient number of countries fall over, the others will follow suit without us even having to bother with them. That's why our strategy is to kick-start a global movement, everywhere, all at once. There will be a D-Day. Planetary malfunction. And then it'll be double or quits."

"Between now and D-Day, we need to be discreet," said Bonnie. "If I were you, I'd get rid of the graffiti on your neighbor's wall. We don't want the cops poking their noses into our network."

Arthur grudgingly agreed. Bonnie and Clyde, impassive, appeared cloaked in an immutable faith in their mission. Had the cold monster that was the ecocidal state produced human beings who were colder still? And would more humane humans follow in their wake? Would the species one day rediscover its joie de vivre?

They, too, were sizing him up. They were waiting for an answer to the question they had refrained from asking. The whole conversation seemed at once absurd and utterly logical to Arthur, the natural culmination of all his work these last years. What had started out as a game with Anne had become the only possible reality. Arthur had always been reluctant to acknowledge the ultimate consequences of his anarcho-stoicism. Extinction Revolution had done it for him.

"I'm with you," he said, without too much further reflection.

Bonnie solemnly held out a hand.

"Welcome."

"What can I do?"

"The coordination committee has tasked us with appointing you France's Predator."

XX

"I'm going to string him up by the balls!"

Philippine was raging. Gathered around the table were Kevin and Mathilde, as well as Anne and her boss, Lupus, with the sharp canines. At that early hour it was still dark outside, and the downlights rendered their faces pallid. Lupus had brought a bag of croissants, which nobody dared touch. The satirical weekly, *Le Canard enchaîné*, was going to run a story that Posthumus, the government's start-up darling and winner of the Next 40 environmental prize, was burning a large part of the waste it was allegedly composting. The article's heading: *There's a Worm in the Apple*. The journalist was having a field day: "The can of worms has been opened"; "after the greenwashing comes wormwashing"; "so you want to be the early bird catching the worm?" In among the wordplay, however, he had provided accurate and incriminating details: the number of tons involved, the incinerator's location, the names of the businesses swindled. He concluded by applauding an anonymous whistleblower, the person Philippine now wished to string up by the balls.

The paper was going to run the story on its website at noon but, in a display of sadistic courtesy, had made it available to its victims the previous evening. Philippine had called an urgent meeting with the crisis management team where Anne was working. They still had a few hours to prepare a response.

"It's like soccer," Lupus explained. "There are three scenarios and three only. Sidestep, defend, or counterattack. The best tactic is to choose one of them and stick to it for as long as possible: nothing is more damaging than changing strategy midgame. We're going to need a few facts before we can choose your best option. To start with, is the article telling the whole truth, some of the truths, or is it all lies?"

"Well, it's a satirical newspaper," said Philippine, "nobody's going to give it any weight. I hadn't ever read it until now!"

"I wouldn't be so sure. For the page two politics in brief, sure, everybody knows that's unverifiable score-settling. But this is an article on page four. That's where the Stavisky story that brought down the Third Republic broke, and the Bokassa diamond scandal that cost Giscard d'Estaing his reelection, as well as the Penelope Fillon fake jobs story that led to Macron's election. On the corporate side of things, there's a whole host of companies the likes of Bouygues, Pechiney, IKEA, M6, and Elf who aren't about to forget the *Canard*. Given your media profile, I can assure you this will be picked up by the media all over the place."

Philippine abruptly snatched a croissant, which she proceeded to stuff into her mouth.

"So, I'll repeat my question. Does the article . . ."

"I don't give a fuck what the article says!" screamed Philippine, spittle flying.

After throwing a glance at Kevin, who had not said a word, Lupus started once again.

"I would just like to clarify our firm's position. We're a little like lawyers. Our reputation is based on our discretion. And we remain unwaveringly in our clients' corner, passing no judgment. However, you have to be transparent with us if you want us to be able to do our job properly, simple as that."

Kevin started to speak, in as considered a fashion as possible.

"The article is telling the exact truth."

Lupus adopted the paternalistic, frustrated look of a doctor to whom one has just confessed a second symptom.

"The truth!" Philippine sighed. "Do you want to know what the truth is? The truth is that we just received authorization to build the Limousin megasite. The truth is we have tens of millions in investments lined up for our next funding round. The truth is we're on the cusp of transforming millions of tons of waste into compost without producing a single gram of carbon emissions. The truth is we're going to save the planet! That's the truth! And the rest of it, well . . ."

Lupus tapped his pen on the table in irritation. He was rising in Kevin's estimations. In all likelihood he was a crook, but at least he was a very professional crook.

"Philippine, we're not on some television talk show here. We're wasting time. So yes, you're burning waste? How much?"

"Two-thirds, or thereabouts," said Kevin.

Lupus ran a hand through his slicked-back hair. Mathilde let out a yelp of astonishment.

"Good. And do you know who the whistleblower is?"

"Sofia?" suggested Mathilde, who had quickly recovered her composure.

"Impossible," Philippine cut in. "She signed a confidentiality clause. And anyway, it's not her style."

"In my opinion," said Kevin, who had long held suspicions, "it could be that dude from R&D at L'Oréal. The engineer who came to the first meeting. He was asking very precise questions about the worms' absorption capabilities. He was at me about it for months. Then Philippine took over dealing with him . . ."

"I mostly let it go through to spam."

"He must have worked out the figures didn't add up."

"How would he know about Thiverval?"

"It's not very difficult to go have a chat with the haulage contractors."

Lupus rubbed his hands together thoughtfully.

"So the source could be pinpointed to a single client?" he asked. "That's something at least. We'd just need to sort out the problem with L'Oréal."

"I think that would be doable," said Philippine.

She wiped the corners of her mouth with a napkin. She, too, was regaining composure.

"Doable? How?"

"We're on good terms with the director of CSR," said Kevin.

"And also, more importantly, my father is the CEO."

Kevin's neck buckled under the shock, overcome. So, Madame CSR was not just a friend of the family. She was an employee of the family.

"You don't have the same name?" Lupus asked. He, too, was visibly surprised.

"No," she replied, coldly. "I took my mother's name. I want to stand on my own two feet. That's allowed, isn't it?"

"Of course, of course. All the same, it's curious that the press hasn't ever mentioned it. At least, not that I know of."

"Journalists are lazy."

"Not all of them."

"Sure. The rest, the ones who come to dinner at our place, they're obliging. Either way, they all keep quiet."

"So, do you think your kind papa could intervene?"

"For once, yes."

"And that the engineer would stop playing whistleblower?"

"Every man has his price, doesn't he?"

Silence. Some things don't need saying. But Philippine said them anyway, with no concern for convention. Despite the repugnance he felt, Kevin couldn't help but admire her.

"So I'll play defense," Lupus concluded. "A cautious, measured defense, no excessive indignation. Acknowledging up front various poor practices from the past but cordoning them off to a specific case. Exceptional circumstances. A teacher's note, some bad buzz in the coming weeks, and we move on."

"All right."

"Anne and Mathilde will work on the press release, and I'll call a few editors to warn them what's coming. They always appreciate the thoughtfulness. I'd also advise you to explain the situation to your internal troops."

Smiling, Lupus stood.

"Now we're making progress!"

Before exiting the room, he placed a comforting hand on Philippine's shoulder and whispered a parting word in her ear.

"This is absolutely not urgent, but we'll also need to discuss our fees . . ."

Philippine nodded. She was feeling relieved and grateful. Lupus knew how to snare his clients at just the right moment.

Kevin found himself standing with Anne in the middle of Posthumus's common area, which was starting to fill with people. Employees were moving back and forth, going about their usual tasks, entirely unaware of the web of lies Philippine had woven around them, and from which, yet again, she would emerge unscathed, balancing her way confidently and skillfully along the threads of her own making. He didn't dare look Anne in the eye. She had said nothing during the meeting. He could well imagine what she might be thinking, she who had beaten the drum for several months at Sciences Po in support of a draft law to protect whistleblowers.

Already back at her computer, Mathilde called Anne from across the room with her customary subtlety and her very particular sense of language.

"You gonna shift your ass? We gotta put this prezo to bed."

"I have to go," said Anne, her voice emotionless.

Kevin could not see how their relationship could survive this disaster. He had only himself to blame. He felt immensely sad, less at losing Anne than at abandoning his notion of a good life, of enjoying a respectable, straightforward relationship with no drama. He was not respectable, and the drama was only just beginning.

To his great surprise, Anne took his hand.

"It's going to be all right," she whispered calmly before going over to Mathilde.

She could not have said anything worse. Kevin went back to his desk and stared at his computer's screensaver sketching spirals. No, it was not all right. He was not all right. Anne was not all right. The world was not all right.

They were not treating waste. They had become the waste. Nonrecyclable waste generated by the production machine.

For the first time, Kevin made a decision. He did not prevaricate. He did not weigh up the pros and cons. He let himself follow his gut. He was not motivated by any concerns about justice, by any sense of heroism, but simply by a violent self-loathing. He wanted to be the young, luminous blond, as desirable as he had once been. If only for a moment. If only in a dream.

He wanted out from this life.

Kevin came up with a precise plan, which he executed swiftly and methodically, and with not the slightest regret, ensuring each of his actions would be irreversible. He called Sofia. He and Philippine were both authorized to execute agreements. Using a PDF document he sent to her, he was able to waive Sofia's obligations under the confidentiality clause. She didn't hesitate for long.

He asked her for all the details. She had retained a copy of the haulage schedule of the trucks that had delivered waste to the factory as well as those that had continued on to Thiverval. Kevin calculated the extent of the fraud to the exact ton, drafted a brief memo that was as factual as possible, and signed it. He attached it to three emails, which he scheduled to be sent the following morning, one to Philippine in which he formally offered his resignation from operational duties, the other to his team to whom he apologized, the third and final one to clients, investors, and journalists in which he limited himself to setting out the facts. He was not about to justify himself to people even more rotten than he was.

Kevin left the premises without another glance at Philippine. Once home, he went online to terminate his lease, then stuffed his sleeping bag and some clothes into a backpack. After Anne had moved in, the apartment had slowly filled up. Sheets, sofas, furniture, crockery, even light fittings, all these useless items had appeared. He was happy to abandon them to their fate. He imagined them being dragged around for decades, move after move, before ending up in an attic, then a yard sale, and finally a dump. How many centuries would it take for these objects to decompose completely and for all their atoms to be tipped back into nature?

At the last minute, just as he was about to close the front door and toss the keys into the letterbox, he remembered he should write a parting note to Anne. It was the done thing. So he did it, taking no pleasure in the task. Anne had devoted the energy of her youth, first with Arthur in Saint-Firmin, then with him in this Parc Monceau apartment, to sowing the seeds for a stable life. She aspired to a modest happiness, without excess. Was she to blame for having ended up with cranks?

Kevin had never been comfortable with a pen. He was unable to write a word of what he wanted to say to her. He wrote out a few cruelly banal lines, concluding with: "It's going to be all right."

Then he withdrew all the cash he could in twenty euro notes, switched off his cell phone, and walked toward the Gare d'Austerlitz to take the first train to Limoges.

* * *

Kevin's original plan had been to stop by his parents' place. Fortunately, the train to Limoges was sufficiently slow to allow a traveler to have a change of heart about everything. Progressing at the rate of a steam train, it struggled to haul the old carriages with their broad, sagging banquette seats into which one sank rather than sat down. Most of the passengers appeared to be heading home, back to another century.

By the time the train had pulled up at Issoudun station, Kevin had abandoned the idea of stopping by the village. He appreciated his parents but had nothing to say to them. The feeling was mutual. They had tenderly raised a beautiful bird and saw no real point in maintaining the whole charade of maternal, paternal, or filial love. As far as they were concerned, family was an ephemeral concept. They probably also thought their son had been led astray. They had heard talk of the Posthumus megasite, only a few dozen kilometers from their own place, which was already generating controversy. They didn't really understand why Kevin would spend so much energy complicating other people's lives. He had abandoned the world of those just getting by every day and had become one of the bosses. The last time they had eaten lunch together, they had all but called him *Sir*.

Having made it to La Souterraine, Kevin had made his decision. He would head south along the GR 654, which would take him through densely forested hills, along ancient Roman roads lined with oaks and hornbeams. He would pass through clearings harboring the ruins of ivy-covered chapels and bread ovens. He would see salamanders slide past in a flash of yellow. Perhaps he would come across beavers, heading back upstream in the rivers. Crossing the plain, he would stop in front of brown cows who would stare at him as they chewed the cud. In the villages, he would slip between stone houses with their shuttered windows. He would go where his steps took him, as he had done as a teenager.

Climbing the cobbled streets of Limoges, he felt the weight of his bag heavy on his shoulders. He stopped in the shelter offered by the double doorway of a porte cochere and took out everything that didn't seem essential: suit, loafers, white shirts, books, and various other bits and pieces. He left them in a pile and continued on his way: people would help themselves. He was wearing battered sneakers, but he didn't care. He had no intention of breaking any records.

Kevin walked for ten or so days beneath miraculously mild skies. He walked as if he were on the run, his step hurried, as if every stride were putting more and more distance between him and his imaginary pursuers. He stocked up in country grocery stores where, next to the checkout, one could always find items that didn't form part of the store's regular inventory: bread, wheels of Tomme cheese, fruit and vegetables. He slept in gites, spent a few nights out in the open, and was taken in by locals. He had only to ask and doors would open. Not every door, of course, but for the most part, his youth and his beauty were sufficient to overcome any hesitation. In farmhouses, he was offered those leftovers that, once upon a time, would have been saved for vagrants, memories of whom were still vivid. He helped with daily jobs and made conversation. He listened to stories that were sad but not despairing. The business of farming was as difficult as it had ever been. Kevin would drink a toast to the future with his hosts. Then he would toss his sleeping bag onto a sofa or into the straw. Life felt deliciously simple.

Crossing the Tardoire River, not far from Châlus, Kevin

realized abruptly that he was no longer a millionaire. The collapse of Posthumus had rendered the shares he owned illiquid and probably valueless. Only a few days earlier, valuation of Posthumus stock ahead of the next capital-raising round had provided him with a virtual fortune of tens of millions of euros. Now he owned nothing more than his bag and the dregs left in his bank account. He was intrigued by the thought, amused, then relieved. He watched the river rush burbling past, sparkling in the dazzling reflection of spring sunshine. Kevin inhaled deeply, filling his lungs, then spat out a great gob of spit, which disappeared immediately into the river. He was rediscovering the privilege of being nothing. How had he been so deranged as to walk away from all this?

Leaving Châlus, Kevin slowed his pace. He was feeling calmer. With nothing more to lose, he no longer needed to be on the run. He lingered to take in the more subtle features of the countryside and its human inhabitants. As he put kilometer after kilometer behind him, the hills flattened out and local accents became more singsong, like vocal exercises growing to a crescendo. The landscape was warming up its voice.

Bad weather took Kevin by surprise as he came into the Périgord. Wearing only a simple canvas jacket, he lacked even the most basic equipment to spend entire days out in the rain. He still had a few things to learn when it came to distinguishing the essential from the nonessential. Warm, waterproof clothes undoubtedly fell into the first category. His feet were soaked and he shivered in the wind. He knew that one day he would have to return to Paris and face the consequences of his actions. The weather told him that moment had come.

Kevin hitched a ride to Périgueux and from there caught the

train. When he arrived in the early evening on the station forecourt, at the foot of the hideous Montparnasse Tower, he turned his phone back on. Unused to lying dormant for so long, the poor creature took its time to revive. Then the beeping started, unable to stop. Every now and again, it seemed to settle, but as soon as Kevin thought he was getting on top of things, the notifications would resume their crazed pursuit, one chasing the other. After several minutes, the pinging grew more sporadic. Kevin was finally able to call one of his former flatmates from Buttes-Chaumont, who offered him a sofa for the night. Then he sat himself down in a brasserie and tried to match his messages to any information he could glean from the internet.

The scandal had lived up to his expectations. From one day to the next, Posthumus had turned into the abhorrent poster child for greenwashing. The press never sang anyone's praises for free; it reserved for itself the intense pleasure of detesting what it had once adored. Gaspard had come up with an editorial denouncing "green hypocrisy." It had to be said, the whole Posthumus affair had come at the right moment. Sick of applauding everybody who wanted to save the planet, the court of public opinion was baying for a spectacular sacrifice. Far from satisfying those calls or attenuating the public's response, Kevin's widely distributed admissions had only exacerbated the hatred directed at him. One could, in a pinch, excuse true crooks, those who stood by their disdain for society and its rules to the very end. But nobody could tolerate a repentant sinner, at once destructive and foolish, harmful and naive.

The only message that truly wounded him was the one from Marcel Combe, short but sweet: "I'm so disappointed." Kevin hesitated for a long time before replying. What could he possibly write to excuse himself for having destroyed a life's dream? Nothing. He deleted the message, as if, with the tip of his thumb, he could swipe away the sorrow of the elderly professor.

Kevin sensed that people at the neighboring table were casting surreptitious glances at him. He thought he heard muffled snickering. Was he imagining it? Was it possible that during those peaceful days, as a journeyman with the squirrels, he had become notorious, forever an outcast?

Lupus had altered his strategy and moved to counterattack. His target was Kevin. In his different documents, Kevin had stuck to using the first-person plural. All the frauds were presented in the form of a collective decision on the part of the two cofounders. "We." Kevin had wanted to stand by his own blindness and also demonstrate one last hint of classiness when it came to Philippine. Above all, he had been stupid. Lupus had no difficulty drawing out a shameless manipulator from behind the "we." In interviews, Philippine let rip, explaining how Kevin had deceived her, used her, threatened her even. And while he was the one to have sent these messages, it was because she herself had been preparing to talk, scandalized by the extent of the deception. Was not his sudden disappearance the most obvious proof of his guilt?

Philippine had then tried to convince the Buddha and other investors threatening Posthumus with legal proceedings to give her one last chance. The board could fire Kevin, whose resignation email she had been careful not to divulge. More specifically, it could force him to divest his stock from the company for next to nothing. Indeed, the partnership agreement contained a so-called bad leaver clause where, in the event of serious malfeasance on the part of a cofounder, that person could see their shares bought back at a nominal price—namely, several thousand euros instead of the millions of their actual valuation. This strategy would have the double benefit of publicly shaming the guilty party while automatically increasing the number of shares owned by founding investors. Philippine was insisting on the fact that Posthumus's technology was up and running, the megasite property had been secured, and none of their clients had yet filed complaints. This regrettable scandal, which was entirely due to the egomaniacal delusions of one individual, could also be seen as the chance for Posthumus to enter a more professional phase.

The success of this counterattack essentially depended on the response of the Buddha, who would then bring the remaining financiers along in his wake. From the various different messages, Kevin realized that following their meeting at Bercy, Delphine was behind the scenes facilitating the rescue. It was preferable that a business that had recently been supported by Bercy not file for bankruptcy immediately, at least while the minister was still in the job. Discreet signals had even been sent to his American counterpart, thus far in vain. As a final resort, the public investment bank, or BPI, was on standby, ready to intervene.

Impervious to political pressure, the Buddha was in no hurry. So Philippine played her last card. She fronted up at the police precinct to file a complaint against Kevin for psychological and sexual harassment. She did not use the word "rape," but described a coercive relationship that had forced her into submitting to intercourse in the most incongruous places and in the most humiliating positions. She even allowed herself to shed a few tears on the set of BFM Business. She was hoping to force the Buddha into action, particularly in an American context where the victim's word is gold.

Kevin was stunned by Philippine's unbridled Machiavellism. He had not for one moment imagined that Posthumus stood the slightest chance of surviving the scandal. However much he had grown used to the thought of losing everything, he still objected to finding himself coerced into that position. He was sharply aware that he would be spending the next years caught in the cogs of the legal machine, and perhaps his whole life atoning for the faults of another. Running away was not so easy. His backpack now felt weighted with stones.

Kevin did, however, receive a text from Philippine, programmed to self-destruct: *Nothing personal, just business. Love. Ph.* Ten seconds later, the text disappeared. Strangely, Kevin couldn't bring himself to be angry with her. He decided to take the message literally, a love letter. In any case, as much love as Philippine was capable of showing.

All the same, Kevin had to try to reestablish the truth. He called the only person with the power to unravel the knots Philippine had so skillfully tied: the Buddha. To Kevin's great surprise, he picked up after two rings. The sun had just come up over Rosewood Sand Hill, staining the sequoias blood red.

"Kevin! You've been the subject of a lot of talk recently."

In his poor English, which was even more hesitant over the telephone, Kevin set out his version of events. The Buddha had the power to send Posthumus to bankruptcy in just a single email, putting an end to this entire saga.

"Kevin," he said, "I've been thinking a great deal these last few days. The issue is not whether I believe you. I do. I come from the Appalachians, the Limousin of the United States. I saw you immediately for who you are. You're a redneck, a rube like me. A good guy, in other words."

A burst of laughter erupted from the next-door table, preventing Kevin from properly hearing what came next. He pushed the phone up against his ear.

". . . if the others are going to believe you. The answer is no. There's also a second question: Does Posthumus still have the potential to succeed? The answer to that is yes. If it shutters, competitors will immediately appear to fill the space. They'll have no difficulty replicating your procedures. It's not as if you filed any particularly sophisticated patents."

"But it's all built on lies. On bullshit."

"Do I have to tell an expert in earthworms that the whole world is built on bullshit? Bullshit. Wormshit. The job for a guy like me is not to clean up the shit but to use it to grow a few flowers. Capitalism is a pile of trash. There are those who manage to make good compost out of it, and then there's the rest of the world. I think you understand that."

"But where is the justice in all this?" Kevin attempted, without conviction.

"If you wanted justice, you ended up in the wrong job, kid. You should have opened up some agro-ecological micro farm in a dive in the asshole of the world. You turned up with your sweet little face asking for money. You agreed to the rules of the game. So, even if you think you're going to end up paying too much, tell yourself it's still not enough for that most fundamental of sins: wanting to create things in the place of God."

"God or nature," corrected Kevin.

"Whatever you like."

Kevin thought of Arthur. It was too late to go see him.

"You're going to lose money," Kevin threw out in desperation.

The Buddha gave a frank laugh.

"Kevin, really, you know how this goes! You throw money at whatever start-up you like, you make a whole lot of noise about it, the valuation goes up, and at the next investor roundtable, you recover your stake. There's no need for results."

"No need for results . . ." Kevin repeated the words piteously. How long could it continue, this phantom capitalism, making money from businesses that were losing it?

"I'm sorry for you, Kevin. Business is business. My attorney advised me against speaking to you. I did anyway, because it's a beautiful morning and I'm in a good mood. I won't do it again."

At least Kevin could say he'd tried. Now there was nothing left for him to save, neither money nor reputation. He was on the path to disgrace. Perhaps it was for the best. He'd have no other choice but to be free, of society and of himself. Kevin left his backpack in Buttes-Chaumont, then headed off into the night to make love with whomever he found.

XXI

The big day had arrived. The long-awaited message had been sent out by the coordination committee the night before: a thirty-second video, distributed worldwide, about how humus is produced. "The secret to good earth," it concluded, "is rest." Arthur had spent the night on his secure VPN server. Thanks to a complex mesh network for which each section was responsible, Arthur's signal was supposed to set in motion thousands of sleeper cells throughout the territory. According to his most recent estimates, he could expect between one to two hundred thousand Extinctionists in the capital. Attacks on electronic and IT systems had already commenced in an attempt to impede for as long as possible the state's ability to react. At four in the morning, Arthur was pleased to see that his messaging service was no longer functioning.

Over two years, Arthur had managed to build one of Extinction Revolution's most solid branches in the world. There was no denying the French had a talent for covert organizations and knew how to hold their tongue. Apart from the odd alert, nothing had come to light. Intelligence within the territory was still focused on harmless enough calls for climate strikes, which continued to distract both media and politicians.

At dawn, Arthur slipped his semiautomatic pistol into a holster attached to his belt. It was a pretty standard Beretta, which he had learned to use over the winter. His tinnitus, running at maximum volume due to lack of sleep, was sounding a general alarm. He took a few steps outside, onto this land he had tried in vain to regenerate and where shrubs were pushing haphazardly through the brambles. He noticed a few dark patches of earth but attached little importance to them. Then he picked the first blackberries of the season, still very sour.

Arthur was reluctant to look over to Jobard's property. His pulse started racing at the mere thought, his hatred surging, all-encompassing and suffocating. He knew what he would see, where once he had imagined a dense hedge, full of chirping birds: a long graveyard of turned earth, tangled branches, and exposed roots. "The mass grave," as he called it. And he remembered that ever so mild spring day when the police appeared with laborers and excavators to carry out the judge's order. The carnage he had witnessed on his knees, powerless, begging, abusing, blubbering. The sound of wood breaking, of wood crying out. The raucous laughter of the executioners who thought the work was more entertaining than their usual leveling jobs. The smug look of those responsible for implementing the order in the face of the duly chastised offender. The pathetic excuses of the local journalist who hadn't been able to come because he'd had to cover a truck accident in Caen. The night of horror when he had inspected the damage by the light of his headlamp, searching in vain for anything left alive from which he could take a cutting, moving through a suddenly silent landscape, mute in its indignation. The days of bereavement when, drunk with rage, he had sworn vengeance to match the crime, sworn to give no quarter.

Arthur did not so much as turn his head. He set off in the old Volvo. He knew he would never return to Saint-Firmin.

Léa was driving, a map on her knees to avoid having to switch on the geolocation. She disapproved of Arthur's plan more than ever, it was too brutal, and in any event, doomed to fail. Nonetheless she had decided to help him see it through and to protect him as much as possible. Not out of love, or even affection. She considered him a sage, an unreasonable sage but a sage all the same, a satguru, as the Hindus called them, pure and enlightened. She had refused a weapon. She had nothing on her, neither money nor ID. Only an image of Buddha in the form of an amulet.

Arthur watched the asphalt of the highway fly past with an irrepressible anger at the ignorant fools who had devastated the land and with complete contempt for the green bridges intended for the animals' use, pathetic bandages on an open wound. His only consolation was to imagine this same highway in a few weeks' time, once Extinction Now had been triggered. First, nothing, then silence and dread. A ribbon of tar, cold and suddenly useless. Then slowly, cautiously, small mammals, those able to slip under the fencing, would begin to set foot on it once again. Field mice, hedgehogs, stone martens, foxes. To begin with they wouldn't believe it—the Berlin wall had come down! After hundreds of generations living separated, divided, they would once again be able to roam freely over their ancestral land. Then they would circulate the news and whole groups would come hurrying across. Wild boar and deer, impatient, would end up tearing holes in the fencing, and the rest of the fauna would follow. There would be gamboling fawns, leaping easily over the safety barriers. Swallows would make their nests on SOS call boxes, and snails would embellish the tollbooths. Then the vegetation would start to grow back. Ivy would climb over road signs, grasses would slip their way into cracks in the road, moss would spread in damp, gleaming patches. After a few years, things would explode; roots would appear from everywhere to crack open the asphalt. Thirty years later, there would no longer be a highway punctuated here and there by a forest, but a forest scattered with a few remaining crumbs of highway. Like present-day Chernobyl, the sole example of a modern town abandoned by humans and reconquered by nature.

Arthur would not be there to witness this gratifying transformation. He was fully conscious his life would soon be over. Today, either he failed and died holding his weapon rather than in the prisons of a regime bent on ecocide. Or he succeeded and would carry out his duty as a Predator. He had slipped the little white pills into his inside pocket. He would die, like his great-grandfather, resisting.

He took little joy in the absolute certainty of his approaching death, but it was wonderfully liberating. He no longer feared anything or anyone.

Arthur had turned on the old car radio. On France Info, the presenter was growing alarmed at riots that had simultaneously been triggered in several Asian cities, the first to wake up on this historic day. In Tokyo, Seoul, Melbourne, and even Beijing, extremely aggressive crowds had stormed government buildings, catching police off guard. Contrary to what one had grown used to witnessing for almost a century, there was nothing peaceful about these demonstrators. They were shooting real bullets at anybody who sought to block their path. Confusion reigned, compounded by the partial collapse of telecommunication networks. The presenter was wondering about the far right's resurgence when her voice died out in a sputter. Arthur changed stations; nothing more than a crackle. He looked at his cell phone: no bars. He sighed in satisfaction. Signal-scrambling drones had been launched throughout the whole of the Île de France thirty minutes ahead of time. The revolution had arrived early.

"Careful," said Arthur. "People are going to go crazy without their navigation apps."

"They'll still have GPS. It's satellite-based."

"That's not going to give them directions. Nobody knows how to read a map anymore."

Indeed, ten minutes later, the emergency lane was jammed with stationary vehicles. Drivers standing around on the shoulder were waving their phones around, hoping to find a signal.

"Humans. What have we reduced ourselves to?" murmured Arthur. "We're doing rain dances now."

Just before reaching the Porte Maillot into Paris, Léa pointed out two motorcycle police advancing in their rear mirror. Arthur instinctively hunched down into his seat. The motorcycles overtook and motioned to them to pull over.

"Fuck! Accelerate!" shouted Arthur.

"Don't be stupid. They'll catch us in a chase."

"They've identified me, the assholes!"

Léa duly obeyed and cut the engine. One of the policemen dismounted and approached the driver's side. Arthur had pulled out his Beretta and was holding it close to his side, hidden beneath his jacket.

"On my signal," he whispered to Léa, "you throw yourself backward and I'll take him out."

"Shut the fuck up. In your dreams."

Léa rolled down her window. The cop lifted the visor of his helmet. He had a bushy white mustache. An old guy. *That makes it easier*, Arthur thought to himself.

"Do you think you're going to Paris like that?"

Léa heard the click of the safety catch being released. For the briefest moment, the policeman's face froze. Then he picked up where he had left off.

"You're not displaying your Crit'Air clean air sticker on your windscreen."

Léa laughed nervously.

"It's not funny. It's mandatory."

"I'm sorry. An oversight . . ."

"An oversight? We'll see about that!" rumbled the police officer. "It's been a long time since wrecks like this have been allowed into the city. You ought to know."

"We live in the country . . ."

"And you think you're going to come here and pollute us! If everybody did that, the air would be unbreathable."

That's got to be the best, thought Arthur.

"Papers, please."

There were no papers to be had. Not for Léa, nor the Volvo, nor Arthur of course, who was no longer submitting to methods of identification imposed by the oppressor state. Léa started spinning a yarn about her sick mother who they were rushing to visit in the hospital.

"Which hospital?"

"Necker," said Léa, taking a chance.

"I'd be surprised," snickered the officer. "Necker's the kids' hospital. Papers!"

Léa pretended to rummage through her coat pockets to win some time. Arthur was growing agitated. He couldn't spend the morning at the police station. He was expected at Place de la Concorde, the rallying point for the Extinctionists. If he had to shoot to have a chance of meeting up with his comrades, there was no point waiting. Arthur hissed like an angry cat. Léa pretended not to hear the signal.

"So, are they coming, these papers?"

"Léa, move!" Arthur instructed her in a low voice.

At that very moment, the other police officer called out to his colleague.

"Come on, things are heating up in Paris!"

"What about these two jokers? They don't have their sticker . . ."

"Let it go. We've been put on high alert."

"It's your lucky day!" The mustache scowled at Léa regretfully.

The motorbikes pulled away. Léa closed her eyes for a minute before pulling herself together. Then she set off again without a word. Arthur shuddered at the realization that Antares and Acropol, the encrypted national security telecommunication networks, were still functioning. That was not what Extinction Revolution had planned.

Police vehicles had already blocked off the Champs-Élysées, so they took the Grands Boulevards, going past the Opéra and finally abandoning the Volvo outside the Louvre, which had been overrun by the mob. They headed through the Tuileries. The atmosphere was curiously calm. The Extinctionists were all helmeted and armed, ready for war. A smell of tear gas indicated that the first clashes had already taken place. Utterly unprepared for the violence of their opponents, law enforcement had taken cover while they waited for orders.

Arthur and Léa headed toward the garden gates on the Concorde side of the Tuileries. The crowd was gradually growing more compact. As Arthur made his way through, word passed around from mouth to mouth: *Predator! Predator!* People put a hand on his shoulder, encouraged him. *Predator! Predator!* The anglicism now had the ring of a Roman apostrophe. *Predator, Lictor, Imperator!* Arthur allowed himself the pleasure of savoring it. Perched high atop the stone barrier, next to the entrance pillar, a small group of Extinctionists gestured to him to join them. Arthur recognized one of them as the man responsible for coordinating the Western region; he was the only person with his head uncovered. He found a way through to the gravel ramp leading up to them. They handed him a megaphone and suggested he stir up the mob from the pillar. The pillar itself was crowned by a monumental statue, an ephebe dressed in a simple loincloth sitting sidesaddle atop a winged stallion. Mercury mounted on Pegasus. Arthur hoisted himself to the top, gripping Mercury by the ankle. The sensation of the cold marble beneath his palm brought him a brief moment of calm. He raised his head and met the white stare of Mercury, who, centuries earlier, must have witnessed the tumbrels passing by on their way to the guillotine.

Arthur cautiously edged his way around the horse's croup and found himself face to face with a human swell that occupied the whole square and spilled out into the adjacent avenues. The base of the obelisk was covered in slogans: Extinction Revolution, Let's turn off the lights, Life Square. Green flags fluttered everywhere bearing the traditional Extinction Rebellion logo: an hourglass in a circle set against a green background but slightly modified: the circle had been replaced by an arrow, a signal that the time for action had arrived. Arthur pulled himself upright. The noise grew. Was it for him? Really? He brandished a fist. Ovation. That removed any doubt. Arthur switched on the megaphone. He had no idea what he would say, nor any certainty he would be listened to, but he felt carried by an indescribable strength, and the words came out of his mouth without him even needing to stop and think. It was as if he were reciting somebody else's text.

"My fellow Extinctionists! At this very moment, from Paris to Washington, from Cape Town to Moscow, from Buenos Aires to Tokyo, the planet is waking up! Our revolution has finally burst from the ground, like a long underground river rising to the surface, engulfing everything in its path. This revolution is a revolution for life. We are here to avenge the bees, the butterflies, the earthworms. We are here to destroy their roads, their aerials, their factories. We have come to save our own humanity and the natural world around us. Today is the day we leave the Anthropocene behind! Today is the day we give France back to the earth on which she is built!"

The crowd interrupted him with a chaotic clamor. Arthur was astounded at the ease with which he found the rhythm of his words.

"Comrades, this revolution will not succeed with ballot papers, or with flowers. There is no time left for pleasing or persuasion.

We have been given our mandate by the bleeding earth, the depopulating oceans, the yellowing rivers, the dying trees, the disappearing species. Our country is the planet; our language, nature's song; our leader, life itself. Our plan? One phrase: to turn off the lights."

Arthur's tone was prophetic. His rhetoric seemed to be working.

"Each one of you knows the mission you've been assigned. Good luck all of you. Long live life and love, death to the living dead!"

Arthur repeated this last phrase several times in the cadence Salim had taught him.

"Long . . . live life . . . and love! Death . . . to the . . . living dead!"

Little by little, the anthem was picked up by tens of thousands of voices. Arthur reached back to rest a hand on Pegasus's rump to keep from overbalancing. He understood better why Predators had to be eliminated in the Extinction Extinct phase. It is too intoxicating at the apex of the trophic level pyramid.

The Extinctionists dispersed swiftly. They separated out into three groups as planned and moved toward their targets: the nearby Élysée Palace and the Ministry of the Interior immediately beyond it, Les Invalides on the other side of the Seine, the seat of Paris's military governor, and the Senate, a good two kilometers farther along, on the left bank. A more concentrated fourth commando was already at the forecourt of La Défense, working to seize the Électricité de France tower. They would utterly ignore the National Assembly, in front of which riot squad trucks were massing. This was not about Extinction Revolution claiming some sort of democratic legitimacy, but about seizing the nation's command centers as quickly as possible. Once the president of the Republic was neutralized, physically or symbolically, the Senate president would have to be prevented from securing some other replacement. The seat of power would thus be vacant and constitutional order overthrown.

Arthur allowed himself to be borne along by the flood of people heading for the Luxembourg Palace. Having crossed the Seine, they encountered the first barricade. No warning was given. The first row of riot police was decimated, the remaining officers folded immediately with no retaliation. Neither their equipment nor their tactics had been conceived for situations involving real bullets. Extinction Revolution was not the General Workers' Confederation with their harmless balloons, or even the black blocs who were happy to smash a window or two. There was nobody singing here, nobody committing any vandalism. They were killing people instead. It was likely the powers that be, having still not properly understood the nature of the movement, had not yet authorized the use of lethal force.

Heading up Boulevard Saint-Germain, Arthur was hit by memories of his student days. He couldn't help but think of the sweet, peaceful life that might have been, his being the last generation, perhaps, able to burn fossil fuels with relative insouciance, to dance until the party ended. All around him, Haussmann buildings with their comfortable interiors implored him to stop everything, to restore reason, to go home.

A violent crunch interrupted his reverie: a car had been used to crash through the entryway to the Ministry of Ecology. A hundred or so armed Extinctionists now swarmed into the cobbled courtyard of the Ministry building, the Hôtel de Roquelaure.

"Don't shoot!" Arthur instructed.

His order was pointless. A police squad positioned on the

front steps behind some sandbags, likely overwhelmed by panic, was the first to open fire. A couple of Extinctionists fell to the ground. Others answered fire. Bullets crackled like kindling. An explosion put a swift end to the clash: the first grenade. The Extinctionists let out a hideous triumphant cry, no different from any cry of triumph from any other army in the world. They stormed the minister's offices in a cloud of smoke.

"Take her alive!" bawled Arthur, with little conviction.

The only response was the bedlam of broken windows. The ransacking had begun. Arthur imagined the imminent transformation of the vast, freshly mown lawn in the garden behind the building into a temporary encampment.

Arthur looked around. Following his orders, he gestured to his group to continue their advance. Léa was still at his side, dressed for spring in a red dress, her skin pale against the red fabric. It was as if she were sleepwalking. Most of the Extinctionists were masked and helmeted and dressed in black. It was not the well-behaved crowd from the Place de la Concorde. This was a dark, silent pack, ready to rip apart anything in its way.

At the Boulevard Raspail intersection, riot police had erected a deeper barricade by lining up caged trucks. As soon as the Extinctionists arrived, they opened fire with water cannons and sting-ball grenades.

"We're going around!" shouted Arthur, lowering his helmet visor.

They scattered instantly. Those who headed left, toward Rue de Luynes, had no difficulty skirting the barricade, before continuing on their way at a run. The others, heading right, found themselves blocked at Rue de Grenelle and facing street combat with no obvious end in sight. Riot police had entrenched themselves behind heavy bulletproof shields, absorbing the impact while holding firm. Police from the antiterrorist unit armed with sniper rifles had positioned themselves on rooftops and were taking aim at the Extinctionists, waiting for an order that was not forthcoming. Reinforcements were being deployed in adjacent streets to close the trap.

Arthur's troops had already been reduced by half. At a glance, there would have been a thousand or so pouring into Rue du Vieux-Colombier past the bronze statue of César's Centaur, whose enormous balls seemed to tremble at the mob's thunderous steps. Extinction Revolution organizers had hoped for massive support in the major cities under the auspices of their green flag. In Paris, at least, it was far from the case. Passersby fled in panic and shutters rolled down as the Extinctionists came through, finding themselves targeted by people on their balconies hurling eggs and empty bottles. A magnum of Château Angelus exploded at Arthur's feet. The bombardment of messages via the internet before networks were shut down had evidently not worked to arouse enthusiasm.

In the recess of a porte cochere, Arthur saw a riot policeman, asleep. He approached him. His chinstrap was undone and his bulletproof vest half open, as if he had made himself comfortable for a nap. An oily spot on his chest darkened the navy blue of his uniform. His staring expression was that of a child caught by surprise. He must have been calmly preparing for routine maneuvers to encircle a few lefties when he had been finished off at point blank range. By whom? Unlikely anybody would ever know. The random fate of insurrection.

Arthur stood there for a moment, dumbfounded. The policeman's face, still suffused with life, had an affable appeal. One would happily have stopped for a chat had he not remained so still, a little twisted, jaw gaping.

"Fuck!" exclaimed Léa. "This is bullshit!"

Arthur pushed any pity from his mind. This was a man, he thought, who would have had no qualms obeying some distant order to tear down a hedge. He was as guilty as the rest of them, guilty of obedience. This was a real death, and it marked the start of a real revolution.

At Rue de Tournon, Arthur saw the Senate completely barricaded off by a dark blue wall of vehicles, flashing lights, and uniforms. He clocked two armored police vehicles. Now the battle was really heating up.

"Through the gardens!" he barked.

In the rush, nobody had thought to close off the gates to the Luxembourg Gardens. The Extinctionists went in through two different gates with the aim of taking the Senate from the rear. They ran down the paths to converge at the large pond, finding themselves at the back of the building, a veritable palace adorned with colonnades and sculpted pediments. The large clock showed eleven. Arthur gave the signal to attack.

The Extinctionists advanced in disarray. They had no difficulty getting past the low gates, conceived for a Republic at peace. A few dozen meters of exposed path stood between them and the palm-flanked glass doors. Arthur was the first to advance across the gravel. They met no resistance, as if the police had totally abandoned that part of the building. A few meters away, Arthur noticed a garden of perfectly laid out white and yellow primroses. He had time to reflect that these French-style gardens, corseting nature to the point of suffocation, had well and truly had their day. Then he raised his fist: "Long live . . ."

He didn't finish. A hail of bullets fired by assault rifles pelted down in rapid bursts from the Senate building's flat roofs. Dozens of Extinctionists went down instantly. The order had been given.

"Retreat!"

There was no need to say it. All of them rushed back in the direction from which they had come, seeking shelter. Arthur saw Léa jump the barrier in front of him then run toward the pond. He followed in the wake of her great leaping strides, a deer taunting a hunter. Suddenly she lurched backward, arms outspread. She continued on, slower now, carried by inertia.

"Léa, this way!" said Arthur, forking off toward the Medici fountain.

Léa wasn't listening. She was still moving straight ahead. Her legs stumbled against the rim. Her whole body fell headfirst into the pond. She remained immobile, face down in the water.

Arthur didn't hesitate. He jumped into the pond and headed over to her. Her soaked dress was now transparent. On her back he saw her tattoo in the shape of a snake, an eel finally returned to its element. Arthur turned Léa over and lifted her head from the water. Her eyes were half-closed.

"Talk to me!"

Suddenly, she opened her eyes and stared at Arthur.

"I already told you: this is bullshit."

Her voice was surprisingly firm and clear. She then gave a short, loud hiccup, like an interrupted burp. Her face grew still.

"Léa!"

Arthur looked around for assistance.

"Help! Somebody help!"

Nobody answered. Several bodies lay stretched out in the pond, inert, a dark stain forming around them, like ships releasing fuel. A little wooden sailing boat that had been abandoned bobbed innocently about in the middle, near the fountain. Arthur fell to his knees in the water. He no longer heard anything, not the sirens, not the rifle shots, not the shouting. Léa had been his only confidante these last months, his only support. She had been unarmed. The image of Buddha was the only thing she held between her clenched fingers. She knew no evil.

"Léa, I'm so very sorry . . ."

Her expression was stern, full of reproach. This was not her battle. Arthur knew that. It was what made her so pure.

"There was no other way . . ." he murmured, looking for excuses.

Arthur was still caught in a bubble of silence, broken only by his tinnitus, which was louder than ever. He saw circles form in the water around him: a sniper playing at skipping stones. He had no further desire to live, but he had a revolution to finish. He wanted to take Léa with him. He didn't have the strength. He ended up dragging her to the edge and pulling her from the water, so at least she, whose beauty had been so fine, wouldn't be found with the swollen, clown-like head of the drowned.

Arthur ran without looking back, chest bowed forward. He found shelter behind the grotto of the Medici fountain where he was immediately joined by a dozen or so other Extinctionists. They raised their visors in acknowledgment, the medieval military salute. Arthur realized that his presence at the vanguards, like his dive into the pond to help the wounded, had suddenly accorded his role as Predator the legitimacy that could only be won in battle. He decided to forget Léa for the moment. He would do his grieving later.

Among the Extinctionists, Arthur thought he could make out a familiar face belonging to a wrinkled woman dressed in a rainbow-colored poncho. He scoured his memory. It was Arlette, the inspector from the welfare office. He smiled at her. She lowered her head, uncomfortable. Arthur thought she could well be one of his Suppressors.

He pulled a satellite phone from his jacket pocket and tried to contact his various group leaders. Some of his troops were gathered over near the boules pitch, some in the greenhouses, others behind the puppet theater. Arthur gave orders to create a diversion that would allow Extinction Revolution crack shots to take up position beneath the stone balustrades opposite the buildings. From there they would be able to clear the snipers on top of the Senate before the survivors attempted a fresh assault.

The maneuver kicked off. Twenty odd Extinctionists opened fire, sheltering behind statues and trees while the marksmen crawled into position. A swarm of drones flew over the fountain, hovering over Arthur and his comrades who tried in vain to bring them down, before they continued on their way across the Luxembourg Gardens. The sound of gunshots gradually eased. Arthur took advantage of the relative calm to get updates from the other groups. The Élysée Palace had been easily taken: the president, however, was still unable to be located. It was possible he had escaped through one of the tunnels people had always suspected existed. The military governor of Paris had surrendered, but nobody really understood either his role or the point of his capture. The Ministry of Ecology had gone up in flames. And those comrades trapped in Rue de Grenelle had laid down their weapons and allowed themselves to be brought in.

All things considered, Arthur felt he could congratulate himself on a fairly rapid and quite unexpected success. At the same time, he sensed a certain wavering. "What happens now?" was the question he was being asked. Having carried out their mission, the Extinctionists were reverting to their activist impulses. They roamed through the capital, slashing tires and smashing neon signs.

"Tell everyone to get their asses to the Luxembourg. It's a battlefield out here."

Arthur told the gunmen to wait for their comrades, hoping to launch a broader counterattack. The drones continued to circle, rendering hopeless any possibility of hiding. Incongruously, an old lady was walking her dachshund slowly through the gardens, indifferent to the corpses. Some habits are hard to break. Arthur heard his phone ring; alas, the networks must have been restored. He quickly scrolled through the news. The president had made an appeal to the nation from his bunker. The Élysée Palace interiors had been quite effectively restored, including the Louis XV desk, which, in and of itself, had come to symbolize the continuity of the state. In his video, the president was castigating a brutal attempt to overthrow the government, declaring the Republic to be in peril and assuring citizens that the Senate, "the beating heart of our democracy," would be defended, "at any cost." Arthur rolled his eyes. He disliked finding himself in the skin of an ordinary terrorist. He was fighting for much greater ideals than the Republic or democracy. History would prove him right. "I have therefore decided," the president concluded, "in accordance with the powers conferred on me by our Constitution, to declare the city of Paris to be under a state of siege." Arthur knew perfectly well what this entailed, a provision that had never before been implemented under the Fifth Republic: the transfer of powers from the police to the military. Troops would be called in to put down the insurrection. In an hour, at most, the army would have surrounded the Luxembourg Gardens. Time was of the essence.

A few minutes later, Arthur caught a movement over toward the street. Instead of reinforcements, he saw hostile armored vehicles entering the garden. Two large, brand new Scarab tanks. They crawled along, confident of their power. On their roofs, not cannons but a grenade launcher together with a light machine gun, controlled from within the vehicle. The Extinctionists' bullets flew thick and fast, lodging harmlessly in its metal shell and bouncing off its windows. Mindful of the need for urgency, the shooters preempted Arthur's orders and started trying to bring down the snipers perched atop the Senate. Some fell to the gravel paths with a heavy thud. Others managed to take cover.

"We going?"

Arthur shook his head.

"We can't really try to get out of here now," he reasoned.

"The longer we wait, the more chance they'll have to regroup."

"We'd have to blow up the tanks first."

"Don't we have a rocket launcher?"

"No. We wanted to buy some and then, for whatever reason, it never happened."

"That was stupid."

Notwithstanding Extinction Revolution's meticulous efforts to prepare for this day, it was not a military organization. On the ground, any oversights in their planning were manifesting as fatal errors.

"I'll do it," said Arlette.

Everybody looked down. It was a suicide mission. Arlette grabbed two hand grenades.

"Here's where you pull the pin . . ."

"I know how to use them," she answered, dryly.

That's the good thing about Trotskyists, thought Arthur. Were people expecting him to make some authoritative statement? Nothing came to mind, and Arlette left without so much as a farewell, muttering about the revolution's poor management. Even acting the hero, she couldn't bring herself to be pleasant.

Arlette moved easily from tree to tree, then crept up to an oversize flowerpot about twenty meters from the armored tanks and remained crouching behind it. A few shots were fired, although it was unclear precisely where they had come from or who they were aimed at. The only thing now certain was that both sides were shooting to kill.

The machine gun on the first Scarab tank started to swivel toward Arlette. She had probably been spotted. It seemed as if this gunner-less cannon, this soldier-less weapon, was endowed with an unyielding, horrifying will of its own. As much as one might accept being killed by an enemy who will bear that responsibility for the rest of their days, equally, this mindless, anonymous machine pushed the immorality of murder to unfathomable extremes.

Then, issuing a battle cry, Arlette leaped, a laughable yet admirable harlequin. The machine gun took aim. For one or two seconds nothing happened. Human hesitation? Computer glitch? Algorithmic error? Nobody would ever know. The delay proved lethal for the tanks. It allowed Arlette to get close enough to toss her grenades between their wheels. Just as she fell to the ground, ripped apart by bullets, the sound of a double explosion reverberated through the air. In the same instant, Arthur heard a rising clamor coming from the gates to the Gardens. A pack of fellow Extinctionists from some of the other groups had come to join them. Arthur had hoped for many more, but only a few hundred had succeeded in skirting around or breaching the barricades. Smoke billowed around the Senate, hampering the snipers' view. Arthur grabbed the satellite phone and with no further hesitation launched the general offensive. It was now or never. Once inside the Senate building, in the labyrinth of corridors and offices, the balance of power would be reversed.

"Advance!" shouted Arthur, hauling himself upright.

Extinctionists shot forward from all sides. Once again, they leaped over the smaller gates and this time made it as far as the French doors, smashing through them easily. Calmly positioned and waiting for them in the broad corridor were fifty or so robocops from the Search and Intervention Brigade unit of the French National Police, wielding heavy assault rifles. The carnage was swift. The Extinctionists retaliated with their makeshift weapons, toys in comparison with the arsenal of the intervention brigade. Yet still they kept coming, only to be flattened by the wall of fire, collapsing to the ground, one on top of the other. Those who somehow managed to make it deeper into the building were quickly neutralized by police waiting in ambush. Blood stained the marble floor. The bitter stench of exposed entrails started to spread through the place. Arthur, having taken a shot to the shoulder, had found cover behind a stone pillar. He wanted to order a retreat, but nobody was listening to him anymore. It was as if this savage mob were harboring its own ghastly death wish.

Arthur realized things were hopeless. He set off slowly, moving against the flow of the last combatants who continued to rush headlong toward an ignoble oblivion. He raised a hand to his wound: the bullet had only grazed him. He shuffled along, heedless of the screams or the shots being fired. He felt miserable and disgusted. He saw Léa in the position he had left her, already gray-faced. He couldn't help but find her grotesque, a reflection of the entire failed revolution.

It was then Arthur noticed a man who appeared to be calmly watching the spectacle from one of the metal chairs placed haphazardly around the Gardens. He headed over to him, intrigued. The man had long hair that fell in messy waves. His clothes were dusty. One of those homeless men, perhaps, who sunned themselves in the garden, one of the few luxuries nobody could take away. The man turned to Arthur. Their eyes met.

It was Kevin.

All of the bitterness Arthur had harbored over the last years, entire hours spent cursing his friend turned traitor, all of it vanished abruptly. He went over and took a seat next to him.

"What's up with you?" asked Arthur, as if nothing had happened.

Arthur knew perfectly well what was up. Kevin had been given a three-year suspended sentence for fraud and psychological harassment. The sexual element of the offense had not been made out, due to lack of proof. He had at least avoided incarceration, his father's greatest fear.

"I'm getting on with life, more or less," said Kevin. "You?"

A violent explosion came from within the Senate building. Perhaps an Extinctionist, having made it inside, was blowing up everything around him in desperation.

"I'm getting on with death, more or less," answered Arthur.

"We're more or less on the same page, then."

There was the sound of breaking glass and something looking a lot like a senator came hurtling through a third-floor window.

"Waste of time, all this," said Arthur, observing the scene. "You were right."

"No! You're the one who was right. What else was there to do?"

The Extinctionists had at last withdrawn from the palace and were now scattering through the Gardens in every direction. One of them recognized the Predator and came asking for orders.

"Fight to the last," commanded Arthur from his sun-lounger.

"Why did you say that?" asked Kevin, when the other man had left.

"It'll just mean fewer humans."

"True."

Sirens blared from Boulevard Saint-Michel. The racket grew louder. Then the convoy appeared at the gates: fifteen or so trucks used to transport military troops, accompanied by police vehicles. They positioned themselves in front of each of the entrances to the Luxembourg Gardens, securing the zone. Arthur felt his inside pocket to check the tablets were still there. He had never felt so free.

"Beautiful day," said Kevin, tipping his head back to the sun. Arthur considered his face, so beloved and so loathed. He searched for the ephebic features beneath the new hirsute look. One by one, they slowly reappeared. Arthur was then able to switch between his visions of the two Kevins, as if looking at a familiar optical illusion: the one from the terrace at AgroParisTech just letting himself be carried along by life, and this one, in the Luxembourg Gardens, who ten years later had come full circle. He regretted the lost years. He stroked his friend's hand gently.

"I'm sorry about . . ." Kevin started.

"It's my fault . . ." continued Arthur.

Soldiers leaped from their truck and spread out in combat formation, some on the ground, others crouching, ready to spring into action. A helicopter flew past, scraping the treetops with a deafening beating of blades and making Kevin's hair fly up, a whirlwind of hay in the warm air. A voice rang out through a loudspeaker: "Give yourselves up! Lay down your weapons and get down on the ground, hands on your head. You will not be harmed." Arthur made an effort to pull out his satellite phone and repeat to his troops that surrender was out of the question, then switched off the phone and tossed it away.

Extinctionists were running in every direction seeking shelter. Those who still had ammunition made a clumsy attempt to fire at the infantry soldiers who stood their ground. "You don't stand a chance!" warned the voice.

Arthur wanted to get to his feet to respond, but now that his adrenaline had ebbed away, the pain in his shoulder drew a sharp cry. He knelt down, hunched over. Kevin rushed to offer him help. Unsure quite what to do, he laid him down on his side, as people are taught in first-aid courses.

"It's nothing," said Kevin. "I'm going to look after you."

Arthur was overcome by such tenderness. How could there be any thought of looking after him, when he was just going to die? Was it now necessary to make him miss being alive? Kevin lay down in the dust next to him. They looked at each other, profoundly serious.

"This is your last warning!"

Around them was silence. Some Extinctionists were starting to turn themselves in. Among all the bodies lying about on the ground, it was difficult to distinguish between corpses, renegades, and friends mid-reunion.

Arthur pressed himself to Kevin, chest to chest, cheek to cheek, a lost child nestling into its mother. He matched the rhythm of his breath, peaceful and regular. He felt his eyelid fluttering. A calming caress of lashes.

The soldiers started moving into the Garden in columns, unhurriedly, as if it were a foreign theater of war. This was not some law enforcement operation: the enemy had to be eliminated. A few sporadic shots were heard, prompting an immediate reply of rapid-fire bursts from HK416 assault rifles. On the far side of the pond, a wounded man cried out in pain.

Arthur looked at his friend. His golden hair had darkened to a thick mane, coiled, in places, into dreadlocks. Arthur preferred it like this, greasy, smelly, organic.

A troop of about fifty odd Extinctionists sheltering in the puppet theater attempted an escape toward Rue Guynemer. There was a burst of bullets, riddling the replica Statue of Liberty before ripping into the front line of soldiers. The clash lasted a few minutes.

Arthur felt arms closing tightly around him. He started to

weep, there was no sound or sobbing. He allowed all his emotions to flow out, feelings that for so long he had refused to acknowledge. Kevin wiped his face with an old handkerchief.

New sirens were blaring: firefighters. The Senate was ablaze. Flames licked out of the library windows on the second floor, illuminating the cut stone facade.

"Can you hear the titmouse?" murmured Kevin.

Arthur recognized the sharp, two-toned song heralding fine weather. Indifferent to the massacre, the bird was celebrating the sunshine as it searched for a good mate. What did the world look like to it? Branches to settle on, insects to eat, moss and dry grass to make its nest, smells and lights to guide it. Humans running around somewhere beneath the canopy were no more than vague shapes of little interest. What would it retain from the battle of the Luxembourg Gardens? A few scraps of fabric, perhaps, to help protect its eggs from any drafts. Arthur found it reassuring to think that right at that moment, such a different perception of the world could coexist with his own. The titmouse then launched into a series of deeper trills. As he listened, Arthur realized his tinnitus had stopped. His world was becoming clearer. He was no longer weeping. He felt overwhelmed by an immense joy.

"It's a great titmouse," he corrected Kevin.

Calm had fallen once again over the puppet theater. Prisoners were lined up on the sidewalk under watchful surveillance, while military nurses hurried about with their stretchers, offering first aid to the wounded. The soldiers remained alert. They had distributed themselves around the path that circled the edge of the garden and were moving, step by step, toward the center, like hunters organizing a beat. When they arrived at the middle, they would find two worm-like creatures glued one to the other.

Arthur had no intention of appearing before a court of his peers, and especially had no wish to find himself behind concrete walls. He made one last-ditch effort to reach the tablets. He pushed three of them into his mouth and let them dissolve. He felt the tasteless poison run down his throat and swallowed to make sure he ingested the full dose. He knew the convulsions would soon start, followed by a sudden drop in blood pressure, then suffocation, then coma. He clung to Kevin with all his might.

XXII

Kevin loaded the ten twenty-liter bags onto the passenger seat and started the engine. For a year now, he had been living in the rudimentarily equipped, windowless white van. He had installed an aluminum kitchenette serviced by two jerricans of water, a compression refrigerator, a Wi-Fi router, and a mattress onto which he tossed his faithful sleeping bag. His personal belongings he kept in three boxes. He would take a leak on the side of the road and a crap in the bushes. Once or twice a week, he would shower at a highway service station. He didn't understand how he could ever have lived any other way.

Kevin was crisscrossing France, going from one town to another trying to convince mayors, environmental administrators, or municipal services to provide citizens with an innovative and ecological solution for treating their waste. Using the two hundred thousand euros Posthumus had paid him in exchange for signing a nondisclosure agreement, he had been able to kick-start his old individual worm composter project. Customers were still wary, especially in the wake of the Posthumus scandal, but he sold enough to pay for his gas and the few essentials he needed. He had only one investor, with a 5 percent stake: the Barber, who was delighted to be back in the game. Behind the driver's seat he had firmly secured his demonstration worm composter, which he had to be careful not to joggle too much while driving. As and when necessary, he would stock up on worms at vermiculture farms. He had turned into a traveling earthworm sales rep, ready to deal with any and every reaction or objection.

In the evenings, Kevin would seek out a forest road, a riverbank, or a simple place to stop at the edge of a field. Sometimes he would find himself sleeping in a parking lot or at a campsite; he had also suffered his fair share of angry landowners and vicious dogs. Most of the time, however, he managed to find a reasonably bucolic spot. Whenever the forecast permitted, he would sleep under the stars. During those long hours of idleness, he would delve studiously into books he had retrieved from Arthur's place, trying to get to grips with the thinking of those philosophers his friend had discussed with him once upon a time. An already wrinkled recluse reading Seneca by the light of a torch on the side of a country lane.

Kevin put Saint-Firmin into his GPS. A two-hour-and-twenty-eight-minute drive. "In fifty meters, turn right" intoned the robot coldly. Kevin set his car stereo to play the Chaconne from Partita number two on repeat. For those two hours and twenty-eight minutes he was unable to escape the memories haunting him, memories he would have done anything to erase from his thoughts. The death throes he had at first mistaken for an embrace. Those up-rolled eyes like a girl climaxing. His distress when the soldiers, accompanied by their officers, came to take the Predator's corpse away. Several of them had been needed to disentangle the two young men, one rigid in death, the other hardened by love. Yet in the midst of this pain, which still made him gasp for air, Kevin had found a certain comfort. In the chaos of the Luxembourg Gardens, he had played Bach's Partita in his head. He had heard the madman's message, *vox clamans in deserto.* This time, he understood it. He had held his friend with all his strength. He would at least have had this. A brief moment of being one.

When he arrived at the farm, the whole gang was already there waiting for Kevin: Maria looking tearful, Matthieu as surly as ever, Louis conveniently with wheelbarrow to hand, and even a rather radiant-looking Salim, who, given the way events had turned out, congratulated himself every day for not having been involved. Standing a little off to the side, as agreed, was an anti-terrorism officer, easily recognizable by his washed denim jeans and bored look.

"Are you going to help me unload?" asked Kevin, without even greeting them.

He opened the van door and took out the first bag, which he placed in the barrow. Louis and Matthieu each took out another two. Maria wanted to follow but dissolved into tears.

"I can't!"

"Come on," Kevin chided her gently, "it's such good compost . . ."

"Shut up! I think it's . . . oh! Worse than anything! I'd still prefer to be cremated!"

"It's what he wanted."

Once he had been released from the endless interrogations, Kevin had followed Arthur's instructions to the letter. He had retrieved the password to the PDF from the tea cannister, which was still in its place, on top of the fireplace, having miraculously been spared by the antiterrorism raids. He then had to painstakingly negotiate the return of the body, not so much with Arthur's father, who hadn't wanted to hear another word about it, but with the authorities who feared that the Predator would become a martyr to the cause. Kevin had undertaken to maintain the strictest secrecy and had agreed to allow the whole process to be supervised by the police criminal investigations unit.

Once the bags had been loaded up, Louis swiveled the wheelbarrow around and pushed it off in the direction of the field. The others followed in silence, a humble funeral procession. Salim carried a shovel on his shoulder and Matthieu was taking precious care of a plastic pot out of which poked a bare branch. The officer pulled up the rear, vaping. Kevin noticed that after all those years of abandonment, the land had become unrecognizable. It was no pleasant pasture, but it could no longer be mistaken for uncultivated wasteland. The dried grasses from the previous season, mixed with the yellowing remains of rumex and ferns, were already being displaced by the tender green of fresh growth. On this late summer's day, the hawthorn's strings of red beads blended with the yellow heads of parsnip flowers in a pointillist tableau of vivid, blurry color.

In the midst of the brambles, ash trees shot skyward, their light-colored trunks already several meters tall. They must have migrated from the neighboring forest, their seeds smuggled across by helicopter-bladed samaras. These ashes were still scrawny teenagers. They grouped together in clumps of three or four, nestled up against each other to brave their first years. In some places, field maples were taking over, much more solid, their shoulders already broad. Here and there, a few isolated elms and elders. Kevin thought he could smell the slight muskiness of undergrowth. Nature had begun the slow metamorphosis back to its normal state: the forest.

Kevin glimpsed a yellow-winged butterfly, like those one might see in an old book, pass right before him. He recognized the oily ink-black spots of a cabbage butterfly and followed its aerobatics with his gaze. The butterfly hovered between different copses, hesitating, before landing on a thistle. Life had returned.

The procession came to a halt at the old hedge, the remains of which had now been reclaimed by ivy. Kevin grabbed the shovel, took a few steps to choose the best position, and started to dig. The blade glided easily into the soil. The earth was black and glossy. It gave off a heady scent of undergrowth. In one of the clumps he extracted, Kevin noticed a fine group of anecics, writhing and moist, in rude good health. He turned back to his companions. They were all looking at the same thing.

"Well, there you go," muttered Matthieu under his breath, "you just had to wait."

"Everything comes in its own time," Louis added.

"He would have been so happy," choked Maria.

Kevin took the young oak from its pot. A single lonely leaf had appeared like a flag at the tip of the stalk. Kevin delicately loosened the compacted roots and felt the rootlets tickling his fingers.

"It's what was always missing here," said Kevin.

"One thing's for sure," added Louis, "no more need for a hedge with that! There'll be no stopping that oak. In a few centuries' time, it'll be king of the plateau. Its branches will stretch all the way across to Jobard's farm."

Kevin pulled a few stones from the hole then opened the first bag. Maria immediately crossed herself, the orthodox way, right to left. He seized a fistful of the compost, brought it to his nostrils and inhaled deeply. It gave off a strong scent of earth released by the actinobacteria forming the humus. Kevin stood for a moment, thoughtful. Then he tipped the bag into the hole, spread the compost over the bottom of it, and settled the oak onto its new bed. Everyone with their own considered, ceremonious gestures, came to tip in the contents of the other bags. Kevin finished it off with a few shovelfuls of earth, doing his best to level out the soil. He noticed an anecic already making its way toward the miraculous manna of the compost.

"Eat up, eat up," murmured Kevin, moved.

Everybody gathered in a circle around the little sapling, which was holding itself upright, proudly preparing for its new existence. Its rootlets were going to cling to the earth. Then things would be set up for the exchange. The oak would provide the soil with hydrogen and sugar, and from it would extract water, nitrogen, and the nutrients necessary for its slow growth. Its roots were like spoons, continuously stirring the soup of microbes, fungus, and minuscule insects that Arthur had become.

"Personally, I think it's freaky," said Salim finally.

"Why?" Louis objected. "It's just the order of things. I remember what the priests used to say when we were kids: 'Remember you are dust, and to dust you shall return.'"

"And anyway this tree's going to live longer than us, longer than our children and our great-grandchildren."

"That's eternity, for real."

"Better than being under some granite slab in any case."

Maria sang haltingly in her native tongue. A melodic, guttural prayer. It was all the more touching for being out of tune. When she had finished, the officer came over and gave them a threatening look.

"I repeat, the location of this grave must remain absolutely confidential. Otherwise . . ."

"What grave?" asked Kevin. "There's nothing here. Just earthworms."

The officer shrugged his shoulders and went off in a puff of vape smoke, like an ocean liner heading out to sea.

"Will you come and have a drink at La Lanterne?" suggested Maria.

"I didn't think we were allowed to anymore."

"Oh, I don't give a damn now. I do as I please."

"I'll catch you up," said Kevin, without moving.

The others all left, except for Louis, who stopped a few meters away, hands in his pockets, eyes raised to the misty sky. Kevin knelt before the sapling, which looked so fragile with its ridiculous leaf. He imagined how Arthur was going to grow, year after year, ring after ring. His buds. His flowers, dangling catkins for the males, reddish pistils for the females. His acorns like cartridge cases on the fall earth. His first branches, spreading horizontally across this exposed field. His bark, first smooth, then wrinkled, fissured, cracked. The knots in his trunk like blind eyes. His residents constantly stirring, day and night, spiders, ants, bees, caterpillars, squirrels, creepers, jays, robin redbreasts, more plentiful than the number of people living in the largest housing block. His trunk now thick enough to be fully embraced. His shady canopy beneath which one could doze off. His transpiration cooling on a summer day. His forks testing the light in every direction, as if he were a tree comprising a thousand trees, each grown from successive cuttings. His branches reaching for the sky to avoid shading those below. And finally, his perfectly round adult crown, swaying in the wind, tens of meters above the ground.

Bound to the world by water and light, Arthur will witness, over time, the mutation of *Homo sapiens*. Heavily armed fighters protecting water and grain, gaunt carbon-deprived nomads, Gaia-worshiping neo-pagan druids, wide-eyed, flat-footed children playing in the quiet of the village, Minotaurs and Centaurs combining man and beast, all will in turn pass by at his feet.

And one day, when he is old and creaking, he will be uprooted by an overly vigorous gust of wind. Down he will come in a thunderous roar. His smashed branches will become entangled with the soil like hair that has come undone. His worn body, full of holes, will slowly, very slowly, decompose over the centuries. He will lose his branches and his bark. He will be covered in swarming bees, gleaming moss, and meringues of mushrooms. He will provide shelter and nourishment to billions and billions of insects. Then, once more, he will become humus.

In the end, Arthur had succeeded. He had pulled off his very own revolution.

"It's going to rain," said Louis. "We got lucky. Don't even need to water."

A NOTE FROM THE TRANSLATOR

Not long after the wonderful editor of this novel, Alexa Frank, sent my translation off to production, my partner and I hosted a performance of Bach's *Chaconne*, from his Partita No. 2 in D minor. On a glorious spring evening at home in Sydney, Australia, we had turned our living room into a makeshift stage. The piece was performed by a very dear friend, Beatrice Colombis, a truly gifted young violinist embarking on a career as a professional musician in Berlin. If you are reading this note *after* finishing the book, you will understand how irresistible it was to read to our assembled audience of friends my translation of the scene in which Mélanie, concertmaster of the Radio-France Philharmonique Orchestra, plays that same piece to her gathered peers, France's next generation of so-called Young Leaders.

We had guests scattered in a rough semblance of rows, some perched on window ledges, standing in the kitchen, looking through to what might laughingly be described as our concert space. The doors and windows were open to the night breeze, there was the sound of cicadas in the courtyard garden, the odd aircraft overhead, the snickering of bold possums venturing closer to snack on the new season's growth on our maple tree. Some of our guests were no doubt familiar with this astonishing piece of music, while others might never have heard it performed either live or in a recorded version and would, like Kevin, have had no expectation of the beauty and anguish Beatrice was about to draw from the strings of her violin.

I remember the first time I "consciously" listened to a recording of the *Chaconne*. It was on a CD recording of a performance by Josef Suk, and I was utterly baffled by the way in which Bach's polyphony could be rendered by a single person on a single instrument with only four strings. It didn't seem possible. I had enjoyed numerous years of piano lessons as a child, having even endured the weekly ordeal of music theory lessons. I had been taken to classical music performances, been gifted a recording of Bach's harpsichord concerti for Christmas when I had specifically asked for David Bowie's *Let's Dance*. But I had never experienced with my own ears the alchemy of a violinist harnessing the many voices of Bach in one of his partitas for solo violin. Even now, all these years later, having had the opportunity to enjoy many such performances, it seems an impossible feat.

Of all the metaphors used by literary translators to describe the nature of our task, maybe this image, of a musician capturing the voices expressed in a score, is the easiest way to illustrate what often feels like an exercise in listening. Philip Boehm—renowned director, playwright, and translator from German and Polish—has written about the fundamentally musical process of translation, likening it to an actor "hearing" the lines in their head. He described his own technique of "putting his ear to the text":

> . . . I close my eyes and let the music play until I hear the melody and rhythm of the writing. . . . Then I try to find the proper key in English—transposing as needed . . .[1]

Boehm explains how he tries to identify the "musical rests" of the text so that he can replicate those silences, the breaths, in his own translation. Like any musician, a literary translator will *listen* to the text, both in the original and then in her own rendition. Some translators admit they often work aloud, because only then does the musicality of their translation become apparent. Sometimes the task of putting an ear to the text might even involve a literal "listening," perhaps to an audiobook of the original text, that helps draw out an author's decisions and, much like a musician might listen to a selection of performances of the same piece, hearing different voices emphasized, noting the breath, the silences, the dynamics, before making their own performance choices. Translators, too, make micro-decisions at every turn, as we try to honor an author's deliberate choice of phrase length, tense, and vocabulary, listen out for verbs that beat a particular rhythm, capture the legato effect of a string of adjectives. Like Mélanie in her performance of the *Chaconne*, we too are constantly alive to the polyphony of the text.

Translating this astounding novel, I reveled in those frequent shifts in voice and register, from spikey and irreverent dialogue—

1. Philip Boehm, "An Act of Imagination" in *The Art of Empathy: Celebrating Literature in Translation*, ed. Don Ball, National Endowment for the Arts, Washington, DC, August 2014, Produced by the NEA Office of Public Affairs, pp. 25–28 at p. 27.

which had me channeling the sometimes unforgiving yet often similarly idealistic, voices of my own twenty-something-year-old offspring—to the author's acutely observed, almost painterly descriptions of the flora and fauna of Norman hedgerow landscapes that transported me back to the pages of Jean Giono that I read in my college French classes. The unapologetically sprawling ambition of Koenig's work regularly had me shaking my head in wonder as I re-read the product of a day's work during which I might have become an expert in anything from the philosophy of the Stoics, to the reproductive cycle of earthworms, to the ergonomics of scything. On more than one occasion, I found myself thinking about translator Gregory Rabassa's robust retort to an interviewer enquiring whether Rabassa felt he knew enough Spanish to translate García Márquez's *One Hundred Years of Solitude.* Per Edith Grossman's retelling of the story in *Why Translation Matters*, Rabassa is said to have answered that this was certainly the wrong question, with the real question being whether he knew enough English.

When I first read *Lowly Creatures*, which was published in French under the title *Humus*, I remember chortling at the author's wormish wordplay, puns he often based on homophones of the French word for "worm" (*ver*). There are many. I felt a delicious combination of respect, followed closely by a vague panic at how I would do them justice in English and bring a similar smile to our new anglophone readers. Wordplay and puns are often a translator's nemesis. Some, I'm told, love the challenge. I tend to find solving these often-intricate word puzzles to be a bit like doing a cryptic crossword. Either you see it or you don't. And I am not ashamed to admit that there are members of my immediate family and circle of friends whose cryptic crossword skills are better than mine! That said, I feel sufficiently pleased with some of my "solutions" to Koenig's written fun and games to explain the underlying French in this note.

Take the name of Philippine and Kevin's industrial-scale worm composting start-up, which the author had cunningly named *Veritas*. Readers might appreciate the play on the French for "worm" (*ver*), and the association with the Latin for "truth." The name could obviously have been kept in the English, but the author's cleverness would have been lost to any reader not well versed in French or Latin. *Posthumus* came at me like a thunderbolt. Not only did it tickle me to incorporate the original French title (a word shared with English), but I couldn't help feeling a certain synergy between the etymology of the word and the scope and ambition of Philippine and Kevin's start-up.

Fellow translators will also recognize that solving one problem will not necessarily prevent a related issue from rearing its head a paragraph or two later. In this case, it was the name of the Veritas or Posthumus biostimulant, *Vino Veritas*, which was to feature quite significantly throughout the novel. If I had lost *Veritas*, what was I to do with the *Vino*? Oh, how I'd like to claim *Wormentino* as my own, but, if I'm honest, I seem to recall that this victory was more correctly shared, over a glass of wine, with my partner, whose cryptic crossword skills also, I might add, far outstrip my own.

At the time of this writing, the young violinist, Beatrice, is preparing to board a plane for Berlin. In addition to being a spectacular musician, she also happens to read more than anybody of her generation I know. So, I asked if she had had room in her luggage to pack any books. Hans Fallada's *Alone in Berlin*, Jenny Erpenbeck's *Go, Went, Gone*, and the originally anonymous memoir *A Woman in Berlin* were a few titles that featured in her response, books she is at this stage still having to read in their English translation. Better than any guidebook, these translations will offer her a way into that city, into its history, and into the preoccupations of its citizens.

Similarly, I can only hope my translation from the French of Koenig's magnificent *Lowly Creatures* will help illuminate for a new English-speaking audience the preoccupations of an author, a generation, indeed, a society. And yes, perhaps it will underscore differences between cultures, but more importantly, it might just emphasize the commonalities of shared concerns at what feels like a particularly precarious moment in history.

Stephanie Smee

Here ends Gaspard Koenig's
Lowly Creatures.

The first edition of this book was printed
and bound at Lakeside Book Company
in Harrisonburg, Virginia, in July 2026.

A NOTE ON THE TYPE

The text of this novel was set in Fournier, a serif typeface released by Monotype Corporation in 1924. It was based on the typeface of the same name created by French typefounder and typographic theoretician Pierre-Simon Fournier around 1742. With its strong contrast between thin and thick strokes and sparse serif bracketing, Fournier was a "transitional" style of typeface that anticipated the more severe modern fonts that would debut later in the eighteenth century. Its light, clean design presents well on the page, making it a popular choice for printed matter.

HARPERVIA

An imprint dedicated to publishing international voices,
offering readers a chance to encounter other lives and other
points of view via the language of the imagination.